When a killer
plays with fire, someone is
bound to get burned...

THE NEXT TO DIE

Shannon was cold to the bone. It didn't matter what the temperature was outside, internally she was freezing, thinking about Mary Beth.

Could she really be dead? Shannon remembered her glimpse of the blackened body and her insides clenched violently.

Mary Beth was dead. Burned. It was unfathomable.

"Who would do it?" Shannon thought aloud, not really aware she'd spoken.

"The guy who's got Dani."

Twisting her neck, Shannon stared directly at Travis for the first time since climbing into his truck. "Why? You think this is all connected? The fires at my house? Mary Beth's . . . death. *Why?*"

"Her murder, Shannon. Your sister-in-law was killed."

"How do you know?"

"I just do. Ten to one they'll find evidence that the fire was intentional when they investigate."

"But why? What does Mary Beth have to do with Dani? Why the fire at my place?"

"You tell me."

"I can't! You're still blaming me for Dani's disappearance, aren't you?"

"No. But somehow it has something to do with you. Otherwise why the burned birth certificate? Whoever's got my child is flaunting it. Taunting us. Getting off on the fact that he knows more than we do . . ."

Books by Lisa Jackson

See How She Dies

Final Scream

Wishes

Whispers

Twice Kissed

Unspoken

If She Only Knew

Hot Blooded

Cold Blooded

The Night Before

The Morning After

Deep Freeze

Fatal Burn

Published by Zebra Books

LISA JACKSON

FATAL BURN

ZEBRA BOOKS
KENSINGTON PUBLISHING CORP.
http://www.zebrabooks.com

Acknowledgments

You've heard the expression that "It takes a village to raise a child"—well, I believe it. And, sometimes it takes a village to write a book. At least in the case of FATAL BURN. I had tons of help from my friends, relatives, research and promotion people. They've been phenomenal. First and foremost I have to thank my sister, Nancy Bush, who became control central and not only edited this book, but also handled the publicity and accounting, family crises and daily phone calls, all the while writing her next novel, ELECTRIC BLUE. Second, a big thank you to Kathy Baker who has championed me from the get-go. Over more than a few years Kathy has not only enthusiastically sold my books, she's become a real friend as well. Also, let me not forget the fantastic team at Kensington Publishing who unflaggingly support me. Everyone in every department works so hard.

The following people were also integral in the birth of FATAL BURN: Kelly Bush, Ken Bush, Eric Brown, Matthew Crose, Michael Crose, Danielle Katcher, Marilyn Katcher, Mike Kavanaugh, Ken Melum, Roz Noonan, Darren Foster, Bob Okano, Kathy Okano, Betty Pederson, Jack Pederson, Sally Peters, Jeff Rosenberg, Robin Rue, Samantha Santi-stevens, John Scognamiglio, Mike Seidel, Linda Sparks, Larry Sparks, Celia Stinson, Mark Stinson.

If I've forgotten anyone, my apologies.

Prologue

Indian summer
The forest near Santa Lucia, California
Three years earlier

He was late.

He checked his watch and the illuminated digital face glowed eerily in the pitch-dark forest.

Eleven fifty-seven.

Hell!

He'd never make it in time and would draw attention to himself, something he could ill afford.

Picking up his pace, he jogged along the uneven terrain, running downward in this stretch of low wooded hills, far away from civilization.

Far away from discovery.

The sounds of the night crept into his brain: the rustle of autumn leaves in the hot breeze, the snap of a dry twig beneath his hurried footsteps and the thunderous pounding of his own heart, thudding wildly, pumping adrenaline through his veins.

He sneaked a glance at his wrist, the face of his watch

registering midnight. His jaw tightened. Perspiration seemed to pour from every inch of his skin and his nerves were strung tight as an assassin's garrote.

Slow down! Don't announce your presence by crashing through the underbrush like a wounded stag! Better to be a few minutes late than to destroy everything by making a clumsy racket.

He stopped, drew in several deep breaths and smelled the tinder-dry forest. Beneath his dark clothes he was sweating. From the hot night. From his exertion. From a sense of anticipation. And from fear.

He swiped at the moisture in his eyes and drew in a long, calming breath. *Concentrate. Focus. Do* not *slip up. Not tonight.*

Somewhere nearby an owl hooted softly and he took it as an omen. A good one. So he was late. He could handle it.

He hoped.

Once his heartbeat had slowed, he dug into the pocket of his tight-fitting jacket, found the ski mask and quickly pulled it over his head, adjusting the eye and nose holes.

Looking downward he saw the first flicker of light in the shadows. Then another.

Flashlights.

They were gathering.

His heart nearly stopped.

But there was no going back, not now. He was committed. Just as they were. There was a chance that he would be caught, that they all would, but it was a risk they were all willing to take.

He continued his descent.

As a full moon rose higher in the sky, he jogged the final quarter mile through the stands of live oak and pine. Forcing his heartbeat to slow, he slipped around a final bend in the trail to the clearing where the four others waited.

They were all dressed like he was, in black, their faces covered by dark ski masks. They stood about three feet from each other, in formation, what would be a circle as soon as he joined them. He felt all the hidden eyes stare at him as he stepped into the spot that completed the ring.

"You're late," a harsh voice whispered. The tallest was glaring at him. The leader.

Every muscle in his body tensed. He nodded. Didn't reply. No excuse would be acceptable.

"There can be no errors. No delays!"

Again, he inclined his head, accepting the rebuke.

"Do not make this mistake again!"

The others stared at him, the offender. He kept his eyes trained straight ahead. Eventually they all turned their attention to the leader who was slightly taller than everyone else. There was something about him that emanated power, a fierceness that came through—something that said he was a man to be respected . . . and feared.

"We begin," the leader went on, mollified, at least for the moment. With one final glance around the circle, the leader bent down to the ground. With a click of his lighter, he touched the small flame to a pile of twigs which crackled and caught. Small, glowing flickers of fire raced in a predetermined path. The smell of burning kerosene caught in the wind. One sharp point of fiery light became defined, then another as the symbol ignited, a blazing star burning on the clearing.

"Tonight it ends." The leader straightened, taking his place at a tip of one star point. They each stood at the end of one of the projections, their boots dangerously close to the flames.

"No more!"

"Everything's in place?" the person to his right asked in a hiss.

Man or woman?

He couldn't tell.

"Yes." The leader glanced at his watch. There was satisfaction in his tone, even pride, though his voice was still disguised. "You all know what you need to do. Tonight Ryan Carlyle pays for what he's done. Tonight he dies."

The latecomer's heart clutched.

"Wait! No! This is a mistake," another one of the group

argued, as if a sudden sense of guilt had claimed him. Or was it a woman? The dissenter was certainly the shortest of the lot and was wearing clothes baggy enough to be deceiving. He was shaking his head as if grappling with his ethics. "We can't do this. It's murder. *Premeditated murder.*"

"It's already been decided." The leader was firm.

"There must be a better way."

"The plan is already in motion. No one will ever find out."

"But—"

"As I said, it's been decided." The whisper was scathing and cruel, daring the dissident to argue further.

All the unseen eyes turned on the one who had found the courage to object. He held his ground for a fraction of a second before his shoulders slumped in reluctant acceptance, as if there was nothing he could do. He argued no more.

"Good. Then we're all in agreement." The leader shot the protestor one final glance before outlining the simple but effective plan to put an end to Ryan Carlyle's life.

No one asked a question.

Everyone understood.

"We're in agreement?" the leader checked. There were nods all around, aside from the one dissenter. "We're in agreement?" the leader demanded again harshly. The dissenter gave up his fight and hitched his chin quickly, as if afraid to utter even the slightest protest.

The leader snorted, satisfied, then moved his eyes from the objector to each member standing at a point of the star before zeroing in on the latecomer again.

Because he'd arrived a few minutes after midnight, the appointed time? Because of a basic animal mistrust? He felt the weight of the tall man's stare and met it evenly.

"You all know your assignments. I expect you to execute them flawlessly." No one spoke. "Leave," the leader ordered. "Separately. Each the way you came. Discuss this with no one."

As the flames in the star began to spread, searching for

other sources of fuel, each of the five conspirators turned from the fire and disappeared into the forest.

He, too, did as he was bid, rotating quickly, ignoring the thundering of his heart and the sweat covering his body. Inside he was thrumming, his senses heightened. He jogged upward and hazarded one glance over his shoulder. Straining to listen, he heard nothing over the sound of his own labored breathing and the sigh of the wind as it rushed through the surrounding trees.

He was alone.

No one was following him.

No one would find out what he had planned.

Far below, in the clearing, the fire was beginning to take hold, the fiery star splintering and crawling rapidly through the summer-dry grass toward the surrounding woods.

He didn't have much time. Yet he waited, eyes scanning the dark hillside, the seconds ticking away. Finally he heard the faraway sound of an engine starting, and then, barely a minute later, another car or truck roared to life.

Come on, come on, he thought, glancing at his watch and biting at the edge of his lip. Finally the sound of a third engine, barely discernable, revved to life, only to fade into the distance. Good.

He waited for the fourth vehicle to start.

A minute passed.

He lifted his mask and mopped his face, then pulled it over his head again. Just in case.

Another full minute ticked by.

What the hell was going on?

He felt the light touch of fear burn down his spine.

Don't panic. Just wait.

But it shouldn't take this long. Everyone should have been desperate to flee. Through the trees he spied the growing flames. Soon someone would see the fire, call it in.

Damn!

Maybe the leader had changed his mind, considered him a risk after all. Maybe showing up late had been a far worse mistake than he'd imagined and even now the leader of the secret band was stalking him, closing in.

Fists clenched, every sense alive, he searched the darkness.

Don't lose it. There's still time. Again he glanced at his watch. Nearly twelve-thirty. And the fire below was taking hold, crackling and burning, racing through the undergrowth.

His ears strained as the smell of smoke teased his nostrils . . . Was that the sound of a car's engine roaring to life?

Five more minutes passed and he stood, sweating, muscles tight, ready to spring.

Still nothing.

Fuck!

He couldn't waste another minute and decided to risk his plan. Swiftly he began running up the trail again, heading toward the little-used logging road high above, but at a fork in the path, he veered sharply right. Heart pounding, his nerves twisted and jangled, he angled along the side of the hill. His muscles were beginning to ache with the effort when he finally saw the abyss ahead of him, a deep chasm cut into the hillside.

He was close now. Could still make it.

Without hesitation, he found the large tree he'd used as a bridge earlier and carefully eased his way along the rough bark and through the broken limbs to the other side of the cleft. Far below, the fire continued to take hold, the flames glowing brighter, the smoke rising toward the night-dark heavens.

Hurry!

At the root-end of the log, he jumped to the ground, picked up another trail and followed it unerringly to a boulder the size of a man. Five paces uphill he found a tree split and blackened by lightning, cleaved as if God Himself had sliced the oak into two pieces.

At the base of that split trunk was his quarry.

Hands and ankles bound, tied to one side of the tree, mouth taped shut, his prisoner waited.

He flicked on his flashlight, saw that the captive's wrists

were bloody and raw, the skin sawed by the ropes as the man had tried to escape.

To no avail.

"The information was correct," he said to his wide-eyed victim. Sweat ran down the bound man's face and he looked frantically around him, as if hoping for rescue. "They want blood."

Garbled noises came from the tied man's throat.

"Your blood."

The captive began thrashing, yanking at his restraints, and the torturer felt a pang of pity—a small one—for him. The garbled noises became louder, and he figured the captive was bartering for his pathetic life. Eyes bulging, the prisoner was shaking his head violently. *No! No! No!* As if there had been some terrible mistake.

But there was sweet justice in what was happening. He felt the warmth of it spreading through his veins, the adrenaline high in anticipation of what was about to come. Slowly, he reached into the pocket of his pants and withdrew a pack of cigarettes. He shook one of the filter tips out, stuffing it casually between his lips as the pathetic creature tied to the tree watched in horror.

"Oh, yes, they definitely want Ryan Carlyle dead tonight," he said, flicking his lighter to the end of his Marlboro and cupping his hand around the tip. The thin paper and tobacco ignited in a flare. He drew in deeply, tasting the smoke, feeling it curl as it filled his lungs.

The prisoner, his eyes wide, his body contorting, flailed as he struggled, his horrified screams muffled, blood running from his wrists.

"And you know what? I want him dead as well. But in a different way, in a way that better serves my purpose." He found a kind of peace in thinking about the demise of Ryan Carlyle, all the ramifications it would cause.

His captive writhed and squirmed crazily. It appeared he was shouting invectives rather than pleading for his life or screaming in terror. Like a wounded animal, he threw himself away from the tree, stretching the ropes, as if he could somehow get free.

Too late.

The decision had been made.

Reaching into his pocket again, the tormentor came up with a syringe. Holding the cigarette between his lips, he pushed on the plunger a bit, spraying a bit of clear liquid into the night.

The prisoner was in full-blown panic but it made no difference. He was restrained, and it was no problem plunging the needle into his exposed arm and waiting for the drug to take effect. Standing back he watched as his victim's eyes glazed and his movements became sluggish. The captive no longer pulled at his restraints, just rolled up his eyes at his tormentor in abject hatred.

And so it was time.

"Adios," he said softly. He flipped his burning cigarette onto the dry forest floor. Fire immediately raced along pine needles, dead leaves and dry twigs, burning bright red, following a carefully laid trail around the base of the tree.

Snap!

A small branch caught fire.

Hiss!

A piece of moss ignited.

Smoke drifted lazily to the heavens as a trail of flames ringed the tree. He stepped back as the prisoner's head lolled to one side.

"Sorry, Carlyle," he said, shaking his head as the man, almost in slow motion, tried to tear at his bonds, ropes made of natural fiber, restraints that would become nothing more than ash and even if analyzed by the police would contain the same chemicals as the clothes he was wearing. That he had been tethered and bound would be difficult, if not impossible, to discern. Even the drug now rendering him helpless would dissipate and be hard to trace.

He stepped back several steps to stare at his victim,

through a rising, crackling wall of hungry flames. "There's nothing more I can do," he said with more than a little satisfaction. "You're a dead man."

Chapter 1

Three years later

"Help me!" she cried, but her voice was mute.

She was running, her legs leaden, fear propelling her forward through the smoke, through the heat. All around her the forest was burning out of control. Hot, scalding flames spiraled hellishly to the sky. Smoke clogged her throat, searing her nostrils with the hot, acrid smell. Her lungs burned. Her eyes teared, her skin blistered.

Blackened tree limbs fell around her, crashing and splintering as she ran. Sprays of sparks peppered the already-burning ground and singed her skin.

Oh, God, oh, God, oh, God!

It was as if she'd somehow fallen through the gates of hell.

"Help!" she screamed again, but her voice was lodged in her throat, not even the barest of whispers escaping her lips. "Please, someone help me!"

But she was alone.

There was no one to help her this time.

Her brothers, always quick to her rescue, couldn't save her.

Oh, dear God.

Run, damn it! MOVE! Get out, Shannon! Now!

She flung herself forward, stumbling, half-falling, the fire a raging, burning beast, its putrid breath scalding, its crackling arms reaching for her, enwrapping her, sizzling against her skin.

Just when she thought she was going to die, that she would be consumed, the fire, with a roar, shrank back. Disappeared. The black smoke turned into a thick white fog and she was suddenly running through fields of smoldering ash, the smell of burning flesh heavy in her nostrils, the ground an arid, vast wasteland.

And everywhere there were bones.

Piles and piles of charred, bleached bones.

White skeletons of animals and people, all flecked with ash.

Cats. Dogs. Horses. Humans.

In her mind's eye, the skeletons became members of her family and though they were only bones, she superimposed faces to the skulls. Her mother. Her father. Her baby.

Pain cut through her at the thought of her child.

No! No! No!

These were only skeletons.

No one she knew.

They couldn't be.

The smell of death and the receding fire burned through her nostrils.

She tried to back away, to escape, but as she moved, she tripped on the scattered bones. She fell and the skeletons broke beneath her. Frantic, clawing wildly, she tried to stand, to run, to get away from this thick, rattling pile.

Brrrrring.

A siren blasted. As if from the distance.

Her heart jolted. Someone was coming!

Oh, please!

Turning, she saw one of the skeletons move, its grotesque, half-burned head turning to face her. Pieces of charred flesh hung from the skull's cheekbones and most of its black hair was singed, the eyes sunken in their sockets, but they were eyes she recognized, eyes she'd trusted, eyes she'd once loved. And they stared at her, blinked, and silently accused her of unspeakable crimes.

No, she thought wildly. No, no, no!

How could something this hideous be alive?

She screamed but her voice was mute.

"Sssssshannon . . ." Her husband's voice hissed evilly through her brain. *Goose pimples covered her skin despite the heat. "Sssssshannon."* It seemed as if his face was taking shape, the blackened flesh filling in, stretching over the bones, cartilage filling the nose hole, sunken eyes staring fixedly at her.

She tried again.

Brrring! The siren. No—a phone. Her *phone.*

Shannon sat bolt upright in bed. Sweat ran down her back and her heart thundered a million beats a minute. It was dark, she was in her room tucked under the eaves of her small cottage. On a sob, she felt sweet relief swell through her. It was a dream. Only a dream. No, a sick, twisted nightmare.

On the floor beside her, the dog gave a disgruntled bark.

Another sharp blast from the telephone.

"Mary, Joseph and Jesus," she whispered, using her mother's rarely called-upon phrase of abject surprise. "What's the matter with me?" Shoving her hair from her eyes she exhaled shakily. The room was hot, the summer air without a breath of a breeze. Flinging off the damp sheets, she gasped as if she'd just run a marathon. "A dream," she reminded herself, a headache creeping behind her eyes. "Just another damned dream."

Heart thudding she yanked the receiver to her ear. "Hello?"

No answer.

Just silence . . . then something more . . . the sound of soft breathing?

She glanced at the bedside clock: 12:07 flashed in red, digital numbers large enough that she could read the time without her contact lenses. "Hello!"

She was suddenly wide-awake.

Quickly she switched on the bedside lamp. Who would be calling at this time of night? What was it her mother always said? Nothing good happens after midnight. Her heart pounded. She thought of her parents, aging and frail. Had there been an accident? Was someone in her family hurt? Missing? Or worse?

"Hello!" she said again, louder, then realized if there was a problem, if the police or one of her brothers were calling, they would have said something immediately. "Who is this?" she demanded, then wondered if she was the victim of some cruel prank.

Just like before. She cringed as she remembered the last time . . . Suddenly clammy, she recalled playing that crank-calling game at slumber parties in junior high school: call strangers in the middle of the night and whisper something meant to scare.

But that had been a lifetime ago and now, tonight, holding the damned receiver to her ear, she was in no mood for this kind of sophomoric, idiotic joke. "Look, either you answer or I hang up." She could still make out the faint sound of raspy, almost excited breathing. "Fine! Have it your way." She slammed the receiver down. "Creep," she muttered under her breath and wasn't even glad that whoever it was had jarred her out of that awful nightmare.

Damn, but it had been real. So visceral. So disturbing. Even now, she was still sweating, her skin crawling, the stench of smoke still lodged in her nostrils. Running a hand over her eyes, she released a long, slow breath and forced the images to recede. It was a dream, nothing else, she told herself, as she reached for the receiver of the phone again and checked the caller ID. The last number to call in, at 12:07, was blocked. No name. No number.

"Big surprise," she muttered under her breath and tried to tamp down her unease. It was just some bored kids dialing numbers at random, hoping to get a reaction. Right? She stared at the phone and frowned. Who else could it be?

Her dog, Khan, a mixed breed with some Australian shepherd ancestry visible in his mottled coat and mismatched eyes, let out another soft bark from his spot on the rag rug beside her bed. He looked up at her hopefully and thumped his tail on the floorboards as if he expected her to let him onto the bed.

"Are you nuts?" she asked, rolling over and reaching down to scratch him behind one ear. "It's midnight and you and I both need to sleep, so don't even think about getting up here, okay? I just need something for this headache." She rolled off the bed and padded barefoot to the bathroom.

As she stepped into the cramped room, she heard the soft thump of Khan hopping onto the bed. "Get down!" she ordered and flipped on the light. She heard the dog land on the floor again. "Nice try, Khan."

Some dog trainer you are, she thought as she scraped her hair away from her face, holding a handful of curls in one clenched fist. *You can get search and rescue dogs into disaster areas, burning buildings and even into the water, but you can't keep that mutt off the bed.*

Leaning over the sink, she turned on the spigot with her free hand and drank from the faucet, letting water splash against her flushed skin as the remnants of the nightmare burned at the corners of her brain.

Don't go there!

Ryan had been dead for three years and in that time she'd been accused and absolved of killing him. "So get over it," she grumbled, snatching a towel from the rack and dabbing it over her face and chest. The nightmares, her shrink had assured her, would lessen over time.

So far that hadn't proved true. She looked into the mirror over the sink, reflective glass clamped over the medicine cabinet, and cringed. Dark smudges appeared beneath her red-veined eyes. Her auburn hair was tangled, a mess from restless sleep, damp ringlets clinging to her skin. Tiny lines of anxiety appeared in the pinch of her lips and the corners of her eyes.

"The face of an angel hiding Satan's tongue," her brother Neville had said after they'd been involved in a particularly brutal argument when she was around fourteen.

Not tonight, she thought sourly, as she grabbed a washcloth from an open shelf, rinsed it under the water and dabbed the wet rag over her skin.

Neville. She still missed him horribly and that particular knot of sorrow when she thought of him tightened painfully in her chest. Technically, since Neville had been born a scant seven minutes after his twin brother, Oliver, Neville had been the closest in age to Shannon, who'd come along nearly two years later, the last of Patrick and Maureen Flannery's brood of six children. Though Oliver and Neville had shared that special "twin bond," she, too, had felt an intimacy with Neville that she never experienced with the rest of her siblings.

She wished Neville was here now. He'd rumple her hair, smile crookedly and say, "You worry too much, Shannon. It was just a dream."

"And a phone call," she would reply. "A *weird* phone call."

"A wrong number."

"At midnight?"

"Hey, somewhere in the world it's already happy hour. Chill out."

"Right," she muttered, like she could. She soaked the cloth again, wrung it between her hands, then placed it at the base of her neck. A headache, brought on by the nightmare, pounded at the base of her skull. Reaching into the cabinet, she found a bottle of ibuprofen and tossed two pills into her palm before chasing them down with another long swallow from the tap. She saw the bottle of sleeping pills on the shelf under the mirror, the ones Dr. Brennan had prescribed three years earlier. She considered taking a couple, then discarded the idea. Tomorrow morning—no, later *this* morning—she couldn't afford to be groggy or sluggish. She had several training sessions scheduled with some new dogs and she was supposed to sign papers on her new place—a bigger ranch. Although the move was still weeks away, the deal was falling into place.

Remembering the property she was going to buy, she felt another jab of distress. Just last week, when she'd walked the perimeter of the ranch, she'd felt as if she was being watched, that there had been unseen eyes hidden behind the gnarled trunks of the black oaks. Even Khan had seemed edgy that day. Nervous.

Get over it, she mentally berated herself. Unlike most of the dogs she trained, Khan wasn't known for his intuition. No one had been following her, watching her every move. She wasn't in some kind of horror movie, for God's sake. No one had been hiding in the shaded forest that surrounded the place, no sinister being had been observing her from the outcropping of rocks on a nearby hillside. No one, other than herself, had been there at all.

She was just antsy about plunking down all of her inheritance and savings on the new place. And why wouldn't she be? Her brothers had all been against her plan and each had enough nerve to tell her the vastness of her mistake.

"This isn't what Dad would have wanted," Shea had pointed out the last time he'd stopped by. His black hair had gleamed blue in the lamplight as he'd stood on her porch while smoking a cigarette, staring at her as if she'd lost her mind. "Dad spent his entire life scrimping, saving and investing and wouldn't want you to squander your share on a run-down, overgrown farm."

"You haven't even seen the place," she'd charged, undeterred. "And don't pull out the violin and crying towel. Dad always trusted my decisions."

Shea had given her a dark, unfathomable look, drawing hard on his cigarette and giving Shannon the distinct impression that she hadn't known their father at all.

"Dad always backed me up," she said, her voice faltering just a bit.

"I'm just tellin' ya." He blew out a plume of gray smoke, then tossed his cigarette butt into the dust and gravel of the lot separating the house from the barns and other outbuildings. "Be careful, Shannon, with your money and yourself."

"What the hell's that supposed to mean?"

The cigarette smoldered, trailing a tiny wisp of smoke.

"Just that sometimes you're impetuous." He cocked his head and winked at her. "You know. All part of the Flannery curse."

"Don't even go there. That's the biggest load of bull I've ever heard. Just a way for Mom to get back at Dad. Flannery curse? Come on, Shea."

He lifted a dark brow. For a second he'd looked like one of those caricatures of Satan with his knowing leer and upraised eyebrows. "I'm just saying."

"Yeah, well, I'm buying the place and that's that."

Now, a week later, she wondered what that was all about. It was almost as if her brother had been warning her.

And Shea hadn't been the only naysayer. Oh, no! Her other brothers had weighed in over the past few weeks, grown men who seemed to think they still held some sway over her. She snorted in disgust as she remembered Robert advising her to put her money in the bank. But she would only earn some pittance on it. Robert! The man was running through his share of the inheritance like water, buying a sports car and going through a major midlife crisis that included ditching his wife and kids. As for Aaron, her oldest sibling, he'd already lost some of his money on speculative stocks. Not to mention that weekend in Reno and the rumors of him having been up thirty thousand dollars at the blackjack table, only to end up losing and playing double-up to catch up. It hadn't worked and Aaron had been touchy about it ever since.

Then there was Oliver, who was pledging all of his money to the church and God. Of course, she thought, frowning, wondering if Oliver's sudden renewed faith was because of her. Guilt dug a deeper hole in her heart as she remembered that after the accident, when Ryan had lost his life and Neville had disappeared, Oliver had turned ultrareligious, to the point that he'd applied to the seminary and now was studying for the priesthood. Her part in his newfound faith was murky. Unclear. However, her being accused of her husband's murder had been a factor.

Shannon shrugged it off, wouldn't revisit that familiar but forbidden territory.

She suspected her brother Shea was the one who'd been careful with his share of the inheritance. But then, he was always careful. With his money. With his life. A secretive sort, who trod softly but heavily armed. He not only carried a big stick but a bazooka and grenades as well.

Who were her brothers to offer up advice? They could spout their negative opinions until hell froze over, but she'd do what she thought best. She was nothing if not as stubborn as they were.

It was probably all their negative vibes that had made her nervous the last time she'd walked the overgrown acres. That was all.

Then why, suddenly, was she so anxious? Not sleeping? Jumping at shadows? Awaking from god-awful nightmares?

She grimaced and dropped her washcloth into the sink. Maybe it was time to visit her shrink again. It had been over a year since she'd felt strong enough to end the weekly sessions that had helped her sort out her life.

Though she didn't much like the thought, maybe she truly was one of those people who needed therapy just to keep functioning.

"Great," she muttered.

Lord, it was hot. The temperatures had been teetering around one hundred all week, the evenings barely cooling into the high eighties. All over town there was talk of a serious drought and, of course, the escalating threat of fire.

She refused to gaze at her reflection again. "You'll look better in the morning," she said, then wondered if there was enough foundation in the warehouses of Revlon to make her appear fresh-faced. She couldn't begin to imagine how many drops of Visine it was going to take when she slipped her contact lenses into her eyes in a few hours.

Her mouth tasted foul. She rubbed some toothpaste over her teeth, rinsed, then twisted hard on the handles of the dripping faucet, listening as the old pipes groaned in protest. Still the scent of smoke and fire lingered.

Dabbing her mouth dry with a hand towel, she wondered why she couldn't get the acrid odor out of her nostrils.

At that moment she heard Khan growl. Low. Warning.

Still holding the towel she glanced through the doorway and saw a gray-and-brown blur as he leapt onto the bed.

"What the devil?" she asked as he stared out the window.

Only then did she realize what was wrong. The smoke still lingered in her nose and throat because it was more than just a conjured image in her dream. It was real.

Her heart nearly stopped. She raced across the floor as Khan, body stiff, hackles on end, began to bark wildly.

Oh, God, what was it?

Fear crawled up her spine. She peered anxiously through the screen and saw nothing but the night. A sliver of moon was rising over the surrounding hills and beginning to lighten the five acres abutting her property, an expanse of arid, weed-infested fields that was about to be turned into a subdivision. A sudden gust of dry wind, bearing hard from the east, stole through the valley, shook the branches of the trees near the house and rustled the already dead and dying leaves.

Nothing seemed amiss.

Nothing seemed out of the ordinary.

Except for the smell.

Her fear deepened.

Khan growled again, his head low, eyes peering through the open window. Suddenly aware that her naked body was silhouetted against the lamp glow, she clicked off the light, then scrounged blindly in the drawer of the nightstand for her glasses. All the while her gaze moved over the shadowy, moon-dappled ground. She saw nothing . . . or was that a glow in the south pasture? Oh, Jesus. Her throat closed. She found her glasses, knocking over the bedside lamp as she yanked them from their case. In a second she had them perched over the bridge of her nose and was squinting into the darkness.

The glow was gone . . . there was no eerie light, no crackling flames . . . but the thin smell of smoke lingered. She could taste it on her tongue.

Could it be from *inside* the house?

Then why was the dog looking out the window?

She reached for the phone, intent upon calling Nate Santana, who lived above the garage, then remembered he was gone for the week, the first vacation he'd taken in years. "Damn." She clenched her teeth. There was no one else she felt she could call about a possible emergency at midnight. Not even her brothers, who still, after three years, thought she was slightly off-kilter.

Every muscle tense, she hurried across the hardwood floor to the dormer that poked over the roof on the other side of the room. She cautiously peered through the window that gave a view over the front of the house, across the gravel lot to the barns, kennels and sheds. Squinting through the wash of eerie light from the security lamps, she saw nothing disturbed, nothing that warranted the dog being nervous.

Maybe Khan heard an owl or a bat.

Or sensed a deer or raccoon wandering across the back fields.

And you, you're just edgy, reacting to the bad dream and weird phone call . . .

But it didn't explain the slight hint of smoke still lingering in the air. "Come on," she said to the dog. "Let's investigate." She headed down the steps without snapping on any lights and Khan flew past her, nearly knocking her over, his claws clicking noisily on the stairs as he led the way to the front door. Once in the small foyer he stood, nose to the door, muscles taut.

By now she wasn't buying his act.

She stood on her tiptoes and peered through the small windows cut into the oak panels of the door. Outside the night was still, the wind having died quickly. Her truck was parked where she'd left it in front of the garage, the doors to the sheds and barns were closed, the parking lot empty. The windows in Nate's apartment over the garage were dark.

See? Nothing more than your imagination working overtime again.

She tried to relax, but the knot of tension between her shoulder blades didn't loosen. Her headache raged on—unfazed by the pain relievers she'd downed.

Shannon walked into the kitchen and looked through the larger window with its view of the parking lot and small paddocks, which she used as training grounds for the search and rescue dogs she worked with. The dogs in the kennels weren't barking, no sound issuing from the barn where the horses Nate trained were stabled. No one was lurking in the shadows.

Khan, unmoving, whined near the door. "False alarm," she told him and silently chided herself for being such a coward.

When had *that* happened? When had her sense of adventure dissolved? She, who had grown up with all those older brothers, who had never shown any fear and insisted upon doing everything they did, who had never been frightened of anything. When had she turned into a scaredy-cat?

Shannon had grown up around these parts. She'd been a tomboy. As a child, she'd been nearly fearless. She'd learned to ride a two-wheeler bicycle before her fourth birthday, and by the time she was eighteen, she'd driven her oldest brother's Harley—south down Highway 101—along the entire length of the rugged California coastline. She'd ridden horses bareback as a child, even entered barrel-racing competitions at a local rodeo. At fifteen, behind her parents' back she and two friends had hitchhiked to an outdoor concert at Red Rocks Amphitheatre outside of Denver. Later, she'd survived an accident where she'd been at the wheel of Robert's new Mustang convertible. The car ended up in a deep ditch, nose and engine first, and had been totaled; she'd managed to get out of it with a broken collarbone, a sprained wrist, two black eyes and a battered ego. She suspected that to this day, Robert had never forgiven her.

It was no wonder that when she'd fallen in love, she'd fallen fast, hard, and hadn't believed for a second that anything but wonderful things would come of it.

"Idiot," she muttered under her breath when she thought of Brendan Giles, her first love. How foolish and head over heels she'd been, crushed when it had ended . . .

To dispel her dark thoughts, she opened the refrigerator and rummaged behind a six-pack of Diet Pepsi to find a chilled bottle of water. Snagging the water, she closed the refrigerator, once again plunging the kitchen into darkness. Resting her hips against the counter, she pressed the cold plastic bottle against her forehead as sweat continued to run down her back.

Air-conditioning. That's what she needed. *Air-conditioning and a way to keep idiots from calling her in the middle of the night.*

Khan finally gave up his vigil, trotting by her and scratching at the back door. His hackles were no longer raised and he glanced over his shoulder at her, eyes pleading, as if he couldn't wait to go out and lift his leg on the first available shrub.

"Sure, why not?" she muttered. "Knock yourself out." Still holding the bottle to her head, she unlatched the back door. "Just don't make a habit of this. It *is* the middle of the night." Khan rocketed outside and she followed, hoping for some relief from the heat. Maybe a breeze would kick up.

No such luck.

The night was hot and still.

Breathless.

Shannon took one step onto the porch when her gaze caught something out of place, a piece of white paper tacked to one of the posts supporting the overhang from the roof.

Goose bumps chased a quick path up her spine even though the paper might be nothing. Someone leaving a note.

At night? Why not just call . . . ?

Her blood chilled. *Maybe whoever had left the piece of paper* had *phoned.*

She stepped backwards and leaned inside the kitchen, slapping at the wall until she hit the light switch and the porch was suddenly awash with incandescence from the two overhead lightbulbs.

She froze.

Her gaze riveted to the paper.

"Oh, God."

Shannon's insides turned to water as she stared at the scrap of white. It had been singed, the edges curling and black. And someone had tacked it to the post with a green pushpin.

Heart thundering in her ears, Shannon stepped closer. The charred paper was a form of some kind, she realized. Adjusting her glasses she read the smudged, partially burned words that were still visible in the middle of the document.

Mother's name: Shannon Leah Flan—
Father's name: Brendan Giles

She gasped.

Her breath froze in her lungs.

Date of Birth: September twenty-thr—
Time of Birth: 12:07 A.M.

"No!" she cried, dropping the water bottle and hearing it roll off the porch as if from a distance. *September twenty-three!* Her mind raced. Tomorrow. No, that was wrong. It was already after midnight, so today was the twenty-third of September and the call . . . Oh, God, the phone call had come in at precisely 12:07. Knees buckling, she leaned against the porch rail, her gaze scouring the darkness, searching for whoever had done this to her, whoever had wanted to bring back all the pain. "You son of a bitch," she bit out through clenched teeth. Despite the hot night she was chilled to the core.

Thirteen years ago, on September twenty-third, at exactly seven minutes after twelve midnight, Shannon had given birth to a seven-pound baby girl.

She hadn't seen the child since.

Chapter 2

He stood before the fire, feeling its heat, listening to the crackle of flames as they devoured the tinder-dry kindling. With all the shades drawn, he slowly unbuttoned his shirt, the crisp white cotton falling off his shoulders as moss ignited, hissing. Sparking.

Above the mantel was a mirror and he watched himself undress, looked at his perfectly honed body, muscles moving easily, flexing, and sliding beneath the taut skin of an athlete.

He glanced at his eyes. Blue. Icy. Described by one woman as "bedroom eyes," by another as "cold eyes," by yet another unsuspecting woman as "eyes that had seen too much."

They'd all been right, he thought, and flashed a smile. A "killer smile," he'd heard.

Bingo.

The women had no idea how close to the truth they'd all been.

He was handsome and he knew it. Not good-looking enough to turn heads on the street, but so interesting that women, once they noticed him, had trouble looking away.

There had been a time when he'd picked and chosen and rarely been denied.

He unbuckled his leather belt, let it fall to the hardwood floor. His slacks slid easily off his butt down his legs and pooled at his feet. He hadn't bothered with boxers or jockeys. Who cared? It was all about outward appearances.

Always.

His smile fell away as he walked closer to the mantel, feeling the heat already radiating from the old bricks. Pictures in frames stood at attention upon the smooth wood. Images he'd caught when his subject didn't realize he or she was on camera. People who knew him. Or of him. People who had to pay. The kid, the old lady, the brothers. All caught on film without their knowledge.

Fools!

Behind the pictures was his hunting knife. Bone-handled with a thin steel blade that could cut easily, slice through any living thing. Fur, skin, hide, muscle, bone, sinew—all cleaved easily with the right amount of exertion.

The knife was his second choice for a weapon.

His first was gasoline and a match . . . but sometimes that just wasn't enough.

He tested the blade against his palm and sure enough, though he barely touched his skin, a thin trail of blood emerged, drops of red that formed the shallowest of slits that ran parallel to his lifeline.

He saw an irony in that and ignored the other tiny scars on his palm, evidence of his fascination with the blade. He watched the red trail widen and ooze and when there was enough blood to form a thick drop, he held his palm over the fire. Feeling its heat, nearly burning his skin, he stared as the red droplet plunged downward to sizzle and burn as it met the eager flames.

"Tonight it starts," he vowed, having completed the first phase of his plan, the hint warning her that he was afoot. Within the hour he'd start the next phase by traveling steadily north. And by evening the next step would be accomplished. He'd start with the old woman—what did she call herself? Blanche Johnson? Yeah, right. He snorted at her ridiculous attempt at anonymity. *He* knew who she really was, disguised as that silly old piano teacher in her knit scarves. And she would pay, just as Shannon Flannery would. Just as the rest of them would.

He fingered the knife. He'd start with Blanche; and then, once he'd lured the girl away, it would be Shannon's turn. Shannon and the others. He let his gaze wander over the pictures until they came to the slightly larger, framed shot of Shannon. Jaw tight, he stared at her gorgeous face.

Innocent and sexy, sweet yet seductive.

And guilty as hell.

He traced a finger along her hairline, his guts churning as he noticed her green eyes, slightly freckled nose, thick waves of unruly auburn curls. Her skin was pale, her eyes lively, her smile tenuous, as if she'd sensed him hiding in the shadowy trees, his lens poised at her heart-shaped face.

The dog, some kind of scraggly mutt, had appeared from the other side of the woods, lifted his nose in the air as he'd reached her, trembled, growled, and nearly given him away. Shannon had given the cur a short command and peered into the woods.

By that time he'd been slipping away. Silently moving through the dark trees and brush, putting distance between them, heading upwind. He'd gotten his snapshots. He'd needed nothing more.

Then.

Because the timing hadn't been right.

But now . . .

The fire glowed bright, seemed to pulse with life as it grew, giving the bare room a warm, rosy glow. He stared again at his image. So perfect in the mirror.

He turned, facing away from the reflection.

Looking over his shoulder, he gritted those perfect white teeth, gnashing them together as he saw the mirror's cruel image of his back, the skin scarred and shiny, looking as if it had melted from his body.

He remembered the fire.

The agony of his flesh being burned from his bones.

He'd never forget.

Not for as long as he drew a breath on this godforsaken planet.

And those who had done this to him would pay.

From the corner of his eye, he saw the picture of Shannon again. Beautiful and wary, as if she knew her life was about to change forever.

But first, he needed bait.

To get the woman to do his bidding.

He smiled to himself. How fortunate the daughter was living in Falls Crossing, a small town in Oregon on the banks of the Columbia River. He knew it well. Had visited. Had waited. Had watched.

It was fate that the girl and the old woman calling herself Blanche knew each other, that they were in the same place, that he could kill two birds with one stone . . . or maybe with two matches.

The flames in the grate crackled and spit.

How foolish they all were.

The girl.

The old lady.

And Shannon.

All feeling secure with their lives, their secrets, their lies. Didn't they know that no one was safe? Not ever?

If they were foolish enough to believe otherwise, then they were all in for a very big, very ugly surprise.

He sheathed his knife and felt anticipation thrum through his veins. He'd waited long for this. Suffered. But now it was his turn. Tonight he'd set the wheels in motion.

But it was just the beginning.

He had a few little details to take care of and then he'd be on his way.

Look out, he thought, smiling evilly, glancing down at the knife blade to see the reflection of the fire in the long, thin blade. *I'm coming, Shannon, oh, yes, I'm coming. And this time I'll have more than a camera and an old birth certificate with me.*

* * *

"What the hell were you thinking?" Aaron demanded, jabbing a finger at the burned scrap of paper lying on Shannon's kitchen table. It, along with the pushpin, was protected in a plastic Baggie on the scarred oak surface, lying next to the newspaper and matching ceramic salt and pepper shakers in the shape of Dalmatian dogs.

It was sweltering in the kitchen even with the oscillating fan droning loudly as it shuffled the hot air from one side of the room to the other. Khan was lying near the back door, positioned on a small rag rug, watching Shannon closely, as if he expected her to miraculously come up with some kind of table scrap.

Shannon snapped the dishwasher closed and pushed the START button. The motor clicked, the water started to run and she finally turned to face her brother. "What was I thinking? I don't know. I was reacting mainly, I guess."

"For three damned days."

"Yeah. That's right. For three days."

The other night, after finding the note and once she'd gotten her wits about her, she'd donned a pair of latex gloves that she used when she cleaned the dog kennels, removed the partial birth certificate from the post and dropped it, along with the pushpin into a Ziploc bag.

"Why didn't you call me when it happened?"

"Look, Aaron, I didn't know what to do, okay?" she admitted, wiping her hands on a worn kitchen towel. "It . . . it was a shock."

"I'll bet." Aaron shoved a hand through his thick hair, paced to the refrigerator, opened the door and yanked out a beer. Seeing that the can was marked Lite he scowled, then popped the top anyway and pushed himself up onto the counter, where his long khaki-clad legs swung in front of the loudly thrumming dishwasher. Droplets of sweat were visible on his forehead and temples.

Shannon's oldest brother was the spitting image of their father. Same square jaw. Same intense, don't-bullshit-me blue eyes. Same straight nose—his nostrils flaring over his trimmed moustache when he was irritated. Exactly the same red-hot rage that could flash at any given moment. Aaron's quick temper had gotten him kicked out of the army, out of the fire department and into anger-management therapy with a local psychologist, whom he'd stopped seeing over a year ago.

Currently he was flying solo, as he called it, running his own private detective agency, which was a one-man operation tied into a secretarial service.

Now, his gaze never leaving his sister, he took a long swallow from the can, then asked, "So does anyone else know about this?"

"Just whoever left it."

"And you think he called."

"He or she. Yeah. It was all intentional. Someone wanted to freak me out and they did—man, did they ever. So that's why I called you—"

"Eventually."

"Look, I could have called Shea, but I didn't want the police involved, at least not yet, not until I know what's going on. And I could have called Robert, but I didn't think this was something the fire department would be interested in. Nothing was burned or damaged."

"Except your peace of mind."

"Amen," she whispered, shaking her head.

"So by process of elimination, you decided to call me."

"You seemed the logical choice."

"Since when were you ever logical?" he said with a bit of a smile.

"I don't know, maybe since I finally decided to grow up." She found a rubber band on the windowsill, bent over and pushed her hair into a ponytail. Straightening, she stared out the window. She'd fed the dogs, made sure they were secure, then seen to the horses before calling her brother. Now dusk was encroaching, casting long shadows across the parking lot and outbuildings, though the temperature refused to drop. "You're a PI. I figured you could look into it."

Aaron took another swallow from his beer and, looking over his shoulder, followed her gaze. Hitching his chin toward the garage and Nate Santana's darkened apartment, he asked, "Santana's not around?"

"No."

"Convenient, don't you think?"

"Coincidence." She bristled and wondered, not for the first time since calling Aaron's cell phone, if calling him had been a mistake. Truth to tell, that's why she'd put it off. She didn't want to rely on any of her brothers, didn't want to appear unable to handle her own problems, didn't need their meddling. So she'd waited, then decided she needed Aaron's expertise and now, of course, she was second-guessing herself all over the place.

"I thought you didn't believe in 'coincidence.'"

"I don't."

"But you don't find it strange that the first time Santana's gone for a few days, this kind of thing happens?" He hooked a thumb toward the plastic-encased scrap of paper lying near the ceramic dogs on the table. "I figured the two of you were close."

"We're partners, that's it."

"He moving up to the new place with you?"

"I don't know, but not into the house." She sighed and threw her brother a don't-start-with-that-again glare. "It's not like that between Nate and me, not that it's any of your business."

"It is now."

"Okay. Right. But Nate and I are just business partners. We're not lovers, okay? If that's what you're hinting at. As for him moving, I don't know yet. We're still talking."

Aaron grunted, possibly to imply that he didn't believe her, but didn't voice it. Good. His eyes were more sober than ever as he asked, "You ever contacted your kid?"

"What?" she asked, startled.

"The baby you gave up, the one that just had the birthday, have you ever contacted her?"

"No! I mean, I don't even know where she is."

At that thought she felt the same painful pang she always did when she remembered giving away her only child, never seeing her baby after that one brief glimpse of the infant in the hospital. Coupled with that dull ache was the sear of guilt for not being strong enough to raise her child alone. No matter how many times she'd told herself she'd done the right thing, that the little girl was far better off with loving parents who desperately wanted a child, the doubts still stole into her thoughts, into her dreams . . . Sudden, hot, unwanted tears touched the back of her eyelids.

Her voice, when she spoke again, was a rasp. "I've thought about it. God, I've wanted to. But, no, I haven't even tried. Haven't put my name on one of those Internet lists or filed with the agencies that help adoptees find their birth parents."

"But you've thought about it?"

She nodded.

"Did you tell anyone?"

"No." She cleared her throat. "I figured I might do it in a few years, when she's an adult."

Aaron rubbed his chin. "What about Giles?"

"Brendan?" she repeated, even though she'd anticipated that her ex-boyfriend, the father of her baby, would be brought up.

"Yeah. You heard from him?"

"No . . . Never."

Aaron's forehead furrowed as if he doubted her. The dog, realizing there was no treat in store, stood and stretched as he yawned, his black lips pulled back to show his teeth.

"Never," she repeated, the old wounds opening and raw. She saw a speck of water on the counter and rubbed it dry with her finger.

"He's the kid's father."

"I *know*, Aaron, but remember, he took off when he heard I was pregnant. Left the country."

"You think." He hopped off the counter and landed lithely on the old, cracked linoleum floor.

"I know. The whole town knows." She held up her hands and blew out a long breath. "Let's not drag him into this."

"I'd just like to talk to him."

Not me, Shannon thought. She never wanted to see Brendan Giles again for as long as she lived. "He's a coward and wasn't interested in the baby, not in the least. But if you can find him, great. Go for it." The muscles in her face tightened as she remembered their final confrontation about her pregnancy. She remembered how his handsome face had twisted into something hideous, how his lips had curled, almost in revulsion, how he'd said the words that had burned into her brain and broken her already-fragile heart. "You know," she admitted now, "Brendan had the nerve, the unmitigated gall to suggest that the baby might not be his."

"It's a normal guy response."

"No, not a normal guy. It's a coward's way out."

"You could have insisted upon a paternity test."

"Why? So he could be forced to do something he didn't *want* to do? To claim the baby? To admit responsibility to me? No, Aaron, that wasn't an option."

"At least you didn't end up marrying him."

He said the words and they settled like lead in the hot kitchen. Because they both thought of Ryan Carlyle. The man she *had* married. The one she'd been accused of killing. Probably a worse choice than Brendan Giles. Boy, could she pick 'em. No wonder she'd avoided any serious relationship since Ryan's death.

Aaron checked his watch. "Mind if I take this?" he asked, picking up the plastic bag.

She shook her head and he pocketed the Ziplock with its damning burned slip of paper, then bent down to pat Khan's head. "So, for now, let's just keep what's going on between you and me," he suggested. "We'll tell Shea later, if we need to, but until we know more, let me poke around and see what I come up with." He finished his beer, crushed the can and left it on the counter. The humorless grin he flashed her reminded her again of their father.

Aaron started for the door, Khan at his heels, then stopped and faced her, his smile fading. "You know, Shannon, I don't like this."

"You and me both."

"I'll see ya later."

He gave her a quick hug, patted Khan's head again, then walked outside into the hot, dry twilight. Darkness was fast encroaching, the security lamps starting to glow. Aaron jogged to his car and slipped inside, starting the ignition as he lit a cigarette. The engine revved, and he tromped on the accelerator.

Shannon watched as the taillights of his Honda faded through the trees. The darkness seemed to swallow him up. Quickly Shannon closed the door and checked the lock. Her fingers automatically reached for Khan's collar, holding him close. It was good to have him. It was good not to be completely alone.

Chapter 3

"Forgive me, Father, for I have sinned." Oliver Flannery bowed his head. He was naked, kneeling on the forest floor, and doubting the vows he would soon take. He'd worked so hard for his goal: to become a parish priest, to follow the calling, to devote his life to God.

And he was so unworthy.

So damned unworthy.

He felt the hot whisper of the night caress his back, as if a demon straight from hell was breathing against him.

How many people had he lied to?

How many laws of God and man had he broken?

He'd come here, to the forest, where he'd first heard the voice of God, not a human voice booming into his ear, but something quieter, almost meek, that had started inside him and swelled to a noise as loud as the roar of the surf.

He'd climbed atop an outcropping of rock high upon on a hill and had considered hurling himself over. As he'd stood, naked as he was now, poised to end his life, his toes stretched over the sharp edge, the voice had come to him. Speaking softly at first, calming him, slowing his rapid heartbeat.

Give yourself to Me, Oliver. I will heal you, and you, in turn, will heal others. Trust. Have faith. Abandon all earthly possessions. Follow Me, Oliver, and I will forgive you for all your sins.

"All?" he'd whispered so long ago.

Trust in Me.

He'd wavered, eyes closed, feeling the urge to jump, the seductive pull of the dry creek bed a hundred feet below. He lifted his arms, intent on free-falling when God had said, *I forgive you.*

Oliver's eyes had flown open and he looked down to the valley floor, a dizzy sensation sweeping over him as he'd stepped back, his heart knocking, sweat running down his sternum and spine. What had he been thinking? Had God really spoken to him? Or was he going mad, the guilt that had been gnawing at his soul finally taking over his mind?

Trust, the voice commanded again. *Give yourself to Me.*

Oliver had fallen to his knees, tears running down his face, and had vowed to become God's humble servant from that moment forward.

But he'd failed.

Everything he'd done had been a lie.

And once again he considered the easier path, the quick way out. But killing oneself was cowardly. And a sin.

Another sin.

His jaw tightened as he reexamined his sorry life.

Lowering himself even farther so that he was lying prostrate in the grass and leaves, he desperately begged that God would heed his prayers.

Forgive him.

Guide him.

But in the darkness, with a slit of a moon rising high in the starry night, he heard only the sound of his own traitorous heartbeat and the sigh of the hot wind rustling dry leaves, rattling the brittle branches of the trees overhead.

Sweat collected everywhere on his bare skin and a cold whisper of fear congealed his blood.

The voice of God was silent.

The only sound was the demons whispering in his brain. Taunting him. Tempting him. Telling him that which he already knew: he was unworthy.

"Help me," he cried aloud, anguish and pain ripping through him, guilt seeming to squeeze the breath from his lungs. His fingers clawed at the dry earth, leaves and twigs, and dead grass compressing into his powerless fists. Tears fell from his eyes as he thought of Jesus on the cross, how He'd died for Oliver's own sins.

Was that fair?

No.

And yet he couldn't control the restless demons warring for his soul, couldn't stop the hot impulses pounding through his blood.

In desperation, he looked up at the heavens, to the stars and the thin, nearly imperceptible fingernail of the moon. Was God listening? Did He care?

Oliver closed his eyes and let his face fall to the earth where dust billowed up his nostrils and clogged his throat.

"Please, Father," he implored in agony, "help me."

But he heard no sounds of comfort.

Found no answers.

The demons laughed.

Tonight, it seemed, God had truly forsaken him.

For the first time in her life, Dani Settler ditched school.

She felt a little guilty about it and she hated missing PE, the last period of her day, her favorite class. Even the teacher, Mr. Jamison, was cool. One of the few cool teachers at Harrington Junior High.

But she had to do this. *Had* to. Even though it was only the third week of school.

Hitching her backpack onto her shoulder, she left by a side door near the gym. She walked rapidly past a row of arborvitae that prevented anyone in the school office from seeing her—especially nosey Miss Craig, the pinched-faced attendance person—then dashed around the bus barns.

So far, so good, she thought, already sweating. It was late September and there wasn't the breath of fall in the air. Just dusty, dry leaves and overhead, in an intensely blue sky, the fading vapor trail of a jet heading east. The sun was beastly, sitting above the mountains and sending out shimmering waves of heat. Still she increased her pace to a jog. She had forty minutes to get to the cybercafe and back before the buses were scheduled to leave for the day. She'd be marked absent for PE, her dad would be called, but she'd be home and ready with her excuse before he could get really mad.

She crossed her fingers at that thought. Hated when she made Dad angry, hated it worse when she disappointed him. But this time she felt that she had no choice.

Never looking over her shoulder Dani just kept jogging along a side street, then cut through the park, the bottoms of her Nikes slapping the asphalt trail where fir trees stood tall and green, offering shade, and the oaks were already shedding their leaves.

Her plan was pretty simple. Once inside the cybercafe and seated at a computer, she would log on to a server using her new free Internet account. It was one she'd opened at her friend Jessica's house, giving the server fake information about herself. Jessica knew nothing about her new name, nor did Andrea, whose computer she also used. They thought she was always DaniSet321, the cybername and e-mail address everyone knew her by, the one she used when she was instant messaging or e-mailing her friends.

No one imagined that she had another alias because every time she used someone's computer, she logged on as DaniSet321, then, when no one was paying any attention, she switched to the other name. She figured she was pretty safe and wouldn't get caught because Andrea and Jessica's older brothers had installed antispyware. Between that and some other programs, information got buried so deep on the hard drive "it would probably blow up the CIA's computer if they ever tried to sort through all the layers of information," Stephen—Jessica's pimply, technogeek older brother—was proud of saying. She tried to forget that she'd often called him a "moron of unchallenged proportions" and had to trust him this time.

So Dani had taken a chance that she wouldn't be found out and nearly a year ago she'd started surfing the net as BorninSF0923. So far it seemed that no one around here was the wiser. Her new name was designed to attract the attention of someone looking for her. She knew she'd been born in San Francisco and her birthday was September 23.

She felt a little guilty about deceiving her dad, but if he found out, he'd flip and he was stressed out enough as it was. Though outwardly cool about being a single parent, she knew it bothered him, a lot. Recently he'd started dating again and the thought of him getting married to someone other than Mom really blew. She was glad he was getting over the pain of Ella's death, but Dani wasn't that thrilled with the prospect of a new "mother," who probably would have a couple of kids and an ex-husband and other relatives to muddy the water.

But Dani had her own mission. Ever since her mother had

died, her curiosity about her biological roots had grown into what she now realized was an obsession. She was getting so close! Not that the people she hoped to find—those related by blood—would ever replace her parents. No way! Thinking like that was just plain stupid.

Nonetheless she had the driving need to know where she'd come from. Who were her birth parents? Where, exactly, had she been born? What were the circumstances? Did she have any siblings, even half brothers and sisters? Were her mother and father married? Had they been? Were they even alive? In prison? Had she been the result of a one-night stand, or maybe even a rape? At that thought she withered inside, but she kept on jogging down the back alleys toward the river.

It had taken nearly a year but finally someone in the chat rooms she visited had indicated there was hope of finding her birth parents, or at least learning who they were. That person was BJC27, a woman who claimed she had been adopted and had struggled for years to find her birth parents, both of whom were alive and whom she'd finally, at the age of twenty-seven, met. Though her father still denied that he had sired this daughter, her mother had cried when they'd reconnected and introduced her to her two half brothers. It had been the most profound experience in Bethany Jane's life and she'd since dedicated her free time to helping others do the same. She and Dani, under the guise of BorninSF0923, had started e-mailing. Bethany Jane was certain she would be able to help her and had been looking into private adoptions in the San Francisco area that took place thirteen years ago.

Dani had been suspicious at first, wary of a fraud. She'd even gone so far as to check out BJC27 through her server where, in the user profiles, she'd found Bethany Jane was from Phoenix, single, was in her early forties and was a librarian at a small college. Though Bethany had given her nothing but her first and middle names, Dani had checked her out. She'd gone to the college's Web site and seen that

Bethany Jane Crandall did work at the library. Her picture was included. A Google search brought up several Bethany Jane Crandalls, but this one was linked to the library, a reader's group, and an organization that was called Birth Writes and was dedicated to working for and with adoptive families.

Good enough.

The last message Bethany had left BorninSF0923 was to assure Dani that she'd found the names and addresses of her birth parents and was going to send documents of proof over the Internet. Dani couldn't take a chance on having them sent to the house or even to her friends' homes, so she'd decided on the cybercafe located on the north end of town.

And she was almost there! The smell of the river, a deep, dank odor she'd grown to love, reached her and as she crossed the streets of the town, she caught glimpses of the Columbia rushing steadily westward. Sunlight spangled the ever-moving gray water, catching in the frigid current as it slashed a sharp, swift canyon between the states of Washington and Oregon.

Over the years her dad had shown her how to respect the river. He'd taken Dani windsurfing, fishing and boating on the Columbia's ever-changing surface. They'd ridden horses on the steep ridge overlooking the river's chasm, they'd pitched a tent near the falls.

She felt another sharp pang of guilt. Travis Settler had done everything he could to teach her about living in the wild, taking care of herself and preserving nature. She knew how to man a canoe, hunt with a bow and arrow, track and make a campfire. He'd shown her which plants and grubs were edible, and which were poisonous. All in all, he'd done everything in his power to make her strong and self-sufficient.

And how was she repaying him?

By lying to him through her teeth!

Yet she'd come this far and wasn't about to turn back. She was too close to the truth.

As she passed by a Dumpster behind the Canyon Café,

she scared a cat who had been sunning himself. Hissing, the tabby scurried off the top of the large green box and slunk into the adjoining parking lot, where it hid beneath a dirty white van with Arizona plates. Dani probably wouldn't have noticed that the van was from out of state, except for the game she and her dad had played for years when they took road trips. Each would try to outdo the other, spotting new and different plates as they drove. Hadn't she seen a van like this across from the school yesterday afternoon?

With the cat glowering from beside a back tire, Dani slowed to a walk and shoved the sweat out of her eyes with the back of her wrist. She slipped into the shade of an awning covering an empty loading dock for the hardware store. Quickly, before anyone came through the open back door, she slid off her backpack, unzipped the main compartment, reached in and retrieved her disguise, which she felt she had to use just in case she came across anyone she knew. It wasn't much, but at a passing glance no one would recognize her. Just in case she messed up and her dad started asking questions.

Besides, though she'd never seen anyone spying on her, lately she'd had the weird feeling that she was being watched and followed. She worried that her dad had sensed something was wrong and was tailing her. Which was just stupid. Her guilt eating at her for deceiving him.

Shoving those uncomfortable thoughts aside, she put on a tattered Yankees' baseball cap and oversized gray sweatshirt she'd taken from the school's lost and found. Next she withdrew a pair of cheap dark sunglasses she'd bought at the drugstore. She completed the outfit with a pair of blue sweatpants that someone had left in the locker room two days earlier.

Her shoes would have to do. She wouldn't change out of her favorite Nikes. Just in case she had to make a quick getaway. Beyond the obvious dishonesty, there was something about her scheme that made her nervous. Probably because she looked like a total dweeb. The fact that she did look so

nerdy and overdressed for the hot day might cause someone
to notice her more than if she'd just left well enough alone,
but she was committed to her plan.

She crammed her hair into the cap, drew the bill down
over her eyes, slid the sunglasses onto the bridge of her nose
and sweltered in the huge, stinky sweatshirt. Then, to make
sure she wouldn't attract attention should her cell phone
ring, she turned it off and slipped it into her pocket.

So it was now or never!

A yellowjacket buzzed around her head and she swiped at
it while glancing around to make certain that no one had witnessed her transformation. Her palms were sweating and she
bit at her lip, her nerves showing, no doubt, because she'd
been lying to everyone she knew. Even to her best friend,
Allie Kramer, whom she was supposed to meet after school,
right before they got onto their buses.

If she made it.

*Hurry, hurry, hurry! And don't get wet feet now. Just do
it!*

But the paranoia, a feeling that she was being observed
from some hidden window or crevice, remained with her.

Dani had resorted to lying to her father on other occasions when she'd thought he was being ridiculously overprotective. Her cell phone had made it so convenient. She was
able to call him and tell him she was somewhere she wasn't,
or diffuse any upcoming fight by calling him first and explaining before actually admitting anything face-to-face.

Taking a deep breath, she slung the backpack onto one
shoulder just as she heard the sound of voices emanating
from the open door of the hardware store. And they were
getting louder. Someone was definitely coming. Someone
who probably knew her and her dad. Crap! She flew off the
loading dock and tried not to think about how disappointed
her father would be if he found out what she'd been doing.

Dani hated sneaking around behind his back, but ever
since her mother's death, he'd been more closed-mouthed
about her birth parents than ever, always saying, "When

you're older, eighteen, if you still want to know, I'll help you."

Eighteen? That was five years from now. She could be dead before then.

No, she couldn't wait, she thought as she rounded a corner. Since there was no traffic she jaywalked across the street, past a tavern named the Not Whole. How dumb, she thought, eyeing the neon beer signs in the window and the pock-marked door.

Tucking an errant lock of hair under her cap, Dani wiped the sweat from her neck. Well, it wasn't her fault that he'd gotten all weird and overprotective when Mom had died. Jesus, all of a sudden he'd started acting like she would break or something, all of a sudden he was angry if she brought up questions about her birth, all of a sudden he drank a lot more until, finally, he'd started dating again. And *that* was another nightmare. Dad getting all dressed up and combing his hair and splashing on skin bracer and cologne for God's sake.

Yuck! Sick!

Dani shuddered at the thought. She used to be able to talk to him about anything but when it came down to the big question—*Who am I really?*—her father just plain shut down. His blue eyes darkened, his lips pinched and the cords in the back of his neck appeared to stick out. It was as if he didn't trust her with that knowledge, afraid she'd up and leave him when she found out the names of her biological parents.

But she couldn't wait any longer, even though she knew Travis would blow a gasket. He'd find out that she'd missed her last class, but she had her excuse down pat: she was having menstrual cramps and was too embarrassed to tell the teacher. Her father wouldn't want to discuss that subject any too deeply. She'd beat the school to the punch and tell her dad about missing the class once she got home. He'd warn her never to do it again, the school would call, and he might go so far as to ground her for a couple of days. Probably he'd just lecture her.

But it would be worth it. Finally, she would have some answers.

She rounded a final corner to the cybercafe, checked her watch and found she was right on time. The Wireless Gorge, as it was called, was a little old house that had been converted to a warren of small offices. Sizzling pink neon announced that the place was open for business and other hand-painted signs listed their services: e-mail, fax, copying, printing and the like.

Palms sweating, Dani walked inside where the air was dry and the rooms were stuffy despite several fans busily moving the air around. The guy who ran the place was sitting in front of one of the dozen computer monitors all connected in a tangle of wires, modems and keyboards. He called himself Sarge and she thought he was somewhere in his sixties, though it was hard to tell with anyone over forty. He sat in the tattered secretary's chair he always seemed to occupy. Though he was obviously going bald, he pulled what remained of his hair into a ponytail and the clamped gray strands clung together and snaked down the back of his camouflage jacket. At the sound of the door opening, he glanced over his shoulder.

"I just want to check my e-mail," Dani said in a rush.

"Go for it." He pointed to the sign that showed what the price would be per fifteen-minute segment, then turned back to his computer monitor where, it appeared, he was playing an engrossing game of chess.

Good.

He'd barely given her a passing glance.

Dani wedged her way around a stack of copy paper and into what had once been the dining area of the little house, which now housed five glowing monitors. She found a computer in the back corner away from the windows and quickly logged on using her new cyberalias.

There was one message from BJC27.

Dani's heart pounded as she opened the e-mail and wondered why there was no attachment. Bethany Jane had written only three partial sentences:

> *Sorry. I'm having trouble with my e-mail attachments today. Will send ASAP.*

Dani couldn't believe it. The woman had *promised* she'd send everything today. *Promised!*

What a flake! She silently seethed for a second and quickly replied:

> *Pls send as soon as u can!*

Then she logged off. What a waste of five bucks! She left a bill on the counter and hurried outside where the heat hit her like a blast furnace.

She'd gone to all this trouble for—what?

Nothing!

Not one darn shred of information.

She'd have to lie to her dad and come up with another way to come down here, but only after she'd checked on Jessica's computer to see if an e-mail *with* an attachment had come through. She couldn't risk downloading it at her friend's house, so only when she knew the attachment had made it through would she come back and spend another five dollars.

Angry and deflated, she was peeling off her sweatshirt when she noticed the white van parked in the alley. She probably wouldn't have thought much about it, but it seemed like it was the same dirty one she'd seen across from the school.

Nah . . . this one had Idaho plates, but it looked a lot like the van she'd seen the tabby cat hiding beneath. It had the same dirty exterior. Same make and model. As she was passing, she noticed one door wasn't quite shut. Then she heard something . . . like a puppy whimpering. Geez, did someone have a dog in that tin can in this heat? What kind of moron would do that? She paused for a heartbeat when she saw a flash in the corner of her eye, something lunging at her.

She started to run, but it was too late.

A man leaped from behind the van and grabbed her in a viselike grip with one arm. He smashed a rag soaked with something awful over her mouth.

No! Oh, God, no!

She bucked away from him, but he was too strong.

If only she could round on him, she could kick and strike, landing blows that would incapacitate him. She writhed and tried to break free, to no avail.

Fear and adrenaline raced through her bloodstream.

She tried to scream but only took in more of the sickening smell. It filled her nostrils and throat. Frantically she kicked but hit nothing in her attempts. Whatever the hell the noxious stuff on the rag was, it weakened her, made her woozy, and within seconds she couldn't move, was barely awake.

In a daze she realized she was being dragged into the van.

No! Dani, don't let this happen. Fight! Run! Scream!

She flailed wildly, but her arms and legs were like rubber and any blow she landed was weak. Darkness welled at the corners of her brain, dragging her under.

In one last attempt, she swung her arm at his face, but only managed to slap him feebly, her fingers scraping down the side of his jaw without an ounce of strength. Her arm felt like it weighed a thousand pounds.

As he hauled her into the van, she noticed that there was no dog, no scared, overheated puppy in the darkness, just a cassette player hidden in the back.

She'd been fooled.

This guy had been waiting for her.

And she didn't doubt for a moment that he was going to kill her. As her eyes closed, she caught a glimpse of something else in the van.

A black plastic garbage sack, tied with a yellow ribbon.

And from the bottom of the bag, through a tiny hole, leaked a thin, dark stream of something that looked like blood.

Sickened, she rolled her eyes up at her captor, fearing she was about to die, certain that his face was the last she would ever see, and then, blackness.

Chapter 4

"It's been days," Travis Settler muttered through tight lips, fear for his missing daughter congealing in his blood as he sat idly, impotently at his kitchen table. "A damned lifetime."

He closed his eyes. Leaned back in the old dinette chair. Tried to quiet the rage and anxiety roiling deep in his gut by counting to ten. When that didn't do any good, he kept on reeling off numbers in his head. Eleven, twelve, thirteen . . . At seventy-nine he quit, opened his eyes to find Shane Carter, the sheriff of Lewis County, sizing him up.

Carter was a tall, rangy man who could have, in another century, been a cowboy. A bushy moustache that matched his near-black hair covered his upper lip and he had those hard brown eyes that could cut to the center of a man. Right now they were staring straight at Travis. "We're working on it," he said.

And the third man in the room, Lieutenant Larry Sparks, of the Oregon State Police, nodded his agreement.

Sparks was leaning a shoulder against the wall of the kitchen alcove, sipping coffee and frowning. Not a speck of humor showed in Sparks's dark gaze and the lines etched into his face said it all: everyone was worried. Beyond worried.

They all felt it, the disquiet of knowing that with each passing day they were losing ground. Over the stove, the old clock ticked off the seconds, emphatically reminding Sparks that time was rapidly fleeing.

"We'll find Dani," Carter said, conviction underscoring his words. "Just like we're going to nail the bastard who killed Blanche Johnson."

"When?" Never in his life had Travis felt so impotent, so totally worthless. Not even when his wife had died three years earlier. That had been painful. Unfair. Wrong. But this . . . "Hell!" he ground out before Carter answered his question. Because the sheriff couldn't respond. No one knew when . . . or, oh, God, *if*, she'd be located. No one knew a damned thing! They'd used tracking dogs. They'd used the Explorer Scouts along with the police and all the neighbors to search the town and surrounding wooded hillsides of Falls Crossing. They'd put up posters, called in the media, begging the public for help. And the police and FBI had questioned the students and staff of the school.

Still they'd found nothing. Not a damned thing.

And he was going out of his mind.

The police had gone over her room, inch by inch. They'd even taken his computer, hoping to find some indication that Dani had been surfing the Web, logging onto the Web sites where pedophiles trolled for unsuspecting prey.

Travis's guts squeezed so hard they ached. If some perverted bastard so much as touched one hair on her head . . . He couldn't go there—wouldn't. The authorities hadn't found any evidence on the hard drive that Dani had been searching for anything other than the humane society and related dog sites, always looking for another pet to rescue and bring home. As if three cats, a dog, two horses and even a box turtle weren't enough.

He glanced over at the box turtle's cage, an elaborate terrarium that he and Dani had created together. It now sat beneath the laundry room window, the turtle hidden inside his "house," a cutout plastic tub. His striped head, feet and tail were all tucked inside his shell. Travis could relate. At times he wanted to hide away; others, like now, he was so anxious and keyed up, he needed to do something, *anything!*

Rage and fear, his constant companions since learning that his daughter was missing, were eating at him, getting to him, and he couldn't stand another minute—make that second—of sitting around and waiting. As the clock ticked loudly and the empty refrigerator hummed, Travis Settler thought he would surely go out of his mind.

"No one has any idea where my girl is," he said, his voice rough. "Except for the son of a bitch who grabbed her." For a minute he couldn't breathe. He thought of Dani, his only child, with her untamed brown hair, smattering of freckles across her nose and wise-beyond-her-years eyes. She was tough—he'd raised her tough—but, Jesus, she was a kid, just a kid. Alone. With some kind of psycho.

Maybe she's just run away, as the police have suggested. Maybe her disappearance has nothing to do with Blanche Johnson's murder.

God, he only wished he believed for even a heartbeat that Dani had gotten a wild hair and set off for parts unknown, that she was safe, just rebellious.

But that was all hogwash. He knew it. Probably the police did, too.

His teeth gnashed in frustration and dread wormed its way through his soul. What was she going through now? Where the hell was she? Was she hurt? Or . . . or worse? A lump filled his throat. His eyes burned. But he wouldn't think the worst. Not yet. What was it his aunt had always said during trying times? "Where there's life, there's hope." Well, damn it all to hell, there had better be life . . . Oh, fuck . . . A hole the size of Wyoming filled the space where his heart had been.

He glanced at the corner of the table where he was sitting, to the phone, the one that the FBI had installed with a separate headset. It sat silent. Mocking him. Daring him to believe that his daughter was safe.

Dear God, Dani, where are you?

He unclenched one fist to shove it through his hair.

For the first time since leaving his special forces unit in the army nearly eighteen years earlier, Travis felt the need for quick action, a decisive plan, a no-holds-barred attack on whoever the hell it was who had stolen his child. His jaw grew so tight it hurt and his hands clenched into fists, only to open and curl up, open and curl, over and over again.

Finally he said the words that he'd been afraid to say earlier. "Whoever's got her isn't going to call. There won't be any ransom demand."

"It's still early," Carter began, then, with a cutting glare from Travis, didn't finish his thought. Carter wasn't a man who could lie easily. That much Travis understood; the sheriff just wasn't any good at platitudes. Thank God.

"It's not early." Travis shoved back his chair, the legs scraping on the scarred hardwood floor of the small cabin where he'd made his home for over a decade. "You know it. I know it. Lieutenant Sparks—" Travis hitched his chin to Sparks who sipped from a chipped brown mug. "He knows it, too—don't you, Sparks?"

The lieutenant didn't answer. He slid a look at Travis, then glanced away, then glowered into his cup. Sparks was another man who wasn't going to lie.

His gut churning, Travis walked barefoot to the window where he'd stood so many mornings, drinking coffee, half-listening to the morning news from the television in the living room while Dani, upstairs in her room under the eaves, roused. He would wait here, gazing outside, occasionally spying a black-tailed deer wander across the yard or a raccoon peering through the branches of the trees as dawn streaked over the hills. All the while Dani, never particularly happy to wake up, reluctantly got ready for school. It didn't take long. At thirteen, unlike a lot of girls her age, she wasn't into boys yet. She still eschewed makeup and hair coloring and those idiot teen magazines, which, he understood, would all come crashing into his life before he was ready . . . or at least he'd always expected they would.

If he thought hard right now, he could almost hear the distinctive thump of her feet hitting the floorboards as she hopped out of bed, the sound of water running through the old pipes as she brushed her teeth and then groggily stepped into the shower, the trip of her sneakers as she hurried down the wooden stairs. Invariably her backpack would be slung over one shoulder, her hair still damp, eyes bright and eager for whatever the new day would bring. She'd be wearing worn-out jeans and a hooded sweatshirt, an outfit her mother would have forbidden, had she still been alive. Then Dani would grab a granola bar and a box of juice on the run—another practice Ella would have railed against.

Pausing only to pet the dog, Dani would pile into the pickup behind the steering wheel and he'd let her drive the length of the lane before they'd exchange places and he'd haul her into town and deposit her beneath the wide awning of Harrington Junior High.

Jesus, would he ever hear those sounds again? Those simple, mundane, everyday noises that announced his daughter was alive and well and happy . . . even carefree.

He glanced toward the bottom of the stairs as if expecting her to appear, to end this nightmare he was living. Then he gave himself a swift mental kick. *Stop it! She's not here! Someone nabbed her and it's your fault for not being vigilant enough!*

"Quit blaming yourself," Shane advised as if he'd read Travis's mind.

Travis cut the sheriff an icy glare.

Carter had the luxury of handing out advice. He didn't have a kid, couldn't understand. No matter how close Carter had gotten to Jenna Hughes's daughters, it wasn't the same as actually being a father.

"It won't help," Carter said.

"Nothing much has," Travis muttered, glowering at the phone, silently daring it to ring.

"He's right," Sparks said. "Won't do a lick of good."

"What will? Waiting around here like dime-store dummies?"

"No . . . just letting us do our job." Sparks's cell phone rang and he snapped it to his ear.

Travis couldn't help the bit of hope that leapt into his chest. He stared at the state trooper as he answered, "Sparks."

Please let it be Dani . . . Please let it be that they found her, that she's safe, that, just as the police suspected, she was a runaway and hasn't been hurt and . . .

Sparks caught his gaze and probably noticed the glimmer of hope in Travis's eyes. The lieutenant gave a quick shake of his head and set his mug on the windowsill as the person on the other end rattled on. All Travis's hopes withered. Sparks nodded and checked his watch as he spoke into the cell. "Got it." He clicked off the phone, shoved it into the case clipped to his belt. "Gotta run. Accident up on 84. I'll be in contact." Squaring his hat onto his head, he paused as he reached for the door handle. His gaze found Travis's. "Hang in there."

"All I can do."

With a nod to Carter, Sparks took off, the screen door slapping shut behind him.

Through the window Travis watched the lieutenant leave. Sparks's state-issued Jeep rolled down the driveway, leaving a wake of dust to settle onto the sparse gravel.

Fear, black as midnight, stole through Travis's blood as he glared through the glass to a scene he'd once found tranquil: a view of stands of old-growth timber, thick ferns and remnants of a split rail fence some long-ago owner of this property had built. The posts were rotting, the few remaining rails gray and sagging, yet Travis hadn't had the heart to tear it down. The old fence spoke of another time and space, less complicated, overly romanticized, but still steadfast and true, now long gone.

He frowned.

Now the landscape was dominated by two Federal agents who had nodded to Sparks as he'd driven off.

One of the Feds was leaning a hip against a dusty, unmarked car that glinted under the sun's harsh rays. José Juarez was a short, wiry man whose emotions were under such tight rein he seemed almost detached. Cold as hell, but, Travis suspected, deadly as a coiled snake. The other one, Isabella Monroe from the local field office, was forever restless, her eyes darting from one person to the next, suspicion in their slate-gray depths. Tall and a little too slim, with angular features and impossibly high cheekbones, her hair pulled back in a knot at the back of her neck, Monroe was pacing beneath the sagging bows of an ancient cedar tree, all the while concentrating on the cell phone jammed to her ear.

Useless.

What had they done to find Dani? Nothing. Not one damned thing. "Even they know there won't be any ransom," Travis said, staring at the agents who had already told him that they would be pulling up stakes soon, probably today, not that they still wouldn't check in, and that someone, probably Monroe, would stop by daily, but they wouldn't be here around the clock.

Even the press, so hungry at the outset of the story, had backed off, the calls and visits to his house having petered off as the reporters caught onto the scent of other, more interesting stories. A blessing.

"Everyone's doing what they can," Carter offered.

"Well, it's not enough, is it?" Travis failed to keep the rage out of his voice. Why Dani? Why had she been abducted sometime before her last class of the day? He'd spent the past sleepless nights asking himself that same question and still didn't have an answer.

The police were continuing to work on the theory that she was a runaway. They'd brought it up several times. But she'd never left before.

There's always a first time. They hadn't said it, but he'd seen the suspicion in their eyes and knew that he, too, was a suspect, the single father, no, the *adoptive* single father. Travis didn't kid himself; he knew his entire life was being studied under a microscope, every little misstep he'd made—from crashing his fist into Tommy Spangler's face at sixteen and being suspended from high school, to the dismissed insubordination charge in the army—was being scrutinized, picked apart and put back together again, only to be reexamined.

Fine.

He had nothing to hide.

He just wanted his daughter back.

Rubbing a hand over his beard stubble, he thought back to the afternoon she'd come up missing.

Dani called in the morning, told him she'd forgotten her overnight backpack and asked him to bring it to her at the home of the piano teacher, where she was taking the dreaded lessons that she despised, lessons her mother had started when Dani was five and lessons Travis, as a form of penance to his wife, had insisted Dani continue.

So he'd driven to Blanche Johnson's house, a tall Victorian with gingerbread trim and flower beds teeming with petunias and geraniums in splashes of bright pink and red. He'd expected to hear piano music drifting from the open windows.

Instead he'd found Shane Carter and Jenna Hughes, Allie Kramer's mother, already parked and waiting outside. Travis's pride had still been wounded, because he'd been interested in Jenna for quite a while. But she'd chosen Carter and so he'd walked up to Jenna's Jeep carrying Dani's overnight bag, a smile frozen on his face.

"Emergency call from Dani," he'd said in explanation, and then whatever other conversation they'd shared had been lost as he'd smelled it: that first whiff of smoke hovering in the late summer air.

His memory came back to him in bits and pieces after that. He recalled sprinting up the steps of the wide porch, finding the front door ajar and racing inside. His heart had been knocking wildly as he'd faced more smoke, all if it roiling from the back of the house. Fortunately the blaze had been little more than a grease fire in the kitchen, one he'd quickly killed with the fire extinguisher he'd found hanging on a hook near the back door.

But the gruesome discovery, the one that still sent splinters of fear shooting through his body, had been finding Blanche Johnson's mutilated and very dead body. She lay in a pool of her own blood behind the couch in the parlor, the room where she gave her lessons. Sheet music was scattered over the floor, the piano stool was empty.

Blanche's face was a pasty shade of white, her glassy eyes open, the carpet beneath her stained a dark, spreading red. Scratched deep into the wall, in what looked like blood, were the words that had haunted him from the moment he'd seen them: Payback Time.

Now he closed his eyes, knew he was living every parent's nightmare and he wanted to crack, to crumble into a million pieces, but more than that he wanted his kid back.

And to kill the goddamned bastard who had taken her.

All the talk of her being a runaway was just plain crap. Dani had her independent streak, sure, but she wasn't into that kind of rebellion.

Yeah, and what do you know? his conscience nagged.

Deep inside he realized he wasn't equipped to be a single parent and a part of him wondered if what was happening was the result of some flaw within himself, if the God he'd shunned completely since his wife's death three years earlier was finally getting around to punishing him.

Payback Time, he thought for the thousandth time. Who did this? What did it mean? For God's sake, why was Dani the victim?

Travis couldn't shake the images of that day, the afternoon that he'd lost his daughter. A terror unlike any other had consumed him as he'd stared at the scarred wall with its dire warning. A deep, punishing fear for his daughter had gnawed at his guts as he'd driven to the junior high school where Jenna's daughter Allie had been pissed as hell for Jenna being late. Her slim shoulders were propped against a post, her arms crossed over her chest indignantly. She'd been waiting under the canopy near the front doors of the school.

The piano lessons had been cancelled, Allie had explained, and she was furious that her mother hadn't gotten her call and had left her waiting.

Travis hadn't received any such call from his daughter.

No communication whatsoever even though she had a cell phone.

He'd barged into the school, demanding answers of a smug secretary who'd wanted to alert him to the fact that his daughter had missed one of her classes.

Travis had come unglued. Things had only gotten worse as, upon questioning, it became evident that neither the smarmy secretary, the principal, nor anyone else at the friggin' school had any idea what had happened to his daughter.

What they'd discovered was that Dani had missed her last period of the day—PE, her favorite class, with Mr. Jamison, her favorite teacher—and not one of the students or staff at Harrington Junior High had remembered seeing her leave.

There had been no clues and all attempts to reach her on her cell phone had failed. Police interviews with her friends and acquaintances had turned up nothing, no indication of what had been going through her head, nor had anyone known of anyone she had contacted.

It was as if she'd been snatched out of thin air.

Except for the bizarre death of Blanche Johnson, who died from a blow to the head and had left bacon on the stove . . .

Payback Time.

That message echoed through his brain over and over again. Had it been intended only for Blanche or did it include Dani as well?

What did it mean?

So far the police had no leads as to who had killed Blanche Johnson and, Travis knew, as each hour passed the chances of finding the murderer lessened, the clues, if there were any, got colder. The press had been hounding him; reporters from as far away as Denver and Seattle had called and he, through the local television station, had put out a plea to whoever had kidnapped his child. But there had been no response.

Just dead air.

Dead.

Anguished, fists clenched impotently, he stared sightlessly out his window and realized that Carter was watching him, witnessing the agony ripping across his face, the fear gnawing at his soul. Thankfully Carter didn't offer up any platitudes and didn't so much as mouth the "I understand," that Travis found so insipid. No one, except for a parent who had lost a child, could begin to fathom the extent of his fear, his desperation, his goddamned dread that he'd never see her again.

He had to do something. *Any*thing. To get his daughter back. And with each tick of the clock, he realized that it was up to him. He couldn't rely on the Feds, or the state police, or the local sheriff.

He would have to take matters into his own hands.

Dani was *his* child, *his* responsibility, and when he thought of her—alone, hoping that he would rescue her—he felt weak and unworthy and knew he had to take action . . . any kind of action.

"I can't stay here another minute," he admitted, turning to face Carter.

"You have to. In case she calls."

"She's not gonna call," Travis said flatly. "We both know it."

"You—"

"I've got to find her." He jabbed a thumb at his chest. "Me."

"Leave it to the professionals."

"Who? Mutt and Jeff out there?" He hitched his chin toward the two FBI agents. "They're convinced she's a runaway and I know in my gut that she's not." He didn't mention that he was a licensed PI, that he knew the ropes. Carter already knew that.

The sheriff seemed about to argue. Instead he nodded curtly. "Don't do anything stupid," he advised, dark eyes focusing hard on Travis.

"I won't."

Carter's cell phone trilled. He answered quickly and for a second Travis experienced that same incredible jolt of hope, his anxious mind grabbing on to the slim chance that it was news of Dani, that she was all right, that . . .

Carter's face told him all he needed to know. Listening intently, the sheriff gave a quick shake of his head. Travis's hopes melted like ice in the desert. It was no use. They weren't going to hear anything. And anyway, they were wrapped up in Blanche Johnson's murder.

Without another look at Carter, he started for the back bedroom, his room, the one he'd shared with Ella, and in his mind's eye he was already packing. And he knew where he'd start looking for Dani, a lead he'd given the police that they were "looking into."

Well, he'd do more than take a peek; he'd scrutinize the hell out of the one person he'd feared all of Dani's life: her birth mother, a woman he'd kept track of all these years, a woman he knew was far from being a saint. In fact, she'd literally gotten away with murder a while back. He'd read about it, and knowing her name, knowing who she was, he hadn't been able to resist seeing her in person.

He'd been in San Francisco on a job, tracking down a deadbeat dad for a client, so he'd decided to make a quick side trip to Santa Lucia. He, like the press, had camped out near the courthouse steps. Reporters wielding microphones and cameras like artillery had been situated strategically. Curious onlookers had huddled together under the trees. It had been early spring, light from a lazy sun sending rays through the leafy trees, guarding the plaza and dappling the ground.

Travis had found a madrona tree and leaned against the peeling bark of the bole. Soon after five o'clock the crowd began to stir and he'd moved for a closer look. The courthouse doors opened and he saw her, the accused, looking much smaller than he'd expected. She'd been dressed in a conservative navy blue suit that Travis suspected the law firm had chosen, and she'd been flanked by several broad-shouldered men, her brothers, Travis had guessed, noting the family resemblance. Along with the brothers, an older man—with a shock of white hair, black-framed glasses and a pinched expression—had also been with her. Travis had guessed him to be Shannon's attorney. His expensive-looking briefcase and impeccable gray suit, tightly knotted blue silk tie and starched white shirt had all screamed "legal eagle."

The men had shepherded her down the steps and toward a parking lot adjacent to the marble-faced building. Shannon Flannery had managed to hold her head high, her little chin thrust out, her eyes shielded behind dark glasses. With her entourage around her as if she was some kind of damned celebrity, she'd headed toward the cars and hadn't paused for a comment to the throng of reporters.

The cameras had rolled, microphones had been jabbed closer, questions hurled from the reporters.

"Ms. Flannery, do you plan to take the stand in your defense?" one tall blond woman had shouted as she'd motioned to her cameraman to get a specific shot.

Another voice, male this time, had yelled, "Ms. Flannery, you claim to be innocent and yet your attorney has brought up allegations of abuse, which sounds like a defense against the charges, as if you were involved in the death of your husband."

"What about the fact that you have no alibi?" a younger man, with a thick red moustache and a face flushed with excitement, had asked. He'd been standing near Travis and had acted as if he was about to get the story of his lifetime. An image of wolves circling a wounded deer had come to

Travis's mind. "People wonder what you were doing on the night your husband was killed," the man said.

Shannon had stiffened, then slowly turned, her gaze behind those shaded lenses zeroing in on the eager reporter. She shoved the glasses to the top of her head to hold her curling auburn hair away from her face. And it was a beautiful face with bold but even features. Her eyes, deep-set and a startling shade of green, had narrowed between a sweep of thick, dark lashes. Sharply arched brows had been nearly mocking and her lips, soft and pink, were a knife blade of quiet, suppressed fury. Despite the warning hand her lawyer placed over her arm, she responded. "No comment," she said slowly and clearly, as if everyone around her were either deaf or stupid. Her eyes, sparking with intelligence, landed unerringly on the reporter standing near Travis.

"But where were you that night?" the man asked again, unbowed.

The lawyer whispered something in Shannon's ear, but she didn't pay him any attention. "No comment," she repeated.

As she ducked down to climb into the waiting car, her gaze shifted to Travis. As if she'd intentionally picked him out of the crowd.

It had probably been his imagination, but the sounds of the street, the reporters, the traffic, the pigeons on the square—all had seemed to hush.

The skin on the back of his neck prickled in apprehension and he felt as if bands had suddenly tightened over his lungs.

He'd been startled at what he'd seen in her expression— pain, worry, and something else, a flash of determination that had cut him to the quick. This woman was no stranger to agony. But neither did she seem to be a half-crazed woman who had snapped and killed her husband. Shannon Flannery seemed to know exactly what she was doing at all times.

She seemed steadfast and sure.

Capable of murder?

Maybe.

Her gaze had been a dare and as she'd stared at him, he'd felt an unlikely emotion steal through his bloodstream, a yearning to know more about her, a concern that went far beyond a casual interest in the birth mother of his child.

Still staring at him, she'd lowered her sunglasses. A long moment passed, then she slid into the open door of the waiting car. He'd felt it then, the slight change in the atmosphere, an altering of his thoughts. For the first time he'd noticed the sweat that was running down his temples and collecting on his palms.

Travis had watched the car drive down the street until it had rounded the corner at the first stoplight. Long after the crowd had dispersed he'd stood and stared at the spot where he'd last seen the Mercedes.

Something inside of him had shifted.

Something dark, something he didn't understand, something he didn't want to consider, had thrummed for a heartbeat before disappearing.

In the shade of the tree, he'd thought of Ella, not six months in her grave. Ella, with her short blond hair, wide smile and apple cheeks. She'd been wise and happy, and a friend who had turned into his wife, then his lover. A kind woman. A churchgoing woman. A safe woman. A barren woman.

And a hundred and eighty degrees from Shannon Flannery.

Guilt had driven a painful stake into his heart and from that moment forward, he'd felt a frisson of trepidation whenever he'd heard Shannon's name. He'd started a file on her that he kept locked in his den, and late at night he would sometimes sort through it.

It sounded crazy now, but that day, nearly three years earlier, he'd had a premonition, an inkling that their paths would cross again. Had it been because of Dani? Or was it something he'd rather not consider?

Whatever the reason, he'd been right.

He intended to chase her down.

Because of his daughter.

Her daughter.

A girl missing.

His muscles tightened as he remembered that after his trip to San Francisco, upon his return, Dani had begun asking dozens of questions about who her birth parents were. She'd never said "real" parents, and she'd always tried to be sly about her questions, never asking them directly, but he suspected her interest ran deep. Though he had no proof, he'd even thought Dani had tried to find the woman, had maybe stumbled upon the documents of her adoption that he'd kept hidden in that locked file. Dani, though the apple of his eye, was smart and sly, could pour on the charm, feign complete innocence, even when she was scheming something behind those wide eyes.

One time he'd caught her on their home computer in a chat room for adoptees searching for their natural parents, and he was certain that, though she'd pretended disinterest since then, she'd found a way to keep searching.

Damn. He should have talked to her, been open about it, but he'd just thought she was too young.

So, even if it wasn't Shannon Flannery who had come searching for her, perhaps Dani, in her attempts to locate her birth mother, had either taken off, or somehow been lured away.

Don't even think like that, he warned himself. The truth of the matter was that he could be all wet. Maybe Shannon Flannery had long ago gotten on with her life and had not a whit of interest in the baby she'd given up for adoption. Same with Dani's biological father, Brendan Giles. But that weak lead was the only one Travis had at the moment.

Of course he knew where Shannon resided. From the moment at the courthouse when he'd seen her in the flesh, Travis had kept up with Shannon's whereabouts. He'd told himself it was to prepare for the day when his daughter would demand to meet her birth mother, but he wondered now, scooping his shaving gear from the bathroom sink into a small nylon bag, if his fascination with her had a deeper, as yet unfathomable meaning.

He wouldn't think of that now. Nor would he dwell on the fact that he and Dani had recently celebrated her thirteenth birthday.

Now he didn't know if he'd ever see her again.

Travis's guts twisted as he yanked down a duffel bag and threw in a couple pairs of jeans and the first two shirts he found hanging in his closet. Then, with an eye on the door, he reached up to the top shelf and pulled down a locked metal box.

Inside was his gun.

A Glock. Forty-five caliber. Big enough to blow a substantial hole in anyone who got in his way. He probably wouldn't need to be armed. He was planning on dealing with the birth mother of his child, for God's sake. And yet, he believed in being prepared. For anything. Maybe Shannon wasn't in this alone. And hell, maybe she wasn't a part of it at all. She was just the first and only lead he could come up with.

But someone had his kid.

And when he met whoever it was, he wanted to make certain that he tipped the odds in his favor.

He held the weapon and it felt good in his hands, just the right weight. He curled his fingers over the smooth handle, sticking his index finger through the trigger loop.

The pistol was unloaded.

He found the shells, pocketed them, then tossed the gun into his bag. His pickup was already equipped with everything else he might need: night vision goggles, small telescope, hunting knife, camouflage jacket and other pieces of equipment he'd become familiar with during his stint with the army.

He zipped the bag closed.

He was ready.

One last time he peered through the blinds to the FBI agents standing near their cars.

Useless!

He'd always known that if you want a job done right, you do it yourself.

As soon as Frick and Frack left for the day, he was outta here.

What if you're wrong? What if Shannon Flannery has nothing to do with Dani's disappearance?

Then he'd keep looking. Endlessly. Until he found his kid.

Chapter 5

Who was *this creep?*

Carefully, not daring to let on that she was awake, Dani cracked open an eye and studied her abductor. It was night, he was driving, the features of his face illuminated by the greenish glow of the dash lights, the big tires of the truck humming over the asphalt of the interstate.

She was scared, more scared than she'd ever been in all of her thirteen years, and a part of her wanted to fall into a bajillion pieces and cry aloud, wailing for her father. But she didn't, wouldn't give the jerk the satisfaction. Oh, she let him think she was even more terrified than she really was, just to make him believe that she wouldn't fight back, that she was too much of a wuss to try and figure out a way to escape, but all the while her mind was working and she was intent on not letting her terror paralyze her.

No way.

She knew that if she was going to get out of this alive, she'd have to rely on her own wits and ability.

But she was handcuffed, her wrists bound together in front of her, which really complicated things.

She'd taken tae kwon do since she was four, had a black belt and won a lot of competitions. She knew how to ride a galloping horse bareback, shoot a .22 pretty straight, and her dad, who'd been with some elite army group, had even demonstrated to her where the vulnerable points were on a man if anyone tried to grab her.

But she'd been stupid, not on her guard when this jerk had nabbed her right outside the cybercafe. The cybercafe! Crap, she'd been an idiot. She felt her face burn with embarrassment. She'd always felt that she was fairly street-smart, that she could hold her own in almost any kind of competition or fight, but this . . . this weirdo had tricked her. She was convinced that he'd pretended to be BJC27, or had somehow found out about Dani's e-mailing Bethany Jane Crandall. But how? She'd been so careful.

Now she felt like a complete and utter idiot.

But she couldn't worry about that right now, not when she had to figure out how to escape. How she'd gotten into this mess was over and done with. She'd made a mistake—maybe even the blunder of a lifetime—but she wasn't dead yet and she was working on a plan to free herself. She just hadn't figured out all the details. And she wasn't going to forget about the bloody knife she'd seen in the back of the van, the one that he'd hidden when they'd pulled over and he'd thought she wasn't looking. Then there was the huge black trash bag stuffed to the gills—with something. She didn't want to think there was a small body curled up inside the opaque plastic, or the remains of another child he could've nabbed.

She nearly gagged at the thought.

Please, God, help me.

She started to worry her lower lip, a habit that had started when her mom had gotten sick. Now she stopped the gentle gnawing and refused to show any sign of weakness or that she was awake. She had to lull this jerk into complacency.

Through nearly closed eyes, she studied his features in the eerie green glimmer of light. Straight nose, deep-set eyes, hard-as-steel mouth, a beard shadowing his jaw. He kept the speed between fifty-five and sixty. The radio was turned on to an all-news channel. She'd gleaned that the transmission was from a station in Santa Rosa, California, which made sense. She'd been keeping track of the mileage, casting glimpses at the odometer when she could, and she figured, from what she'd seen through the window, that she was somewhere in Northern California.

He hadn't driven the easy way, though. Originally, he'd headed east, crossing into Idaho where, just after midnight on the outskirts of a tiny little town about forty miles from Boise, if the highway signs could be believed, he'd pulled into a long, rutted lane that led through tall, bleached grass and a straggly thatch of skinny, dead-looking trees. Grass and weeds had brushed the undercarriage and the van had bucked and bounced over rocks and potholes. The long drive had opened to a patch of knee-high yellow grass surrounded by a few desolate and obviously abandoned buildings.

He'd parked near a dilapidated garage with a sagging roof and boarded-up windows. After one swift glance in her direction, he'd climbed out of the van and there, in the weak moonlight, stretched. He was tall. Kind of muscular and she'd figured his age around thirty, maybe even close to forty.

She'd watched him approach the garage, all the while scrounging in his pocket. He had come up with something that glinted in the weak light. A key. Quickly he'd unlatched a padlock and the old doors of the garage had creaked open. He'd returned to the van, opened the back doors and pulled out his duffel bag, tool box and two boxes.

Oh, God, she'd wondered, did he plan on the two of them staying here? Her skin had crawled at the thought of spending any time alone with him in the neglected two-storied farmhouse that was, in her estimation, straight out of a horror film.

How would she get away?

Where would she go?

She still had her cell phone, turned off and hidden in her bra. She'd managed to sneak it out of the pocket of these grotty sweatpants when he'd thought she was still knocked out from that awful-smelling stuff he'd used to subdue her and before he'd clicked on the handcuffs. But she worried that if she did reach for it, she might drop it. And, at this point, she hadn't yet tried to retrieve it for fear that if she managed to turn it on, he might hear the sounds the phone emitted as it engaged. It was an old phone, didn't have a GPS chip like the new ones.

But it had been risky to try to use it that night, so at first she'd decided to wait to save whatever little battery life it had left until her hands were uncuffed so that she wouldn't fumble and drop the phone. She'd planned to use it only when she was absolutely certain she'd be alone for more than a few minutes.

At that point, she'd figured, she'd have only one shot at calling her dad.

As she'd sat in the truck, she'd craned her neck just a bit, glancing through the window to the isolated, sagging buildings. Even in the pale moonlight she'd seen that the paint on the farmhouse siding was cracked and peeling, rust running from hinges that were rotting. A screen door banged with the bit of wind that stole over the dry landscape. One corner of the roof had collapsed entirely.

What had once been a shed and pump house was a tumbled pile of bricks and a crumbled roof.

It was so quiet out here.

Aside from the thump of the screen door, Dani had heard nothing over the sound of her own breathing.

It was as if they'd stopped at the very ends of the earth. She shivered despite the heat and swallowed back the fear that had been rising in her throat. How long would she be here with him? she wondered while casting a worried look into the back of the van where the dark plastic bag still lay.

She had the unlikely urge to reach behind, untie the yellow ribbon holding it closed and open the damned thing.

What stopped her was the fear that she would open the sack to display a dead girl, eyes open, staring lifelessly up at her.

Her insides turned to water at the thought, but she was horrifically fascinated with the bag and its contents. The blood that was leaking from it had stopped and coagulated to stain the soiled carpet. Silently, using both hands, since they were locked together, she reached back for just a second and touched the plastic. It gave under her fingertips, so there had definitely been something squishy inside.

Her imagination ran wild.

She had to rein it in.

Don't do this, she mutely reprimanded herself. *Forget about the stupid bag and try to find a way out of here!*

She let out her breath and turned her eyes away from the back of the van.

Don't think about it . . . at least it doesn't stink . . . not yet. Now, find a way to get out of here or get help. Not the phone, you could drop it, you'll have to wait, but do something!

With her own admonition spurring her on, Dani worked fast.

Eyes trained on the windshield, she tried to open the glove compartment, to search for some kind of papers—like the vehicle registration or an insurance card or *any*thing that would give her some kind of clue as to who he was or what he wanted. Her other hope was that she would unearth some kind of weapon or something that could be used as a weapon. If only she could find a jackknife or a screwdriver . . . but the glove box was firmly locked.

Time was her enemy. Sweating, feeling the seconds for her chance to escape ticking rapidly away, she frantically searched for some kind of tool in the darkened interior. A hammer, or wrench, or file—some object that she could hide and would give her an edge over the bastard. But there was nothing! Not even a damned fountain pen or pencil to use to poke him in the nose or eyes or throat or anyplace she could reach.

Damn!

Looking up, she spied him heading into the garage.

Go, Dani!

Fumbling with the hem of her shirt, she dug her fingers into her bra. Carefully, one eye on the windshield, she pushed the phone, which was pressing against the underside of her left breast, to the middle of her bra, then up and over the small piece of lace. But the phone, wet from her sweat, slithered into her hands and then slipped, tumbling toward the floor. No! Gasping, she caught the cell in her damp fingers.

Thank God. Her heart hammered wildly as she cradled the phone in one hand and flipped it open with the other. The digital display illuminated, music starting before she was able to mute it. Slowly, oh, God, so agonizingly slowly, the phone came to life.

Great! she'd thought, her heart leaping as she peered through the windshield and double-checked the whereabouts of her captor.

He was still in the garage.

She hoped she might have a few minutes free.

The LCD on the phone's face showed that there was some battery life left. Not much, but some.

She expected to hear that she had a million messages from her dad, but the screen faded before ever coming to life. With mounting dread, she realized there were no bars—there was no cell tower nearby. Her phone wasn't able to transmit or receive!

No!

That was impossible!

But true.

Her insides crumpled. Damn it. She couldn't leave the van to move around and try to find if there was any coverage, even roaming coverage, in the area. Wanting to cry she snapped the phone closed, turned it off, managing to worm it back into her bra again where it then stayed lodged safely, if painfully, against her breast.

She hadn't let her disappointment overwhelm her. She'd wanted to give up, but she'd made herself fight through it. Maybe there would be another moment when she would be able to try and call.

She tried to just sit and wait, but her insides were screaming. She had to do something to help with her own escape! But what? What could she do?

She searched the cab, her gaze scouring the dash, the cup holders and the driver's seat before landing on the ashtray, where dozens of crumpled cigarette butts were squished into the small container. The tray was so full, it couldn't shut.

And each one carried some of the creep's DNA on it.

Good.

Without thinking twice, she inched her body to the middle of the van and tried to pick up one of the smoked cigarettes with her joined hands. If nothing else she would somehow, someday, get the Marlboro Lights butt to the police, and they could run what was left of it through the lab and their databases and somehow be able to nail his sick hide, just like she'd seen on those true crime shows. And if it turned out that she wasn't able to talk . . . if she was found really, really hurt, or . . . even . . . She swallowed hard and recalled the garbage bag in the back of the van with its sickly trail of blood seeping from the corner. Oh, God . . .

Dani didn't want to think that the jerk-wad might actually kill her, that he might use his long-bladed knife on her throat. She nearly lost control of her bladder when she considered it, so she stubbornly pushed that horrible thought aside and had gnashed her teeth until they ached. She decided if the son of a bitch tried anything with her, he'd be in for a surprise. Though she was playing the part of the scared, witless little girl, she planned on fighting him tooth and nail before he so much as scratched her skin.

In the dark interior, she inched closer to the driver's side of the van.

The handcuffs hampered her movements. She was running out of time.

Still, she had to chance it. Couldn't just play the scared little girl forever. But she'd have to be careful, so that she didn't spill anything out of the ashtray and make him suspicious.

She licked her lips. Told herself it was like playing Pick-Up-Sticks, a game she'd played with Allie Kramer. The object of the game was to withdraw one plastic stick from a nest of jumbled plastic sticks without disturbing any of the rest. She was pretty good at it. But thin plastic sticks played for fun were a lot different from cigarette butts jammed into an ashtray.

Wiping her sweating palms on her pants, she held her breath. Carefully she attempted to extract one of the smelly, squashed butts from the full tray. Just as her fingers clamped over one filter tip, a loud roar had cut through the night, the sound of a huge engine sparking to life. Twin beams of light glared from the open doors of the garage. Startled, Dani jumped. And that's when cigarette butts had rained to the floor of the vehicle—in plain sight.

Dear Jesus, she'd be caught!

She'd been about to try and retrieve them and force each back into the tray or brush them under the seat when a black truck rocketed out from the garage, its headlights blazing like the eyes of a monster.

Dani sat frozen, sweat seeming to curdle on her scalp.

As she watched, the creep parked his truck on the far side of the garage, then jogged across the open space to the van.

Her heart seized.

Oh, no!

He would see the spilled cigarettes and guess what she'd been doing!

His boots crunched ominously on the sparse gravel.

Fear crawling up her throat, she stuffed the cigarette butt into her pocket and silently prayed he wouldn't notice anything wrong. She was sweating from the exertion and a case of nerves, but forced herself to pretend to just be scared to death.

Which hadn't been hard.

Though she'd barely been able to draw in a breath, she tried to figure out how to keep him from seeing what she'd done.

She had to distract him!

That was it!

Before he realized anything was amiss.

Her heart thudded so loudly she was certain he would be able to hear it. The cigarette butt in her pocket felt heavy as a stone. Oh, this was a dumb plan! He was going to see the scattered filter tips on the floor and know what she'd been doing. He might even search her and find her phone!

He climbed inside and cast her a quick, harsh look that had turned her insides to water. Without a word he flicked on the ignition, drove forward into the long, weed-choked drive, then stopped and rammed the gearshift into reverse. Flinging one arm over the back of the seat, his fingers nearly brushing the back of her collar, he checked the mirrors, then stared over his shoulder as he eased the van backward, quickly wedging it into the dilapidated garage.

Dani could scarcely breathe.

She wondered if he would leave her there. Handcuff her to the door, gag her, abandon her and let her die in that dark, smelly, rat hole of a van with the dead girl in the trash bag behind her.

Oh, Jesus!

Her mouth was chalk.

Or would he take her with him?

Either option was bad.

She held her breath and waited.

The van was so large that there were mere inches between the exterior and the walls of the old building. But somehow, with little effort, he managed to park it without scraping the fenders. When he braked the taillights illuminated the small garage in an eerie red glow. Dani withered inside as she caught a glimpse of the cobweb-infested walls of ancient two-by-fours.

With a satisfied grunt, the creep slammed the transmission into park and cut the engine. "Come on, let's go. Get out," he ordered. He clicked off the autolock mechanism that kept all the passenger doors secured, allowing her door handle to work. As he opened the driver's door, the dome light flicked on. He turned toward her—intense eyes narrowing a fraction. "Don't try any funny stuff." Then he stepped into the small space the door opening allowed and his gaze swept the van's interior.

Dani froze.

"I said, let's go!" He reached in and grabbed his pack of Marlboros, an old gas receipt and a notepad. That's when he spotted the quashed cigarette butts spilled onto the floor near the accelerator. "What the fuck?"

His gaze cut swiftly to her face. Dani pretended not to notice as she feigned to struggle with the door. As if for leverage, she then "accidentally" kicked the dash, her foot hitting the overflowing ashtray. Other cigarettes tumbled out. "I can't get out," she mewled, the pitiful sound of her voice making her cringe inside. She hated acting like a pathetic, scared little kid. Even though she was frightened, all she really wanted to do was have a chance to kick him where it counted and scratch out his sicko eyes.

"Christ, you're an idiot," he growled, jabbing a finger at the telltale butts. "What were you doing? Trying to escape?" His lips flattened over his teeth and his eyes blazed with an evil light.

Dani shivered inside.

"Don't get smart, kid." He slammed the driver's door shut and strode quickly around the back of the van.

Dani unlatched the passenger door and nearly fell out. As the bottoms of her sneakers hit the earthen floor of the garage she felt his fingers against her nape, twisting in the collar of her jacket. The smell of earth and years of dust filled her nostrils and she thought she heard wings, those of bats or an owl, overhead.

With hardly any effort he jerked her off her feet. "Listen," he snarled against her ear, his rough beard scratching her cheek, his breath still laced with the smoke of his last cigarette. "You'd better do as I say or you'll regret it!"

Her skin rippled in revulsion. She thought she might pee her pants. Worse yet, her cell phone began to slide against her wet skin.

He yanked her away from the van, slammed the door shut. With her feet still struggling to find purchase as he pulled her with him, he growled in her ear, "I'm warning you one last time. Don't fuck with me. You got it? Do *not* fuck with me!" He shook her hard and the phone slid farther.

No!

Desperately she tried to tighten her arms closer to her body. But she could feel the cell slip.

As he dropped her to her feet, she lost her balance, tumbling against the fender of the van, feeling the hot metal of the hood as the engine ticked and cooled. The phone slid to the floor of the garage. She cringed, waiting for discovery.

"Now, move it, kid. We don't have much time."

He was nervous as he pushed her forward and slammed the van's passenger door shut. But in the scuffle, he didn't notice her cell, wedged tight against the tire. She'd wanted to dive for the phone but knew he'd catch her. She'd wanted to run, to scream, but any attempt to get away from him at that point would have been futile. The abandoned farm was so remote and desolate no one would ever hear her.

So, she was forced to remain passive. *Help me,* she silently prayed as she stumbled toward the black truck. *Help me . . . Please, God, help me!*

She wished fervently that she hadn't skipped Sunday school any chance she could. When her mother had been alive Dani had been forced to attend, but once Mom had died, Dad hadn't pushed the whole church thing. And she'd been glad that she hadn't had to get up early on Sunday mornings to listen to the teacher, Jewel Lundeen, with her saccharine-sweet smile and iron will—a woman who'd forced her to memorize Bible verses and then, if she'd forgotten them, would kindly but firmly remind her how important it was for her to learn the Word of the Lord.

Worse yet, Mrs. Lundeen had seemed to really get off on stupid crafts like making Jesus puppets and putting on a play with the little figures of Jesus and all the disciples. Jesus walking on water. Jesus casting tiny bits of bread into the cellophane lake. Jesus turning the minuscule jugs of water into grape Kool-Aid.

It had been so inane, but as she was being shepherded toward the big black truck with its canopy, by a man who scared her half to death, Dani so wished she'd paid more attention. It wasn't that she didn't believe in God. She just didn't believe in all the foolish little rituals and so, once her mother had died, her dad had agreed that she could give up the Sunday-morning tradition as long as it was replaced with doing something outside, in nature.

Which had been way cooler.

Or so she'd thought until she sat in the passenger seat beside the sick bastard who'd kidnapped her. If only he wasn't so careful! If he would make a mistake. Her heart sank as she watched him take the time to close the garage doors and lock them securely before climbing behind the wheel of this newer vehicle, and turn its nose to the road: a roundabout route that eventually led south.

Now, after days that felt like months, she knew she was in California; she'd heard enough talk radio to prove that. She sent up another prayer and fervently hoped that God was listening. That He would forgive her.

That her dad would find her.

Her abductor wasn't making it easy, though.

Every day or so, he switched license plates, first on the dirty white van and now on this truck. Originally, the truck had been equipped with Idaho plates. That had changed when he'd driven east, toward the Montana border, and stolen the back plate off an SUV from Washington state.

And all the while on their zigzagged course across Wyoming, Colorado, and Nevada, she'd kept the cigarette butt hidden. He had a porta-potty that he kept in the back of the truck under a canopy and when she told him she needed to go to the bathroom, he'd uncuff her and let her into the back, always staying right at the tailgate.

Food was bought at drive-thru restaurants or at gas stations, always late at night, and each time he watched her like a hawk, his knife always a visible threat.

During all the hours since he'd forced her into the van, he'd never once blindfolded her, and that was a worry. All the cop/detective/forensic shows she'd seen on television suggested to her that if he wasn't worried about her seeing his face, then he would probably kill her so she couldn't identify him.

Her throat closed at the thought, but she didn't fall victim to her fear. He'd kept her alive this long. He hadn't so much as touched her except to pull her in and out of the van, and when he did cast a glance her way, he didn't seem to see her. It was as if she was nothing more than cargo that had to be dealt with.

He was silent. Serious. A simmering anger evident in the way he gripped the steering wheel, or flattened his lips whenever they had to slow or stop for road work. When he talked to her, it was to bark orders and remind her that if she did as he told her, she wouldn't get hurt.

So far he'd kept his word.

What did he want with her? No. She didn't even want to think about it.

As if he sensed her staring at him, he quickly glanced her way. Her eyelids drooped and she feigned sleep, leaning against the glass of the passenger door window, all the while wanting to scream.

"I know you're awake," he said.

His voice was deep and rough, scratching against her ears like sandpaper. She hated him. *Hated* him.

"No use pretendin'. So quit staring, okay?"

He pushed on the lighter in the dash, she heard the familiar click, then the rustle of cellophane as he unwrapped another pack of cigarettes. Marlboro Lights. The lighter popped as he braked and she heard him fiddling with it, then she smelled the familiar, acrid scent of smoke. He inhaled and rolled down the window, the fresh air quickly filled with the smell of burning tobacco.

As the tires hummed over the dry pavement and bugs splattered against the windshield, Dani tried to figure out how to escape. At the next rest stop? When he pulled over to sleep? But how? He always handcuffed her.

Every problem has a solution. Sometimes you just have to work hard to figure it out.

She could almost hear her father's voice. He'd told her often enough. Whenever she was having trouble at school with her friends, or she was certain she wouldn't pass the next math test, or when her fishing line was caught on the overhanging branches of a tree leaning over the river.

Tears welled in her eyes. Dad was tall. Strong. Honest. And tough. Really tough. Even when Mom had died, he'd managed to hold himself together.

She swallowed back a sob, pulled herself together with an effort. Chancing another glimpse of her captor, Dani considered her father again. He would come for her. She knew it. But when? And how? This guy wasn't about to leave any kind of trail, especially since he changed the vehicle's plates at every opportunity. What were the chances he'd be pulled over?

Dani's hands, cuffed together at the wrists, curled into fists.

Somehow her dad would find her.

He had to.

And soon.

Chapter 6

Armed with a bit of knowledge and a lot of suspicion, Travis parked his truck a mile and a half from Shannon Flannery's home. He'd driven twelve hours straight from his home in Oregon to Santa Lucia, California. He'd already passed by her lane leading off the main road because he didn't want to be seen. Much as he'd like to burst into her house and demand answers, he figured he'd better watch her place for a while and scope out the surrounding area, to try to determine whether Dani was anywhere nearby.

It was night. A smattering of stars and a quarter moon offered little light and though there was a thin layer of clouds wafting over the black heavens, the temperature was simmering several degrees above eighty.

Stealthily, wearing black and carrying a backpack, he jogged through the back streets and overgrown lots, scaring a cat hiding in the shadows and causing a dog down the street to start barking its fool head off.

He cut through a couple of back alleys and around an old, abandoned rifle range until he came to a warped chain-link fence that surrounded the property next to hers. New NO TRESPASSING signs had been posted and he ignored them, rimming the fence line, moving within the night shadows to the far side where, he saw through a few scraggly oaks, warm light emanating from the windows of a house. Shannon Flannery's property, where she trained search and rescue dogs.

He'd have to be careful.

Quiet.

Stay downwind.

He circled around the field until he was standing in a sparse copse of trees at the fence line. Less than a hundred feet away was the house. Her house. Hoisting himself over the fence, he landed lithely on the other side, then he crept along the shrubbery to the two-storied cottage. She was home, he heard her voice floating through an open window. But from his position, he could catch only parts of the conversation.

". . . Telling you . . . I just don't know . . ." she was saying emphatically, her voice low and calm.

She paused as if listening to a response.

Then he saw her, walking past the window, a phone to her ear. He didn't move a muscle.

". . . Sorry . . . look, Mary Beth, Robert doesn't tell me anything, you know that . . ." Another pause. She stopped dead in her tracks and walked to the window, her eyes searching the field where he stood. Her red hair shone in the illumination from an overhead light, her eyebrows drawn together in concentration, a frown pulling at her full lips.

His heart thudded, certain she would see him. Instead, using her free hand, she lifted the hair off her neck and nodded, as if the person on the other end of the line could see her.

"I don't think that's a good idea . . . Right . . . I can't explain what's going through his head. I think—" She closed her eyes, threw back her head and sighed. Her throat curved backward, a smoothly tanned column above the V of her blouse and just a hint of the hollow between her breasts.

His own throat tightened seeing the sweat that was drizzling down her neck and into that dusky cleft. For the first time since leaving Falls Crossing he realized how foolish he'd been, how he'd been grasping at straws. What could this woman possibly know about Dani? What were the chances that Dani had linked up with her . . . ? What had he been thinking driving like a madman down here, certain that this woman was somehow behind his daughter's disappearance?

His jaw slid to the side.

". . . I wouldn't do that if I were you, Mary Beth. Listen, I know I'm not a good one to give advice, but—"

Again she was cut off and as it happened her eyes flew open, her head snapped up and she flushed scarlet. "That's it. I don't have to take this from you or anyone else. Goodbye!" She clicked the phone to OFF. Clenching her teeth for a moment, she muttered something under her breath and moved away from the window.

Travis let his breath out of his lungs.

Now what?

He ran a hand through his hair and was about to leave when he noticed something. A movement. Near the corner of her house.

A person or a shadow? He couldn't tell.

He crouched, automatically hiding. Had she spotted him and slipped noiselessly outside? He reached into his bag for his night vision goggles, all the while his eyes trained on the spot where he'd thought he'd seen someone beneath the trees.

But the image was gone and as he unzipped his bag, pulled out his goggles and trained them on the area where he'd thought he'd spied a person, there was nothing, just a big water trough and a tall spigot.

Sweating, he moved the glasses over her small compound. The sound of crickets chirping nearly drowned out the soft hum of the freeway a few miles off and the rumble of a train on distant tracks.

He heard no footsteps, saw no one scuttling around the edges of the buildings or hiding in the trees.

Just his own case of nerves getting the better of him.

He took one more sweep through the goggles, then carefully put them into his bag. Rocking back on his heels, he wondered what his next step would be. Would he stake out her place, watch whoever came and went?

What if she wasn't in the least connected to Dani? That was certainly possible. Just because she was his daughter's birth mother and Dani had been interested in finding her natural parents, might not mean much. Maybe it had been a gigantic leap to think that Shannon Flannery had somehow lured and nabbed his daughter away, the leap of a desperate, impotent man.

Christ, he thought. Here he was, alone in a field, spying on a woman he didn't know, a woman who was probably innocent. But what other option did he have? He'd called back to Falls Crossing six times since he'd left, talked to the authorities in charge of the investigation.

No phone call had come in.

No new clues had been found.

Not a word from whoever had his little girl.

Son of a bitch, he thought, *son of a goddamn bitch!*

Standing, he turned away from Shannon's house and zipped up his surveillance kit.

What good would upsetting this woman's life do? Just because he was desperate didn't mean that—

BOOM!

An explosion blasted.

The earth shook.

Glass shattered.

What the hell?

Travis's head whipped back, his eyes trained on Shannon's house.

It was intact.

But a building near the cottage, a shed of some kind, was suddenly afire. Flames shot out of the roof, sparks flew high only to rain down on the tinder-dry ground.

Travis started running.

He yanked his cell phone from his pocket.

Dialed 9-1-1 on the fly.

One ring.

"Nine-one-one, what's the nature of your emergency?" the dispatcher asked.

BAM!

Another explosion blasted and the roof of the shed blew into a million pieces. Fire leapt to the sky. Darkness scattered in the wake of curling, wild flames crawling toward the heavens.

Dogs howled.

Horses screamed.

"There's a fire," Travis yelled into the phone as he ran. "And two explosions at Shannon Flannery's place." He rattled off the address he'd memorized less than a week earlier. "Send trucks. Emergency vehicles." Smoke billowed to the night sky. Flames crackled greedily. Sparks ignited in the dry twigs, leaves and grass.

"Is anyone hurt?"

"Don't know yet. You got that address?" he yelled.

She repeated it back to him.

"Emergency crews are on their way."

"Tell them to hurry!" Travis clicked off the phone and using both hands on the top rail, propelled his body onto Shannon's property and started running again.

BOOM!

The windows rattled.

The doors shook.

Shannon, climbing the stairs, grabbed the rail. "What the hell was that?" she whispered, her heart instantly pounding. Fear propelling her, she flew back down the steps.

With a sharp bark and growl, Khan ran to the front door. Growling, scratching, the hackles on the back of his neck stiff, he started barking, sounding the alarm.

Shannon peered through the windows near the front door.

Her blood turned to ice.

Shifting light and shadows chased away the darkness. From the corner of her eye, she caught sight of the tack shed, only a few feet away from the stable. Flames ascended through the roof and into the sky. "Oh, God, no!" she cried.

She dove for her cell phone and yanked it from its charger. *The horses! The dogs!* She punched out 9-1-1 and was on her way through the kitchen. On the first ring, the dispatcher answered.

"Nine-one-one dispatch. What is—"

"This is Shannon Flannery," she yelled into the phone as she yanked the fire extinguisher from the wall near the back door and gave her address, repeating it. "There's been an explosion and now a fire in the shed at my house! It's bad! Send help now!"

"Is anyone injured?"

"Not yet! You got that address?"

"Yes."

"Good. Inform Shea Flannery with the police force. He's the fire investigator and my brother!"

She hung up and stuffed the phone in the pocket of her jeans.

BAM!!!

Another explosion rocked through the house. *Oh, God, please not the animals.* She thought of her trucks with their half-full gas tanks and the horses and dogs trapped in their shelters. *Jesus, no! Please, no!*

She flung open the door. A great, roaring wall of flame was already chewing through the shed's old timbers, shingles and insulation. Heat radiated in searing waves toward the sky. Thick black smoke surged upward in horrifying clouds, burning her nostrils, searing the back of her throat. Through it all the worried neighs and startled barks of the terrified animals split the night.

If only Nate was here.

If only the fire department was here!

How far out was she? Five minutes? Ten? By that time every old wooden building on her property could be involved.

She yanked on her boots and engaged the extinguisher, knowing it was too small to begin to snuff out the flames that were consuming the shed. But the pressurized carbon dioxide would be able to slow the fire's advance, laying down a thin sheet of retardant that wouldn't ignite.

Khan growled and stuck close to her. Shannon forced

him to stay inside, ignoring his worried whining. She could hear him barking and scratching frantically at the door as she ran the length of the porch.

Never breaking stride, she swung the nozzle of the fire extinguisher at the ground where sparks were catching on the twigs, leaves and brush. A thick plume of retardant plumed outward over the ground.

From the corner of her eye, she saw the man running toward her. She swung, CO_2 spraying in front of her, and he quickly zigzagged away from her.

"Hey! Watch out!" he yelled over the roar of the flames.

"Who the hell are you?"

"I saw the fire. Called 9-1-1. Thought I could help."

Camouflaged in dark jeans and gloves.

Like hell.

She swung the extinguisher at him again and he backed farther away. Hands over his head, he danced away from the freezing retardant. "You can go at me if you want, or you can trust me!" he yelled. "I'm here to help."

"I don't know you!"

"And I don't know you, either, but you've got a helluva problem."

A ceiling beam in the shed gave way and with a groan the roof caved in. Sparks erupted into the night. The stranger was right. There wasn't much time.

"You'd better leave now," he ordered, motioning to the extinguisher. "That isn't going to do much."

"It'll have to!" she declared, heading for the door of the stable. He was right on her heels, but kept his distance, aware that she could shoot him with CO_2 should she decide to.

"What do you think you're doing?"

"Getting the stock out." She grabbed the handle of the door and yanked it open. From inside came the frightened sounds of horses whinnying and whistling. Hooves pummelled the straw-covered floor of the box stalls and over it all the fire raged hot and high, boiling loudly. "Who did you say you were?"

"Doesn't matter. Really, you should get out of here. This whole place, the buildings, the trees, the grass, could go up in a matter of seconds."

"I will."

"I mean now!"

"I can't!" She didn't have time to argue. Rounding on him, she saw his features in the gold reflection of the flames and wondered again who he was, this tall man with broad shoulders, intense eyes and features that looked as if they'd been carved out of granite. He stared down a nose that looked as if it had been broken at least once. "We don't have time," she yelled at the top of her lungs. "Either you help me, or you get the hell out of my way."

"What can I do?"

She didn't think twice. "Go to the next building, it's the kennel," she ordered, pointing at the long, low building wedged between the stable and garage. "Let the dogs out, okay? I don't care where they go, just get them the hell out of there!"

He was already turning.

"There's an extinguisher by the door. After you set the dogs free, use the extinguisher on whatever you can, then crank up the garden hose. It's attached to the west wall of the house!"

"Got it!"

She stepped through the door into the pandemonium of the stable.

Horses were rearing, screaming in terror as the smoke blew into the stable. Through the windows she saw the fire, growing and billowing higher, reaching toward the sky with wild, hellish fingers, casting blood-red shadows that leapt and jumped inside the stables. Its sound was a distant, background roar.

Still carrying the extinguisher she slapped at the light

switch. Nothing happened. "Damn it!" She swatted it again, to no avail. Sweating, she jogged the length of the corridor that separated the two rows of stalls.

The horses were in a froth, legs striking the stalls, eyes wide, white-rimmed and rolling. The odors of urine and dung mixed with the scents of sweat and fear and the overpowering, ever-present smell of smoke.

"Shh," she said to the animals in a soothing voice, the lie coming easily, "it's all right."

Where the hell were the fire trucks?

She flipped the light switch at this end of the building.

Again nothing happened.

"Hell."

She'd just have to work in the dark. She didn't have time to try and find a flashlight, knew the building like the back of her hand anyway.

Hurry! Hurry! Hurry!

She eased along the wall. By feel, she unlatched the wide, double doors to the paddock and shoved hard. They flew open. Banged against the exterior walls.

Shimmering reddish light from the fire crept inside on a cloud of black smoke. Quickly she wedged the doors open to the protected side of the stable where the paddock was long and deep with a gate at the far end, should she need to evacuate the animals.

She started back inside.

BAM!

She jumped.

The door at the far end of the building, the one through which she'd entered minutes earlier, slammed shut.

"Hey!" she shouted, but there was no answer. Her heart, already thudding, kicked more frantically. Either the wind had caught the door or the stranger, whoever he was, had shut it.

But why?

Oh, Jesus, she couldn't worry about that now. She had to get these damned horses to safety.

Holding the extinguisher under one arm, she started working her way along the corridor, retracing her steps. Unlatching first the stall on her right, the box that housed Nate's black gelding, she said softly, "Come on, boy," but the big horse needed no further coaxing. In a blur of lathered black hide, he shot out of his box, steel-shod hooves echoing on the concrete, black tail billowing behind him.

One down, seven to go!

Sweat ran down her face and arms. She unlatched the stall across the corridor and a feisty little roan bolted. So frantic was the mare that she scrambled on the concrete, getting out of the stall, scraping her side and almost losing her footing as she, too, galloped outside.

So far so good.

The air was thick and Shannon was beginning to cough, but the horses were escaping. As she reached the next stall she heard the dogs barking and hoped fervently that the stranger who had appeared in the parking area was releasing them.

Who in God's name was he?

Why was he here, seemingly waiting for her in the parking lot?

Had he set the fire?

Oh, for the love of St. Mary, Shannon, don't think about that now. Just get these animals out!

She unlatched the stall on the left side and a white mare with a gray muzzle and stockings flew through the opening. Two more followed quickly.

Adrenaline pumping through her veins, she kept at it, unlatching the stalls one at a time, avoiding a stampede or getting run over by the horses. Two bays, plus a black and a gray shot out of their boxes, horseshoes clanging on the cement over the crackling roar of the fire.

Just one more!

Thick clouds of smoke roiled inside and she was coughing—half-blinded as she reached the final stall. She opened the door and expected the frightened mare to bolt through, but the horse cowered in the corner, backing up and trembling, her dun coat awash with sweat, lather flecking her hide.

"Come on, girl," Shannon said, slipping inside and setting down the extinguisher to free both hands. She could always come back for it. Right now it was crucial to get the horse out of the building. "Time to get out of here." The mare snorted and shook, ears flicking nervously, eyes wild. Softly, Shannon clucked in encouragement, easing forward, intent on reaching for the mare's halter.

She reached up.

Crash!

A window blew, spraying glass.

The horse squealed and lashed out with a foreleg. Shannon sidestepped the blow. "Nuh-uh, Molly. Calm down . . . come on now." She talked low and evenly, showing no fear, when inside she was screaming for the buckskin to get out, to run with the others, to follow the damned herd! "Let's go," Shannon said, her boots crunching on the shattered glass, the heat searing her skin.

In the background, over the ghastly roil of flames she heard the first faint shrill of sirens. *Emergency vehicles! Thank God! Hurry! Before it's too late!*

Moving slowly but steadily, she held the horse's gaze, then lifted her hand to the halter. She didn't have time to find a lead, she just had to get the frightened mare out of the damned box and outside. "Here we go," she said and grabbed hold of a leather strap.

The horse flung her head up.

Shannon didn't let go.

Pain scorched through her shoulder.

The mare reared, nearly pulling Shannon's arm from its socket.

"No!"

A heavy black foreleg lashed out.

Shannon, still holding the halter, tried to twist away.

One hoof grazed her temple.

Pain exploded behind her eyes.

She started to fall backward but didn't let go.

Then a hoof pounded her already-wrenched shoulder, and scraped down her body, seeming to hit every rib before crunching against her hip. Pain careened down her side and blackness curled at the edges of her consciousness.

"Stop it," she muttered and held onto the halter as if her life depended upon it. If she let go now, she'd never be able to grab hold of it again, never be able to save the horse. "Come on, now," she insisted, ignoring the pain searing through her body. Fingers clamped over the leather straps, she gently pulled, fighting the urge to black out, leading the balking, sidestepping mare through the open stall door.

Outside the fire roared. She saw the ever-growing blaze through the windows, snapping and crackling as flames spread their vile heat.

From the corner of her eye, she saw a shadow.

A figure of a man inside the stable. *Oh, God, had that idiot who'd appeared a few minutes ago not gone to save the dogs?*

She turned her head to face him, but there was no one there, nothing but her own imagination playing tricks on her.

The mare sidestepped and tried to rear again, but Shannon, arm screaming in pain, held fast. She had to focus, couldn't be distracted. Her first priority was to get the horse outside to the paddock away from the fire, then she'd check the kennels. Concentrating on the open door at the far end of what seemed an impossible distance, she kept moving. If she could just make it outside, if she could fight the blackness starting to surround her. Her shoulder screamed in pain and she felt a stream of blood, where the mare's hoof had scraped her skin, flow down her side.

"Come on, come on," she whispered, more to herself than the mare, "you can make it."

The yawning entryway loomed ahead of them. Just a few more feet! Beyond the doorway the night sky was an ominous orange. Smoke brought tears to her eyes and made her cough, but she placed one foot in front of the other. She heard the baying of the dogs and prayed that they were safe, that the stranger had set them free.

Who was the guy who'd appeared out of nowhere? Angel of mercy? Good Samaritan who'd just happened to be in the area? Or was he somehow involved with this horrifying blaze? What had he said his name was?

He hadn't. At least she didn't think so. Her mind was fuzzy, she could barely breathe. She forced herself to keep moving. They were so close . . . so close . . .

She didn't have time to wonder further who the stranger was, didn't even want to consider that he might somehow be related to the conflagration that she saw through the windows, now burning wildly, flames leaping into the heavens, sparks threatening the roof of the garage and Nate Santana's apartment.

Nate! If only he was here, she thought again, nearly deliriously. If only she could fall in love with him . . . if only . . . Her thoughts were confused . . . she thought she heard her name as if through a tunnel . . . *Keep moving! Focus! It's the pain and smoke. You need air! Just get the damned horse out of here!*

God, it was hot. Sweat prickled her scalp. Ran down her back. The heat was so intense, the pain in her arm debilitating, her legs feeling like rubber. "Come on," she urged. She tried to run the last few feet, one foot in front of the other, when the mare, suddenly realizing that freedom lay ahead, threw back her head and ripped the halter from Shannon's fingers.

Shannon started to follow, took one step toward the open door, when she saw movement from the corner of her eye.

Her heart jolted.

A dark figure, carrying a long pole, sprang.

The man she'd seen earlier!

With a weapon!

NO! She feinted left, dodging away.

But her movements weren't sharp.

She was sluggish. Nearly tripped on herself.

Too late!

Whack! The thick handle of a pitchfork crashed into the side of her face.

Pain splintered through her cheek, sending off needles of agony into her eye. *No . . . Oh, God, no!*

Blood erupted through her nose and skin.

She threw up a hand to protect herself and staggered backward, trying to reach the open door, hoping to catch a glimpse of the bastard's face, but it was obscured, hidden in the shadows of a hood.

"Shannon!" a male voice yelled, as if from a distance. Her attacker? Stunned, she reeled, trying to run, her legs wobbly, blood pouring down from her face and down her throat. She could barely see and every breath she took felt like she was taking in fire.

Only a few more steps!

"Shannon!" the male voice again yelled from somewhere outside the building.

"In here. Help!" she cried, but the words were strangled, muted over the rush and whoosh of the fire.

She took another step toward the door.

CRACK!

The back of her head seemed to explode.

She pitched forward, landed on the cement.

He came at her again, this dark figure silhouetted by the red, shifting, eerie light through the windows.

She screamed.

He raised his club again and she tried to zero in on his face, but it was covered. As he lunged, intent on striking her, she forced herself to roll to one side, then leap up. Dizzy, spitting blood, she grabbed the end of the pitchfork before he could beat her.

Her fingers surrounded the smooth wood handle and she put her weight into it, hoping to drive the tines into the bastard's chest or neck. But her fingers were slick with sweat and her own blood, and she couldn't hold on. As if she weighed nothing, he twisted the pitchfork and she lost her grip, her boots slipping in the blood.

He yanked it away and she fell back. Her injured shoulder slammed into the concrete. A hot, searing pain ripped down her arm, ricocheting through her body.

Writhing, she let out a scream and rolled toward the open door, away from her attacker. Blackness pulled at her, begging her to leave consciousness and agony behind, but if she did she knew whoever had done this to her would kill her. Would beat her with the handle of the pitchfork or drive the sharp, long tines into her body.

Sirens!

Loud. Piercing. The wail of sirens cut through the night air.

If she could only hang on . . . help was on its way . . . she curled into the fetal position, protecting herself from the blows she knew were coming, and closed her eyes. It was so hot . . . she couldn't breathe . . . *Stay awake!* . . . *Don't pass out!* . . . but she was losing the battle, the pull was so great . . . *For God's sake, Shannon, don't let go!*

But it was useless, the pain too intense. She lay on the floor, spent, her blood seeping onto the concrete. With no last thought she gave herself over to the enveloping blackness . . .

Chapter 7

Travis unlatched the last kennel.

A German shepherd hurtled past him, nearly knocking him over in the darkness, racing to follow the pack of Border collies, Labs and a couple of mutts of undecipherable lineage that he had freed.

He'd managed to get all of the anxious, howling dogs out of their cages despite the fact that the kennel had been plunged in an eerie darkness, pierced only by the hellish red glow seeping through a bank of small windows. None of the lights had worked.

Nonetheless, all the dogs were now free and running wildly through the fields and into the woods. Through the door he saw them racing away from the fire that climbed higher and higher into the night sky.

He thought of the man he'd seen seconds before the first explosion. Who the hell was he? Travis had no doubt that the son of a bitch had set the blaze intentionally. But why?

Sweating, carrying the fire extinguisher he'd found in the kennel, he jogged across the paddock and closer to the fire, spraying retardant on the ground near the burning shed while looking for Shannon, searching the shifting shadows, feeling the blistering heat from the blaze.

Where was she?

With the horses?

Still in the stable?

He didn't see her anywhere outside but he noticed the small horses racing back and forth in a far corner of the field. They were anxious, their eyes wide, their heads high as they sniffed the air and whinnied in fright.

Shannon wasn't with them. Or nearby.

Again he swept his gaze around the nearby buildings.

Had she gone back to the house?

No, he decided, still blowing retardant near the base of the burning building. After releasing the horses, she would have run to the kennel to make certain he'd taken care of the dogs. She'd been adamant about saving the animals.

Sirens screamed in the distance and another horse, a panicked, yellowish animal with black stockings, mane and tail, careened out of the stable. The mare barreled past him at breakneck speed, dark legs flashing as she beelined for the rest of the herd now huddled and restless at the far end of the paddock.

Was Shannon still inside?

"Shannon!" he yelled, one eye on the door, the other on the plume of retardant he was shooting toward the shed. Slowly, he eased toward the stable.

He thought she might have gone out the other door at the front of the building, the one where she'd entered, the smaller door that faced the parking lot, but as the flames roared higher and far he heard in the distance the wail of a siren, and he had a bad feeling.

A real bad feeling.

He didn't know how many horses were on the premises. The small herd that was snorting and pawing might be all the horses, nonetheless, he moved toward the open door, feeling the heat char his lungs, tasting the smoke in his mouth.

All the while he scanned the landscape, the buildings, the connecting paddocks, porches and walkways.

The sirens screamed closer, the noise nearly deafening.

His canister was suddenly empty, the few last gasps of retardant sputtering out.

"Shannon!" he yelled again, spying a hose coiled on the outside of the stable, only a few feet from a watering trough and spigot. Still watching the door, he jogged to the building, tossed the empty fire extinguisher onto the ground, then unwound the hose. Losing no time, he attached the hose to the spigot, twisted the tap on full bore and turned toward the stable, intending to spray down the roof. "Shannon!"

Where the hell could she be? Still inside? With an injured horse?

"Hell!"

He had to find out. Dropping the hose, he let it wriggle and writhe on the ground like a dying snake.

He was two steps from the doorway when he heard her scream.

A sharp, piercing cry of sheer agony.

Fear jolted through him.

"Shannon!" He ran into the yawning open doorway and into the darkness.

She was less than ten feet from the door.

A crumpled heap in a pool of blood.

"Jesus, no!"

He was at her side in a second.

She was beaten, blood covering her face, running onto the concrete. Oh, God, had she been trampled? He knelt beside her, feeling the heat of the fire, hearing the growl of huge engines, the sound of gravel being crushed beneath thick tires.

Fire trucks!

Emergency vehicles!

Paramedics!

Oh, God, please, let the paramedics be here!

Heart in his throat Travis felt for her pulse, checked her airway and listened for her breathing over the sounds of men shouting, boots crunching, the fire hissing.

She was alive, breathing on her own, her pulse steady and yet she was out cold, blood gushing from a wound in the back of her head. "Here!" he screamed at the top of his lungs. "I need help over here!" He wanted to move her, to drag her from this dark, smoke-filled building, but he didn't dare for fear of injuring her further.

Where the hell were the EMTs?

"Shannon!" he yelled, trying to wake her without shaking her. "Shannon Flannery!"

She didn't move. In the dim, reddish light, he saw that her once-beautiful face had been battered. Blood was flowing and crusting from her nose and mouth, bruises surfacing over what had so recently been flawless skin. He tore off a piece from the hem of his T-shirt and held it over the worst of the cut, feeling the blood wet and sticky as it oozed through the wad of dark cotton. With his teeth and free hand, he ripped off more of his shirt and tried to staunch the flow of blood at the back of her head, conscious that she might have a neck injury and careful to barely move her.

"Help!" he screamed again.

God, would they not search the buildings?

For a second he let go of the soaked wad of cloth and her chin and reached into his pocket for his cell phone. He didn't dare leave her, but he'd call damned 9-1-1 again and have them call and relay a message to the EMTs that there was an injured woman in the stable who needed immediate attention.

He'd pulled up his antennae with his teeth when he heard the sound of footsteps.

Thank God!

"In here!" he yelled.

Someone was running toward him.

Relief washed over him.

Still kneeling, the cell phone in one hand, he glanced up, expecting a fireman or EMT, but the tall man who stopped only inches from him was wearing sun-bleached jeans and a tattered T-shirt. He glared down at Travis with dark, suspicious eyes.

"Who're you?" he demanded.

But Travis ignored the question. "She needs help."

"I can see that." The stranger was on his knees in an instant.

"Shit," he muttered, touching her gently yet familiarly, as if he was accustomed to placing his hands on her body. Travis's gut knotted and he felt a spurt of jealousy shoot through his blood. He ignored the ridiculous sensation, hoped whoever the hell this guy was, he could help her.

"You with the fire crew?"

The dark-eyed man didn't answer, his concentration completely on Shannon, eerily so, as if the rest of the world, the horrific fiery blaze, the scattered, panicked horses, the rescue workers, this whole hellish scene, were removed.

Carefully this man touched and probed. "Shannon," he whispered in a voice barely audible. "Wake up. Can you hear me?"

"She's out," Travis said impatiently.

The man didn't so much as flick him a glance.

"I'll get help!" Though he was hesitant to leave her, Travis ran to the far end of the building and tried to open the door. It didn't give. Hell! He fiddled with the deadbolt, heard the latch spring, then shouldered open the door. Emergency vehicles were scattered around the lot—a county sheriff's rig, a pumper truck, a fire engine and an ambulance. Firefighters in helmets and fire-retardant gear were already twisting on nozzles, dragging hoses, shouting to each other as they surrounded the blaze.

"Hey, you!" shouted one firefighter, a short, wiry man wearing a protective jacket, trousers and helmet. His face was stern and set, eyes drilling through the clear shield of his visor. He held a halligan tool in one hand, his self-contained breathing apparatus strapped to his back. "Anyone inside?" he asked, pointing toward Shannon's house.

"I don't know." He thought of the man running from the fire. Where the hell had he gone?

"I don't think so, but I've got a woman hurt in the stable. She needs medical attention—now!"

The firefighter pointed out the paramedics emerging from the ambulance.

Travis flagged them down as firefighters dragged hoses closer to the blaze and great streams of water began pouring over the burning shed and surrounding buildings. The angry fire spat, sizzled and hissed as if enraged by the onslaught of gallons of water.

"There's a woman, the one who owns this place, Shannon Flannery, and she's unconscious," Travis explained as the EMTs pulled their equipment cases from the ambulance. "Head wound. Facial cuts. Maybe internal injuries."

"What about you?" the female EMT asked, already following Travis as he ran toward the stable. She was short and slim, her partner, a stocky man jogging beside her, was only a few inches taller.

"I'm fine."

"You don't look it," she said, frowning, and he glanced down at his jacket, shirt and jeans, all of which were colored by splotches of blood—Shannon's blood.

"It's not mine," he said as he reached the door. "Down this corridor. The lights aren't working."

"No problem." The man turned on a huge flashlight that illuminated the concrete path bisecting the building. All along the corridor were bloody footprints.

"Don't step in those!" the male EMT ordered, but it was too late. Travis saw that the footprints had already been smeared by his own boots as he'd run through the dark seeking help. Knowing whatever evidence had been in those tracks was probably lost, he sidestepped the footprints to the spot near the far door where Shannon lay inert, the tall man in attendance.

He didn't move away from Shannon even when the EMTs closed in.

"Stand back, sir," the woman ordered. "Sir!"

The second EMT was already opening his case.

Reluctantly the man eased away from Shannon and the stern, small woman wearing protective gear took control. "God," she said in a whisper. "This is Shannon Flannery?"

"Yes," both men answered and Travis cringed at the sight of Shannon's battered face. He'd seen his share of wounds in his day, watched his share of fights but Shannon's contusions, the cuts and bruising on her face, the blood everywhere, caused his gut to clench.

The female EMT looked up. "Either of you related to her? Husband?"

"No," Travis said and the other man shook his head.

"Do you know if anyone else is injured?" she asked, kneeling next to Shannon as her partner reached into his medical case and yanked on a pair of latex gloves.

"I don't know," Travis answered. "I haven't seen anyone else."

"Anyone else live here?" She pulled on her gloves and was already examining Shannon, checking her breathing and pulse.

"I do, but I wasn't home. Just got back," the tall man answered.

Nate Santana, Travis realized, and another unwanted and uncalled for sense of jealousy sang through his blood. He'd known about Santana, of course, had read about him in some of the articles on Shannon. Supposedly the guy was some kind of horse trainer, a "horse whisperer," if you could believe what the Internet said about him.

But nowhere in any of the articles he'd read had Santana and Shannon Flannery been romantically linked. A little tidbit the press hadn't reported. Now, Travis guessed, by the look of concern on his face, the way he'd touched her and talked to her, Santana was more than Shannon Flannery's partner. He probably lived with her and was her lover.

Tense, Travis hazarded a glance at the tall man with the black hair and eyes as dark as obsidian. Deep grooves were evident around the corners of his mouth and crow's-feet fanned out from his eyes.

"Does anyone else live on the premises besides you and Ms. Flannery?" the male paramedic asked.

"No."

Just outside the open door, firefighters tackled the blaze, yelling at each other, working together, a kind of fascinating ordered chaos as they battled the blaze. More water was pumped onto the fire. Smoke and steam rose to the night sky.

"Any guests or visitors?"

The tall man glanced at Travis. "None that I know of."

"Okay, so what happened to her?" the female EMT asked as her partner radioed to someone that there were no other people known to be on the premises.

"She was setting the horses free, afraid this building might go up. I went to take care of the dogs . . . I wasn't here, but I thought maybe she'd been kicked or trampled by a horse . . ."

"This is more than a kick," she said, glancing up at both men. "How long has she been out?"

Travis said, "Five minutes, maybe six or seven."

Quickly and efficiently, the female EMT bandaged Shannon's head, frowning at the cut on the back side, then tore open Shannon's blouse and bandaged the scrape that sliced down her ribs. "Surface laceration," she said to her cohort before shining the beam of a penlight into Shannon's eyes. "Shannon Flannery!" she yelled. "Shannon!" No response. "Let's take her in, careful of the shoulder."

She frowned as they unfolded a stretcher. Into a recorder, she said, "The victim's suffered multiple contusions on the face and head . . ." She rattled off more of her vital signs, then snapped the recorder off. "Looks like someone beat the tar out of her." She stared down the corridor to the smeared trail of blood, then said, "Let's get her to the hospital."

Travis's insides twisted. What the hell had happened to her in those few minutes they'd been separated, when Shannon had gone into the horse barn and he'd run to the kennel? He stared down at what had so recently been a heart-stoppingly beautiful face, at the dark bruises, bandages and blood on what had been flawless features. The paramedics stabilized her neck, then carefully placed her on a stretcher.

The paramedic was right. Shannon looked as if someone had swung a baseball bat at her and connected. Because she'd stayed in the stables, because she'd cared enough about her animals that she'd risked her life for them.

His jaw slid to the side and he felt like a fool.

"You two, tell the investigators what you know about this fire," the female EMT ordered, then she and her partner hoisted Shannon from the ground and carried her away from the fire, down the alley between the garage and stable to the waiting ambulance.

"Let's start with you," Santana suggested, his black eyes narrowing on Travis. Suspicion and plain-old distrust were evident in the set of his jaw. "Just who the hell are you and how is it that you happened to be here when the fire broke out?"

Chapter 8

Shea stepped on the accelerator. Pushing the speed limit, siren blaring, the lights on the cab of his truck flashing, he drove furiously through the empty city streets to the outskirts of town where his sister lived.

He couldn't believe what Melanie Dean, the dispatcher at the 9-1-1 center, had told him. That there was a fire at Shannon's house, on which both his sister and some man had called in. Melanie said the second call came from a cell phone registered to Travis Settler from Falls Crossing, Oregon. A few minutes later the center had received other calls from people who were driving by or lived close enough to smell the smoke and see the flames.

He braked to turn off the main road and cracked his window. The acrid smell of smoke, soot and wet, scorched wood hit him full force. It was an odor he'd grown up with.

One of his uncles had just retired from the San Francisco Fire Department after nearly forty years of service, another uncle had died on the job, fighting a wildfire in Southern California in the eighties. Shea had been with the Santa Lucia Fire Department before jumping ship and taking the fire investigator job with the Santa Lucia Police Department a few years back.

It was in the Flannery blood.

All of his brothers had, at one time or another, been associated with the fire department, but now, only Robert remained, upholding the Flannery family tradition of actually fighting fires.

Through the trees, he saw lights and within seconds he'd rounded a bend and stopped in the clearing that was the parking lot. Ahead, close to the stable, was what remained of a two-storied tack shed now reduced to charred rubble. Illuminated by the headlights of a remaining pumper truck, a few lanterns and heavy-duty flashlights, three blackened walls stood. The roof had collapsed, one wall was gone, all the windows blown. Smoke still rose in thin wisps from the smoldering, soggy mass. Fortunately, it looked like none of the other buildings had been involved. The stable, kennel and garage, even the house, probably had some smoke damage, but all in all, Shannon had lucked out. The shed was the least important of all the outbuildings that now stood with yellow crime scene tape roping off the area. Even the house was declared off-limits.

Killing the engine and hitting the emergency brake in one motion, Shea swore under his breath, then climbed out of his rig. The night had a bite to it, seeming as tense as his own stretched nerves. The ground was wet from the runoff of the hoses and his boots slogged through gravel, dirt and debris. Several firefighters remained, cleaning up, putting equipment back into the one remaining truck.

A van from a local news station and two police cars were parked at odd angles, squeezed into the neck of the lane on this side of the tape and leaving enough room between them to allow the big fire trucks to come and go.

The reporters who remained were already packing up, and Shea scowled when he thought of the headlines that would appear in the *Santa Lucia Citizen* or the sound bites that would lead into the story on the eleven o'clock news.

No doubt this fire at Shannon's house would turn out to be another link to the past, to the time when Shannon Flannery had been on trial for murdering her son of a bitch of a husband. Shea's jaw hardened when he thought of Ryan Carlyle. The bastard got what he deserved. So let the story die.

It would kill their mother, Maureen, if she had to relive the scandal all over again.

"Hell," he muttered as he walked up to the cops, got the information that Shannon had been taken to Santa Lucia General and that no one knew yet what the cause of the fire was. That much he figured. Finding the source of the blaze was his job—well, his and the investigator for the Santa

Lucia Rural Fire Department, which covered not only the city but the surrounding hills as well.

As Shea worked for the PD he was often at odds with the fire department's investigator who, in Shea's opinion, was a supercilious prick, all about advancement, getting press for himself and smiling for the camera. Cameron Norris might have degrees in criminology and business crammed up his ass, but he didn't know that ass from a hole in the ground when it came to fires. And the dick had never been satisfied that Shannon hadn't started the fire that had killed her husband.

The two cops were talking, still guarding the premises and keeping at bay anyone who happened to drive by: neighbors, concerned friends, lookie-loos, reporters and anyone else wandering up to the lane to watch the fire burn who weren't all that interested in or aware of preserving the scene for the investigation. All they wanted was a chance to be close to the fire. That's the way it was and always had been; everyone had a fascination with the burning, wild beast that could devour and destroy. It was a living, breathing thing that man needed to survive yet feared as instinctively as death.

He flashed his badge at the cops, who barely looked up, nodded and went back to their conversation as they waited for the crime-scene team to show up and start collecting evidence.

One of the firefighters who was locking equipment into the truck spied Shea and peeled away from his job.

His brother Robert.

Even in his protective gear, Shea would recognize him anywhere.

Though all of Patrick's sons resembled him, Robert was the one who was what all the relatives referred to as "the spitting image," even down to his quick, straight-backed gait. "What the hell happened?" Shea demanded once Robert was within earshot.

"Don't know." Robert unclasped his strap and pulled off

his helmet, then lowered his hood to reveal sweat-dampened hair and a face covered with grime and soot. Slightly shorter than Shea, Robert was blessed with the same wavy black hair, intense blue eyes and knife-edged jaw that every Flannery brother shared. "A call came in about an hour ago." He let out a breath and rubbed the back of his neck. "Man, I couldn't believe it was Shannon's place. Heard the address and nearly peed my damned turnout pants."

"But you didn't see her?"

"No. Just heard that she was pretty messed up. Cuddahey caught a glimpse of her." He glanced back to the fire truck where Kaye Cuddahey was working with a nozzle. Shea knew her. Tall and good-looking, with a sharp tongue, three kids and two ex-husbands who weren't worth fifty cents added together.

"Smoke inhalation? Burns?"

"No. The word is that she was messed up, probably trampled by the horses. Cuddahey said she looked like she'd been beaten with a Louisville Slugger."

"Beaten?" Shea repeated, his skin crawling as if scorched by flame. "By whom?"

"Don't know yet."

"But it doesn't make sense." He scratched at his chin. "She's always real careful around the animals. They trust her." He trained his gaze on the blackened heap that had been the shed. Why had the building gone up so suddenly? And why would it look like someone had bludgeoned Shannon?

Shea's back teeth ground as he ran through the possible scenarios in his head. Horses. It had to have been the frantic horses who, in their crazed panic to run to safety, had knocked her down and galloped over her, their heavy hooves cutting and bruising her, even breaking her bones and nearly killing her. Yeah, that had to be it.

Or was it something else? his mind nagged.

Something much more sinister.

The night got under his skin . . . the smell of doused fire, the hush of the wind, the feeling that something very wrong was happening.

He stared at the smoldering ruins and wondered how all of this had happened. His eyes narrowed under the glare of the harsh security lights and remaining lanterns. Everything looked worse in the fake blue light. More forbidding. More malicious.

A bad taste climbed the back of his throat.

An old fear took shape in his mind.

He didn't like the turn of his thoughts. Ugly thoughts that traveled into deadly territories he didn't want to explore. Ever.

"Because of the fire," Robert was saying, "my guess is that the horses probably panicked as she was letting them out. Deep down, they're wild animals and the fear of fire's pretty damned primal. She could have slipped. One could have knocked her down. The rest could have trampled her."

"Maybe," Shea allowed, but he wasn't buying it. At least not all of it. Shannon, like everyone else in the Flannery family, knew about the dangers of fire. She would know how her animals would react. Despite her own fear, she would have been extremely careful.

Something felt off about all of this.

Way out of kilter.

"Where was she found?"

"In the stable." Robert nodded toward the building less than fifteen feet from the rubble of the shed. "Near the back door, the big one that leads to the corral."

Yellow tape surrounded the long two-storied building. Shea had been in the horse barn a couple of times when she'd taken in a particularly nasty animal that Santana was working with. The stables could house up to a dozen horses with six stalls on either side of a center walkway that opened to the parking lot on one end, a large paddock on the other. Near the back door were several closets for leads and bridles, the tack that was used on a daily basis, as well as feed grain and a locked cabinet of veterinary medicines. Overhead was the loft that, depending upon the time of year, was filled with hay and straw.

The wall closest to the remains of the shed was blackened, several windows shattered.

"Lucky she didn't lose it as well," Shea thought aloud.

"Or any of the stock."

"Where are the animals?"

"In a pen out beyond the paddock. Santana rounded up all of the horses and locked them in a corral on the far side of the paddock, the one farthest from the fire. Then he located the dogs and has them kenneled in cages away from the scene, out near the lane, just so nothing gets any more disturbed than it already is before the crime scene team and the arson dicks have a look."

"What about Shannon's dog?" Shea asked as he studied the area that the arson squad would have to evaluate: a sodden, seared mess.

"Khan? We found him in the house. Unharmed and pissed as hell that he was cooped up when all the action was out here. Now he's with the other dogs."

"Santana's taking care of him, too?"

"Yep." Robert's eyes held Shea's for a second and though neither said a word, the unspoken sentiments toward the man who lived and worked with Shannon passed between them. Neither Shea nor Robert trusted Nate Santana as far as they could throw him.

"Swell guy," Shea said and the corners of Robert's mouth tightened in his soot-streaked face. "Where was Santana when all of this happened?"

"Good question. Maybe up in his studio. He showed up after she managed to get the horses out. But I got the feeling from something Aaron said the other night that he was supposed to be away for a while, that Shannon was alone this week."

The bad feeling in Shea's gut just got a little worse. Gnawed at him. Already things weren't adding up and the crime scene guys hadn't even started picking through the ash and debris yet.

"Look, all I know is that he and another guy were here trying to help Shannon before the EMTs arrived," Shea said.

"What other guy?"

"A guy from out of town. Named Settler, I think. Didn't catch any more than that."

The fire truck behind him rumbled to life. "Beats me. I never saw him, never heard his name. But the captain has it. Look, I'd better get back." He motioned toward the last fire truck and the hoses being folded by a couple of other fire-fighters.

"So who's at the hospital with Shannon?"

"Oliver," Robert said, mentioning their younger brother. "I called him when I figured out it was Shan."

Oliver, too, had been a firefighter once, but had given it up and now was only a few weeks away from taking his final vows as a priest, if you could believe that.

Shea didn't understand Oliver's latent calling to serve God, but their mother had been delighted to finally have a priest in the family. Maureen had so little interest in life, had become so filled with a creeping despair in the past few years that Shea thought Oliver should go for it, become a goddamned priest. Take the vows. Swear off sex and sin for the rest of life. Hell, someone should break out of the family's seemingly unbreakable tradition—or was it obsession?—of fighting fires.

"After Oliver talks to the docs and sees that Shannon's okay, then he'll tell Ma."

"That'll be fun," Shea said sarcastically. This might be the final blow for their mother. It wasn't enough that she'd raised hellions like their father, even her daughter couldn't stay out of trouble. It seemed to be a Flannery family trait, or the curse, as Maureen O'Malley Flannery called it.

All the Flannerys had been born with wild streaks. All had skeletons locked firmly away in their closets. All had a penchant for trouble—whatever it may be. "Just as long as Shannon's all right, nothing else really matters," Shea muttered.

"If you say so."

"What's that supposed to mean?"

"Only if someone did happen to beat the crap out of my sister, I think that stupid bastard is gonna pay and pay big time."

"The law will handle it," Shea said.

"Yeah, right." Robert snorted, the smile on his blackened face without a trace of humor. "And I think I'm about to be canonized by the pope himself."

"Hey, Flannery, how about a hand over here!" Kaye Cuddahey, wearing her most put-upon, I'm-friggin'-tired-of-doing-all-the-work-for-you-lazy-male-asses expression, waved at Robert. She and Luis Santiago were slamming doors shut on the rig as it idled. She looked pissed as hell as she glared at Robert.

"See ya later," Robert said and hustled back to the truck. A few seconds later the big rig rambled down the lane.

Shea walked around the scene, eyeing the rubble, trying to imagine the conflagration that had erupted. So far they didn't have answers, but that would change. Once it was cool enough, he and some of the people from the police crime lab as well as the fire department's investigator would sort through the piles of ash, glass and charred remains to figure out exactly what had happened. Maybe Shannon could give an explanation, or Santana, or the other guy, the stranger. What had the name been? Settler? Christ, who was he?

Shea returned to his truck, donned protective covers over his boots, pulled on gloves and hauled his flashlight with him. He stepped over the yellow plastic tape and walked through the open door of the stable.

With a flip of the switch, the entire length of the building was awash with bright fluorescent light. His stomach curdled as he saw a pool of dark, crusted blood. Instead of going through the building, he carefully picked his way around the back where he stood outside and studied the dark, drying puddle. It too was blotchy and smeared, whatever evidence might have been there probably destroyed as Shannon was tended to and then moved.

Squatting, he stared down the corridor, trying to imagine what had happened. Where were the bloody hoofprints? If horses had trampled her, they would leave impressions behind. But they were missing. There were other prints however, soles that were the size of a man's shoe or boot.

His gut twisted and the feeling that things were going from bad to worse got a whole lot stronger. Through the far door he heard the approach of another vehicle. Headlights appeared.

The crime scene team had arrived.

Soon, maybe, they'd have some answers.

From a sun-bleached bench on the back porch of the cabin, he watched the dawn break and sipped from a bottle of Coca-Cola. It was warm, the weather hot enough that there was no early morning chill, just a searing, dry wind that seeped through the surrounding hills, chasing down the dry arroyos and creeping through the forest.

Flaming streaks of light were rising over the mountains to the east. Vibrant oranges and golds pushed the edges of night back to the far corners of the earth, reminding him of fire . . . always fire.

A jackrabbit hopped through the bracken of this rundown old shack, a place no one had occupied for decades. A crow cawed from the branch of a spindly oak. Overhead the wasps were just coming out of their muddy nests built under the eaves, thin black bodies crawling from narrow holes, warming themselves.

This was his haven.

A spot no one knew about.

Not even those close to him.

If there were any.

He took another pull from the bottle.

The kid was inside. Locked in a room where the only natural illumination came in through a skylight. The windows were nailed shut and covered with plywood, the door locked from his side.

So far she hadn't complained.

Scared little twit. But a pain nonetheless.

Hard to believe that the frightened wimp of a kid was Shannon Flannery's blood kin. Her daughter.

His gaze returned to the slowly lightening sky and he pushed thoughts of the girl out of his mind as he stared at the brilliant colors.

Reminding him again of the fire.

Reminding him of her.

His blood ran hot at the thought of her.

He'd been close enough to smell her, to sense her fear, to hear her breath escape in a startled "ooph" as he'd struck. Licking his lips, he remembered the feeling of the impact, just powerful enough to break her skin, to crush a few small bones, but not to pulverize her, not to permanently mar her beauty, not to have her in the hospital for weeks.

Not to kill her.

Not yet.

He'd known when he'd started the fire that she would go for the horses. Either after the dogs or before, but he counted on the fact she would save the beasts before waiting for help to come.

And so he'd waited. Hidden behind a barrel of grain, the pitchfork close at hand, he'd counted the seconds, heard his own breathing, felt his pulse accelerate. Through the window he'd watched his work, felt the explosion that had shattered windows and rocked the ground. Seen the horses panic, pacing in their stalls, working into lathers. He'd stared at the rapidly spreading flames as they'd feasted on the old timbers, chewing hungrily through the dry roof, burning hot and wild.

Oh, God, it had been perfect.

Even now, he could feel that hot surge of excitement whispering through his bloodstream.

The second explosion had put the already-frightened animals into a wild, unleashed frenzy. They'd squealed and kicked at their stalls, while the dogs in the kennels bayed and whined mournfully.

Best yet, from his vantage point he'd been able to see the house, watched as the door had opened and she'd appeared with a pathetic little fire extinguisher. Just as he'd expected. Her auburn hair had been wild and free, her face without much makeup twisted in fear, her body thin and supple, small and athletic with high breasts and a tight, perfect little ass.

Frightened, scared spitless, but still in control, she'd flown out of the house, across the gravel lot, toward the stable.

Everything had begun to work perfectly.

Except a man had shown up out of nowhere.

Someone unexpected.

Someone who'd been hiding nearby.

The proverbial fly in the ointment.

His smile disappeared as he remembered the interloper.

Fortunately, Shannon had talked him into releasing the dogs while she'd dealt with the horses.

As the stranger had taken off for the kennels, she'd thrown open the door of the stable and started running to the far end. Again, predictable. It gave him enough time to close the door to the parking lot and latch it, cutting off her escape, assuring him that they would be alone. That the stranger wouldn't return and interrupt them.

Now, he took a long swallow of Coke as the sun crested the eastern hills, a blazing ball of fire that gilded everything and pushed away the lingering vestiges of night.

His tongue flicked to the edges of his lips as he remembered waiting to pounce. How his muscles had ached, his blood singing with anticipation, something akin to lust flowing through his body.

It had taken all of his patience to wait as she'd unleashed the animals one at a time, working her way backward, toward him and the balking mare, the fidgety buckskin he'd already frightened by flicking a butane lighter in front of her face, close enough to singe the bristles on her nose. The horse had reared and screamed in terror, still smelling him as he'd waited, still sensing the lighter with its long, hot flame.

So by the time Shannon reached her, the dun-colored mare was out of her mind with fear. In a lather. It had taken all of Shannon's skills to get the horse out of the stall. Even then the animal had managed to wound her.

And she hadn't so much as let out a sound.

So brave.

So filled with a sense of righteousness.

And so doomed.

The pitchfork had been handy and thorough.

He could have killed her if he'd wanted to; but that would ruin his plans. And much as he tasted the blood lust, he had to be patient.

There were others who had to pay first. He drained his bottle and tossed it into the bracken, startling a nest of finches that fluttered and swooped at the disturbance.

He wanted Shannon to survive until after the others died. If she couldn't witness their deaths, then, at the very least, she would experience the pain of the loss, imagine their torment, know that she, too, would not survive.

No one would.

Chapter 9

Shannon felt like hell.

Her entire body ached.

Her face pulsed with pain.

The back of her head felt as if it might explode.

And above it all, she had trouble waking up, her eyelids felt as if they were weighted down and when she licked her lips, her tongue was thick and awkward, her mouth tasting sour, her teeth scummy.

She heard voices—hushed, muted voices—and felt fingertips upon her bare arm.

Tentatively she squinted out of one bleary eye, only to slam her eyelid closed against the harsh rush of light.

"She's rousing," a woman's soft voice said.

It took a second, then she realized she wasn't home in her own bed, but that she was in a hospital. Fragments of her memory returned in sharp, painful shards. She remembered the panic of the fire in the shed, running outside barefoot, the stranger waiting for her, the frightened, frenzied horses, the crackling terror of the fire and then the attack, the vicious, excruciating assault.

"Ms. Flannery's coming around," the woman's soft voice said again. "See if Dr. Zollner is still here."

"I saw her about ten minutes ago in B wing," a younger voice responded.

"Good. Find her if you can. Let the doctor know that Ms. Flannery is rousing."

Shannon was still caught up in the memories that were returning. Who had been hiding in the stables? Who had tried to kill her?

Her heart raced, she began to breathe unevenly as she recalled the pain, the fear, the sheer horror of it all. Had the man who attacked her set the fire? And the Good Samaritan who had just happened to show up after the explosions and fire—who was he? Friend or foe? Had he started the fire, then, when she'd come out of the house, pretended to want to help her, only to wait for her in the darkened stables ready to spring and attack? Had he told her his name?

Her head pounded as she tried to think, to make sense of it.

"Shannon?"

The female voice—a nurse's voice, Shannon guessed—was closer. "Shannon, can you hear me? Shannon?"

"Yes," she forced out, though her mouth tasted like soot and one cheek throbbed.

"How're you feeling? Can you open your eyes?"

Wincing, Shannon blinked a few times before she was able to force her eyelids open and focus on the petite nurse with short, streaked hair, wire-rimmed glasses and dimples.

"How're you feeling?" she asked again, gentle fingers rimming Shannon's wrist as she took her pulse.

Horrible!

In pain!

Like I've been run over by an eighteen-wheeler that took one pass, only to come around for another.

"Compared to what?" Shannon managed, her voice little more than a whisper.

The corner of the nurse's mouth twitched. "That bad?"

"Worse."

"After the doctor examines you, we'll up your pain med," the nurse said, her dark gaze compassionate. "Do you know where you are?"

"The hospital."

"Not just *any* hospital, mind you. You're an official guest of Santa Lucia General, the best in the Bay area . . . Well, at least that's what we're supposed to tell you."

Shannon rotated her head slightly and saw she was in a private room with pale green walls, sterile medical equipment, a television mounted on the far wall and a short counter that was already laden with vases of cut flowers and potted plants.

People had already sent gifts?

That took time.

She felt a moment's panic.

"How long have I been out?" she asked, spying the IV flowing into her arm.

"You were brought in the night before last."

She looked out the window. It was twilight, the lights of the parking lot beginning to illuminate as dusk darkened.

"What happened? What about my horses?" Adrenaline chased away whatever was making her feel so drowsy and thick in the head.

"I'm sure they're fine." The nurse stuck a digital thermometer under Shannon's tongue, took her temperature, then wrapped a blood pressure cuff around her arm.

Shannon could barely wait while the nurse stuck the cold stethoscope inside her arm, then marked her chart.

Trying to remain calm, Shannon said, "Is my purse here? My wallet? My cell phone?"

"I don't think so. You came by ambulance. Emergency. From a fire. You didn't have any personal items with you other than your clothes and watch."

Shannon glanced at her wrist.

"It's in the closet."

"I need a phone," Shannon said, beginning to panic. Surely her brothers would have seen to her livestock. They would have called Nate, or if unable to reach him, get hold of Lindy, who did the books and would be able to find someone to come in and make sure the horses and dogs were fed, watered and exercised. "And then I have to get out of here."

"There's a phone on the bedside table," the nurse said, "but you've had family members camping out in the waiting room. One of them, the tall policeman—"

"Shea."

The nurse nodded. "He told the staff to let you know that your family is taking care of everything, including your home and business and animals. You're not to worry and just get well."

"Not worry?" *Fat chance.*

"Is he here?"

"I don't know, I think maybe one of them is, but your mother went home."

Shannon let out a long breath. The thought of her family camping out in the hospital, making certain that her place was secure, worrying about her, caused her headache to pound even more painfully. She imagined her mother praying, her arthritic fingers caressing the worn beads of her rosary as Oliver consoled her. Robert would be impatient: he had his own problems to deal with, chiefly with his family, and was trying to avoid any face-to-face confrontations with his wife, Mary Beth. Aaron would be angry, a hothead ready to go out, find whoever had done this to her and run him to the ground. Shea, as always, would be the voice of reason, calm, but quietly furious.

"Hello, Shannon." A tall woman in a white lab coat strode into the room and introduced herself as Dr. Ingrid Zollner. Her sun-streaked hair was clipped away from her face, her features were strong and the lines near the corners of her eyes and mouth suggested she'd spent a lot of time outdoors. Her smile was tired and forced.

After asking a few of the same questions as the nurse did, Dr. Zollner examined Shannon, checking her peripheral vision, the amount of pain she was experiencing, then the bandages on her face, scalp and abdomen. She explained to Shannon the extent of her injuries.

"You were brought in unconscious with a concussion from a blow to the back of your head and multiple contusions. Fortunately, and I don't know how, but you have no broken bones. Your shoulder is strained and you have bruised ribs."

She examined the wound in the back of Shannon's head again. "All in all, I'd say, you were pretty lucky."

"Lucky?" Shannon repeated as the nurse adjusted the IV drip. "You know, that's not exactly how I feel."

"It could have been much worse." The doctor was completely sober, her forced smile disappearing. "As I said, lucky, as in no brain damage. No surgery for facial reconstruction. Considering the savageness of the attack, yeah, lucky."

Shannon saw no reason to argue the point.

Folding her arms over her chest, Dr. Zollner said, "The police would like to speak to you and I told them that if you agreed, they could have a few minutes, no more. They've been fairly insistent, but if you're not feeling up to it, I'll have them wait."

"No reason to put it off," Shannon said. "And then, can you tell me when I can go home?"

A blond eyebrow arched. "Soon."

"How soon?"

Zollner eyed Shannon speculatively as a pager went off. She pulled it from her pocket, saw the number, frowned, then dropped the pager into her deep pocket again. "You can probably be released tomorrow morning," she said to Shannon. "I'd like you to get one more night's rest here, where we can monitor you. Even though I said you were lucky, a concussion is serious."

"I know, but I have animals to take care of. I have—"

"You have to heal," the doctor said firmly as she started for the door. "I'm sure someone can take care of your pets."

"No, you don't understand—"

But Dr. Zollner was already gone, leaving Shannon alone with the nurse.

"Great," Shannon muttered.

"I'll see what I can do," the nurse said with a wink. "Dr. Zollner's very busy. In the meantime talk to the detectives, and I'll tell your family that you're awake and they can see you soon. Maybe after you've had something to eat."

The mention of food caused immediate hunger pangs. "I'd like that," Shannon said.

"A good sign." The nurse exited and the painkillers began to kick in.

Within minutes two detectives, Cleo Janowitz and Ray Rossi, slipped through the partially opened door. Janowitz was model-thin and nearly as tall as her partner, somewhere close to six feet. Glossy, straight black hair fell to her shoulders and her gold, almond-shaped eyes were sharp and intense. She was pretty, but there was nothing soft or warm about her. The smile on her face was thin.

Rossi could have been a young Kojak: large nose, big brown eyes, shaved head . . . His soul patch and apple cheeks took something away from the image.

"Ms. Flannery," Janowitz, obviously the lead detective, began, "I know that you're not feeling all that great and so we'll try to be brief, but we'd like to ask you a few questions about the other night."

"Go ahead." Lying on the bed, with an IV drip pumping into her arm and her bandages restricting her, Shannon pushed the button to raise the head of the electric bed a little higher. It was a weird feeling to be interviewed here, in the hospital, with the door to the room ajar, the nurses' station visible through the opening.

"You know that arson is suspected in the fire?" Janowitz asked as she delved into a small black shoulder bag. She retrieved a pen and small tablet with a spiral binding and pages covered in a bold scrawl. Rossi pulled a recorder from his pocket and set it on a table near her bed.

"I figured," she said, her worst fears confirmed. Since she'd already found the burned birth certificate on her porch and been attacked in the horse barn, she'd known someone was out to do her harm. She just didn't know who, or why.

"The crime scene investigators are still evaluating the evidence, and, I think, so is the fire investigator for the department, Shea Flannery. He's your brother, right?"

"Yes."

"He's out in the waiting room, but we wanted to talk to you first."

She began to feel a bit of relief in knowing that at least one of her brothers was nearby. Though they often drove her crazy, she had to admit it was reassuring to have a family to rely on. "What do you want to know?"

Janowitz was staring at her with those intense gold eyes. "We assume from your injuries that you were attacked by an assailant. We found a pitchfork with blood on the handle, boot prints, some with blood on them as well. And all the injuries you sustained can't be explained by a horse striking or trampling you as we first suspected."

Shannon inhaled slowly. "Someone was waiting for me in the stable." She remembered the overwhelming sense of panic as the flames snapped and glass shattered. The frenzy of the horses and the wild barking of the dogs. The fear that heightened as the man struck. "He jumped me."

"Can you describe him?" Janowitz asked.

"A little, but it was dark and I thought, I had the sense that he had on a mask of some kind. I think he was around six feet tall and muscular—athletic, I'd say, but again, that's more of an impression than anything. As I said, it was dark and it all happened so fast . . ."

"Did you see what he was wearing?"

"No . . ." She slowly shook her head. "Dark, maybe black clothes? I don't know . . ."

"Jeans?" Rossi asked, prodding her.

"Maybe. Maybe not."

Rossi said, "Long-sleeved shirt? Jacket? Gloves?"

"I . . . I can't say, not for certain."

"Did you have any other impressions of the assailant? Was he wearing cologne, or did he smell like gasoline?"

"No—just sweat. He smelled of sweat, I think, maybe, but mostly what I smelled was smoke from the fire."

"Did he say anything? Call out to you? Would you be able to identify his voice?"

"No. Didn't say a word," she said.

"How did the attack start?"

She swallowed. "As I said, I think he was waiting in the

stables until I was the farthest from the door that I'd opened for the horses. Most of the animals were already out. One of the mares, Molly, balked at being released. She was frightened and wouldn't budge. I had to grab her halter and physically pull her. She reared . . . struck me . . ." Shannon reached for her water glass. Rossi handed it to her.

Clearing her throat Shannon explained everything she could remember, and as she did Janowitz asked more questions and took notes in her small spiral-bound pad while Rossi listened without so much as another comment.

No, Shannon hadn't seen any vehicles that she didn't recognize.

No, she hadn't observed anyone on the premises who shouldn't have been there.

Yes, sometimes she did feel that she was being followed or watched. She couldn't really explain the sensation.

No, she had no idea who left her the burned piece of her daughter's birth certificate, or who had called at exactly 12:07 on the thirteenth anniversary of that birth, but yes, she did think all the events, including the fire, were connected.

Shannon yawned, suddenly tired. She moved her shoulders and felt a stab of pain in her ribs. She didn't want to think about the fire any longer, couldn't really concentrate.

But Janowitz wasn't quite finished. "There was a man, a stranger on the premises. The one you ran into as the fire broke out."

"Uh-huh." Shannon nodded, remembering the tall man who'd appeared from the shadows, the one she'd sent to release the dogs from their kennels. It had been too dark to get a good look at his face, all she had were vague images of a tall, athletically built man with sharp features. "I didn't get his name."

Janowitz checked her notes, flipping back a couple of pages, but Shannon guessed she really didn't need to remind herself. If nothing else, the female detective seemed focused and, Shannon bet, had a razor-sharp memory. "Travis Settler."

The name meant nothing to her. "Settler?"

"You don't know him?"

She shook her head. "No. But . . ." She thought about catching the first glimpse of his shadowed face and the sensation that she'd seen him somewhere before. She wanted to dismiss it. Everything had been so crazy, but the detective was staring at her expectantly, waiting for her to finish her sentence. "Okay, when I saw him that night . . . I had this . . . this strange feeling that I'd met him or seen him somewhere before. Kind of a déjà vu thing." Which was impossible. Where had she seen him? "But I'm not sure about that."

"He's from Falls Crossing."

Shannon shrugged. "Where's that?"

"In Oregon. Near the Washington border."

"Never heard of it."

"Not many people have." A hint of a smile tugged at the corner of Janowitz's mouth. So the hard-nosed detective did have a sense of humor.

"And you've never met Travis Settler before?"

"No, I don't know anyone by that name," she said and turned her head to glance out the window to the leafy branches of an oak illuminated by the security lights. Was the name familiar? She didn't think so. "Should I know him?" Shannon asked, looking at the detective again. She noticed a hint of doubt in the detective's gaze, as if Janowitz knew something she didn't. And the other guy—Rossi—his scowl had deepened around the small stripe of blond beard visible on his chin.

"Wait a minute," Shannon said, her pulse escalating. "What's going on? Who is this Settler guy?"

Janowitz ignored her question. "Do you think Travis Settler was the one who attacked you?"

"No . . . I . . ." She didn't really know, did she? She'd thought he'd gone to free the dogs, but he could have pretended to run to the kennels, then hidden. "I don't know, but . . . No, I don't *think* it was him. Why would it be?"

"Who do you think it was?"

"Beats me. It was dark. I'd already been injured by the mare."

"Tell us about it again," Janowitz said, her steady gaze missing nothing. Suddenly Shannon felt vulnerable. Lying here in the bed, an IV dripping into the back of her right wrist, her left arm taped to her side, her face patched with bandages. These people, the police, knew a whole lot more about what had happened to her, to her property, than she did and they acted as if she was hiding something.

"I saw the fire," she began wearily. Her strength ebbing, she nevertheless reviewed every step of that awful night: grabbing the fire extinguisher, running to the stable, meeting Settler, the mad panic as she raced through the horse barn, then backwards through the stalls to avoid being trampled, Molly's resistance, her shoulder feeling as if it was ripping apart, the horse rearing and finally getting the crazed mare almost to safety, when she was suddenly jumped from behind.

"So there weren't any lights in the stable?"

"They weren't working."

"The circuit breaker had flipped," Rossi interjected.

"What?" Shannon asked.

"The reason the lights wouldn't come on in the stable was that the bank of circuit breakers for the building had either tripped off, maybe because of the fire, I don't know, or someone had switched them off intentionally. Did you flip the breakers?"

"No, of course not . . ."

Janowitz said, "The breakers had flipped in the kennels, too."

Shannon's heart nearly stopped. How premeditated had the attack been? How long had the guy been watching her? Walking on her property? Setting this up? She shivered as if the room temperature had dropped twenty degrees.

The arson wasn't what was the most terrifying; she'd suspected that someone had intentionally set the blaze—a "fire-bug" as her father used to call them. But the fact that she, personally, had been targeted, that was something else.

"Ms. Flannery," Detective Janowitz asked, her voice a little softer, "do you have any enemies, anyone who would want to hurt you?"

Shannon closed her eyes. A dozen names came to mind, people who had hurled insults at her. Slurs. Thought she'd literally "gotten away with murder" three years ago. She'd thought—no, hoped—that most of the bitterness and hatred had eased over the years . . . Now she wasn't so sure. A headache pounded despite the IV drip with its painkiller. All the old feelings, the anger, the grief, the fear, converged on her again. Who would want to see her harmed? Where did she begin? Ryan's family would be a good start. His mother, father and assorted cousins had sworn vengeance after the trial. His girlfriend, Wendy Ayers, had nearly spat on Shannon after the verdict was announced. Wendy clearly had considered Ryan hers even though Shannon was still married to him at the time of his death.

And there had been others as well, people he'd known, worked with, friends who couldn't believe a man with his Irish charm and good looks could ever raise his voice, let alone his fist, to his wife . . .

Her stomach knotted with the memories. "You work with my brother, Shea. I think he can give you a list."

Janowitz wasn't about to be put off. She stepped a little closer, a pucker forming between her dark eyebrows. "But how about you? Who do you think would want to do you harm? An ex-lover, or someone you worked with? What about Nate Santana? He was supposed to be gone that night, but he suddenly showed up."

"It wasn't Nate," Shannon said firmly, though deep inside, didn't she, too, have questions about the man she'd hired, the man she'd spent so many hours with, the man who told her so little of his past? She knew he cared for her, though, and couldn't believe he would be a part of this kind of violence . . . or could he?

"Are you involved with anyone?"

"No . . . not now. My ex-husband, Ryan Carlyle, is dead, but I'm sure you know all about that."

"What about the father of the child you gave up for adoption?"

"Brendan?" She let out a quick little snort of disgust. "He took off when I told him I was pregnant, nearly fourteen years ago. Never heard from him again. His parents said he went to Central or South America."

"No other boyfriends?"

She shook her head and felt herself color. "Nothing serious. I've been involved with two men since . . . since Ryan's death. The first man, Reggie Maxwell, said he was from LA, turned out he lived over in Santa Rosa, with his wife and three kids. As soon as I found out, I ended it." Her hand fisted at the memory, the fury and embarrassment of being duped.

"And the other guy?"

"Keith Lewellyn, a lawyer from San Francisco. Corporate law. We dated five, maybe six times. Neither of us was that interested in the other. It died a natural and quick death. The people who have the most ill feelings toward me are Ryan's friends and family."

Janowitz waited, pen poised.

Rossi stroked that bit of beard.

The recorder kept taping.

"I'm sure you realize that I was accused of murdering my husband," she said quietly, her fingers twisting the hem of her sheet. "Donald Berringer was the lead prosecutor. I was found innocent but a lot of people weren't happy with the verdict, including Berringer. For nearly a year I got hate mail and of course my husband's family was up in arms." She cleared her throat, looked directly at the two detectives. "I received death threats. I reported them."

"Do you know who sent any of them?"

She grimaced, then told them about Ryan's family, especially his first cousins, the Carlyle siblings, who had been so vocal in their belief that she had killed him. Liam had written letters to the editor of the local paper. Kevin had glared at her whenever he saw her, purposely intimidating her. Mary Beth, Shannon's sister-in-law, had accused her of murder and testified against her. And even the usually quiet Margaret had shunned her.

Then Shannon mentioned Wendy, Ryan's girlfriend, but admitted that most of the hate mail had been anonymous.

"The threats slowly ebbed. I thought whoever was behind them had found a new cause to champion, a new target, and I was relieved. It was . . . difficult." She cleared her throat. "I haven't had any trouble in a year, maybe eighteen months. I thought it was all behind me."

"What happened to you might not be linked to your husband's death," Janowitz said, her mouth softening a bit. "It seems more likely that it has to do with the child. The baby you gave up for adoption. She's missing."

"Missing?" Shannon's head snapped up, the weariness she'd been beginning to feel suddenly gone. "What do you mean? Missing from where?"

"Travis Settler, the man who was outside your house when the fire started, is your daughter's adoptive father. He's in Santa Lucia because the girl didn't come home from school over a week ago, two days after you received the burned birth certificate."

"My—baby?" Shannon whispered, stunned, unable to quite grasp what Janowitz was saying. Her head pounded.

"Yes. The girl that was born thirteen years ago. The baby listed on the birth certificate you found on your porch."

Shannon felt as if her world was cracking.

Janowitz's gaze held hers. "I think it's more than a coincidence."

Chapter 10

Dani peeked through the crack between the door and the doorjamb, just a slice of light that filtered into this room from the next. The little gap allowed her a view of the main living area and the fireplace on the far wall. It was built out of old, crumbling rock and had a thick mantel, upon which were framed photos. They looked like pictures of people's faces, though she couldn't make out their features. She wasn't able to view the entire length of the mantel, so she wasn't sure how many he had, but she could see three.

He also kept his hunting knife on the mantel along with a box of wooden matches, a lighter and a pistol—all items Dani could use if she ever made good her escape.

And she was working on that. She had a plan.

Above the mantel was a cracked mirror. Some of the silver had come off the back and the lines running through it caused some distortion, but in the reflection Dani could see his face and part of the living area, including the door she was locked behind.

Though she was now imprisoned in this small room, she'd been allowed to walk through the rest of the cabin every once in a while. The dilapidated house consisted of this bedroom, a foul-smelling bathroom, a tiny, unused kitchen and the main living area—the room just outside her locked door, where he spent most of his time when he was here.

The bad news was that he locked the door to "her room" whenever he stepped foot out of the shack; the good news was he was gone a lot, so she could set her plan for escape into motion. And though so far he hadn't been rough with her, hadn't indicated that he would hurt her, she sensed it was just a matter of time. He was using her for some vile, criminal purpose and she was determined to thwart him. To save herself. She'd do whatever she had to, because though she was still playing the part, she wasn't about to just roll over. If he tried to hurt her or kill her she was going to give him the fight of her life. Acting cowardly now might buy her some freedom, but in the end, she figured, it wouldn't save her.

So she was figuring a way to get out of this dump. Her quarters consisted of the small bedroom, a closet and a porta-potty, the kind used for camping. The windows of the room had been boarded shut from the outside, but there was a skylight that allowed in some natural light and, with the illumination, a peek-a-boo view of the heavens. A rag rug covered most of the rotting floorboards. He'd given her a cot with a sleeping bag, and a pillow without a case that gave off a weird odor so she never used it—couldn't imagine what kind of cooties were inside or who else had laid their head on the scuzzy thing.

As near as she could figure there was absolutely no insulation in the wood walls and so the place was sweltering most of the time. If it hadn't been for the skylight, which he opened with a long pole that fit around a crank, she was certain she would have suffocated or roasted to death in this pit.

Now, it was night. Dark outside, though she thought she saw a hint of moonlight. It was quiet. Just the sound of insects buzzing and chirping outside.

And the creep was going through his sick ritual. Through the crack in the door she watched him again.

Each night he went through the same motions that he was following now. He bent down and, using the long-necked butane lighter, he lit the fire. It was the same kind her dad used to ignite the lighter fluid in their barbecue at home.

Her stomach twisted as she thought of her dad and she felt her chin shake as she gave in to the fear, the dread. She closed her eyes. What if he couldn't find her? What if this sicko had covered his tracks so well that even her father— with all his hunting and tracking experience and the skills he'd learned in the special forces of the army—had no idea where she was?

Where was her dad now? Was he still coming for her? Had he given up? . . . No . . . not her dad. Travis Settler would move heaven and earth to find her; she knew that much. She just wished he'd show up. And she wished to heaven that she'd never, ever started trying to find her birth parents. That's what had started this . . . It was all her fault.

She blinked back her tears and told herself she had to quit being a baby, pull herself together and stay focused on how to thwart this weirdo.

For now, she pressed her eye against the crack and watched the perv do his thing.

The yellowed newspaper and small twigs in the blackened firebox caught fire instantly, eager flames rising to lick the kindling and small logs he'd piled on the grate.

Satisfied, he placed the small torch onto the mantel again, then stood barefoot in front of the blackened stones and stared at his reflection in the mirror.

Then the really weird stuff happened, just as it had for the past three nights. It was as if he got off on the fire, or on seeing his image in the mirror or something equally bizarre.

As the fire crackled and hissed, consuming the dry wood, he slowly took off his clothes, almost as if he was performing in some kind of bizarre striptease. All for his own benefit.

Dani had never seen an actual stripper in action, of course, but she'd heard all about it from a friend, whose single mother had gotten one of those sexy messengers for her fortieth birthday who came, sang and took off his clothes. Her friend had said it had been really, really gross even though the messenger had been a "hottie" in his twenties. He had taken off his tie, tuxedo and shirt all the way down to a little thong-thing.

Now, watching this whacko undress, Dani couldn't agree more. Still she watched, fascinated, trying to figure this loser out.

First he unbuttoned his shirt, then, his gaze never leaving the mirror, he dropped the shirt onto the floor. She sucked in her breath and bit her tongue as she stared at his back. The sight of his shoulders made her cringe. Scars slashed across his muscles, burn marks covered his skin and made it look slick and stretched too tight, while the rest of his body was smoothed and toned. What had happened to him? And what was with this strange routine?

Not knowing she was watching, he kept at it. He unzipped his jeans and let them slide down his legs, then kicked the dirty Levi's away. If he wore underwear, it came off in the same quick motion. She never actually caught a glimpse of jockeys or boxers or anything. Then he stood naked, facing the fire, away from her, his body tanned except for his scarred back and muscular butt.

He was in good shape, she could see that. His flesh was taut. Not an ounce of flab was visible, just a hard, honed body with that horrid, disfiguring burn across his shoulders and halfway down his back. She couldn't see the front of him, other than his face, didn't know if the scars went down the front. But his face was unscarred and handsome, in an evil way. Blue, blue eyes, thick black hair, defined jaw and thin, cruel mouth.

She finally understood what women meant when they called some guy a "handsome devil." Dani could believe he truly was a devil.

He reached toward the mantel, grabbed his small bottle of oil and slowly started rubbing his body all over, along his neck, down his arms, over his torso, making his tanned skin glisten a shiny gold in the firelight.

It was like he was into himself to the point of being obsessed.

Now the fire was burning bright, eager flames dancing and snapping, red-hot coals winking from the black ash. He smiled at his reflection and touched himself . . . down there.

Sick, sick, sick!

She thought he might jerk off and decided she didn't want to watch *that!*

But instead he peed, sending his stream into the fire,

spraying urine on the flames as his eyes moved from his own reflection to watch the fire hissing and recoiling under the foul-smelling onslaught.

Dani almost heaved.

She clamped her teeth together, determined to watch all of it, hoping to somehow figure out what made him tick.

As soon as he was finished peeing, the rite was over.

Just like that.

As slowly as he'd stripped, he pulled on his clothes in a rush, almost as if to make up for lost time. The fire sputtered and died, red embers still winking in the ashes as he yanked the shirt over his head and pulled up his pants.

Dani shrank back and crept to her cot, crossed her fingers that he wouldn't guess she was faking it and feigned sleep. As she did every night. She knew he was coming. He always checked on her, opening the door enough to allow light to spill on the cot and her face. Sometimes it seemed as if he stared at her forever.

She always pretended that she wasn't awake, her eyes were closed, but not squeezed shut, her mouth was slightly open and she tried to breathe evenly. Sometimes she even rolled over while he was staring, then sighed. All the while she was trembling inside, afraid that he could see through her ruse, and that he might change his routine and step into the room, move across the short distance to the cot, lean down and touch her . . .

She felt nauseated at the thought but forced herself to appear relaxed. Whatever happened she had to go with it, to the point that she knew she could wound him, debilitate him or outrun him.

So far he hadn't stepped a foot into her private cell.

In fact it was almost as if he could barely tolerate her.

She still had no idea who he was and any attempts to draw him into conversation were met with steely-eyed resistance and tight lips.

During this whole time, he'd barely strung two words together when talking with her and then it was always just to bark an order.

"Get into your room."

"What're you lookin' at?"

"Eat and shut the fuck up."

During mealtimes he allowed her to sit at a table and choke down the stuff he had—canned beans, canned spaghetti, canned stew—all of which he cooked over the fire that he pissed on each night. It turned her stomach, but she forced the food down, determined to keep up her strength, determined to escape from this boring, hot, hell of a prison. He gave her bottled water and sometimes a Coke.

In the brief periods of time he'd allowed her out of the room she'd checked out as much of this cabin as possible, each avenue of escape, the few windows and two doors. There was no television. No phone. No electricity. The shack was primitive and decaying, the door on her room latched with an old-fashioned hook-and-eye lock that looked as if it had been there for half a century.

Her forays out of the cell were short, only long enough to eat or stretch her legs, but he was beside her constantly, his eyes trained on her, his muscles tense as if he was ready to pounce on her if she made one misstep. That thought, of his hands on her again, of the smell of him close, kept her in line.

She wondered where he went every night after the strange peeing ritual. He was gone for hours, often until late the next day, as if he was living somewhere else, or had a job, as if he had a double life.

He was a freak. That was it. She listened as he prepared to leave—just as he did every night. First he latched her door, locking her into this miserable room, then he would walk outside, his boots making the old porch boards squeak. After that his footsteps would fade away and about a minute or two later the sound of a truck engine would spark in the distance.

She knew he parked the truck away from the cabin in an

old lean-to shed off the road. She'd seen its leaning, cracked boards on the night he'd brought her here. Since then, she'd never even caught a glimpse of his truck. The few times he'd let her outside, he'd been close beside her. In those few precious minutes, she would try like crazy to figure out where they were. Since she'd never seen that they'd crossed any more state lines she was pretty sure they were still in California. They'd passed through small towns and vineyards and had driven through the Valley of the Moon, so they were probably somewhere in that area her dad called "wine country." But where was that?

From the cabin she heard no sounds of traffic, not even the rush of cars on a distant freeway. But in the middle of the night she'd be awakened by the sound of a train thundering past. The tracks couldn't be too far away, she figured, because the whole cabin shook. The clank of wheels and the roar of the engine were deafening as the train rushed by.

Now, wondering where the train went to, where it came from, how close the next station or railway yard was, Dani lay sweating on the cot, counting off the seconds with her own heartbeats. She hardly dared breathe as she waited for the sound of the pickup truck's engine to ignite in the distance. Crossing her fingers that he was really taking off for the night and hadn't just left for a few minutes to get something from the truck, she strained to listen.

She wanted him gone.

Forever.

She wouldn't die here.

No, she'd get out of this hot, airless prison.

She just needed some time.

A lot of time.

By herself.

So she could work out her plan.

Then she heard it, the catch and cough of a truck's engine.

Thank God.

Dani relaxed. She had a few hours, maybe more. In the near darkness, she rolled off the cot and crawled unerringly into the tiny closet where she'd discovered what she hoped would be her salvation. She couldn't see anything, but she felt with her fingers all around the floorboards until she found it, that one warped board with the nail working its way out of its hole.

She smiled to herself. The perv hadn't noticed it, thought the room was secure. *Think again, jerk-wad!*

Using one of her socks as a glove, she grabbed hold of the nail head and began wiggling and pulling. Back and forth, back and forth, tugging slightly, hoping to ream out the nail hole and make it bigger, all the while urging that rusted, ancient spike from the rotting wood.

Sweat collected on her forehead.

Ran down her arms.

The rusted nail head poked through her sock and she doubled the cotton over, still feeling the sharp edges of the head dig into her fingers. She didn't care, worked through the discomfort, even when she felt blood welling.

The nail, if she could just extract it, was her ticket to freedom.

"I don't care what strings you have to pull, or whose butt you have to kiss, but get me out of here," Shannon said from her hospital bed.

Her brother Shea, all six feet one of him, wasn't buying it. He stood inside the open door of the small room and shook his head. "I don't think that's a good idea."

"Probably not, but do it anyway. You're with the police department, twist some arms, make some calls, lean on someone, but for God's sake, get me out of here." She was already shifting on the bed, swinging her legs over and trying not to cringe at the pain in her shoulder and ribs. They seemed to be the worst, even harsher than the cut on the back of her head that had required a patch of her hair to be shaved and seven stitches to close the wound.

The meal the nurse had rustled up—clear broth, red Jell-O, and a wimpy pressed-turkey sandwich—lay untouched on her plate. Her hunger had fled when she'd learned about Travis Settler and his daughter. No, check that, make it *her* daughter.

"It doesn't work that way," Shea was saying, but she wasn't going to take no for an answer.

"Well, either you work things out with the powers that be here at Santa Lucia General, or I go AWOL." She slid her feet onto the floor and found that her legs supported her.

"Shannon, listen to reason."

"You listen, okay? The arson detectives spilled the beans that the guy I ran into during the fire is my daughter's adoptive father. He's claiming that she's missing."

"It's true."

"You checked? And you didn't tell me?"

"I thought I'd wait until you were released."

"Consider me outta here. So my daughter really is missing?"

His lips pinched at the corners, but he nodded. "Yeah. She's been missing for a while. The reason Settler is down here is because he thought you might have something to do with the abduction."

She felt her gut tighten. "Swell guy. He loses track of his kid, then immediately thinks *I* had something to do with it? *Me!*" She pointed a finger at her own chest. "The woman who trusted that whoever adopted her would take care of her, keep her safe, protect her, love her? The person who hasn't seen her in thirteen damned years?" Shannon's voice cracked a bit. She fought back tears and cleared her throat. Right now she couldn't afford to get too emotional. Now, more than ever, she had to be clear-headed, in control. "What about his wife?" she asked. "Where's she in all this? The attorneys told me when I agreed to give the baby up, even though it was a private adoption, that my little girl was going to be raised by a married couple, one that really wanted children and for some reason or other couldn't conceive."

"The wife is dead."

All the air in the room seemed to be sucked out by a vacuum.

"Oh." A little of Shannon's rage dissipated. For the briefest of seconds she felt a pang of compassion for the single father who obviously had to deal with his own grief as well as his child's. Who knew what he had suffered? "What happened to her?"

"The wife? Not sure. Illness of some kind, I think. She's been gone a few years. Now it's just Settler and the daughter."

"Whom he lost!" Again her anger reached flash point. What kind of father loses a kid? *Her* baby? Rationally she knew that children could be abducted, or run away, that it was a tragedy that happened every day, but not to *her* daughter, not to the precious baby she'd given up against her better judgment! She'd fought the idea, but in the end she'd been persuaded that giving the baby to a loving married couple desperate for a child would be best for her daughter's sake, for her well-being. The couple would be able to give the baby everything she wanted and needed . . . And it had turned out badly. Shannon's eyes burned. She tried to get a grip on herself. "This is just so wrong," she whispered, swallowing hard.

Refusing to wince against the pain that thrummed from her head down through her torso, she walked carefully across the small room and opened the closet door. Inside was an old yellow terry-cloth robe that one of her brothers had obviously found at the back of her closet at home. The robe had seen better days and was beyond shopworn. The cuffs were ragged and there was a coffee stain on one lapel that had never quite faded. Her blood-soaked boots had been tossed, and there weren't any shoes, just a pair of worn, navy blue mule-type slippers.

"Perfect," she muttered flatly. Annoyed, she slid her feet into the scuffs.

"I suppose I can't talk you out of this."

"Nope."

"You seem to have forgotten that you've always been the baby, Shan." Shea looked for all the world as if he was frustrated out of his mind. He scrabbled in his pocket for his pack of cigarettes before remembering where he was. He let his hand drop to his side.

"Yeah, well, let's not think of me as the baby of the clan. Or the only sister or any of that bull. I'm a grown woman and it's time I quit relying on the rest of you."

"Except for me pulling strings to get you out of here."

She had the grace to smile. "Nobody said I wouldn't still use you whenever I could."

His eyes narrowed thoughtfully. "So who put you in charge?"

"The son of a bitch who tried to beat the crap out of me," she said, cinching the belt of her robe over the stupid hospital gown. She had no option but to wear it out of the place. "So do whatever it is you have to do to spring me and let's go."

"You want me to take you back home."

"Eventually, but we have a stop to make first."

"A stop?"

"You know where Travis Settler is, don't you?"

Shea's lips tightened. "I can't take you to him."

"Sure you can."

"Shannon, I'd strongly advise against you having any contact with the man. We haven't ruled him out as a suspect."

"I don't care."

"Listen to me. You could compromise the investigation," Shea insisted, again reaching for his pack of cigarettes only to leave it in his pocket. "I can't let you talk to him."

"I don't see why not. I just want some simple answers,

you know, like where the hell is my daughter? And since when do you go by the rules anyway? Since when does anyone in this family?"

He was standing in front of the door, the proverbial brick wall.

"Either you help me with this or I do it on my own," she said, walking to the bedside table and the phone. "I'll call Nate. I know he's at the house taking care of the animals and I bet he'd come in an instant. Or I can call a cab. Or you can just drive me where I want to go." She picked up the receiver and Shea threw up a hand.

"Shit! When did you get so damned hardheaded?"

"Flannery family trait," she shot back. She didn't bother explaining that from the moment she saw the fire in the shed she'd decided to take matters into her own hands. She now knew that the horses were safe, the dogs were fine and her house was still standing. But her daughter was missing. She couldn't sit idly by.

"Fine. You win," Shea growled. "I'll start the paperwork to get out of here. I'll put in my two cents' worth, but you talk to the staff, get your instructions and prescriptions. After that, I'll drive you to your place to get your things . . . some clean clothes and your purse. If you're going to meet Settler, you may as well not do it in a hospital gown."

"All right," she agreed, silently admitting he was right. She didn't want to go off half-cocked and look like a lunatic to boot.

Shea wasn't finished. "Listen, I don't know this guy and I don't trust him. So I'm not dropping you off or anything like that. We'll go together. That's the deal."

Shannon didn't hesitate. She dropped the receiver. "I'll take it."

It was time she met Travis Settler face-to-face.

Chapter 11

Turning off all the lights in his small motel room, Travis fiddled with the blinds and looked out the window. Across the asphalt lot, past a row of minivans, sedans and SUVs, parked on the street was an unmarked police car. The same silver Ford Taurus he'd caught tailing him earlier in the day. So much for a covert operation, he thought, and scowled to himself. He closed the blinds, turned the air conditioner to MAX/COOL, flipped on the television, leaving it muted, then flopped onto the bed with its thin mattress and floral-print quilt.

What the hell had happened at Shannon Flannery's place?

It didn't take a rocket scientist to realize that someone had not only torched the shed but had used the fire as a trap and a distraction. Shannon had been so busy trying to save her livestock that she'd almost gotten herself killed by an assailant.

She'd been set up.

The television, on an all-news channel, showed the president, smiling, holding up a hand to the press while his Secret Service bodyguards stood between him and the crowd of protestors.

Travis barely noticed. He swiped the sweat from his forehead and tried to make sense of the fire. Sure, the arsonist could have been intent on torching the place, a random act, and when Shannon stumbled upon him, he'd panicked and beaten her while trying to escape . . . But that didn't fit, Travis thought. No . . . There was more to the story than met the eye.

What did he know about Shannon Flannery? First and foremost she was Dani's birth mother. She'd never married the father and had given the baby up for adoption, a private adoption, through the law firm of Black, Rosen and Tallericco, which had dissolved over ten years ago.

He also knew that she'd been charged with her husband's murder. According to all the records the marriage had been rocky and there had been a restraining order filed against Ryan Carlyle by his wife. There were rumors of affairs and some speculation that he'd been a criminal known as the "Stealth Torcher" because of a string of intentionally set fires that had not occurred again since his death.

Some people thought that Carlyle had been caught in his own trap. That he'd died in the forest fire that he'd set, slipped on a rock and broken his ankle as the fire had blazed around him.

Others thought his wife, fed up with being cheated on and beaten, had lured him into the woods, somehow disabled him and then set a fire. The ensuing blaze had not only killed him, reducing him to little more than ash but had also taken some five hundred acres of California wilderness with it and sent three firefighters to the emergency ward.

So what does the fire at Shannon Flannery's house have to do with Dani?

Nothing!

Not one damned thing!

This had been a wild-goose chase.

Nothing more.

Stretching across the bed, he opened the minifridge that doubled as a nightstand and dragged out a beer that he'd picked up earlier along with a nine-dollar pizza that was eight dollars overpriced. The damned thing had tasted like cardboard topped with too little burned mozzarella cheese.

Today, all the while he'd been running his errands including spending time at the offices of the newspaper, then hitting the library before picking up the six-pack of Coors and the bad pizza, the police had followed him in that dirty silver Taurus. Not that he blamed them, he supposed. After all, he *had* been at the fire, and though he *had* called 9-1-1, the call could have been his cover. His clothes *had* been smeared with her blood and she didn't know who he was. Plus, all the damaging evidence they'd found in his truck.

He twisted off the cap from his bottle of beer, then zinged the cap across the room to land hard in the trash basket under a scarred desk.

The police had questioned him for nearly an hour, then let him go . . . But still they tailed him.

He didn't blame them for zeroing in on him, but it was a pain in the backside.

As he took a long pull from his bottle, he wondered who had been behind the attack? Who would want to destroy her property and nearly kill her?

He'd always considered Shannon Flannery his enemy, a woman who could seek out the daughter she'd given up thirteen years ago, a woman with the power to throw his life into total chaos. He wasn't even certain that the private transaction through attorneys had conformed to all of the adoption laws of the state. For years, Travis had feared Shannon would change her mind, that she might find a way to try and reclaim her daughter and that Dani could be stripped from him.

After Ella's death, his fear had been stronger, to the point of near paranoia, but now . . . observing Shannon Flannery in action, seeing her trying to save her animals, only to be beaten savagely, he found himself softening to her.

Maybe she wasn't the enemy.

Then who was?

Who had his child?

He drained his beer and left the bottle on the nightstand. If he could only find his kid. That's all he wanted. Just Dani back home.

His throat thickened and a muscle ticked in his jaw. He flipped open his cell and punched the speed dial button for Shane Carter. Though he was certain Carter would have called him had there been any news about Dani, Travis felt the need to check in, the need to hear something, *any*thing.

One ring.

Two.

"Carter," the sheriff answered.

"It's Travis. Just wondering if there's anything new." God, he hated the sound of desperation in his voice.

"Nothing yet," Carter said, then cleared his throat.

"No ransom call?"

"Nope."

"No new evidence, no leads?" he persisted, wishing for just a glimmer of hope.

There was a bit of hesitation before Carter said, "Not really, but we're checking on something."

"What's that?" Travis asked, his heart knocking in dread. Oh, God, please don't let it be that they'd found the body of a girl, that even now the lab was trying to ID her. He squeezed his eyes shut and held the receiver in a death grip.

"Earl Miller, who works over at Janssen's Hardware store, thought he saw a white van with out-of-state plates on the day that Dani went missing. He can't remember anything else about the van, just that the license plate was from Arizona and that he thought, but wasn't sure, that the van was a Ford. He didn't catch a glimpse of the driver, but another person, Madge Rickert, was walking her dog and saw a similar vehicle parked on a side street not far from the school earlier that same day, around eight-thirty. She remembers because she was trying to keep her Chihuahua from lifting his leg on the back tire."

"That's about the time Dani got to school."

"He could have been looking for her."

"Jesus." Travis's lungs were so tight he could barely breathe. Even though he'd thought he'd prepared himself for the evidence that she'd been abducted, the news brought with it a soul-jarring, desperate fear.

"Look, Travis, we don't know anything yet. This might not lead to finding her, but right now, it's all we've got. We're checking with Blanche Johnson's neighbors again, asking if anyone saw an unknown van with out-of-state plates."

Travis nodded. Neither of them believed it was coincidence that Dani had disappeared the day Blanche Johnson was murdered. "Keep me posted."

"I will and in the meantime, you'd better think about keeping your nose clean," Carter advised. "I've been getting calls about you from the Santa Lucia PD."

Travis flicked a glance toward the window where the blinds were snapped tightly shut. He didn't have to check. He knew the cop car was still parked near the curb on the other side of the street. "I figured."

"I had to tell them what's going on up here and why I think you're in their town. Sounds like you got yourself into some trouble."

"Some," Travis allowed. "What did they say?"

"A lot. About the fire. About the fact that you were found at the scene of an attack against the woman who's the natural mother of your child." Travis steeled himself. The news was only going to get worse; he was certain of it. "Look, I assured them you were a stand-up guy hell-bent to find his daughter, that you wouldn't resort to any kind of violence." He paused. "I didn't lie, did I?"

Travis picked up the remote, turned the television off. "I didn't start the fire, if that's what you mean, and I sure as hell didn't beat the living tar out of Shannon Flannery. But someone did. And yeah, I was there."

"With a surveillance kit that included a hunting knife, night vision goggles and a loaded .45."

"I have a license to carry."

"I know, but the police are interested. More than interested. And there you were at the scene of the crime with your truck parked over a mile away. When they looked inside the pickup, with a warrant, by the way, they found a lot of stuff that didn't look good including a file on Shannon Flannery complete with pictures, notes and articles from newspapers about her. It seems to them that you might have an obsession with the lady, that you had all the makings of a stalker."

Travis closed his eyes. He knew this, of course, but hated his nose being rubbed in it.

"You know why."

"But they don't."

"I told them."

"It's their job to be suspicious."

Travis nodded to himself. He caught a glimpse of his reflection in the mirror mounted over a small, battered dresser. He appeared haggard. Tired and unshaven. His hair stuck up at odd ends from where he'd continually run his hands through it in frustration, and the lines around his mouth and eyes were deeper than usual. Sweat was beading around his hairline and he looked like he hadn't slept or eaten in days.

He said, "I thought it would be best if I didn't go up and beat on her door and make all sorts of accusations before I saw for myself if Dani was around. Thought I'd scope out the place first. Get my bearings."

"And Dani wasn't there."

"Nope." Travis rubbed at his eyes with his free hand. Conjured up his daughter's face. Where the hell was she? *Where?* What sick pervert had her? What was he doing with her? Images of a dirty white van, a torture chamber on wheels, slid through his brain. Oh, God, was she tied up, was the guy hurting her? Torturing her? Forcing her into having sex with him?

His insides shredded and he thought he might throw up. A white-hot fury stormed through his blood. If he ever caught one glimpse of the creep who kidnapped his daughter, Travis would kill him. No questions asked.

"So you don't think Shannon Flannery has anything to do with her kidnapping?"

"No." Travis's voice was raw. "Not anymore."

"Then you'd better explain all that to the authorities and get your butt out of there. If they'll let you."

He closed his eyes again, listened to the air conditioner rattle and wheeze. "Meaning?"

"You're a suspect, Travis. In the fire. In the assault. That's the bottom line."

"For the record, I think this is a bad idea." Shea was behind the wheel of his truck, driving out of the hospital parking lot.

"You and the rest of the world." From her position huddled against the passenger door of his truck, Shannon shot him a glare. "I got the message already, okay? You're not backing out of your end of the deal."

"Fine."

She was strapped into her seat belt and tried to pretend that every lurch of the vehicle didn't send a stab of pain ripping across her shoulder and rib cage. Clutched in her hand was a plastic bag with a bottle of Vicodin from the hospital pharmacy and two pages of instructions from a disgruntled Dr. Zollner. But Shannon didn't want to take any of the pills until she'd had a talk with Travis Settler. She still had narcotic medications running through her bloodstream so she wasn't as sharp as she'd like to be, and she didn't want to add to the fog in her brain.

"Do I look that bad?" she asked.

He crooked an eyebrow. "Worse."

"I think you're supposed to be more supportive."

"And I think you're supposed to go home and rest."

She glanced in the mirror. She was beyond a wreck. Shea hadn't been kidding. And though she didn't want to waste a second, she needed to avoid looking like the maniac she saw in the reflection. "Give me a few minutes and I'll pull myself together. Then I want to see this guy face-to-face."

"You got it." Shea punched in the lighter and found his pack of Marlboros on the dash, shook out a cigarette with one hand, drove with the other. "Okay, Shannon, this probably isn't the best time to bring this up, but I want to know why you didn't come to me about the burned birth certificate and crank call you received last week."

"I told Detectives Janowitz and Rossi."

"Today."

"Yeah."

"When you had no choice, but you didn't bother calling me earlier."

"It wouldn't have prevented the fire."

"Probably not."

The lighter clicked. Shea cracked the window on his side of the truck, lit his cigarette, then drove through the business section of town, heading past an old Spanish-styled hotel with its red-tiled roof, potted palms and high, arched ceilings cut into soft gold stucco. Lights blazed on the hotel grounds, splashing illumination up the walls and displaying the terra cotta tiles of the roof and lush vegetation near the entrance.

"So why should I have called the police?" she asked, sensing that Shea was spoiling for a fight.

"Because you were being harassed. You could have put the department and me on alert."

"I didn't want to make a scene."

"You mean you didn't want to make headlines," he clarified, slowing for a red light near a mom-and-pop grocery, "again." He brooded and smoked, waiting for the light to change as his big truck idled. Twice he checked his watch.

A group of kids on skateboards—wearing knit caps despite the fact that the temperature was still near eighty, shouting and laughing—cut through the double lanes of stopped traffic, their slim, dark silhouettes thrown in sharp relief by the bright headlights of the vehicles.

Shannon said deliberately, "I thought I'd have Aaron look into it first."

Shea cut her a glance and took another drag on his cigarette. "Why Aaron?" Smoke curled from his nostrils as the light changed and he stepped on the accelerator.

"He's a PI, to begin with, and he's not affiliated with the police department like you are, or the fire department like Robert is, or the priesthood—"

"Like Oliver, yeah, I get that. But Aaron is a PI only because he wouldn't be able to cut it as a cop. He got his ass kicked out of the fire department and he's no saint, so the church wouldn't want him."

"Your point?" she asked as they pushed the speed limit toward the outskirts of town.

"That he wasn't exactly a prime choice."

"Apparently not," she muttered, flipping down her visor to shade her eyes. "Because he obviously couldn't keep his mouth shut."

"Hey. For once he did the right thing. Besides, as you said, you already told Janowitz and Rossi." He squashed the rest of his cigarette into an overflowing ashtray.

Shea was right, of course, but that didn't mean it didn't rankle that Aaron had spilled his guts to her other brothers.

They drove in silence through the suburbs and past a few small ranches until they passed the vacant acres earmarked as the new subdivision.

The next driveway was hers. Shea eased on the brakes as he turned into the long lane. Shannon didn't know which was worse, the jars to her body as the truck bounced along the uneven lane, or the assault on her emotions as she spied the blackened wreckage of the shed, the sooty exterior wall of the stable and her little home still standing, blessedly unharmed.

The security lights were blazing, casting pools of blue light. Yellow plastic tape still warned that the area was a crime scene. And the place seemed empty. Still. Lifeless.

"Where's Nate?" she asked, searching the parking lot for his SUV. The Explorer wasn't parked in its usual spot. Nor were any lights glowing from the windows of his apartment over the garage.

Shea lifted a shoulder. "Beats me."

Shannon felt a whisper of dread slide through her. "I'd better check on the animals."

"I'll take care of it. You go upstairs and change."

"You sure?"

"Yep."

With her scuffs pushing through the muck that still remained, she made her way to the front door. The house was locked and she had no key.

"Wait. I'll get it." Shea used a key from his ring and opened the door, the key she'd given him when she was still married to Ryan. It seemed eons ago, now.

As she opened the door, she expected Khan to hurl himself at her, but the cottage was empty. And silent. No clicking toenails on the stairs, no eager whines, no wiggling body begging for her to pet him. Only the hum of the refrigerator and the drip of the faucet in the kitchen. Shannon snapped on a light and stood in the foyer. Everything was as she'd left it, and yet it seemed different, almost surreal. As if she hadn't been inside in years, rather than days.

She walked into the kitchen, twisted hard on the faucet and spied her bananas and apples now rotting in a basket on the table. Her cell phone charger was in place and her purse, on the end of the counter, looked undisturbed.

Shea was still standing in the doorway, on the other side of the threshold. "Everything okay?"

"Yeah. Except for Khan."

"Either Santana's got him or he's with the others," Shea guessed.

"Probably." But it didn't feel right. Everything looked the same, but the atmosphere in the cottage had lost its warmth, its coziness. She rubbed her arms as if chilled, though she was still sweating from the heat.

"I'll go look for him when I check the other animals, you . . . go on, get cleaned up." He glanced at his watch again. "Can you handle the stairs by yourself?"

She forced a smile she didn't feel. "I think I'll manage. Am I keeping you from something? A hot date?"

"What?" He looked up sharply. Caught her expression and grinned. "No . . . Nothing. A habit."

She wasn't sure he was telling the truth but wasn't in the mood to argue. Not tonight.

"I'll leave the door open. Yell if you need me," he advised and turned abruptly, heading toward the stable at a quick jog. He seemed jumpy. Out of sorts. But then so was she. No doubt her whole family was.

She made her way upstairs, one painful step at a time and once in her bedroom, where the bed was still unmade, she made a stab at cleaning herself up. She washed her face, ran a wet cloth over her body, slapped on sheer lipstick and a bit of mascara, then, with some difficulty, pulled on a pair of jeans and a knit top. She couldn't bend over without a lot of pain, so she stepped into a pair of flip-flops, then tried and failed to tame her hair. It was wild and curly and in the back, there was a large patch missing where her head had been shaved and a neat row of stitches held her scalp together. With gentle fingers she swept the hair over the delicate spot, secured the unruly curls into a ponytail and surveyed her reflection with a wry look.

She looked marginally better, but she wasn't out to win any beauty contests.

Not that it mattered, she just wanted to square off with Travis Settler.

She was on her way downstairs when she heard an engine barreling up the drive. Headlights cut through the night as she stepped outside. She expected to find Nate Santana returning with Kahn, nose poking out the window, in the passenger seat.

Instead she spied her brother Robert's new sports car, a BMW with a silver finish that looked nearly liquid in the lamplight. He'd bought the thing the weekend he'd moved out of the house that he'd shared with Mary Beth and their two kids. In Shannon's estimation the flashy car was just one more symptom of his malaise known as midlife crisis.

Robert wasn't alone. Aaron was in the passenger seat and as they climbed out of the sleek vehicle, Shea appeared in the doorway of the kennel and half-ran to catch up with his siblings.

"So what's this?" Shannon asked, her eyes narrowing in

suspicion. "An ambush?" Eyeing the stern expressions on each of their faces, she added, "By the Brothers Grim? That's with one *m*."

"Funny," Robert muttered.

"So where's Oliver?" Shannon asked.

"With Mom . . . or at the church," Robert said. "You know how it is, the Lord's work is never done."

"What's up?" she asked, her accusatory gaze landing on Shea. "Don't you guys gang up on me and try and talk me out of meeting Settler, cuz it's not gonna work."

"We just want you to have all the facts," Aaron said.

"Like the fact that you told these two what was going on"—she wagged her finger at Robert and Shea—"even though we had an agreement?"

"Because of the fire."

She was still irritated as all get-out. "So what's on your minds?"

"Let's go inside and sit down," Shea suggested and Shannon realized why he'd been checking his watch every two minutes. This had been a setup. He'd suggested she come home to change, just so they could all work her and try and get her to change her mind. Great. Just like when she was a kid, the youngest Flannery of six, and the only girl.

"Make it quick," she suggested as they filed in and sat stiffly at the kitchen table. Half a dozen tiny fruit flies hovered over the basket of apples and bananas.

"The investigators found something odd in the fire," Shea began. "At the point of origin, where obviously some kerosene had been poured there was a pattern in the burn path and it was placed upon a slab of concrete, something that wouldn't burn."

"Meaning?" she asked, not liking the sound of this.

"That whoever started the fire made this impression on purpose, knowing we'd find it." Shea reached into his back pocket and extracted a small tablet. "The trail was in this shape, see . . . almost like a diamond, but part of it is cut off."

She stared at the design and shook her head. "So?"

"So it's the same kind of pattern that was on the birth certificate you found on your porch. The original's with the lab, but here's a copy and look, the charred edges are very similar to the burn pattern we found in the shed. I'm betting the paper was sprayed carefully with some kind of invisible retardant so that it wouldn't burn completely and would retain this shape." He pointed at the two images.

Shannon's throat went dry as she saw the copy of her baby's birth certificate, now placed on the table near Shea's drawing.

"Not identical," he said, "but similar."

Her heart knocked as she stared at the symbols. What kind of macabre prank was this? . . . No, not a prank. A warning. A statement. A *bold,* taunting statement. "But there's something in the middle of the burn pattern," she said, pointing to Shea's tablet. "A number six . . . or nine."

"Definitely six," Aaron said. "If we use the birth certificate as the template, and assume that the printing on it is upright, not upside down, then the burn pattern should have the same form, with the cutoff peak of the diamond at the top. Like this."

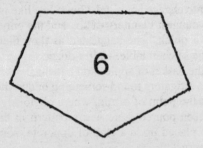

Despite the sweltering heat trapped in the little house, Shannon's blood seemed to turn to ice as she stared at the two images: two blackened threats somehow tied to the child she hadn't seen since birth. "What does it mean?" she asked in a whisper. Her three brothers, who looked so much alike they were oftentimes confused, were staring at her, their blue eyes dark with anger, their thin lips even more compressed, their square jaws set and hard.

Shea said, "We hoped you'd know."

Slowly she shook her head. "I have no idea." Fear skittered down her spine. "Who would . . . ?"

"We'll find him," Aaron insisted, but she saw no such assurance in Shea or Robert's eyes.

"Maybe this is something we should show to Travis Settler." Her stomach tightened painfully and her mind spun, trying to figure out how the adoptive father of her child could have anything to do with the fire, with the charred missive left on her porch. "It seems like more than a coincidence that he's in Santa Lucia, my daughter's missing, and part of her birth certificate was left on the porch on her birthday."

"He was in Oregon when the birth certificate was left," Shea said.

"You're certain?" Aaron asked.

"Looks that way. We're double-checking with the Oregon State Police and the local sheriff."

"But he did just happen to be here when the fire broke out," Robert said.

"That he did." Shea nodded.

Shannon squared her shoulders. "So then, there's no reason to wait, is there? Let's go talk to him."

Chapter 12

The last person Travis expected to see on the other side of his door was Shannon Flannery, but there she stood under the overhang of the porch that surrounded the rooms of the

motel. Her face showed evidence of the beating she'd taken—
cuts and swelling, some mottled bruising that no amount of
makeup could hide, though it didn't look as if she'd bothered. She was surrounded by three men who dwarfed her,
three men who, though not identical, appeared enough alike
that it didn't take a geneticist to figure out they were brothers. Two of the six-footers were the same men he'd seen escort her down the courthouse steps during her trial; the third
obviously another Flannery sibling.

"Travis Settler?" she asked, green eyes narrowed as she
craned her neck to stare him full in the face. Her arm was in
a sling and she stood stiffly. He remembered the gash in her
side, the wound on the back of her head. There were also
small pools of blood visible in the whites of her eyes. "I'm
Shannon Flannery, but you already know that, don't you?
We met at my place, after someone torched it."

"That's right."

"I asked you your name but you didn't give it."

"There wasn't time."

"Right," she said, uninterested in hiding her cynicism.

He didn't blame her. His excuse sounded as lame as it
was.

"Looks like we need to talk, Settler."

He glanced at the stern-faced men and she quickly
pointed each one out in turn. "My brothers: Shea, fire inspector with the Santa Lucia Police Department." He was
the tallest with the same black hair as the one she next introduced. "Robert, he's a firefighter with the local fire department." Her gaze flicked to the last brother. "Aaron is a
private investigator."

Aaron gave a nearly imperceptible nod. He was the shortest by about an inch, thicker in the body with slightly
hunched shoulders. A bushy moustache covered his upper
lip and something dark and unfathomable lurked in his gaze.

In an instant, Travis didn't trust him.

The jury was out on the other two.

"I heard you were the guy at the fire the other night," she said, "and that you're my daughter's adoptive father and that she's missing." She was shaking now. Anger snapped in her gaze, fury set her jaw. "What the hell's going on?"

"I think I made a mistake."

"A pretty damned big one. Are you going to invite us in or are you going to make me stand here in the parking lot?"

So far the men with her hadn't said a word, just stared at him as if he was Satan incarnate. He thought about the small motel room with its one chair, two double beds and limited space. He couldn't imagine being crushed into it with this small firebrand of a woman and her three looming, suspicious brothers.

"How about we take this to the restaurant?" he asked, hitching his chin toward El Ranchito, the eatery associated with the motel. "I'll buy you all a drink."

Shea's eyes narrowed a fraction. Distrusting.

"The room's too small," Travis explained as he walked back inside, grabbed his wallet off the desk, then stepped outside where the night was warm and close, the thrum of traffic ever-present. He closed the door behind him. "That okay with you?" he asked Shannon and ignored the goons who were with her. He'd deal with her. Fine. But not the whole testosterone-laden group of them.

"I'll pass on the drink," she said, scrutinizing him. "The restaurant's fine."

"Good. Let's go."

They walked across the parking lot and into the cool, dark interior of the restaurant. Travis held open the swinging doors to the bar for Shannon and her fleet of Flannerys, then found a large corner table near the window, away from both the shaved-headed men who were playing pool and the group wearing baseball caps while watching sports highlights on the television mounted over the bar.

They all slid into chairs and Travis noticed that Shannon grimaced as she sat down directly across from him. She stared at him across the dark, scarred wood. Two of her brothers sat on either side of her. Shea positioned himself on one end.

Travis hardly knew where to start.

Before he could utter a word, a waitress appeared and, seemingly unaware that the small crowd was in anything but a party mood, chatted and took orders, then swung over to the bar.

"I owe you an apology," Travis began. "Yes, I am Dani's father. My wife and I adopted her thirteen years ago." His lungs tightened and the weight in his chest was nearly unbearable. "You're right, she's missing, there are very few clues as to what happened and I got real sick of sitting around and waiting for a call that wasn't going to come."

"And what if it does?" Shannon asked, her face pale beneath her bruises, her lips barely moving. "What if whoever took her tries to get in touch with you?"

"There are people who will answer the phone."

"What if the kidnappers refuse to talk to anyone but you?"

"I have a cell. They'll be directed to me." He felt suddenly tired and old, his looming failure as a father settling hard on his shoulders. "They're not going to call, Shannon."

Her shoulders stiffened at his familiar use of her name. "Because you think she's a runaway?"

"No." He shook his head. "Dani's never shown any indication of wanting to leave home. We don't fight, well, not much—" he saw the concern in her features, the hunger for any information about the child she gave up. "Look." He spread his hands. "I really don't know what to think."

The waitress returned with four bottles of beer and a club soda for Shannon. Conversation died as a fresh basket of tortilla chips and a small bowl of mixed nuts were placed on the table.

Once the waitress had moved off Travis leaned closer to Shannon. She flinched at his close proximity. "I said I made a mistake, but the reason I did was because I had nothing to go on. All I knew was that my daughter had recently expressed some interest in her birth parents."

"And what did you tell her?" Shannon asked carefully.

"To wait. That when she was eighteen, when I hoped she'd be mature enough to handle the situation, I'd tell her everything I knew."

"But you kept records. You came down here with weapons and equipment. You were sneaking around my house." Her face suddenly suffused with color, her eyes hard. "You spied on me. You thought I took her. And, for all I know, you torched my shed."

"I've done a lot of things, some of them pretty stupid lately, but, trust me, I didn't set the fire."

"You were there," Shea said, fingering his bottle, not drinking from it.

"And you had all kinds of spy gear and weapons and information on Shannon," the shortest one, Aaron, pointed out.

"I jumped to conclusions, because I had nowhere to look."

Shannon pointed a finger at his chest. "So you decide to harass me?"

"I was just looking for my kid." Travis sighed and leaned back in his chair, taking a long tug from his bottle, barely tasting the beer. He held her gaze, ignored the three brothers. "And I was grasping at straws. I'm sorry." He motioned to the sling on her arm. "I had nothing to do with the fire. Really. I drove down from Oregon. That night was my first opportunity to see what was what."

"And instead of knocking on my door, or calling, you chose to slink around the place like a thief in the night."

"I didn't want to start making accusations until I knew a little more about you."

"By spying on me."

"Yes."

"You son of a bitch!"

He pushed himself toward her again so that he was cer--

tain she could hear every word. He could smell the scent of soap on her skin, the lingering smell of antiseptic from the hospital. "You have to understand one thing, Ms. Flannery—" He sensed all three brothers tense, coiled, as if ready to spring. He didn't care. He would almost welcome a physical match so that he could unleash all of his pent-up frustration. Inching his nose closer to Shannon, he muttered harshly, "I would do anything, you got that? *Any*thing to find my kid. So, I apologize if I inconvenienced you, if I bothered you, because, yeah, I did spy on you. And I would do it again. In a heartbeat. *Anything!* If it meant getting Dani back!"

"Ever the protective father." She couldn't hide her scorn.

Her barb hit its mark but he didn't back down. "I just didn't know whether you were involved. I had to rule you out."

"And have you?"

"I think so, but that kind of leaves me with nowhere to turn," he added sourly. "So, as soon as the authorities remove me from the list of suspects in the fire, which is bound to happen soon"—he glanced over to Shea who was seated stock-still at the end of the table—"I'll give up this part of the wild-goose chase and go back to square one."

She swallowed. Travis didn't let his eyes stray down to where the movement of her throat and her escalating pulse were visible. He sat back down in his seat and took another swig from his long-necked bottle, tried not to feel overwhelmed with fear. Pool balls clicked. On the television the scene switched from golf to baseball.

Shannon drew a long breath. "For the record, Settler, I agree with you on one point: I'll do anything, and I mean *any*thing, to make sure my daughter is safe as well." As if seeing the protest rising in his throat, she added tensely, "Just because I gave her up for adoption doesn't mean I don't love her, or that I don't have maternal feelings for her. I gave her up because I did, and do, love her. It . . . It was the best thing for her. I was sure of that or believe me, it wouldn't have happened. Now . . ." Her teeth clenched. Her chin began to wobble. With an effort she took control of her emotions.

"So don't fight me, okay? I'll help you any way I can. And . . . to that end . . . I think I might know something that will help."

Travis stilled, waiting.

Shannon glanced at her brothers. Travis saw the tallest one—the guy from the police department, Shea, give a nearly imperceptible nod.

"You might not have been so far off in coming here."

"What?" Travis's eyes bore into hers. "You contacted Dani? You know where she is?"

"No, no." She held up a hand. "Slow down, cowboy. I have no idea where my, er, your daughter is. Haven't seen her since she was ten minutes old." A shadow passed behind her eyes. Even in the darkened room where men huddled at the bar, hovering over their microbrews, and the strains of some Mexican music were faint, but present, he saw that fleeting umbra of pain.

"Then . . . ?"

She told him. About the weird phone call. About the feeling that she was being watched. About the burned birth certificate, Dani's birth certificate.

He felt as if he'd been kicked in the gut. "Son of a bitch!" Travis hissed. One of his fists slammed into the tabletop, causing the basket of chips to hop. Several heads at the bar swiveled toward them.

One of the men shooting pool said, "Shit!" as his shot careened in the wrong direction. He glared at Travis while the man he was playing against smothered a smile.

Travis didn't give them a second glance. "Who?" he demanded, and she shook her head, lifted a tired shoulder. "Who would do this?" His head was spinning. Dani's disappearance and the charred piece of her birth certificate had to be linked. But how? And why? And who, damn it? No one had mentioned this before; no one had told him that his kid was linked to what was going on down here. For the love of God, where the hell was Dani?

Nerves stretched to the breaking point, he turned his head and glared at the brothers coolly sipping their goddamned beers. The slimy one, Aaron, was popping peanuts like they were pills, like he was an addict looking for a quick fix. The middle guy, the fireman, whatever his name was—Bob, Rob, no, Robert—rolled his bottle between his palms. The third one, the fire investigator, Shea, hadn't touched his beer, nor a single chip. Arms folded across his chest he was scrutinizing Travis intently, like a hawk perched on a high branch, ready to dive at the slightest movement in the grass below.

"You know something more," Travis charged, his voice low as the patrons near the bar turned back to their drinks and sports highlights. "Have you seen her?" His gaze whipped back to Shannon. "Heard from her?"

"No. I had no idea she wasn't safe with her family. When I received the phone call and found the birth certificate, I just thought someone was pulling a cruel prank. As you might have guessed, I've had some, er, trouble with being harassed before. I'm sure you know all about my shady past."

He didn't respond.

"So in an effort to maintain a low profile and figure this thing out on my own, to not stir up the old hornet's nest again, I didn't go to the police." The corners of her mouth tightened. "Instead I asked Aaron to look into it for me as he's a private investigator. I figure you'd understand as you're a kind of PI, too, I gather."

Travis didn't bother with her question. He zeroed in on the brother with the moustache. "What did you find?"

"Nothing. The certificate was a copy. When the fire happened, I turned it over to the police." Aaron crunched on more peanuts.

Shea added, "The lab has it, analyzing the paper, the burn pattern, and we looked over Shannon's place for evidence, footprints, fingerprints, an old cigarette butt, something left. So far nothing. No prints on the scrap of burned paper." He reached into his pocket, producing what seemed to be a copy of the nearly destroyed document.

"Jesus," Travis said staring at the barely legible bit of information. There was just enough left to ensure that whoever was reading it would get the point. "This guy's really working it," he said, glancing up at Shannon. "He wanted you to start thinking about Dani."

She nodded, then rubbed the arm in the sling with her free hand, as if chasing away a chill. "But I had no idea where she was, who she was with, that she was missing . . ."

"He must've counted on me coming down here."

"How would he know that you had information on the birth parents?"

"Lucky guess," Travis thought aloud, staring at the copied remnants of the birth certificate. "Or else he knew somehow."

"From whom?"

"I don't know. My wife and I didn't tell anyone and actually she didn't know as much as I did. After she passed, and Dani started asking more and more questions, I began adding to the information I already had." He didn't admit to seeing Shannon on the courthouse steps, couldn't see how that would help his cause. "But nothing prepared me for this."

"Nothing could," Shannon said as if she, too, experienced his pain.

Which was ridiculous, Travis thought. She didn't even know Dani, hadn't seen her daughter, if she was to be believed, since those first few minutes after her birth.

"Someone wanted me down here," Travis said.

"You think so?" Shea's eyebrows had slammed together to form one black, angry line.

"I'd bet."

"Pretty big leap, if you ask me," Aaron chimed in. His blue eyes charged Travis with a million unspeakable crimes.

"Maybe, but I'm here and the birth certificate was burned here. Not that big a leap."

The brothers didn't respond. Nor did Shannon. Travis had a sense they were still holding back. "So what else have you got?"

"Nothing we can discuss."

"I'm Dani's damned father." His voice was low but intense.

Shannon said, "And you still could have set the fire at my place."

He shook his head. "I was just there. Spying on you, yes, because I was desperate to locate my kid, but I did not torch anything." He was angry now, felt a vein throb in his temple. "And, for the record, I couldn't have been involved in the birth certificate thing, because, according to you it happened on Dani's birthday around midnight, and I was with my daughter that night. She had a sleepover."

Shannon's eyes darkened. She looked away, as if she didn't want to be reminded of the normal activities of raising the child she hadn't seen since birth.

Shea nodded. "We checked. We know. Sheriff Carter vouched for you. His fiancée's kid was at the party."

Travis winced at the memory. Yes, Allie had been at the house, along with six other twelve- and thirteen-year-old girls. Enough to nearly drive him crazy at the time. Now, of course, all he felt was an overwhelming sense of guilt.

"The guy who set the fire was most likely the creep who burned the birth certificate." He remembered the dark figure he'd seen at the fire. "I think I saw the perp that night."

"What?" she whispered, eyes rounding.

"I already told the police." Travis turned his gaze to Shea. "When the two detectives, Janowitz and Rossi, questioned me, I told them about the guy. And by the way, I'm sure that either one of them or some undercover cop is tailing me. Silver Taurus, parked across the street? Pretty damned obvious."

A muscle worked in Shea Flannery's jaw.

"Why didn't you tell me?" Shannon demanded, her fury ricocheting to her brother as she glared at him.

"We're still processing everything. You were the one hell-bent to meet Settler."

"So what else aren't you telling me?"

"Nothing," Shea said quickly.

Too quickly, in Travis's estimation. What the hell was the cop hiding? And what about the other brothers? Though tight-lipped, they, too, appeared to know a whole lot more than they were saying.

"You saw the man who lit the fire?" Shannon asked, turning the conversation back to Travis.

"I witnessed a man who was hanging out around the buildings just before the explosion, but no, I didn't see who he was or what he looked like," Travis said, anticipating her next question. "I had night goggles with me but didn't have time to put them on before all hell broke loose."

"But you actually *witnessed* another man on my property that night?" she asked again as if she hadn't heard right.

Travis nodded. "He looked about my size, dressed in black. I didn't notice any vehicles or anything that made this guy stand out, and no, I couldn't pick him out of a lineup," he said, repeating what he'd told the two skeptical detectives.

"Damn," she muttered, shoving her hair from her eyes.

He noticed the bruises on her cheek again, the redness in the whites of her eyes.

"Could have been Santana," the fireman brother suggested, eyebrows raised, urging Travis to condemn the man.

"It wasn't Nate!" Shannon said angrily, her indignant face flushing. "Get off that, okay? I already told you he would never do anything to hurt me or the animals!" She blew out an angry breath and despite her wounds appeared as if she wanted to strangle each of her brothers in turn.

Travis silently applauded her. But the fact that she was so quick to Santana's defense was something else, something that bothered him. A lot. Far more than it should.

"What about you?" Shea asked. "You think it was Santana? According to your statement you met him when you found Shannon in the stable."

Shannon turned those damning green eyes on him. They narrowed along with her lips as if she was almost daring him to speak the sacrilege.

"Maybe," he allowed, taking another drink from his bottle and watching her as he swallowed. "I couldn't tell."

Irritation flashed in her eyes. "It wasn't Nate," she insisted. "Let's get that straight and we'll all be on the same page."

"Got no alibi," Aaron offered.

"Enough!" she ordered.

Travis, surprised he'd slid off the hot seat of suspicion so easily, was secretly pleased that Shannon's obviously over-protective brothers had no use for Santana. He saw an opening to ask a question that had been on his mind from the get-go. "What about Dani's father . . . her biological father?"

Shannon visibly stiffened. Her voice was calm but she seemed as if she was restraining herself. "He left soon after I told him I was pregnant, before my daughter . . . Dani . . . was born. No one, not even his parents, knows what happened to him."

"Or so they say," Robert interjected as he drained his beer.

"Actually, Brendan might be back." Aaron had stopped eating peanuts.

"*What?*" Shannon's head whipped around. She skewered Aaron with a furious green gaze. "Brendan's back?"

"Hey, slow down. I heard a rumor. That's all," Aaron said, backtracking. "Some people in town have seen someone they think *could* be him. No one knows for certain and it's been so long, his looks could have changed significantly. After you asked me to look into the burned birth certificate, I did some digging. As far as I can tell no one has reentered the country using Brendan Giles's passport, but I'm still checking."

"You knew this and didn't tell me?" she whispered, obviously incredulous. She cut a quick, hard glance at Shea. "And you knew, too? Don't deny it."

"Okay."

"Hell!" she whispered.

Aaron sighed. "I just didn't want to get you upset. Not until I knew for certain."

"Damn it, Aaron, this is my life, my child, my . . ." her voice trailed off and she looked back at Travis again. She picked up her glass and her hand shook so badly that some of the clear liquid sloshed over the side as she lifted it to her lips.

"Dear God," she muttered as she took a sip, then set down the glass. "So everyone's keeping secrets, either to protect someone or because they don't trust anyone or . . . Geez, this is just such a damned circus!"

"Shannon—" Shea started. .

"Don't. Okay?" Her nostrils flared in indignation. "Don't placate me, don't pity me, don't big-brother me and for God's sake, don't lie to me."

Before he could argue, she turned to Travis, her mouth set, her eyes determined. "I wasn't certain I wanted to do this, that's why I didn't say anything earlier. But now . . . Now, I know I have to see her." She let out a long, shuddering breath and closed her eyes for a second, as if to calm herself, to make herself clear. "I mean, I hope you have a picture with you. Of my daughter, I mean your daughter . . . of Dani."

He nodded. "Just happen to."

"May I see it?"

"Shannon, this isn't a great idea," Aaron said.

"He's right," Shea interjected. "It's better for you to think of her in abstract terms."

"Show it to me," she urged Travis. "Please."

Travis also wondered if this was a smart move, but he'd be damned if he'd say so now. Deep inside he felt it was inevitable anyway. Of course she'd want to see her child. Of course her curiosity and latent maternal instinct would get the better of her.

Shifting, he pulled his wallet out of his back pocket and

flipped it open. Encased in clear plastic was last year's school photo. As he spied the picture, he felt a new pang of distress. This year Dani would probably miss picture day, he thought, along with a lot of other events. Something deep inside him ripped painfully. God, he had to get her back and soon. He knew the odds, realized that each hour a person was missing, it became more likely the clues would go cold, the person was less likely to be found.

Jesus, he couldn't think like that. He had to stay positive. Focused. He'd find her. Somehow . . . he just would.

Tentatively, Shannon drew his wallet closer, sliding it over the smooth surface of the table.

"That one, the school shot, was taken last October. It's about a year old," he told her. When she flipped the picture over, to the snapshot of him and Dani sitting on a boulder, proudly holding up their "catch of the day," two silvery twelve-inch trout, he had to swallow hard. He remembered that fall morning. They'd been up before dawn, with stars winking high over the tops of the fir trees and the mountain stream bubbling and gurgling past their campsite. They'd used salmon flies and had each caught his limit. His throat closed and he pushed the memory back into a far corner of his mind.

There were other pictures as well, other school photos, a picture of Dani in a softball uniform that was about three sizes too big, taken when she'd been in the sixth grade. Shannon stared at the posed picture, her lips folding over her teeth, then she traced the edge of Dani's jaw with one slim finger.

As if suddenly realizing what she was doing, she quickly flipped to the next picture, a wallet size of a family portrait that had been posed and snapped when his daughter had been somewhere between five and six. Dani, wearing an impossibly frilly dress that Ella loved and she hated, was sitting on her mother's lap. Travis standing stiffly in a dark suit he barely remembered now, had been told by the photographer to place one hand over his wife's shoulder, so there he stood in a ludicrous pose as Ella forced a smile and Dani lit up the shot. Even through the plastic and even though the photo had aged, Dani's bright eyes, curly strawberry-blond hair, and smile missing a few teeth, showed her impish, tomboy personality in full form. Travis felt his heart clutch and was hit by a sudden thought that it was good that Ella wasn't alive, that his wife didn't have to suffer the heartache, despair and fear that had been his constant companions since the discovery of Blanche Johnson's bloody corpse and the heart-stopping realization that Dani was missing.

Payback Time.

He inwardly cringed. Jesus, what could it mean? What did it have to do with Shannon Flannery and that damned birth certificate?

Fear was an icy snake crawling through his veins.

Shannon studied each picture, almost devoured them with her intent gaze, as if she'd been starved for some kind of information, some mental image of the child she'd offered up for adoption. She clenched her jaw and tears gathered in the corners of her eyes, causing her to blink. Reaching for a napkin on the table she swiped at her nose as she sniffled, and dabbed at her eyes to staunch the flow of tears. Swallowing, she finally slid the wallet across the table. "If . . . If you don't mind," she said and cleared her throat, "I would like a copy or two."

She looked so damned miserable that he forgot all of his resentment, all of his fear, all of his out-and-out paranoia.

"You might want to rethink that," Robert cut in, his own face showing signs of strain. "I, um, I've got kids and I don't get to see them as much as I'd like and . . . It might just be better if you don't know."

"Too late," she said, then looked up at Travis. "If you don't mind."

He couldn't deny her. With her arm in a sling, her face battered, her eyes pleading with a quiet desperation he couldn't refuse. "I'll see what I can do about a copy. In the meantime . . ." Again he reached into his back pocket and, his insides aching, pulled out a folded piece of paper that he handed to her.

"Dear God," she whispered as she unfolded the poster he'd had made. It was a color photograph of Dani. Travis stared down at the image of his daughter with her riot of curls, big green-gold eyes that twinkled above a straight little freckled nose. Her chin was pointed, her mouth wide and smiling in the shot. Above the face in bold letters was the word MISSING. Beside the picture was a description and contact information including his name.

Shannon closed her eyes, touched a trembling hand to her forehead. How often had she seen posters such as this? How many pairs of worried, fearful eyes of parents had she witnessed?

"You can keep it, if you want."

"Thanks."

"Jesus Christ, Shannon, don't even go there!" Aaron cut in. "I think you'd better remember why we're all here."

Good point, Travis thought grudgingly. He didn't like the smarmy bastard, but he had to keep his distance from this woman; she was still a threat. *Not* an ally. Yet, he couldn't help wonder about her and though he hardened himself toward her, he didn't think the tears that had sprung to her eyes were faked. He imagined that every day over the past thirteen years she'd regretted giving up her baby. And somehow she was entangled in this same mess that included him and his daughter. Why else was the burned birth certificate left on the porch on the night of Dani's birthday?

Shannon stared at the poster as if she couldn't get enough of it, then finally refolded the page and stuck it into her own pocket. He finished his beer, and decided that since he was treading on tenuous territory already, there was no reason not to go a step or two farther.

Motioning with his finger toward her sling, he asked, "So how're you feeling?"

"What?" she asked as if lost in thought. "Oh." A faint smile. "How do you think?"

"Like you've been flattened by a semi."

She cleared her throat. "Close enough."

He nodded. Scraping his chair back, he signaled to the waitress. "I think we've covered about everything tonight." He glanced at her. "Any other questions?"

"Just one more thing." She met his gaze levelly. "I might be more help than you think. I train search and rescue dogs, train them to find people. I want to help. With the dogs."

"If you think it would help."

"I don't know. She wasn't taken from here, but if you saw that man . . . if she's with him . . . Do you have anything of hers with you? Clothing? Hairbrush? Anything she handled a lot."

He thought of Dani's sweatshirt stuffed behind the seat of his truck. Could he trust her? What did he have to lose? Maybe it was a mistake to let Shannon Flannery in, but she seemed sincere and he was rapidly running out of options. "Yeah, I think."

She pushed back her chair. "Let's get it."

As if on cue, the waitress came with the check. Shannon tried to snap it up. He beat her to it. "I offered," he said, slapping his credit card onto the small tray. She didn't object and her brothers finished what was left of their beers, then pushed away from the table and stood.

Within two minutes it was over. He signed for the drinks, then started for the door. The Flannery entourage was on his heels as he stepped into the parking lot. The heat of the simmering night hit him full force.

A woman was waiting by a BMW.

"Okay, Robert," she said, venom in her smile. "Where the hell is your whore?"

Travis's gaze swung to the Flannerys. What the hell was this?

Chapter 13

Shannon stopped dead in her tracks.

The night was hot.

Sultry.

The near-empty parking lot radiating leftover heat. Two sedans, a minivan and an SUV were parked in front of the low-lying units of the motel. A few others were scattered in the spots closer to the restaurant. One woman stood waiting.

Mary Beth, her face a mask of scorned fury, was leaning a hip against the fender of Robert's new BMW. Petite, with a killer figure and short, straight black hair highlighted to a shimmering midnight blue, she bristled slightly at the sight of the Flannery family. Dangling from one finger, winking in the bluish lights of the parking lot, was a single key. Mary Beth held the silvery piece of metal and pursed her lips, her threat evident: she intended to scratch the hell out of the Beemer's glossy silver exterior.

Twenty feet away, standing near his own vehicle, was her brother Liam. Everything about him—his stance, his glare, the set of his jaw—suggested he was looking for a fight.

And he'd found one.

Shannon couldn't believe it. This was like some weird, surreal movie, a bad knockoff of a street-fighting scene in *West Side Story*.

And she wanted no part of it.

"Hold on," Robert said to his siblings. He crossed the parking lot at a jog while traffic rushed past and the night, beneath the security lamps, closed in. "What're you doing here?" he demanded, ripping the key from Mary Beth's fingers and pulling her away from his car.

"Looking for you."

"Where are the kids?"

"Like you care!" she feigned shock, throwing her free hand over her chest while he held her other wrist in a death grip.

"Where the hell are Elizabeth and RJ?" he demanded in a low whisper.

"With my sister. Margaret's looking after them."

"So you could hunt me down?"

"That's right." Mary Beth played the part of the wounded martyr to the hilt. Except for Liam lurking in the background, a tall, menacing shadow, as if he was her "muscle."

"Are you out of your mind?" Robert demanded.

"No, honey," she said, sarcasm dripping from her words, "that's you. Now, where the hell is your goddamned whore? In one of these primo, deluxe units?" Her nose wrinkled in disdain as she waved her hand at the bank of doors to the rooms of the cheap motel. "I want to talk to her."

"Cynthia's not here."

"Cynthia," she repeated, hissing the word as if she were a snake. "You sure?" Again, she made a gesture toward the motel where Travis Settler had taken up residence. "I'm supposed to believe that she isn't holed up in one of these rooms?"

"No, damn it," Robert insisted. "Now go home, Mary Beth. Get the kids. You're making a scene and a fool of yourself."

"Me? Honey, you did enough of that for both of us." There was pain in her eyes.

"Mary Beth, please, this isn't the place," Shannon said and took a step forward, but Shea's hand clamped over her good arm, restraining her.

"Yeah, as if *you* would know about that!" she sneered. Mary Beth was on a roll, almost as if she enjoyed the audience. Her eyes returned to her husband. "Don't pretend to care about family pride or reputation or any of that shit. Who's the one driving all around town in a flashy new sports car that he can't afford? Who's been sleeping with a known slut? Ignoring his marriage vows? Ignoring his kids?

Moving into a bachelor pad when he's got a family at home?" she demanded. "Jesus, Robert, you don't give a rat's ass about making scenes!"

Robert bristled. "Mary Beth, stop it!"

"*You* stop it. You're the one who's acting like an idiot!" she lashed out. On the far side of Robert's BMW, Liam moved in closer.

Shannon wanted to drop through the pocked asphalt. This was so over-the-top, so much a part of Mary Beth, who was ever the drama queen. As much as she empathized with her sister-in-law, Shannon despised public displays. She'd had enough to last a lifetime and she was furious with her brother for being such an idiot. Either stay married and faithful to his wife, or get a divorce, but don't flaunt his current mistress in Mary Beth's face.

"This is getting way out of hand," Shea muttered under his breath. Releasing Shannon's arm, he strode across the lot and said to his brother, "Can't you get her out of here?" He hitched his chin in Mary Beth's direction as a car pulled into the parking lot, headlights washing over the group.

"Butt out, Shea."

Shea ignored her. "Listen, Mary Beth—"

"Shut up! This isn't your fight."

"You're making it mine." Shea's eyes narrowed on his sister-in-law. "Take this somewhere private." He turned his gaze to his brother. "Get her out of here, Robert. Before there are complaints. Before someone calls the police."

"Aren't you a cop?" Mary Beth taunted.

"Get her the hell out of here *now.*" Shea ordered. "Or I will have to do something."

"That's the answer, isn't it?" Mary Beth asked, whirling on her brother-in-law. "Just hide the dirty linen in the closet, don't let anyone know. Well, I'm not about to let some whore ruin my life or my kids' lives. We have rights, too!"

Shannon couldn't stand it a second longer. Stepping forward, cognizant of Travis Settler watching her every move, she said quietly, "Shea's right. This isn't the time or the place."

"As if you would know anything about it!"

"Think of the kids."

"Like *he* does?" she said, jerking her arm away from Robert's grip. Tears were running from her eyes now, mascara streaking her face. "Like you do?" She glared at Shannon as Liam moved in closer to stand on the driver's side of the silver car. "That's the trouble with you Flannerys! You only think of yourselves. You don't know what it's like to have a child, to actually raise a kid, to put someone else before yourself!" she accused, her face twisted in pain and hatred. "And when your husband gave you some trouble, did you just shut up about it, huh? No way." She pointed a finger at Shannon. "You found a way to get rid of him, didn't you? Ryan ended up dead. Burned to a goddamned crisp!"

"That's enough!" Robert hissed.

Shannon stared in impotent fury at the raving woman. Mary Beth was wounded, angry, and wasn't going to be satisfied until she'd scratched and clawed at everyone associated with her unfaithful husband.

"Get her out of here," Shea insisted.

Aaron, heretofore lagging behind, put an arm around Mary Beth's shoulders.

"Don't touch her," Liam warned.

"Put a lid on it!" Aaron snapped back, then more quietly to Mary Beth, "Hey, MB, you don't want to be doing this. Let me take you home. We'll pick up your kids at Margaret's."

For a second she seemed to comply. Then a semi rolled past and Mary Beth's head snapped up. "You sick son of a bitch!" She shook off his arm. "Forget it! You're the worst of the lot, Aaron, and that's saying something. And don't try to hit on me!"

"What?" Aaron seemed stunned.

"The dumb-shit routine doesn't work, either. You've tried to get me into the sack for years."

"God, Mary Beth, listen to yourself," Aaron said uneasily but Robert's flash point temper took control of things.

"That does it!" he said to his wife. "Get in the damned car." Robert opened the passenger door of his sports car.

"Why?"

"We'll talk, okay? Just get the fuck inside."

"Don't do it," Liam advised.

Mary Beth appeared about to balk but at that moment the motel manager opened the door of the office and stepped into the parking lot. A squat man about as wide as he was tall, with an obvious comb-over across his bald pate, he glowered at the group huddled near the car. Pointing at Travis Settler, he yelled, "Is there a problem out there? I don't want none of it, y'hear? Take your troubles somewhere else, or I'll call the police." His tiny eyes focused on Robert and Mary Beth. "I'm not kidding! Now get the hell out!"

Robert glowered at his wife. Mary Beth, tight-lipped, her face a mess, slid into the open door of the car, muttering something about "hating to sit where the slut's ass had been." Robert slammed the door closed, then walked briskly to the driver's side, reaching into his pocket for his keys. Quickly, as if he was afraid she'd escape, he slid behind the wheel. Within seconds the engine caught and roared as he stepped on the gas. Without a look over his shoulder, he accelerated out of the parking lot, leaving the rest of them to stare after his taillights as they disappeared around the next corner.

"Fuck!" Liam cast one scathing glance at the Flannerys and headed back to his black Jeep. Within seconds he was in the vehicle and had thrown it into reverse, narrowly missing the fender of a minivan. He jammed his rig into DRIVE and with a screech of tires, sped out of the lot.

"What's his deal?" Aaron asked, staring after the Jeep.

"Who knows?" Shannon couldn't begin to understand anyone in Ryan's family. She glanced at Travis Settler but the man was keeping his own counsel.

"Mary Beth's a head case," Aaron muttered, reaching into

his pocket for a pack of cigarettes and his lighter. He jabbed one filter tip between his lips. "I never so much as came on to her once." He fired up the cigarette and shot a stream of smoke from the corner of his mouth. A drizzle of sweat ran down the side of his face, through one sideburn. "A bona fide nut."

"Always has been." Shea shot a look at Travis Settler. "Guess you got a bird's-eye view of the inner workings of the Flannery family. Sometimes, it's just not pretty."

"All families have their problems," Travis said dismissively.

"Yeah, well, we have more than our share of crackpots." Shea tried to shepherd Shannon into his truck, but she turned to Travis and reminded him, "Dani's things?"

"Right." He started for his truck. "Just give me a second."

When he was out of earshot, Shea muttered, "I don't think you want to get involved in this, Shannon."

"I already am."

"You don't know anything about this guy."

"I know he's my baby's father and that she's in danger. That's enough." She saw another protest forming on her brother's lips, but whatever he was about to say he kept to himself. Which was great. She was tired, getting cranky, and embarrassed by Mary Beth's public display. And that didn't begin to touch on her anger for her other brother. She wanted to strangle Robert.

Travis jogged back to them and offered up a red hooded sweatshirt and a CD case. "It's all I've got with me," he explained.

"Hopefully it's enough, but only if we have some clue as to where Dani is or has been," Shannon said. "Come by my place tomorrow and we'll figure out a plan."

"What?" Aaron asked. Shannon sent him a look guaranteed to cut through granite and he bit back anything further.

"I will," he promised and Shannon, her daughter's things in hand, climbed into Shea's rig.

"If you're going to do this, let's do it right," Shea suggested, digging in the back of his truck. He found a couple of clear plastic bags and Shannon placed the items inside them.

She doubted that her daughter was anywhere near the area, but she couldn't pass up the chance to try and help, even in a small way.

Shea slid behind the wheel, Shannon occupied the middle and Aaron squeezed in beside her, muttering about Mary Beth under his breath as he slammed the door shut. "What gets into her?" he growled.

Shannon just wanted to forget the whole mortifying experience. Though she was far from completely trusting Travis Settler, she'd rather he wasn't a witness to any more of her family's private dealings. She didn't want him to know too much about her. For reasons she didn't completely understand she thought any knowledge he had of her might be dangerous. *He's not the enemy,* her mind insisted, but she wasn't so sure. She was weary and worried and just wanted to go home.

But she couldn't help peering into the rearview mirror as Shea drove away from the motel. She caught Settler's image in the reflective slice of glass and her heart thudded uncomfortably.

Tall, with long, jean-clad legs, some kind of running shoes and a knit shirt stretched across his wide shoulders, Settler stood feet apart, arms crossed over his chest. The dome light of the porch area in front of his motel room illuminated his head, showing off the streaks of blond in his otherwise light brown hair. It was unkempt, a little shaggy and fell over his forehead. His countenance was hard, etched in worry. Intense blue eyes stared after the truck, and she imagined his gaze found hers in the mirror. Which was just plain silly. There was no way he could see into the darkened interior of the pickup's cab.

But her last look at him in the reflection burned deep into her mind: broad shoulders, steely jaw, intensity radiating from him in sharp, sexy waves.

As they'd sat at the table in the restaurant she would have had to be blind not to notice the sharp angles and planes in his face, or the way his skin was tan and weathered. She sensed he was tough, and she imagined if he smiled, it would cut a woman to her soul. But he'd been tense. Worried. The one thing on his mind was finding his daughter. Which only made him more attractive to her.

Attractive?

Lord, what was she thinking?

It had to be the pain meds.

Or the shock of meeting the adoptive father of her child.

Or seeing pictures of the child her infant had become.

She couldn't, *wouldn't* find Travis Settler sexy or attractive or any of the above. So he was intent on saving their . . . his . . . her child. So he'd helped her that night when someone had beaten her so savagely. So he was handsome and sexy as all get-out. But she had to remember: He was the enemy. He'd admitted to spying on her, to thinking she'd somehow abducted Dani.

If he only knew how she really felt about her child.

She closed her eyes and her mind to any other ludicrous thoughts about him; they had absolutely no place there.

Shea cracked his window and the dash lighter clicked.

Shannon leaned her head against the headrest and felt overwhelmingly weary. Her body ached and her mind was reeling. As the outskirts of Santa Lucia flashed past the windows and the conversation between her two brothers swirled around her in clouds of cigarette smoke, she closed her eyes and silently fought the headache that had been building.

Meeting Travis Settler, talking to him and knowing he was the father of her daughter had been difficult, but harder yet had been viewing the pictures of her child. Even now she was shaking inside. She'd eyed those small images and tried to burn them into her mind, but all the while, as she'd viewed the progression of her daughter from infant to teenager, she'd felt this tremendous pain that was as much like loneliness as anything she could name.

You should have kept her. You should have been able to watch her grow up, be a part of her first Christmas. You should have helped her ride a bicycle and a horse, taught her respect for animals. She should have had her First Communion in St. Theresa's where you'd had yours. You should have been holding her on your lap for the photographer, not Travis Settler's wife. Your daughter should have known her uncles and grandparents and most of all you, Shannon Flannery, should have protected her. From this. From whatever horror she is now enduring.

The headache raged and her throat was so thick she could barely swallow. Where was Dani, that little, red-faced, screaming baby Shannon had so reluctantly given away? Was she alive? Waiting for her father or the police to save her? Or had the unthinkable already happened?

Oh, God. Don't think like that. Do not think like that. She's alive. Travis will find her and you, damn it, will help him! You owe your daughter that much!

The pickup bounced over a bump in the road and a jolt of pain blasted through her ribs. The headache she'd fought all day pounded at the base of her skull. She needed to get home, to down some more painkillers and sleep for about a hundred hours.

Then she could face the mess that was her life.

And Travis Settler?

And the whereabouts of his—your daughter?

The dull throb in her head increased.

She'd nearly lost the thread of her brother's conversation, but then she heard Mary Beth's name again.

"A bitch," Aaron pronounced.

"Psycho . . . just like the rest of her family," Shea agreed. "Look at Liam and Kevin."

"Yeah, what the fuck was Liam doing with her tonight?"

"Moral support," Shannon said.

Aaron snorted and streams of smoke shot from his nose. "From him? The guy has the morals of all of the devil's disciples thrown together."

Silently Shannon agreed as the town gave way to rolling countryside. At least about the psycho part of the Carlyles. Ryan's cousins Liam and Kevin were known for their mercurial tempers. Their flash points were quick to ignite and when they did, all hell broke loose. How often, during her marriage to Ryan, had she witnessed the Carlyle brothers' wrath at family gatherings?

The conversation lagged and Shannon realized that Aaron must've asked her a question while she'd been lost in thought about her ex-in-laws.

"What?"

"So, I asked, are you buyin' Settler's story? That he just happened to be at the fire?" Aaron repeated.

"I don't know what to think," she admitted.

Shea braked for a corner. "Me neither."

"I'm not through checkin' him out. I think there's more goin' on with our buddy from Oregon. Hell of a coincidence, him coming all the way from some little town in northern Oregon and landing here, at Shannon's, the night the place gets torched. I don't like it."

"Me neither," Shea agreed.

Aaron had a point, she thought. It did seem more than a little coincidental that Travis Settler was at her place on the night of the fire. But being with him tonight, witnessing his fear, his desperation, his grief for his daughter, she didn't think he would set an intentional fire. And he hadn't been around when she'd received the burned birth certificate. He might be a lot of things . . . But she doubted that he was the arsonist. Thinking of him, she felt a dozen conflicting emotions for the steely jawed man who had raised her child.

Shea slowed the truck and the wheels turned off the county road. Opening one eye to a slit, Shannon spied the trees guarding her lane, the gnarled trunks visible in the splash of illumination from the Dodge's headlights. Soon, she'd be in her own bed. It seemed like eons since she'd slept in the upstairs room of her little cottage, a home she'd once shared with her husband. Ryan. He was long dead now. She was sorry for the pain his death caused his family, but she wasn't sorry that he was no longer a part of her life.

"And don't forget Margaret. Another nut job," Aaron said as he squashed his cigarette into the ashtray. Shannon didn't want to think any more about any of Ryan's cousins tonight. They were a close-knit, clannish family. Years ago, before her marriage to Ryan and before Robert had asked Mary Beth to be his wife, they'd all gone to school together at Saint Theresa's. The Flannerys and Carlyles had often been friends, always acquaintances.

Until she'd made the mistake of marrying one of them.

She looked at the garage, saw the light in Nate's apartment burning in the night and felt a bit of relief. The shed was a pile of ash and rubble and would be for a while, but she didn't dwell on the loss. At least none of the other buildings had gone up in flames.

Because whoever did this didn't want them to . . . He has a purpose. Remember the weird symbol with the number six in its middle. And never forget that he might have Dani as well.

The door over the garage opened and Nate, boots clattering on the steps, hurried down the exterior stairs. With his long strides, he was across the lot before Shea had cut the engine. Beside him, bounding to keep up with Nate's brisk pace, was Khan.

Shannon's heart nearly broke with happiness.

God, she'd missed the dog.

Aaron slid out of the truck, then helped Shannon land carefully on her feet. Khan let out a happy yip as he shot to her side, whining and wiggling, his tail swiping the air frantically and banging against the open door of the truck. Shannon leaned over and scratched him behind his ears and along his back.

"I'm glad to see you, too," she said to the wriggling mass of fur.

"He's been miserable without you. Damned thing whined day and night. Kept wanting to go into the house and search for you. I obliged him a couple of times, then decided he'd just have to tough things out." Nate was serious, his blue eyes dark with the night. "So, how're you doing?"

"Been better," she said, forcing a smile. "Actually I've been a lot better."

Aaron climbed down from the cab. "I think Shannon should get her rest. You'll be here?"

"Yep."

Aaron didn't comment as he and Shea walked Shannon and the galloping dog into the house. But then they started arguing about who should stay with her.

"No one!" she finally had to shout after suggesting twice that she'd be okay. "Nate's next door and you're both a phone call away."

"I'd feel better if someone was in the house with you. How about Lily?" Shea suggested.

Shannon exhaled a puff of air. "Lily's got a husband and three cats. You," she pointed a tired finger at Shea, "have a wife who barely sees you as it is, and Aaron, you and I both know that if you were to stay here we'd be at each other's throats in twenty minutes. Really, I'll be fine," she said, showing them the door. They grumbled and looked unhappy, but they finally headed back to Shea's truck.

As soon as they were gone Shannon bolted the front door, then she pulled the poster of Dani Settler out of her pocket. Staring at the picture she felt something shift in her soul.

"Oh, baby," she whispered. "Where are you?" She gazed tenderly at the image of the fresh-faced girl. She had to be alive. *Had to.* Surely God wouldn't tease her this way by offering her a glimpse of her child only to snatch her away.

"Please let her be safe," she whispered and, for the first time in half a dozen years, made the sign of the cross over her chest.

So far, the Beast—that's what Dani had decided to call him—hadn't discovered her project. She lay on her cot, staring up through the skylight wishing she had another way, an easier way, to make good her escape.

For the past three nights she had worked with the stubborn nail for as long as she could stand, trying to ease the rusted spike out of its hole, forcing it upward.

She knew she was making progress, the nail head was now about a quarter of an inch above the board and easier to move, but it was still stubborn and she couldn't risk making her fingers bleed.

He would notice.

And be suspicious.

If this was going to work she had to be really, really careful.

But she had the feeling that she was running out of time. The guy was getting antsy. She sensed a change in him, saw the restlessness and anticipation in his eyes.

God, he was creepy and that weird rite of getting naked in front of the fire, slathering himself in oil, then pissing into the flames was just plain whacked! So far the routine hadn't changed aside from the fact that he seemed pleased with himself a few nights ago and she noticed some blood on his shirt.

Again she was reminded of the bloodied bag he'd left in that garage in Idaho. Who was inside? What kid had he killed and left to rot and stink in that garage at the abandoned farm?

Don't think like that! Forcing herself off the cot, she crawled into the small, airless closet and tried not to listen to the rats chewing and clawing beneath the floorboards. She took off her socks again and ignoring the fact that they reeked, used them as gloves, doubling the toes over, giving herself extra padding as she started to work removing the nail.

Wiggle, wiggle, wiggle.

Sweat slid down her face, along her nose.

Her fingers hurt immediately, but she kept working.

Working the spike to and fro, pulling it upward, her muscles straining as she tried to keep hold of the small head. So intent was she in her work that she almost didn't hear the engine.

She froze.

He was back?

So soon?

The engine died.

Maybe it was someone else.

Help?

Quickly she eased out of the closet, fumbling as she pulled her socks over her feet, sweating like a pig.

Footsteps crunched on the sparse gravel outside.

Crap!

She turned, banged her head. Nearly yelped. Sucked her breath in through her teeth.

The outside door banged open.

Quickly she crawled back toward the cot.

She heard the latch to her door creak.

She flew onto the makeshift bed and closed her eyes.

The door swung open and a flashlight's beam made a quick, cutting swath across the room.

Dani's heart was thudding, her nerves tight as the piano wires of Mrs. Johnson's old upright.

"What're ya doin'?" he growled and she froze, feigning sleep.

"I said what're ya doin'?" He crossed the room and kicked at the cot's frame.

She jumped, no longer trying to fake him out with the sleeping ruse. He wasn't buying it anyway. "I had to go to the bathroom."

He swung his light over to the empty Porta-Potty sitting near the bed. "Don't think so."

"Cuz I didn't get the chance. I heard you coming in and I knew you'd open the door. I didn't want to be . . . well, you know, squatting . . . when you came in."

He snorted.

Disbelieving.

She couldn't see him. It was too dark. Then he trained the flashlight in her direction and she couldn't make out anything with the harsh, bright beam piercing her eyes.

He swung it from the cot to the Porta-Potty to the boarded window, then up to the skylight. Satisfied they were as he expected, he trained the beam on the closet.

Dani wanted to disappear. What if she'd left something inside? Her socks? What if he noticed the nail head rising above the board?

Her heart was knocking so loudly she was sure he could hear it. She had to do something to distract him. She said the first thing she thought of. "I'm thirsty."

"What?" He swung the beam back at her and she held one hand up to shade her eyes.

"I said, I'm thirsty."

"Tough. You'll have to wait. Until morning."

"But—"

"I said forget it. Christ, you can be a pain in the ass." He stepped out of the room then, and for a second Dani saw his silhouette against the still-glowing embers of the fire. He had something more than the flashlight in his hand, something small and square and . . . she recognized it as a cell phone that he slipped into his pocket.

Oh, God, if she could just get it away from him!

Was there any reception up here in these hills?

Why did he, all of a sudden, start carrying a phone?

Where did he get it?

From his house, stupid. He lives around here somewhere. Remember, he's got some other life. If you can get hold of the phone, you might find out who the bastard is. Be able to turn him in!

Hope flared bright for an instant but quickly died.

He shut the door and latched the hook, then tested the door to her cage before leaving. It didn't budge.

Dani's heart sank.

Once again she was trapped.

Chapter 14

Come by my place tomorrow and we'll figure out a plan. Shannon's offer trailed after Travis as he set about his task. Could he trust her?

He didn't know.

Did he have any other options?

Not a whole lot.

He checked his watch and decided it wasn't too late to call Carter. Though he hadn't expected much, he needed to hear that someone was doing something to help find his kid.

The sheriff picked up before the phone rang twice. "Carter."

"It's Travis. Wondering if there was any news?"

"Not much. You keepin' yourself out of trouble?"

"Tryin'."

"Yeah, right." Carter didn't bother hiding his sarcasm.

"Well, we might have a little more to go on, but it's not much. Remember Madge Rickert?"

Travis knew instantly. "The woman walking her dog who spotted a white van near the school?"

"Yep. Seems as if she got all hot and bothered about what she'd seen and visited a hypnotist in an attempt to remember the license plate."

"Does that work?"

"Sometimes, I guess, though it's not too scientific. Anyway, she had this guy hypnotize her and lo and behold she comes up with a series of numbers and letters for an Arizona plate."

Travis's heart stopped. His fingers tightened over his cell phone. "And?"

"And that plate belongs to a black Chevrolet TrailBlazer, but, get this, the back plate was reported missing about six weeks ago. We called the guy and it turns out he thought he lost it in the car wash. Now, of course, we think it might have been stolen."

Travis leaned a shoulder against the motel room wall.

"It gets better. The owner of the Blazer isn't sure how long the plate had been missing when he discovered that it was gone. As it turns out he'd been on a two-week camping trip—started out in Medford, Oregon, traveled south over the Siskiyou Mountains and camped a few nights around Lake Tahoe."

Travis squeezed his eyes shut. "Pretty much a straight line between Falls Crossing and here in Santa Lucia."

"You got it. The Feds are checking into registrations and recent transactions for white Ford Econoline vans for the years that the description fits, but it's pretty much like finding a needle in a haystack. Sometimes people don't get around to doing the actual paperwork when they buy vehicles. It could go through several hands before someone actually takes the time to register the thing. A lot of vehicles are on the road with no insurance, no proper title or registration."

Travis's hopes sank. "But you're looking for the van."

"Yeah." Carter hesitated. "I don't need to tell you that chances are he's ditched the van already. We figure his MO is to change plates on his vehicles regularly to keep everyone off guard. He probably steals the vehicles, changes the plates and no one's the wiser unless he's stupid enough to get himself pulled over."

"He's not stupid," Travis said and felt a new dread thud in his soul.

"So what have you found out? You talk to Dani's biological mother?"

"Oh, yeah," Travis said, thinking of Shannon and how she'd offered to help him locate Dani. He gave Carter a brief sketch of what had transpired including the burned birth certificate left at Shannon's house.

Carter agreed to pass the information along to the FBI and warned Travis to let the police handle the case. His advice was little more than lip service. They both knew Travis wasn't about to give up. "Just don't do anything you'll regret," Carter said.

"Too late."

"Yeah, I figured."

They talked a few more minutes before Travis hung up. Now that he'd met Shannon Flannery and learned of the burned birth certificate, he had a new perspective on what was happening and a more pointed fear. His hunch that Dani's disappearance was linked to her birth mother wasn't as far off the mark as he'd begun to think.

Ordering himself to emotionally step out of the situation, to think rationally and logically, as if what was happening with his daughter was a case he was working on for someone else, he spent the next four hours sipping beer and organizing everything he knew about Shannon Flannery so that tomorrow, when he went to her ranch, he'd be prepared for anything.

Though the police had confiscated his computer and notes, he had taken backup copies of all the old newspaper articles and his notes, and had kept his computer data on a jump drive the police hadn't found. Earlier in the day, he'd purchased a new laptop and before Shannon Flannery had come knocking on his door, he'd loaded new programs onto the machine and had transferred information from the jump drive onto the hard drive of the laptop.

Working on the premise that Dani's abduction was somehow linked to her birth mother, Travis reviewed what he'd learned. The burned birth certificate proved that Shannon was involved in the kidnapping, even if on the periphery. But how? And why? And was the fire significant? The document had been charred and left for her to find, the shed burned down, her husband killed in a forest fire that had been intentionally set. No one had ever bought the careless smoker or camper theory brought up by the defense. No, someone had wanted Ryan Carlyle dead and burned. Maybe to hide the evidence of murder, or maybe to make a point. Maybe for revenge.

Travis scowled at his notes and clicked his pen a few times as he reviewed the articles about Ryan Carlyle's death, Shannon's arraignment and eventual trial.

So why had Shannon's shed been torched?

He stopped clicking his pen.

Torched.

As in the . . . What had the arsonist been called? The Stealth Torcher? The firebug whom everyone had assumed had been Shannon Flannery's husband, Ryan Carlyle.

Seven buildings had gone up in flames in a two-year span and miraculously there had been only one fatality: a woman by the name of Dolores Galvez, who had been inside an abandoned restaurant, though no one knew why.

No firefighters had been injured or lost their lives fighting the blazes, no surrounding buildings had been destroyed, and though the investigations had indicated that the buildings, all abandoned, might have been set on fire for the insurance proceeds, that was all speculation. The warehouse, restaurant, two old apartment buildings, two residences and an empty private school hadn't been connected, so unless the Torcher had been a freelancer, someone who was paid to burn buildings, the insurance theory didn't hold water. All of the fires had been started with the same kind of remote-ignition device.

With Ryan Carlyle's death, the series of fires had stopped, though it had never been proven that Ryan was the arsonist.

Coincidence?

Travis didn't think so.

What did Shannon know about the blazes?

Were those fires connected to Dani's abduction and the recent fires at her house? He made a note: how was the fire in the shed started? He remembered hearing an explosion. Was it possible the shed fire was ignited in the same manner?

Rubbing the crick in his neck, Travis reached into the minirefrigerator for another beer. Twisting off the cap, he frowned. It was a pretty big leap to think the Stealth Torcher had returned. It would mean that either Ryan Carlyle had not been the Stealth Torcher and so might be innocent of the crimes for which he'd been blamed, or that a copycat, someone with inside information about the original crimes, was now re-creating the Stealth Torcher's crimes.

Damn it all.

He took a swallow from the bottle and sat at the desk again. He wondered if he was missing something, something vital, a connection between what had happened three years earlier and now. He reread the information, sifting through it, this time focusing on the personal side of Carlyle.

Not only had Carlyle lost his life in a raging forest fire, but one of Shannon's brothers, Neville, had disappeared a few weeks after the blaze, never to be heard from again, or so the Flannery family claimed. Soon thereafter, Neville's twin, Oliver, had completely wigged out and been placed in a psychiatric ward for several weeks before finding Jesus and deciding to join the priesthood.

Why would the church want someone so mentally unstable? Travis wondered. He took another swig from his bottle and made a note to check on that angle.

What, if anything, did those two events—Neville's disappearance and Oliver's nervous breakdown—have to do with the fires and, more importantly, Dani's disappearance?

Who had taken his daughter?

Some guy who stole cars, switched plates, probably butchered Blanche Johnson and was connected to Shannon?

Travis's guts twisted and he reminded himself to stay detached, to think like a private investigator, not a father.

What did Shannon know that she wasn't telling him, either intentionally or just because she didn't think it significant?

Was she as innocent as she insisted, as lily-white as she and her brothers claimed?

Travis's eyes narrowed as he thought of her battered yet determined face, the slope of her jaw, the curve of her neck, more visible with her hair scraped away from her face. It killed him, but he saw his daughter in Shannon's features down to the small dusting of freckles across her nose.

His back teeth gnashed and he finished his beer in one long pull.

He started formulating a strategy.

Maybe he shouldn't act as if Shannon was the enemy. Maybe he should cool it a bit, temper his anger and try and get close to her, act as if he was interested in her, to find out how she, either by accident or design, was entangled in all this.

He considered the men in Shannon's life.

Her first lover, Brendan Giles, the biological father of Dani, left the country and never returned.

Ryan Carlyle, her husband, ended up murdered.

One brother, Neville, disappeared.

His twin spent time in the loony bin.

Aaron, the hothead he'd met earlier, had gotten himself thrown out of the fire department . . . Why? Travis circled his name.

Just last year her father died of a sudden heart attack, a man who, though admittedly in his seventies, had heretofore been robust and healthy.

She'd had a couple of other very short relationships in the years since her husband's death: Keith Lewellyn and Reggie Maxwell. Both losers.

Lewellyn was a lawyer and went through women like water; his interest in Shannon might have come from her infamy. The other one, Maxwell, had dated Shannon for only a month and it turned out he was married. That relationship had died before it had started. Reportedly, and this was mainly gossip he'd picked up around town, Shannon had abruptly stopped seeing the guy after three dates, probably when she'd found out he had a wife. At least that's what Travis had been led to believe.

Then there was Nate Santana.

The mystery man.

The guy who had been so familiar with her on the night of the fire, touching her so naturally, taking command as if he alone should be in charge of her welfare. A jolt of jealousy again raced through Travis's bloodstream and he told himself he was being the worst kind of idiot. There was no room for any emotional attachment to anyone right now, least of all Shannon Flannery.

He focused again on the man who lived on Shannon's property. Santana had a reputation for working with temperamental horses. He'd spent some time in prison, albeit wrongly accused of murder. Ostensibly he was her partner but probably also her lover.

It all didn't sit well with Travis.

These days, nothing did.

It was late. Her brothers had left a couple of hours earlier and she'd convinced Nate that she would be fine for the rest of the night. He must have believed her because as she placed a cup of water into the microwave she looked out the kitchen window and saw that the lights to his apartment were no longer burning.

The phone rang. She set the timer on the microwave, then plucked the handset from the wall phone. "Hello?"

"Is he there?" a woman demanded. "Shannon? Is Robert at your place?" Mary Beth Flannery's voice was an octave higher than usual, her words slightly slurred, the rage within her nearly seething through the phone. Obviously Robert hadn't been able to calm her down earlier.

"Of course not, Mary Beth. The last time I saw him was with you."

"He left. With the kids."

"Then . . . Maybe he's at his apartment," Shannon suggested, silently damning her philandering brother. What was the problem with Robert that he couldn't keep his pants zipped up around other women?

"Already checked," Mary Beth bit out. "Damn it. He's with *her and* my *kids! I just know it.*"

"You don't know that," Shannon said, cringing inwardly at the false ring in her words. Dear God, would he actually bring his kids into the middle of this mess?

"Of course I do. Just like you do and everyone at the fire station and this stinking town does, too. Even the kids. Oh, shit . . . This is so horrible . . . so wrong!" Her voice caught on a sob.

Shannon bit back angry advice she knew Mary Beth wouldn't listen to. "I don't know what to say."

"You don't have to say anything." Mary Beth started to cry softly. Once she'd been Shannon's best friend. Now she was a stranger.

"I don't know why I called you," Mary Beth choked out. "Probably because you called me earlier . . . I thought you knew something or wanted to talk . . . Oh, shit. This was obviously a mistake—"

"I'm sorry, Mary Beth. I know this is hard, but I didn't call you . . ."

The microwave timer dinged softly.

"Of course you did. I have it on my caller ID. What the hell game are you playing?"

"But I didn't—"

"Oh, God, Shannon. You're just like the rest of them, maybe worse! Stop lying to me. You and your sick brothers. I never should have married Robert. Never!" She slammed down the receiver, cutting their connection.

Shannon's spine was stiff. *You're just like the rest of them, Shannon, maybe worse.* Mary Beth's words echoed through her head and she gritted her teeth. There were other accusations her sister-in-law hadn't said but remained forever between them: hateful, angry accusations that simmered in the air. Accusations that haunted her life.

"You killed Ryan, I know you did," Mary Beth had told

her once, shortly after the trial, when Shannon had run into her at the deli counter of the local grocery store. "No matter how that lawyer twisted my words on the witness stand, no matter what the judge decided, you killed him just as surely as if you'd dumped gasoline all over him and lit the match."

Shaken by Mary Beth's rage and fury, Shannon had managed to stand firm. "I didn't kill my husband," she denied for the hundredth time while she felt other people staring, women pushing half-filled carts with toddlers in the seats of the baskets, the shocked clerk standing on the other side of the salad case, a scoop of pasta salad stopped halfway to the plastic container in her other hand.

Mary Beth found the decency to lower her voice. "I'm your sister-in-law, Shannon, but that's it, okay? I'm not your friend. Not anymore." And with that she'd pushed her empty cart with its wobbling wheel toward the produce section.

Shannon had been mortified and miserable.

Now she closed her eyes and counted slowly to ten, listening to the wall clock ticking over the soft hum of the refrigerator's motor. "What a disaster," she whispered as she thought about her brothers. All with their Black Irish good looks, thick, ebony-colored hair, glittering blue eyes filled, as her mother had often said, "with the very devil himself." Their cheekbones were high, their eyebrows thick, their jaws looking as if they'd been squared off by a carpenter, then creased at the chin. They'd all been blessed with impossibly white teeth that slashed easily into heart-stopping smiles. But along with those easy, sexy grins and the gleam in their clear blue gazes came trouble. Not only was she the lone female of what their father, Patrick, had often referred to as "his litter," she also didn't resemble her siblings all that much. To a one, the boys took after strapping, outspoken, fire-fighting Patrick while Shannon had a petite frame, auburn curls that refused to be tamed and green eyes that were identical to her mother's. The difference was that while her mother, Maureen, had been frail all her life, nearly dying in childbirth with the twins, Shannon was headstrong and athletic like her brothers. Maureen had been a God-fearing woman who prided herself on sticking to a strict code of Catholic ethics and often told her children the Devil was just over their shoulders. All the boys, except maybe for Oliver, had ignored her dire warnings about sin and punishment. Shannon, much to her mother's humiliation, had eagerly followed in the footsteps of her older brothers and nearly broken every one of her mother's rules. Along with her poor mother's heart. The worst had been, of course, getting pregnant before she was married.

Shannon felt the old tug on her heart when she remembered her father's suddenly weary shoulders the night he learned about Shannon's impending baby. He stood in the den, an unlit cigar clamped between his teeth, leaning against the window casing, his back to her. But she saw his face in the reflection of the paned glass, his eyes turning into marbles of hatred in his suddenly florid face. "I'll kill him," he'd promised.

"No, Dad," Shannon had whispered, holding tears at bay. "You won't."

"That lowlife bastard will marry you."

"No way," she'd insisted. "He doesn't want me. Doesn't want the baby and so I don't want him. There's not going to be a wedding."

Her mother, ashen-faced, sat on an overstuffed wingback chair. "Jesus, Mary and Joseph," she'd said on a weary sigh. "Shannon Mary Flannery, you will marry the father of my grandchild and you'll do it quickly. I'll call Father Timothy right now."

"No!" If she'd ever been certain of anything in her life it was that she didn't want to become the wife to the spineless man she'd thought she'd loved.

"Damned straight, you'll get married," her father grated. He strode across the carpet to stand behind his wife and place a big, calloused hand upon Maureen's thin shoulder. "If I have to chase that boy down with a shotgun, he's going to marry you."

"That's archaic," Shannon argued, her spine stiffening. "I can raise the baby by myself."

"Oh, for the love of Mary! That's not an option."

Her mother shot to her feet and some of the iron will that rarely showed itself in Maureen Flannery became apparent. She pointed an accusing finger at her only daughter and decreed, "I'll speak to Father Timothy and Brendan's mother and—"

"No! Keep her out of this. I'll handle it!" Shannon's cheeks burned. Tears started down her face. She nearly panicked at the thought of dealing with Brendan's parents. They'd never liked her and this situation would only make things worse. Before she could say another word she felt her stomach roil, the hot taste of bile rise up her throat. It was as if the baby she was carrying could hear and understand and was protesting loudly.

She ran out of the room to the tiny bathroom tucked under the staircase and retched and retched. Spent and gasping, she ground her teeth, silently vowing she would do what was best for her child. She knew she couldn't raise the baby herself. Not with her disapproving father and mother, certain the child had been conceived in sin. Not with a passel of brothers often considered immoral hellions even by their own mother. Not with the possibility of running into Brendan on the streets of Santa Lucia.

That night, in the tiny powder room, Shannon had swallowed hard, flushed the toilet and stared at her pale reflection in the mirror over the medicine cabinet. Outside the door her parents continued arguing, her father raging about "young bucks who can't keep their peckers in their pants" and her mother going on and on about "the Flannery curse," something Maureen constantly brought up when things didn't go as planned. Shannon could practically visualize her mother sketching out a quick sign of the cross over her thin chest, just as she always did when she spoke of ill luck.

Even now, nearly fourteen years later, Shannon felt her

skin flush at the memory of confiding to her parents that she'd been three months' pregnant.

"The Flannery curse," she said aloud, thinking of her brother Robert. Still disturbed by Mary Beth's phone call, Shannon removed her cup from the microwave. She found a box of caffeine-free herbal teas that Shea's first wife, Anne, had given her for Christmas long ago. She selected a tiny pouch named raspberry mist and she dunked the bag into her steaming cup. She briefly considered calling around for Robert before discarding the idea.

Mary Beth had been right. His involvement with Cynthia Tallericco was common knowledge in town because Robert had up and moved out of their three-bedroom ranch home and into an apartment. He'd made absolutely no attempt to hide what he was doing. Whereas his other "dalliances" had been clandestine and short-lived, this one was different, this one had staying power. It was out in the open. Public enough to embarrass Mary Beth and their two kids. Robert didn't seem to care. He would listen to no one—not their parents or any of his siblings—not even Oliver, soon to be a member of the priesthood.

Robert steadfastly claimed he wanted a divorce, that he loved Cynthia. And there seemed to be no talking him out of it. It was time for him to move on and for Mary Beth "to get a life." Mary Beth, a staunch Catholic, was refusing, insisting that Robert would "come to his senses" and using their kids as pawns in an ever-escalating war.

When did love become hate? Shannon wondered grimly. Her own marriage had ended in a bloodied emotional battlefield.

Carrying her cup out of the kitchen, Shannon snapped off the lights and climbed the stairs to her bedroom. From the windowseat Shannon was able to view her backyard and over the fence to the property that had just been sold and was slated for a development where "seventy new, affordable homes" would soon be constructed.

Another reason she had decided to move. These five acres

would soon be a part of the suburban sprawl of Santa Lucia. She needed more room to train her animals.

She'd thought the place she'd purchased was perfect, and it would be good to put some of the horrors of this house behind her. As she opened the window and gazed out to the night sky where the moon was rising and the sound of cicadas and crickets whispered up to her, the darkness held forboding.

She looked into the night and felt as if there, hidden in the darkness, unseen eyes were watching her.

A chill skittered down her spine.

The Flannery curse, she thought again. In her mind's eye, she saw her mother as she had been on that fateful day so many years ago, her spirit broken, the look of horror and condemnation upon her face as Shannon had said, "I'm pregnant." That image had never left her.

"Get over it," she told herself now as she took off her shoes and padded barefoot to the bathroom. But her mind swam with images of Dani Settler. Silently she prayed the girl was safe, that soon she'd be with her father again. That's where she belonged, with Travis Settler. Shannon was no part of the girl's life.

Her heart squeezed painfully as she shook out a pain pill from the bottle. Her ribs were beginning to ache and a headache was crawling up her brain. Tossing back the pill, she chased it with water. Then she grabbed her hairbrush and worked the knots from her tangled tresses. She yanked the brush through her hair as if her life depended on it. She felt the need to hurry, as if the more she brushed, the faster and more furious she worked, the quicker her pain would end, the sooner this would all be over. Eventually she tossed down the brush, covering her face with her hands for several long moments.

She was afraid for the daughter she'd never known and now might never meet. Sick with worry.

Blindly, she walked back to her bedroom, saw the tea steeping on her nightstand. All of her thoughts were on

Dani. From her pocket, she withdrew the poster, smoothed the creases with the flat of her hand and propped the picture next to her bed. "Be safe, baby," she whispered. "Oh, please be safe." She fought a new round of tears as she eased into bed and turned out the light.

She'd find Dani. She and Travis. There was a strength to the man, a determination. She would help him find their daughter.

Then what? her mind taunted. *She could already be dead . . . Oh, please, God, no! But if she's not and you find her, are you going to just let her drift out of your life again?*

That, of course, would be impossible.

But, for tonight, Shannon wouldn't dwell on the future. Not now. Not until her child was safe again.

He watched from a distance, his binoculars trained on the compound where Shannon lived. As far as he could tell she was in the house and alone. A perfect time.

He reached into his pocket and pulled out her cell phone, then, knowing he was in reach of the nearest tower to her home, he placed the call.

One ring.

Two.

On the third a woman said, "Hello?"

He waited.

"Hello?"

Again he said nothing.

"Shannon?" the woman guessed. Her voice grew more strident. "Listen, I don't know what kind of weird game you're playing with me, but you'd better stop this shit or I'll call the authorities!" She slammed down the phone.

In the darkness he smiled. *Don't worry,* he thought as he repocketed the cell, *the authorities will be there sooner than you think, sooner than you want.*

It was time to raise the stakes. Tonight. He felt a surge of anticipation through his blood.

Oh, yeah, "the authorities" would soon be on their way.

Chapter 15

"That son of a bitch," Mary Beth said, kicking off her shoes and watching the three-inch heels bounce against the scuffed wall of her walk-in closet, her half-empty closet. When she and Robert had moved into this house five years earlier, the walk-in dressing area had been one of the reasons she'd fallen in love with it. Now the space was a mockery, her "side" filled to the gills with outfits, Robert's empty aside from his old letterman's jacket hanging lopsidedly on a single hanger. She closed her eyes, remembering him wearing the jacket in high school, being such a jock. She'd fallen in love with him so easily and believed the dream of happily ever after.

What a laugh, she thought scornfully. All those Friday-night football games, watching him play, meeting him afterwards, spending more time than she should have alone with him wherever they could find a secluded place.

She'd waited for him through college and even bitten back her disappointment when he'd decided to follow in his father's footsteps and join the Santa Lucia Fire Department.

Another mistake.

From that point on, her life had been hell.

On a sigh she snapped off the closet light. Jesus, it was stuffy in here. The air-conditioning was on the fritz again and Robert refused to pay to have it fixed.

What a jackass.

Mary Beth opened the bedroom windows, then slipped into the living room and did the same. There wasn't much of a breeze, but at least some of the hot air inside the house dissipated into the night.

Robert, Robert, Robert.

Why couldn't she get over him?

Should she divorce the bastard?

So what if her parents, the parish priest and her kids were against it. Would God really blame her?

No, but your children will. They will never get over it.

She blew her bangs out of her eyes and knew she was doomed to stay with her husband until death. And the way she was feeling tonight, that might not be long. God, she'd love to shoot the bastard dead!

Well, not really.

But she would love to scare the liver out of him.

From the get-go there had always been other women. Even as far back as her senior year, when he'd been in college, but she'd been certain once they were married his roving eye would return to her.

Of course it hadn't happened. Then after a while, Mary Beth began to think that maybe a baby would change things—and it had. At least for a couple of years after Elizabeth was born. But the late nights of not knowing where her husband was had started up again. So she'd gotten pregnant again and this time had given him a son.

Surely that would do the trick!

But she'd been wrong. Again.

She walked through the kids' rooms, threw some toys into the toy boxes and scooped up a few discarded clothes, which she carried down the long hallway to the tiny laundry room off the kitchen, just inside the door of the single-car garage.

After tossing the dirty clothes into a basket balanced on the dryer, and trying to swipe down a spiderweb with one of JR's socks, she shut the door and made her way to the kitchen. She'd already decided to tap into the bottle of wine she'd opened earlier—her own special confidence booster. The wine had certainly helped her confront her husband in the parking lot of that run-down, no-tell motel. Shit, what was Robert thinking?

"He's not," she said aloud. "Unless his brain truly is in his dick." She didn't trust him. Never had. Never could.

Oh, he'd sworn he wasn't going to be with that bitch

tonight. When she hadn't believed him and had started screaming at him, even going so far as to slap him once they'd gotten home, he'd acted like it was all her fault.

He'd flinched, raised his hand, but hadn't hit her back. He
just stared at her, his eyes dark and unfathomable, and warned,
"Watch it, Mary Beth. Don't you believe in the Bible? What's
the quote that's appropriate here? 'As ye sow, so shall ye
reap'?"

"If that's the case, you miserable prick, then you're going
to spend all of eternity roasting in hell!"

"Then I'll see you there."

With that he took off in a roar from his piece-of-shit car's
powerful engine. A BMW! When they were up to their eye-
balls in debt! Her fault again, he'd said. Because she didn't
work outside the home and so they had no money.

But didn't taking care of the kids—*his* kids!—count for
something?

"Dick-head," she muttered, pulling a bottle of Chardonnay from the refrigerator and yanking out the cork. She filled
a tall, stemmed glass with the lovely amber fluid, and didn't
dwell on the fact that it had been years since Robert and she
had shared a bottle of wine.

Toting the glass and bottle into the master bath, she
placed them both on the rim of the jetted tub, then peeled off
her clothes. First her tight pants, then her blouse that had
showed off what she'd hoped was just enough cleavage to get
Robert interested. She figured she'd fight fire with fire to get
him back and to that end she'd purchased a low-cut black
push-up bra and a god-awful matching thong. Now, staring
at her reflection in the mirror, she decided she didn't look
too bad for a woman who had borne two nearly ten-pound
babies. She worked out and tried to keep her body toned, but
all she ever heard from Robert were complaints about the
cost of the athletic club and personal trainer who had helped
her form her exercise routine.

There had to be a way to win him back, she determined.
She just had to think of it. In the past, sex had worked, but

this time . . . Oh, hell, this time he acted as if he was in love. *Love!* With a twice-divorced lawyer who had no kids. It was all so wrong.

Angry all over again, she wiggled out of her bra and what no one in her right mind would think of as "panties," and filled the tub with hot water. Turning on the jets of the whirlpool, she decided to take advantage of the fact that the kids were out of the house. She sipped her wine and she doused the water with scented oil and bubble bath, then wrapped a short robe around herself and walked into RJ's room, pulling open his dresser drawer to reach the stash of candy bars tucked inside. She would have preferred imported truffles, but the Snickers and Butterfinger would have to suffice. Peeling off the candy bars' wrappers, she bit into the Snickers and let out a soft "Ooh," for the indulgence she rarely allowed herself.

In just the robe, she walked into her bedroom and found a favorite Dixie Chicks CD. Slipping it into the disc player, she cranked up the volume, then returned to the bathroom where mountains of suds were building into frothy white mounds. Quickly, she finished her first glass of wine, well, third, if you counted the two she'd had before calling Liam and accosting Robert. She poured herself another, nibbled at the chocolate, then hung her robe on a hook near the tub.

Before sinking into the bath, she lit the candles that decorated the sill of the frosted-glass window as well as the tile ledge surrounding the Jacuzzi. Slapping at the wall switch cut off the glaring overhead lights. The candles flickered softly.

The bath looked delicious.

She slipped into the hot water, feeling its silk surround her, seeping into her tired bones. She grabbed some suds and blew them off her palm, smiling a little. Even though it was eighty degrees outside, she loved the heated liquid around her, easing her out of her stress.

She sipped her wine more slowly now.

A dozen little tea candles reflected in the mirror and window over the tub. Despite all her troubles, she felt a bit of hope.

She'd get Robert back.

She always did.

This was just a slightly harder challenge than the last time.

Sadly, she considered the undeniable fact that Robert would never quit cheating. If not on her, then on the next woman in his life.

Shifting in the water, she felt the sweet buzz of the wine in her bloodstream. She'd heard the warnings often enough about not mixing booze with antidepressants. But she'd been taking them since Robert's last affair and she'd never stopped drinking. And so far no problem.

Come on, what could a glass or two of wine hurt?

She sculpted the soap bubbles over her breasts, singing along to the ballad about heartache and sorrow. Soon, she knew, there would be the song about killing off an abusive husband.

Just like Shannon had.

Mary Beth, like everyone else in her family, was convinced Shannon had set up her cousin Ryan. There had been the restraining order and then, when Ryan broke it, pictures of Shannon bearing bruises he'd sworn could not have been made by him.

Well, Ryan had been a piece of work, too.

If Mary Beth had been married to him, yeah, maybe she would have found a way to get rid of him, too. He was an A1 bastard, even if he had been her first cousin.

"Bad blood," her mother had always said when referring to Ryan. But then, who knew how good or bad his blood was? He'd been adopted before Mary Beth had been born.

And, at one time, Shannon had been her best friend. That's why testifying against her during the trial had been so damned difficult. What would she have done if someone continually beat the crap out of her? Just take it? No way!

And how about the fact that in one of the worst incidents, Shannon had miscarried?

Mary Beth frowned. She didn't want to think about Shannon and her problems. Let her deal with them. Mary Beth had her own. Tipping back her glass, she thought she heard a neighbor's dog bark. She twirled the stem in her fingers and sang along as the next song started to play. Midway through the ballad, she sensed something, a breath of the hot summer breeze, slip through the room, shimmering the tower of bubbles over her breasts. She felt a second's panic before remembering that she'd opened the windows to help cool the house.

She was probably imagining the air disturbance. Or, more likely, she was reacting because of the wine. Chardonnay had a way of going straight to her head. That's why she loved it so much. Lately she'd really craved the soothing magic that it brought to her, the way it calmed her nerves after her arguments and fights with her stupid husband. Sighing, she finished the second glass of wine and leaned back against the rim of the tub, closing her eyes, letting the hot water ease some of her tension.

She'd get Robert back.

It was only a matter of time.

Hardly making a sound, he removed the screen from the bedroom window. The room was dark, just a slice of illumination slipping through the crack left by the slightly ajar bathroom door. Music pulsed through the house, which would mask any noises he might make.

His blood was dancing through his veins, thrumming in his ears. With gloved hands he tied plastic bags over his shoes. The loud music was the perfect cover as he walked noiselessly across the carpet. Standing in the shadow of the bedroom, smelling the scent of her perfume mingle with the odors of soap and bath oil, he felt a thrill of anticipation. He peered through the crack. She was lying in the tub, eyes closed, unaware that he was near, not knowing that she was breathing her last. The water lapped at the fringe of dark hair at her nape and traces of mascara stained her cheeks. Her lipstick had faded, most of it smudged upon the rim of the empty wineglass sitting on the ledge of the tub.

The jets of the Jacuzzi were rumbling, water pulsing around her, the pile of bubbles on the water's surface beginning to diminish. He saw her breasts through the suds, large dark areolae only partially hidden, nipples puckering. She was wearing nothing but a necklace, a thin gold chain from which dangled a cross of tiny diamonds that glittered and winked in the flickering light.

Her skin was slick and wet and he imagined running his hands over the most intimate parts of her. He licked his lips, feeling those nasty old sensations of lust rise in his blood. His cock even twitched a bit, anxious for the feel of wet skin against it. In his mind's eye, he saw himself rubbing it against her glossy skin and could almost feel the bath oil begin to coat the entire length in warm droplets that she would smooth with her hands.

At the thought he nearly groaned aloud.

He was breathing hard, his blood running hot with want, but he forced the carnal thoughts from his mind.

No!

Not her.

Not this one.

Not now.

Not ever.

He had work to do.

Death to dispense.

Mary Beth Carlyle Flannery was only the beginning.

Sweat collecting over his brow, he carefully reached forward and pushed the door open just a little farther, enough that he could squeeze through.

She didn't move. Her eyelids didn't so much as flutter. Dark lashes continued to rest against the tops of her cheeks in smooth, twin arcs. If she sensed a change in the atmosphere, she didn't show it. Yet he was cautious. Wary. Hardly daring to expel a breath.

He stepped closer to the tub.

The floor creaked.

"Robert?" she mumbled as her eyes drifted slowly open.

He leaped forward, his hands instantly around her neck. Startled, her eyes flew wide. She flailed and started to scream. With all his power, using his body as a weight, he shoved her head beneath the water.

She kicked and clawed at him. Her hands swiped his wet suit. Her legs churned the water, slammed against the sides of the tub. She was strong. Muscular. Bucked upward. With adrenaline pumping through her veins she had the strength of an athlete. She wrenched and writhed, gasped and coughed, grabbed at his wrists attempting to loosen his grip, trying to wound him, desperately seeking to get away.

He held on.

Forced her downward, until the back of her head cracked against the bottom of the tub and her short black hair swirled and danced around her face.

Mary Beth gurgled, churned and thrashed.

Candles flew off the edge of the tub, sizzling into the water, clattering onto the floor, creating waxy pools. She tried to fling her entire body out of the tub, but he held her down, feeling her panic, watching her eyes bulge in desperation.

Frantically, she twisted and turned, trying to squirm away, to wriggle from his grasp.

It was no use.

Water slopped over the edge of the tub, suds flew onto the walls and floor.

She was stronger than he'd anticipated, but his hands held her firmly against the bottom of the tub, steadily cutting off her air.

He could see the look of horror on her face beneath the water, suds floating and dissipating on the surface.

He smiled.

Under his hands he felt her strength ebb. Her movements became sluggish and weak. Still he held on, while the damned CD kept playing, loud, the singer's voice echoing through his head.

All struggling ceased.

At last it was over.

Mary Beth stared at him from beneath the water's surface, big eyes glassy.

He held her down for another three minutes, until he was certain that she was dead.

Then he let out most of the water from the tub, so that her body was partially exposed. Satisfied that she was positioned just so, he draped a towel over the tub's rim and into the water. Next, he took the belt of the robe that was hanging near the tub and pulled it so that it touched the water on one end, but was still secure in the belt loop of the pink wrapper.

Working quickly, he poured bath oil over the water, and then, to make certain it would ignite, reached into his pack and found a bottle of his own mix of oils, ones that were certain to ignite quickly. He poured the entire contents into the water around Mary Beth.

The CD stopped abruptly.

Silence surrounded him.

He froze.

Had someone come in? Had he missed the sound of another person entering because of his absorption in his task and the damned music?

Holding his breath, not moving a muscle, he waited. His heart thudded, sweat covered his body beneath his wet clothes.

But there was nothing other than the hum of the refrigerator from the kitchen, the gurgle of water still running down the pipes from the tub and outside, a few houses down, the sharp, staccato bark of a small dog. As if the damned mutt knew something was going on.

Hurry, damn it. You don't have any time to waste.

Deciding he was alone, he finished his job quickly.

Using a tube of Mary Beth's lipstick that he found on the

counter in a special little rack, he drew a figure on the mirror, then reached into his pouch again and found a special little package that he left in the sink.

The rest was easy. With a final look at Mary Beth, he dropped a lit candle into the tub.

Flames shot upward and crawled across the water's surface, finding the towel and belt. Dark smoke, acrid and thin, rose upward, burning his nostrils and growing in intensity with the flames that fed eagerly, crackling and hissing as they met water.

Mary Beth was ringed in fire, the room brightening to a shifting gold hue. He had to leave. Now. Away from the fascination of watching her hair singe or her skin start to burn.

Moving quickly, he left the way he'd come in, slipping through the window and into the night, stealing along the shrubbery and fence rows, hiding behind a garage as a car passed, the predominant bass throbbing over the roar of a big engine as a pickup, jacked high over huge tires, commandeered by a teenaged boy, flew past.

He flattened against a fence and the kid missed him by inches.

Once the truck had passed he caught his breath, then took off at a sprint. He was down an alley at a dead run and four blocks away from the fire when he heard the first shriek of a siren cutting through the night.

Too late, he thought, sliding into his truck and breathing hard. *Too damned late.*

Sirens wailed in the distance.

Fire!

Shannon's eyes opened and she trembled inside.

Something was wrong. Terribly wrong. Glancing at the clock she realized she hadn't even been in bed for two hours, asleep for less. In the darkness she climbed to her feet and walked to the window to stare outside.

It's not your place. You're safe.

Drawing a breath, she headed downstairs, just to be sure. She heard Khan's paws hit the hardwood floor. He trailed after her down the steps. As she walked out the front door the dog was beside her, sniffing the air and stretching.

Nothing was burning.

Nothing out of the ordinary.

And yet she felt a chill, a quiver from the inside out. She stared at the rubble of the shed and told herself that she was jumping at shadows, that there were fires every day. She couldn't start flipping out just because she heard a siren.

And yet . . .

Walking inside the house she went directly into the kitchen, picked up the telephone and dialed Shea's cell phone. It rang four times before she was thrown into voice mail.

"Give it up," she told herself, but even as she did, she punched in the number of Aaron's cell and on the third ring he answered.

"Shannon," he said, sounding wide awake and a little breathless. She could tell from the sounds other than his voice and the way the connection cut out that he was driving. Of course he knew who she was before she identified herself. He had caller ID on his cell as well as his personal phone. Aaron, the private investigator, had every gadget known to man. Including a police scanner.

"I know this sounds crazy, but I heard sirens and I just had this weird feeling, almost a premonition that the fire might be . . . Oh, I don't know, related to what happened here the other night." She heard herself and shook her head, as if he could see her. "God, now I sound paranoid."

He hesitated.

Long enough to cause Shannon's heart to leap to her throat. "What is it?" she demanded.

"Robert's house."

"What!"

"Calm down, I think they might be able to save it, or most of it. I already talked to Shea."

Shannon's worst fears gelled. "But we just saw Robert and Mary Beth a few hours ago."

"I know."

"Was anyone home?" she asked, fear darting through her body. The kids had been taken to Margaret's place earlier, and Mary Beth had called . . . from where? Maybe Robert and Mary Beth were somewhere else . . .

"Don't know."

"Oh, God!"

"I'm on my way. You stay put and I'll call you the minute I know anything."

"Like hell, Aaron."

"Don't go to the fire."

"Yeah, right."

"Shannon, really. You know the last thing the fire department needs is more spectators."

"Robert's my brother, too," she said angrily. "Mary Beth and the kids are part of my family . . ." She silently prayed that they were safe, still with their aunt Margaret. With anyone. Not at home. That no one was at home. Shannon hung up while Aaron was still trying to talk her out of going to the fire.

Hastily she pulled on a pair of jeans and a long-sleeved T-shirt, then tied back her hair with a rubber band. She left Khan behind and was in her truck and driving away within ten minutes. She considered alerting Nate but decided against disturbing him when she realized his Explorer was missing, not parked in its usual place.

Had it been in front of the garage when she'd returned from town with her brothers? She thought so but couldn't remember. And right now she couldn't take the time to sort it all out.

She punched the accelerator and the truck lurched forward.

Another fire.

At a member of her family's home.

What were the chances of that happening? Fear spurred her on. She ignored the speed limit as she drove into town and down the familiar streets, smelling the smoke, seeing lights flashing before she turned onto the street where her brother and his wife had lived for years.

Dread pulsed through her. All her thoughts centered around her brother and his family. Images flashed across her mind: Robert and Mary Beth's wedding reception . . . Mary Beth still in her full-length beaded dress, long finished with the rites of cutting the cake, toasting their marriage. Their first dance together. Mary Beth's tears of joy. The birth of their daughter, Elizabeth, and her christening down at St. Theresa's church. She remembered the day Robert Junior was born a few years later. Shannon had waited outside the delivery room to welcome her nephew into the world. Her mind then flashed to the family get-togethers, sometimes on the Carlyle side, sometimes on the Flannery, where Robert and Mary Beth had either cuddled like newlyweds or not been speaking because of their most recent spat.

She pulled around a final corner and faced what looked like utter chaos.

At the block nearest Robert's house the street had been cordoned off. One fire engine and two trucks were parked in front of Robert's house and the nearest hydrant. Police cars, their lights a swirl of red and blue, were parked in the street. Dozens of neighbors and lookie-loos who had followed the big rigs stood by. Across the street was parked the inevitable news van, a reporter already positioned in front of the blaze.

Shannon arrowed her truck into a spot too narrow for it, scrambled out, and ignoring protests from her ribs and shoulder, walked briskly down the street.

Flames were shooting toward the sky, black smoke billowing into the heavens. Shannon's stomach roiled. *Please, God, let them be safe. Please, please, please.*

Firefighters had the situation in hand. Hoses snaked across the street and the lawn. Men and women in protective gear hosed down the roof and surrounding houses. A great hiss and steam rose over the roar and crackle of flames.

Despite the pain in her ribs, Shannon jogged down a now-wet and shimmering street. Smoke made her cough as she wended through the knots of people who were looking, staring, fascinated by fire and the sense of impending tragedy.

She reached the police barricade and was rebuffed. "No one past this line, ma'am," one burly guard insisted.

"But this is my brother's house!"

"No one past the line, ma'am."

"Is anyone inside? Please, do you know?" she demanded, frustrated, her eyes searching the helmeted firefighters covered in protective jackets, hoods and pants, all looking the same. Was Robert among them?

Of course not. It wasn't his shift. You saw him only a few hours ago.

What about Mary Beth?

Her gaze shot to the garage where the door was shut. She couldn't divine whether a car was inside. And the kids . . . Oh, sweet Jesus, the kids. Surely they were safe. They had to be.

"Is . . . Was anyone inside?" she repeated.

"Listen, lady, it would be best if you just went home. You'll know soon enough," the cop told her.

"No way. Where's the police fire investigator? Shea Flannery?"

Another officer, with a narrow chin and pencil-thin moustache, hitched a thumb toward what appeared to be the command center. "I think he's over there, but you can't cross this line."

"I'm the sister of the owner of this house! My family might be inside!"

"All the more reason to stay back."

She felt a hand on her elbow and spun quickly, expecting that some macho member of the Santa Lucia police or fire department was intending to escort her away. Instead she found Travis Settler at her side. A part of her wanted to crumble, to fall into his arms and pound her fists in frustration. She just needed someone to hold her, to tell her it would be all right.

Instead she looked up at him. "What're you doing here?"

"Heard the sirens. The motel is only half a mile away. I thought . . . Christ, I don't know what I thought." His eyes were dark with the night. "But with the fire at your place, I just had to come and see, and now . . ." He shook his head, deep lines of concern bracketing his mouth.

"It's a nightmare," she whispered, the smoky, damp air filling her nostrils. She spied Shea talking with the fire captain and noticed Aaron weaving his way through the crowd toward her. Everywhere there was a fine mist, spray from the hoses.

"I got hold of Robert," he said, and Shannon felt relieved knowing that her brother was safe. "He's on his way."

"What about the kids? Mary Beth?"

"The kids are still at Margaret's. He left Mary Beth here."

"Here . . . !" Her hand flew to her mouth, though she told herself not to imagine the worst. Mary Beth might have escaped the blaze. "Has anyone seen her?"

Aaron's eyes were somber and she felt Travis's hand, still on her arm, hold on a little tighter. Little lines of concern dimpled between Aaron's eyebrows. He looked about to remark on it when his eyes shifted again, to a spot over Shannon's shoulder, and his jaw clenched. "Stay here," he said and took off at a fast, resolute clip. He angled past a group of men and women in slippers and robes, their faces blank as they remained mesmerized by the spectacle.

Shannon craned her neck and saw the object of Aaron's quest.

Robert had left his beloved BMW idling and was running through the crowd. His face was twisted in horror, his eyes dark with fear. Though Aaron, keeping stride with him, was talking, Robert didn't seem to hear. His gaze was fixed on the house, his gait increasing as he pushed past people, ignoring the cops, heading for the front door.

"Mary Beth!" Robert yelled, his voice raw with emotion.

A burly firefighter blocked his path at the door. "Nobody goes in," he said, then squinted in recognition. "Robert?"

"My wife's in there!" Robert dove at the door, pushing past his fellow firefighter, who stepped aside.

Shannon barreled in behind him, with Travis and Aaron at her heels.

"Mary Beth!" Robert leaped up the stairs, two at a time.

Shannon felt her eyes tear from smoke but she pressed on, up the stairs, into the hallway where two firemen kneeled on the floor.

She stopped short before the two men.

One was zipping a long, black bag. The other was cradling a body, so singed and charred that the corpse was barely recognizable as Mary Beth.

"Jesus!" Aaron whispered in awe.

"Don't look," Travis warned Shannon, but it was too late. She stared in disbelief and horror at the blackened remains of what had so recently been her sister-in-law—a vital, young mother.

Nausea burned up her throat and denial screamed through her brain. These seared remains couldn't be Mary Beth! Couldn't! Shannon staggered back to the threshold of her nephew's room and wretched violently, Travis at her side, Aaron standing stock-still, his face chalky.

"Clear these people out!" someone ordered.

All the while the fire hissed in its inevitable death throes, smoke and ash billowing out through smashed windows.

And above it all, over the sound of the bullhorn, radios, barked orders and stomping boots was a keening wail that cut Shannon to her very soul.

In the soot-stained hall she saw Robert, standing between two firemen, fall to his knees.

Chapter 16

"Come on, I'll get you out of here," Travis said.

Her stomach still roiling, her ribs aching, Shannon said shakily, "No, I've got to be with Robert. I can't leave." Her mouth tasted foul and she felt like she'd been pulled through a wringer both ways.

"There's nothing you can do here."

"I can't leave."

"Your brothers can take care of him now."

"I just want to talk to him . . . to . . ." She lifted a hand helplessly, watching as Shea arrived in the crowded living room and pushed through a small knot of firefighters to crouch at Robert's side. Robert was openly crying, his face the color of the ashes upstairs, his body sagging under an unbearable weight. What could she possibly say to ease his pain, to balm his guilt?

"He's right," Aaron agreed, his gaze, too, fixed on their two brothers. Robert on his knees. Shea squatting beside him, speaking in low tones.

"But I want . . . to help."

"Fine." Aaron said. "What you can do is call Oliver. He can go over to Mom's, unless you want to."

Shannon felt weak inside again. "She'll have to know," she agreed tonelessly. "But I don't have a cell. Mine's missing."

Travis whipped a phone from his pocket. "Use mine."

She didn't hesitate. "Thanks." She turned her attention to Aaron. "I'll call Oliver and we can go over there together," she said and glanced up at Travis. "I can't go home yet."

"I get it." His hand on her arm didn't relax. "I'll drive you."

"I've got my own car."

Aaron argued, "Really, Shan, don't drive, but I need to stay here. Maybe he can help." Aaron sent a speculative look at Travis, then focused his gaze on his brothers.

Reluctantly, Shannon dialed Oliver's number. It was true: though she could be of little comfort to Robert, his brothers, always close, would be able to circle the proverbial wagons. Her brothers, singly or en masse, had often tried to protect their only female sibling, but she had never quite broken into their inner circle, never had been trusted or included on the same level. She figured it was because she was the only daughter of Patrick and Maureen as well as being the youngest of the siblings, an outcast on both counts.

Now she pressed Travis's cell to her ear, smelled the lingering scent of his aftershave and waited as the phone rang six times before going automatically to voice mail.

"He's not picking up."

Aaron scowled. "I thought priests were on duty 24/7."

"He's not a priest yet," Shannon said, then added, "I'll go see Mom."

Aaron's eyes grew sober. "You sure, Shan?"

"Positive." She turned her gaze to Travis. "I think I'd better do this alone, but . . . thanks."

He released her arm and she picked her way through the firefighters to the door. Outside, the crowd seeming to have grown rather than shrunk in the few minutes since she'd arrived. Sidestepping the curious, including a man in pajamas with a dog on a leash, as well as puddles of water and sludge and cars and trucks parked at odd angles, she made her way to her truck. The last thing she wanted to do tonight was face her mother, but someone had to be with Maureen Flannery when she learned that her daughter-in-law had perished in a fire.

She didn't feel that she could wait for morning, lest her mother was up early and caught the news or some acquaintance should call to offer condolences.

Shannon braced herself.

Though her mother had dealt with her share of accidents and deaths, and the ever-present force of a blaze, Maureen would no doubt fall into a million pieces upon learning that the mother of two of her grandchildren had died.

Or been killed?

Didn't someone nearly take you out? Hadn't he started not just one fire, but two, if you count the fire that burned Dani Settler's birth certificate? She grew cold inside at the thought that somewhere out in the darkness was a sick, twisted killer, a criminal who was holding Dani Settler hostage.

If the girl was still alive.

Shannon's knees trembled. She refused to think that the girl was anything but living. Captive, but still breathing.

She wouldn't let her mind wander into those murky, frightening waters. Right now she had to deal with her mother. "One battle at a time," she told herself.

And what about Mary Beth's parents? Her brothers and sister? Her children? Who would tell them?

Shannon's heart seemed to weigh a ton as she thought of her niece and nephew growing up without their mother. Robert might remarry, but a stepmother wouldn't replace Mary Beth, at least not in her children's eyes. Shannon couldn't help but think of her own situation, of the daughter she'd never met, might never even see, and wondered again how all this fit together. It seemed unlikely that the fires weren't connected, and yet the idea that they were somehow linked, even set by the same person, also felt wrong. Glancing over her shoulder, she caught a glimpse of Travis Settler, still standing near Aaron, still watching her make her way to her vehicle. Instead of the sensation being weird or creepy it was somehow calming. It felt right. As if he was reliable.

You don't even know the guy. He showed up at the fire at your house, too, remember? And now you think you can trust him? That you might be able to rely on him? Somehow Travis Settler, no matter how concerned he seems, no matter how attractive and sexy he appears, is mixed up in this. Don't trust him. Do not trust him. Remember: the deadliest snakes are usually the most interesting.

She climbed into her truck and found that it was blocked

in. Several cars, a news van and a police vehicle were in the way. "Hell," she growled under her breath.

She looked back at the crowd through her bug-spattered and now-misty windshield. Drops of condensation drizzled down the glass, distorting her view, making everything seem more surreal than it already was. Through the shimmering glaze, she spotted Travis, a head taller than most of the on-lookers, pushing his way past the crush of the crowd toward her truck. She rolled down the window.

Her stupid heart kicked up a beat or two and she silently berated herself for her reaction.

"Come on," he said, now at the driver's door. "Lock this up and we'll use my rig. I won't intrude, really."

"Fine. Let's do it." She couldn't stand another second of doing nothing. "Where's your rig?"

"A couple of streets over."

"Smart," she admitted and followed closely at his side as they made their way along the dark alleys to a nearly deserted street. His truck was parked across from a grade school, the one Mary Beth and Robert's kids would have attended had it not been that Mary Beth insisted they be enrolled at St. Theresa's, the parochial grade school that bled into St. Theresa's junior high and high schools that all of Robert and Mary Beth's siblings had attended.

Travis unlocked his truck for her, strode around to the driver's side and slid behind the steering wheel. The dome light clicked off as he closed the door and started the engine. "You'll have to point the way," he said, easing the Ford into the empty street.

"Right at the next intersection, then left at the light and follow that road until you reach Greenwich, which is about a mile and a half, I think," she said. "Another right. It's about four blocks down from where we turn."

He glanced at her, flashed a small, understanding smile in the darkness. "Just let me know if I make a wrong turn."

She glanced up sharply, wondering if his words had a double meaning, seeing the questions in his intense blue eyes, then decided she was overreacting. The long day and horrific tragedy were getting to her. Dear God, she dreaded what was to come. Her mother, always into theatrics, would absolutely fall into a million pieces.

They drove in silence, Travis not bothering with the radio, Shannon not caring that there were no words between them. They passed dark houses, parked cars and light poles. They met a few vehicles and a gray tabby cat darted in front of the car, only to slink into the shadows when Travis swerved to miss it.

"Geez!" he growled.

Shannon watched the feline hide in the shrubbery as they passed. She was cold to the bone. It didn't matter what the temperature was outside, internally she was freezing, thinking about growing up with Mary Beth.

Could she really be dead? That vital, vibrant, opinionated woman? Shannon remembered her glimpse of the blackened body and her insides clenched violently, warning her that though her stomach had been emptied, she could still dry heave. Wrapping her arms around herself, almost glad for the life-affirming small jab of pain in her ribs, she fought the nausea.

Mary Beth was dead. Burned. God, it was unfathomable.

"Who would do it?" she asked herself, not aware she'd spoken.

"The guy who's got Dani."

Twisting her neck, she stared directly at Travis for the first time since climbing into his truck. "Why? You think this is all connected? The fires at my house? Mary Beth's . . . death? *Why?*"

"Her murder, Shannon. Your sister-in-law was killed."

Shannon shook her head, fought the chill of certainty as it clawed up her ribs. "How do you know?"

"I just do. Ten to one they'll find evidence that the fire was intentional when they investigate."

"But why? What does Mary Beth have to do with Dani? Why the fire at my place?"

"You tell me."

"I can't!" She wedged herself in the corner, farther away from this man, and stared at him, wondering what made him tick. Yes, she knew he was concerned about his child, worried sick even, but beyond that, what did she know about him? The answer was simple: not a whole helluva lot. Yet, here she was riding with him, on her way to give her mother the horrible news that Mary Beth was dead. "You're still blaming me for Dani's disappearance, aren't you?" she accused.

"No." He was adamant. "But somehow it has something to do with you. Otherwise why the burned birth certificate? Whoever's got my child is flaunting it. Taunting us. Getting off on the fact that he knows more than we do."

"But what would be the point?"

"I don't know."

"Oh, turn here." She motioned to Greenwich Avenue, a street lined by trees that were overgrown, their shallow roots buckling the sidewalk.

Travis cranked on the wheel and headed down the narrow road that split perfectly formed city blocks, the two-storied, post-World War II houses looking like cookie-cutter replicas of each other. Some had bricks or stones to accentuate the siding, others had been remodeled several times.

Shannon's parents' home, which she pointed out to Travis as they approached, had the same tired exterior it had started with over half a century earlier. The siding had been painted a different color each decade and now was a shade of soft green that had blistered from too many years in the sun. The roof needed to be replaced and the single-car driveway was choked by weeds and grass that were bleached and dry, matching the patch of front lawn.

"Want me to walk you in?"

"I can handle it."

"Then I'll wait."

"You don't have to."

"I know. But I will."

She was about to argue but, in the dark, close interior of the pickup's cab, she saw the resolution in the hard set of his jaw. There was no talking him out of it. Besides, she didn't have the energy or the time.

She glanced at the house again. She couldn't put off the inevitable. "Do you mind if I use this again?" she asked, still clutching his cell phone.

"Go ahead."

She dialed quickly, punching out the numbers. Just after the second ring her mother answered. Maureen's voice was groggy, but still there was an edge to it, as if she'd woken from a deep sleep and, realizing it was late, knew that no good news was coming over the wires. "Hello?"

"Hi, Mom, it's Shannon."

"Shannon? What's wrong?" Her voice was sharp now, alert. Full-blown worry edging each syllable. From the truck Shannon witnessed the upstairs window of her mother's bedroom illuminate as Maureen snapped on a bedside lamp. "Are you feeling all right? Your head okay?"

"I'm here at the house. Let me in."

"Ohmigawd, what happened?" Maureen asked and through the blinds Shannon saw a silhouette: her mother getting up and reaching for the robe she always kept draped over one of the tall posts at the foot of the bed.

"Just open the door, Mom, and I'll explain."

"Oh, Lord, what now?"

Shannon hung up, handed Travis his phone and opened the door of the truck. By the time she'd crossed the lawn, the porch light was switched on, locks and latches clicked open and the front door, behind a screen, swung inward. Her mother, small and frail, red hair covered in some kind of net, a worn chenille robe cinched around her waist, stood on the other side of the screen door. "What happened?" she demanded, fear crowding her features as she fumbled with the hook that latched the screen door.

Shannon had practiced what she was going to say. "It's Mary Beth, Mom. There's been an accident." She slipped inside the house where the odors of dust, Pledge, bacon grease and onions lingered. She was instantly awash with memories of growing up with all of her loud, boisterous older siblings: Shea and Robert sliding down the banister; Aaron surreptitiously seated on the back porch, his pellet gun aimed at the bird feeder; Neville and Oliver building a tree house in the apple tree out back, only to abandon it for a fort upstairs in the attic. And Shannon in the thick of it all. Though her mother had tried to interest her in cooking and quilting, gardening or even writing, she was the one begging to be the next in line to sit in a box at the top of the stairs as her brothers pushed it forward to bounce down the wooden steps, or to engage in water-balloon fights in which she inevitably commandeered the hose.

How often had Maureen described her home as a "madhouse"?

Now the place was tidy, not a book out of place on the shelf. The only noise came from the cuckoo clock mounted in the front entry hall as it ticked off the seconds of what remained of Maureen's life.

"What about Mary Beth? Is she hurt? What?" Maureen demanded.

This was the bad part. "She's dead, Mom. An accident."

"*Dead! What? No!*" Shock drained all the color from Maureen's face.

"Yeah, Mom, it's true."

Maureen began to quiver. She braced one thin shoulder against the door frame. "But I just saw her . . . Oh, Lord . . . What happened?" she asked as the truth sank in. "The kids?" she asked as a new panic invaded her.

"Elizabeth and RJ are fine. With Mary Beth's sister, Margaret."

"And—"

"Robert's okay." A lie. Physically he was fine, Shannon knew, but emotionally he was a wreck.

"But what happened?"

"A fire."

"Saints preserve us!" Maureen's bony hand flew over her chest and quickly she made the sign of the cross. "Another fire?" she whispered, spitting it out as if it was an epitaph. "Jesus, Mary and Joseph," she said, then unconsciously, with quick movements, making another sign of the cross. "It's the Flannery curse."

"There is no such thing, Mom."

Maureen narrowed her red-rimmed eyes on her only daughter. "Tell that to Mary Beth." She headed stiffly into the kitchen, snapping on a trail of lights in her wake. Shannon followed in time to see her mother rummage in a catch-all drawer for the pack of cigarettes she kept for emergencies. Maureen had quit smoking during each of her pregnancies, taking the habit up again once each baby had reached the third month of his or her life. She finally quit for good when Shannon was five, but, whenever a crisis developed, Maureen was quick to find the pack she kept "just for emergencies" and light up with the matches she hoarded for the same purpose.

Now, fingers shaking, she unwrapped the cellophane, shook out a filter tip and managed to strike a match. "Tell me what you know."

"Nothing yet," Shannon admitted.

Maureen lit up, drawing the smoke in deeply as she waved out the match. "Where was Robert?"

"I don't know."

"With that Tallericco woman? Your lawyer?"

"She wasn't my lawyer, she just helped me with the adoption," Shannon said and experienced a small shock as she connected the dots. She'd used the San Francisco law firm of Black, Rosen and Tallericco when giving her baby up for adoption and Cynthia Tallericco, a full partner at the time, had taken an interest in her case. Though an associate had helped her through most of the paperwork Cynthia had consulted and consoled her.

Now, twice divorced, and no longer with the firm, Cynthia had moved to Santa Lucia and somehow connected with

Robert. Their affair had been running white-hot for three or four months, and Robert had moved out of the home he'd shared with Mary Beth and the kids less than six weeks earlier.

And now Robert's wife was dead, killed in a fire, and the daughter Shannon had given up—through the law offices that Cynthia Tallericco had worked for—was missing. What were the chances of that being a coincidence?

The doorbell rang and Maureen visibly started. "More good news?" She took a final puff, turned on the tap to douse her cigarette, then tossed the wet butt into the trash under the sink. As the bell pealed again, she maneuvered spryly through the long hallway, where the walls were covered with framed pictures of her children, to the front foyer.

Shannon expected to find Travis on the other side of the wooden panels, but instead her brother Oliver's face peered through one of the three small panes of glass that ran across the top of the door.

"Thank goodness," Maureen declared as she unlocked the door again. As soon as Oliver was inside, she fell to pieces. "You heard?" Maureen asked, tears raining from her eyes. "About the fire and Mary Beth?"

"Aaron called and left a message." Oliver managed a thin, patient smile without a trace of warmth. He glanced at his sister and something odd danced in his eyes for just a second, something out of place. He wrapped a comforting arm around his mother's slim, now shaking shoulders. "I came as soon as I could."

"Thank you."

"Why don't we pray together?"

"Yes."

"Shannon?" He looked at her expectantly.

Shannon couldn't imagine kneeling on the old carpet in the living room while Oliver stood over them and prayed. It felt wrong, just as his embrace of the church had. He'd always had a religious bent—she'd known that—but after the fire that had taken Ryan's life, and after losing his twin,

Oliver had been sent to a psychiatric hospital, a broken man. He'd come out quoting scripture and talking about his calling, and even suggesting that he communed with God. Shannon had never gotten used to it. While everyone else in the family seemed to go along with Oliver's new religious intensity, she'd thought it was just plain weird.

Her brother Aaron's assertion that Oliver's fervor was "because of Neville—he misses his twin," hadn't offered a complete explanation, in Shannon's opinion. "Those two, they were like half of a whole," Aaron reminded her. "Then Neville disappears and Ollie, he can't function, at least not right."

"Do you think he knows what happened to Neville?" Shannon had asked.

Aaron just shrugged. "Doubt it." He'd shaken his head. "It's the damnedest thing."

On that, Shannon had agreed. She'd wondered if Neville had run off, like Brendan, or had an accident while out hunting or had been killed. It was so weird. Neville was just . . . gone. The press and the DA had been convinced that Neville had helped Shannon plot her husband's murder. That together they'd found a way to drug Ryan, haul him out to the woods and set the fire that was supposed to cremate him and destroy all evidence of murder. But they'd been sloppy, hadn't understood about modern forensics, had screwed up.

Neville, the theory continued, disappeared so that he wouldn't have to testify against his sister, nor incriminate himself.

But it was all conjecture.

Never proven.

And a pile of garbage.

But something had happened. Something Shannon didn't understand. And whatever it was had eaten at Oliver until he'd snapped and somehow started conversations with God.

"I'd better go," she said now to her mother, wondering at the stranger her younger brother had become.

"Is the man outside waiting for you?" Oliver asked.

"What man?" Maureen turned to Shannon, who sent Oliver a look guaranteed to crucify him.

"I had to get a ride over here. I was at the fire and my truck got blocked in."

"So why didn't you invite him in? Who is he?" Maureen wanted to know.

"His name is Travis Settler. It's complicated and really, really late."

"Are you dating him?"

Shannon almost laughed. Dating Travis Settler? Dear Lord, how much simpler that sounded than the truth! "No, Mom, he's just a fr—an acquaintance who offered to drive me over."

"A Good Samaritan," Oliver said and Shannon felt a little sensation of disquiet. Hadn't she mentally referred to Travis as a Good Samaritan after she'd been attacked? Now, knowing him a little better, she realized he was anything but. He'd come to Santa Lucia with a single-minded purpose. He'd hidden in the shadows of her house spying on her. He'd thought she'd stolen his child, for God's sake. He'd saved her only because he'd been on the property, lurking, trying to ferret out the truth. She'd even thought he might have been the man who'd attacked her, but she'd changed her opinion of him in the ensuing days. Nearly trusted him.

Nearly.

But not quite.

"Sure," she said, eager to end the conversation. "A Good Samaritan. That's what he is."

And then she left. Before her mother could ask any more questions and before she said or did anything she might regret.

She let the screen door slap behind her and found Travis outside, leaning against his fender and staring at the house. The lights of the town splashed into the heavens and only a few stars peeked through the lingering cloud of smoke that hovered above the ground and tainted the air.

"You had company," he said.

"My brother Oliver."

"The one who wants to be a priest. Yeah, I know."

"What is it you *don't* know about my family?" she asked as he opened the door of the truck. He looked about to help her climb into the interior but she shot him a glance that said all too clearly: back off. The last thing she wanted was to rely on him, but because of the pain in her shoulder, she had more than a little trouble getting inside and once in her seat waited for the agony to subside. "Are there any secrets we Flannerys have managed to keep from you?"

"More than your share," he admitted. He smiled faintly, in a way that made him seem particularly attractive. Shannon looked away, disturbed by her own thoughts as Travis slammed the passenger door closed.

She surreptitiously watched him walk in front of the truck: long strides, straight back, slim hips . . . the kind of trouble she didn't want or need.

She mentally shook herself. What was wrong with her? Why was she so aware of him?

Strapping on her seat belt, she nearly gasped. The belt was tight. Binding. And when it gripped, it pushed painfully against her ribs. All of her pain medication had worn off hours before and she was feeling ragged around the edges, her ribs, shoulder and the back of her head hurting her enough to cause a dull ache to run through every inch of her body. She was exhausted, worried and grief-stricken.

What else could go wrong?

Don't even go there!

He climbed inside the cab, shut the door behind him. The dome light clicked off and she was suddenly, again, in a small confined space with him, so close that she could smell his scent, touch his jean-clad leg if she let her hand drop.

His profile was visible in the weak light thrown off from the dash and the bit of illumination seeping through the windshield. Travis Settler was strong, even handsome, with a hard jaw, straight nose and deep-set eyes that seemed to miss little. His mouth was razor-thin, a scratch cut into the sharp angles of his chin. A bit of beard shadowed his chin. His hair was mussed and unkempt and all around him was a sense that he was pure, don't-give-me-any-bullshit male— tough, coiled, ready for action.

He rammed his truck into gear and pulled away from the street. She noticed the strap of his watch, nothing fancy, just a functional, no-frills timepiece on a sexy, strong wrist—a wrist that was currently poised over one taut, jean-clad thigh. She could imagine the sinewy muscles beneath the jeans. And the hard flatness of his stomach. And the strength in his hands and fingers.

She caught herself.

What the hell was she thinking?

She must have been more tired than she realized.

He cast her a quick look and in that heartbeat she knew he'd seen her checking him out. Wanting to melt into the cushions of the seat, instead Shannon straightened and arched a "so-what" eyebrow in his direction, hoping he didn't notice the wash of heat flooding her face. But she had to roll down her window to get some air.

So he was overtly male.

So he was sexy.

So it had been a long time since she'd felt a spark of interest in any man.

So what?

Hadn't she learned her lesson about men? Or maybe the pain meds hadn't quite left her system and her brain wasn't functioning properly. Tonight, of all nights, with Mary Beth so recently dead, her own body not yet recovered from her recent attack and her daughter, *his* daughter missing, the last thing—the very last thing—Shannon should be thinking about was sex. Or sexy men. Or what it would feel like to have one of those big, calloused hands scale her ribs and touch her breasts.

She shivered. Was this what being faced with one's own mortality brought on? Sharpened awareness? Heightened desire for intimacy? She couldn't feel this way about Travis Settler . . . especially not Travis Settler.

Angry at herself, Shannon readjusted the band holding her ponytail away from her face and snapped the elastic into place. She needed some space from him, had to break the intimacy that the small environs of the cab seemed to create. Hopefully the open window and the rush of air would help to destroy any familiarity between them—imagined or otherwise.

Do not trust this man, Shannon. Do not. You know nothing about him other than that he's Dani's adoptive father and he knows everything about you.

As the rig picked up speed and the air whistled by, pulling some unruly hairs from the restraint of the hair band, she winced as she moved her shoulder, biting back the urge to swear. When the pain had passed, she slowly let out her breath. Surreptitiously she cast another glance at this stranger who had inserted himself into her life, this man who was her daughter's father.

His maleness swamped her senses. She felt weak and vulnerable. She inwardly groaned. It wasn't right.

His gaze was focused through the windshield as he drove, but he was as aware of her as she was of him. Twice he flicked a glance at his mirrors before changing lanes on the nearly deserted streets, but she guessed that he was observing her from the corner of his eye, that anything she did, any small gesture or movement wouldn't go unnoticed.

"Okay, so I know some things about you, about your family, but not everything," he said into the silence that had enveloped them. Shannon turned to him, glad to be yanked from her thoughts. "For instance, I don't know why whoever has my daughter wants to bring you into it. I don't know why one of your brothers became a priest or why his twin disappeared. I have no idea why whoever has Dani has started setting fires and worse yet, I don't know who the murdering bastard is or what he's done to my kid!" All of a sudden his calm cracked. "Something's going on down here, something that doesn't make sense and something that scares the hell out of me. I'm sick with worry, feel impotent as hell, and yeah, I'd like to know everything about anyone remotely connected to you and your family since the son of a bitch who kidnapped Dani is interested. You're my only link to her and by God I damned well want to know every little thing about you because it might help."

"But you don't think I had anything to do with the kidnapping," she clarified as he braked for a stoplight.

"Not anymore." Illumination from the traffic signal cast a red, unworldly glow into the truck's interior.

"Good." She didn't know if she believed him or not, figured it didn't matter. She forced herself to look away from him and through the windshield to the night, still thick with smoke.

At the turn to Robert's house, Travis continued straight, on a beeline out of town. "Hey, wait! You missed the turn," she said, her eyes swinging from the deserted street leading to her brother's house to Travis's profile.

"You're in no condition to drive."

"What? Are you out of your mind? I can't just leave my truck. Where the hell do you think you're going?"

"To your place. You can call one of your brothers to pick up the truck or get it in the morning."

"It'll be towed by morning."

"The way I hear it you have connections in the police department."

"No way! Turn around. Take me to my damned truck and don't go all macho on me, okay? I can't do this. You don't have to act like John Wayne in some bad flick from the fifties, telling the little woman what to do. I can drive my own truck home."

"Too late."

Shannon's mouth dropped open. "You're unbelievable!"

"You look like hell and I've seen you wince and try to

pretend that you're not in pain, but it's not working, okay? It's been a long, hard night and I think you need a ride home."

"I don't care what *you* think *I* need, Settler. This is my life! Mine!" Angrily, she poked a thumb at her chest. "And it's my truck and my decision and . . . Oh . . ." A pain shot through her ribs, cutting off any further argument. Almost as if to drive home his point. She sucked in a sharp breath, squeezed her eyes shut and silently cursed her weakness. "Fine, all right," she muttered when she could breathe again. Glancing up at him she looked for any signs of a smirk, but found none, just a serious gaze that cut from her to the road. "Take me home. Do your worst."

His lips faintly twitched.

He almost smiled.

Almost.

Chapter 17

What the hell had come over him?

Who was he to tell her what to do, to refuse to take her to her damned truck, to boss her around?

Travis, slowing for the turn into her lane, couldn't believe what he'd done. There was just something about her that forced him to take charge. He'd known she was in agony, not only mental anguish but also pain from her injuries. Still, he had no right to take over her life.

And yet he hadn't been able to stop himself.

Even when she'd about come unglued he'd ignored her protests. Which was unlike him. He wasn't one of those men who thought they knew best, who was always pushing other people into his way of thinking, who disregarded anyone else's point of view.

But here he was, driving down the lane leading to her house, fingers wrapped around the steering wheel in a death grip as he wondered what he would face at her doorstep.

An irate Nate Santana?

One of her brothers?

He steeled himself for whatever confrontation was headed his way, but when he rounded the final bend and the beams of his headlights illuminated the house, the place looked serene. No cars or trucks were parked in the lot. No interior lights flashed on when he pulled to a stop.

He cut the engine andyanked on the emergency brake.

"Thanks for the ride . . . I guess," she said, unbuckling her seatbelt and opening the door. The overhead light switched on and he saw how pale she was. The cuts on her face, though healing, were pronounced, the bruising under her eyes deepened by dark smudges from lack of sleep.

"Get some sleep. You can get your truck in the morning."

"My truck! Could I use your phone one last time? I'm sorry. I've lost my cell." She lifted a helpless hand, then dropped it. "Haven't had time to find it, and my head's so over-loaded I'm afraid I'll forget this call by the time I get inside."

"No problem."

He handed his phone to her and she punched in a number.

She was still seated in the truck, one leg resting on the running board, her faded, worn-out jeans stretched tight. "Hey, are you still at the scene . . . ? Yeah, really awful . . . I can't imagine, and Robert . . . I know . . . Look, I saw Mom, and she was pretty upset, but Oliver came over to pray with her, or whatever it is they do, and I think she'll be okay . . . Hmmm . . . Listen, could I ask a favor? Can you move my truck? I was blocked in. Couldn't get it out . . . I caught a ride . . . from Settler." She glanced at him quickly, then nodded, as if whichever brother was on the other end of the line could see her. "No worries. I'm okay . . . The keys are in the ignition. I'll see ya tomorrow. Thanks, Aaron." She flipped the phone closed and handed it to Travis. "Mission accomplished." Sliding out of his truck, she stood and faced him through the open door. "Thanks."

"No problem."

"No, I mean for everything." She offered him the ghost of a smile, a hint of warmth. Her otherwise beautiful face was now wracked with grief, pain and sheer exhaustion.

"You're welcome."

"I'd ask you to come in," she said lifting a hand, only to drop it to her side. She didn't finish her thought but he knew he'd overstayed his welcome as far as Shannon Flannery was concerned.

"Another time. I'll be back tomorrow. I mean, later today."

"To see if we can get the dogs to pick up Dani's scent."

He nodded, sobering as he thought of his missing daughter. He realized with a tiny jolt that the more he was with Shannon, the more he recognized her resemblance to Dani. He glanced to the house. "You got someone to take care of you?"

"I've got Khan." She smiled. The first genuine one he'd witnessed. At whatever she saw on his face, her smile deepened.

"Okay, Hot Shot," she said, "you're the one who's been digging around in my personal life, the guy who's been checking me out with field glasses and Internet research. Do I have someone to take care of me?" She slammed the truck's door shut, looking at him through the open window. "You tell me. It'll be on the test tomorrow."

She lifted a hand in good-bye, then she made her way to her door, unlocking it and slapping on the exterior and interior lights before bending down to the mutt of a dog at her feet. The ball of fur with the ragged ear wiggled and whined as she looked up at him, smiled again, then slipped inside and shut the door behind her. He heard the lock slide into place with a loud and definite click.

So where was Santana? Travis wondered as he fired up the engine. Why wasn't he with Shannon tonight? Since he hadn't driven with her to the fire, why wasn't Nate Santana, her lover, waiting up for her?

As Travis turned his truck around in the gravel lot, he checked for another vehicle, but the parking area was empty. Santana could have parked in the garage, but Travis had a feeling the guy wasn't on the premises. He glanced at his watch. It was late. Hours after midnight. Where was he? And where had he been on the night Shannon had been attacked?

Trying to make sense of it all, he scanned the outbuildings, his gaze landing on the blackened rubble of what had been the shed.

Who was behind this?

Jesus-God, where was Dani?

Frustration and fear gnawed at him. Swearing beneath his breath, he punched the accelerator, the tires spraying gravel in his frustration.

The days were slipping through his fingers. The monster who had his kid was getting bolder and more deadly. Now another woman was dead and Travis was damned sure that Mary Beth Flannery's demise was somehow linked to Dani's disappearance.

He only hoped his daughter was alive.

Oliver was alone.

The cathedral was empty, almost eerily so.

Quickly sketching the sign of the cross over his chest, he knelt on the cold stone floor, his knees aching immediately, an old soccer injury unforgiving.

He embraced the pain. Wished he could endure more. Then perhaps, the evil would be banished from his soul for all of eternity.

Instead it lingered, an oozing, dark cancer spreading through him.

"Forgive me, Father, for I have sinned," he prayed desperately.

High over the altar, the Son of God looked down on him. Wounded, bleeding, a crown of thorns upon His head as He suffered on the cross. Jesus was unmoving. Cast in plaster and paint. Staring.

Oliver made the sign of the cross again and begged the Spirit to enter him. Pleaded for goodness to fill him. Craved for forgiveness.

But his eyes strayed to the floor beneath the windows where shadows played and danced.

Brilliant beams from the rising sun pierced the stained glass and cast splintered, colorful images upon the cold stones of the cathedral's floor.

The patterns of color reminded him of the kaleidoscope his brother Neville had been given.

How many hours had he stared through the eyepiece to watch the dancing, changing, swirling patterns? But Neville had been selfish with the toy he'd bought with his birthday money and he'd hidden the intriguing tube in a slit in the mattress of his upper bunk.

Oliver had found it.

And kept it.

When Neville discovered his treasure was missing, he'd accused Oliver of the crime, but Oliver had lied and sworn he'd seen Aaron hanging around their bunks, poking and prodding. Oliver had convinced Neville that Aaron was the culprit and Neville had never guessed differently.

But then Aaron had always been such an easy target.

Oliver had then hidden his prize in the bole of a hollow oak tree at the edge of the park three streets over from their house. There had been a path through a patch of woods and old-man Henderson's backyard that led to the small, dedicated piece of land where a rusted swing set and a jungle gym near a baseball diamond was considered a playground. But there had been the one special tree. He'd spent hours in the limbs of the gnarled oak, looking through the magical glass and letting his mind spin with all the distorted images.

He'd never confessed his sin to his twin.

But then, he'd never confessed a lot of his sins. For he was poisoned inside. He knew it now. The torturing thought burned through his brain. He whispered a prayer, but his eyes strayed to the patterns of color on the floor that reminded him of other places. Dark haunts. Creaking corridors with stained glass images of Jesus and Mary and the disciples . . . He felt a weird, nearly seductive tingle move through his blood and he thought of the dark place . . . the lonely place . . . the spot where in his sickness he'd been sent to recover.

A hospital they'd called it.

Our Lady of Virtues.

But he knew better.

Hospitals were for healing.

That place—with its dripping faucets, creaky stairways and hidden, evil hallways—was for harming. A cool breeze would creep through the apse, as if something cold and unholy had passed by. He'd felt it more than once.

He glanced down at his wrists, saw the scars, now twenty-five years old, and felt a violent rumble deep in his soul. He hurriedly bent his head and once more began to pray.

Fervently.

Desperately.

Needing God to hear him and keep the demons at bay.

But it was a lost cause.

The demons would return.

They always did.

The phone blasted beside her bed and Shannon reluctantly reached to answer it. She gave up on any hope of sleep. It was only nine-thirty in the morning and she'd already endured a call from her mother, saying she and Oliver would be over later in the day with Shannon's truck, another call from Lily, shocked at Mary Beth's death, and a third from Carl Washington wanting an interview. She'd no sooner hung up on the reporter when the phone rang again.

"Hello?" she answered tensely, ready and armed to tell Washington to quit harassing her.

"How are you?"

Travis Settler. She recognized the strong voice immediately. Stupidly, her pulse jumped a bit and she remembered how she'd seen him last, in the pickup, in the dark, so close she could have touched him.

She scooted back on the bed and rested against the headboard. "I'm okay."

"You get your truck back?"

"One of my brothers is bringing it over."

"Good. I thought we should get started with the dogs."

He sounded anxious. She didn't blame him. "Give me an hour. I've got a few chores to do."

"You got it." He hung up and she pushed herself off the bed.

"No rest for the wicked," she muttered and Khan lifted his bad ear but didn't move from his spot on the quilt. "Yeah, I'm talkin' about you." She ruffled his coat, then headed for the shower. Her headache was still drumming in the back of her skull and her eyes felt gritty. The few hours of sleep she'd caught between nightmares of Mary Beth had been few and her shoulder ached a little.

The hot water of the shower felt good and she managed to wash her hair without getting too much shampoo in her eyes or disturbing the stitches on the back of her head. She left her hair alone, deciding to let the damp curls air dry, then brushed her teeth and swiped on lipstick and mascara.

The image in the mirror staring back at her wasn't exactly Hollywood-glamorous but was fresh-scrubbed, which would just have to do.

She dragged on a pair of clean, worn jeans, and pulled a V-neck T-shirt over her head. Her ribs and shoulder felt better than they had since the attack.

"Clean living," she told Khan as he stretched on the bed. She ducked into the bathroom and shook out a Vicodin from the bottle. She thought about the day ahead. Travis Settler was first on the docket, then she'd have to deal with her dogs, her mother, her brothers and who knew who else. Closing her fist around the tablet, she decided to hold off on taking anything stronger than over-the-counter stuff. She didn't want to spend the rest of the day dull-witted. She wasn't much of a pill popper, and she wanted to wean herself as quickly as possible off the medication. If the pain got to be more than she could handle, then, okay, she'd take a dose, if not, she'd "soldier on," as her father had so often said.

Her father.

She thought fleetingly of him and wondered what he would say or do in a situation where fires were being set, people dying . . . Patrick Flannery had been a man of action, oftentimes bending or nearly breaking the rules to serve his purpose. More dedicated to his career than to his wife and six children, he was a no-bullshit individual whose hard drinking and rule breaking had eventually cost him his job.

"Oh, Pop," she whispered, conjuring up his face and almost hearing him say, *Buck up, Shannon. Life's not always easy, but it's always interesting.*

Unfortunately, sometimes "interesting" meant painful. She had only to remember the horrid image of Mary Beth's burned body being hauled out of her home.

Shannon put the tablet back in the bottle, shoving it into the medicine cabinet and shutting the mirrored door.

She settled for a couple of ibuprofen. "Breakfast," she explained to Khan, swallowing the pills dry, then leaning over and chasing them down with a drink from the tap.

With the dog leading the way, she headed downstairs and started making coffee. As the machine gurgled and dripped she fed Khan and glanced out the window. The sun had long risen and through an open window she felt a warm, dry breeze, the promise of yet another day where the temperature pushed a hundred degrees in this year of drought and fear of forest fires.

Like the year that Ryan was killed.

She tried not to remember that breathless, hot Indian summer where there was talk of electrical brownouts, low reservoirs of water. The fires had been relentless, crackling and feeding in the surrounding hills.

And with the heat and fear came quick tempers and anger. She'd seen it in Ryan's face, known that telling him she intended to divorce him would only add to his rage, that the restraining order she'd managed to get was in his eyes little more than a piece of paper.

There had been no getting away from him, nor from his fury. Even her brothers hadn't been able to protect her. Nor had they been able to keep her baby safe. No one had. Her throat tightened as she remembered a time she'd sworn to forget. She squeezed her eyes shut at the thought of her second pregnancy, and the old sadness and anger invaded her soul. Her fingers clenched around the edge of the counter. How she'd wanted that child, even though he had been fathered by her estranged husband, had been created in a loveless marriage that had been rapidly and surely crumbling apart. That child, her son, Ryan Carlyle's son, had been the one good thing to come from the unhappy, violent union. She bit her lip. Like a whipsaw, guilt cut through her because if she looked deep into her own soul, and faced the naked truth that stalked her relentlessly, she knew that she wasn't sorry that Ryan was gone. Maybe not even sorry that he was dead.

After fishing in the refrigerator for some creamer to no avail, she poured herself a cup of coffee. Sipping, she searched for her cell phone but couldn't find that either. Then, with Khan barreling ahead of her, she walked outside and noticed that Nate's truck, again, was missing, not parked in its usual spot. She started to worry about him. That worry changed to perplexity when she went to check on the horses and saw

that they'd already been fed, watered, then let outside where
they were currently grazing on dry bits of grass or standing
next to each other, swatting flies with their tails.

She glanced at the windows of Nate's apartment. Where
was he? In all the time that she'd worked with him, he had
been an early riser, taking the animals out at dawn, depending upon the season. Lately his schedule had been off and
he'd been gone more than he'd been on the premises.

It was true they both did their own things with the animals and rarely checked in with each other . . . Yet this was
far outside the bounds of their usual routine.

Weird.

So out of character.

Or was it? What did she really know about him? Not a
whole helluva lot when you got down to it. So what was he
up to? What was with the odd hours?

Realizing she couldn't do anything about it now, she decided to talk to him later, if and when he showed up during
her waking hours. Whatever his reasons for his odd hours,
they were his business.

Unless he's somehow involved in the fires . . .

"No way," she muttered, angry with herself. Opening the
door, she was immediately greeted by a series of excited
barks, yips and even baying from Tattoo, the lone blood-
hound that was a part of her pack. One by one, she greeted
the dogs, then let them outside for exercise. "You all get another day off," she explained, "except for you," she patted
Atlas's broad head, a huge German shepherd with a head the
size of a bear's. She was rewarded with a nose against her leg
as he begged for more. To the other dogs she warned, "But
look out, cuz tomorrow, we're back to work. Serious work,"
she said, grinning at the animals. "Got it?"

Tattoo gave off a deep bark.

Cissy, an intense border collie whose face was half white
and half black, barely listened. She was focused on stalking
Atlas. The larger dog didn't intimidate her in the least and

now Cissy, eyes trained on Atlas, lay in wait, her body immobile and pressed into the ground as the big dog ignored her and relieved himself on a fence post.

"Sorry, Cissy," Shannon said. "I don't think Atlas 'gets' you. It's a male thing."

The border collie cocked her head as if she was truly understanding, while the others, after running off some energy, swarmed around Shannon's legs. There were only five dogs, aside from Khan, all of which she owned. Usually she had at least twice as many, those she trained and those she boarded, but, over the past three months, in anticipation of moving, she'd whittled down the number of dogs on the premises to those she owned.

As they stretched their legs, rolled in the dry grass and sniffed around the pen, Shannon couldn't help but look over the ruins of the shed, dark and ghastly, an anomaly on this bright day. Who had started the fire that had ruined the shed that held only leftover feed, tack that wasn't used and a few pieces of nearly forgotten equipment? Why?

She glanced to the paddock where the horses were grazing and noticed Molly, nose to tail with a dappled gelding. Both horses' tails were switching, their ears in constant movement as they swished at bothersome flies.

Who was the culprit who had set the shed afire, then waited to assault her? Remembering the attack, she tensed, feeling the man's strength, sensing his rage.

She bit her lip and her eyes narrowed thoughtfully. If her assailant had wanted to kill her, it would have been a simple matter of shooting her while she was trying to set the horses free. If the would-be assassin had been worried about noise, the gun could have been silenced. Or he could have jumped her and slit her throat, or used the pitchfork to impale her rather than beat her senseless.

No, killing hadn't been his motive.

Otherwise he would have torched the house, not the shed. Whoever he was, he'd wanted her to be afraid, to know that he had some kind of power over her, enough power to steal her only child and taunt her with the fact that he'd kidnapped her.

So it has to be someone who knows how important the child was to you, how difficult it was to give up the baby. A relative? A friend? Confidante?

It wasn't as if she'd kept her pregnancy a secret. A lot of people in this small community had known.

So what does kidnapping Dani Settler have to do with Mary Beth's death? Shannon asked herself. Why had the bastard gone to such great lengths to spare her, but then make certain Mary Beth died? Horribly.

Shannon stared at the debris that had been her shed, the yellow tape now flapping in a slight breeze that had kicked up the dust and blown a few dry leaves across the field. She leaned against the top rail of the fence. Her thoughts, as they had all night, turned to Mary Beth. Shannon found it incomprehensible that her sister-in-law was dead.

Atlas came up and nuzzled her leg. Patting his wide head, she managed a smile. He was her best tracking dog. Confident but not aggressive, social but not to the exclusion of listening to commands, Atlas had the intelligence and nose to be an excellent search and rescue dog as well as a tracker. "Good boy," she said, rubbing him behind the ears. "We'll work together later. I promise." His long tail wagged.

She glanced up at the sun, stealing upward in the morning sky, already promising the day would be another scorcher. She felt disjointed and achy, but she toughed it out, didn't want to be groggy or distracted when Settler appeared.

She kenneled the dogs. As she was heading back to the house she heard the phone ring. Jogging as fast as her injuries would allow, she made it into the kitchen by the fourth ring, picked up, and shouted over the prerecorded message on her answering machine, "I'm here. Just give me a sec." She managed to disengage the recorder as she read the caller ID message. It was Shea. "Hey," she said, bracing herself against the counter. "What's up?"

"A lot," Shea said. Shannon could hear the strain in his voice. "First off, it looks like Mary Beth was murdered."

Travis had told her as much but she started shaking inside anew. "It's just so hard to believe."

"Because I'm family, it was suggested strongly that I relinquish the investigation to someone else. You'll probably get a call from Nadine Ignacio, she's been my second in command and she'll do a good job."

"You're being relieved of your duties?"

"No one's saying that," he said, sounding faintly bitter. "I'm still the chief investigator, but I'm just to steer clear of anything to do with fires that involve my family members including the one at your house. It's a conflict of interest."

"This gets worse by the second."

"I was told it was to protect me."

"You believe that?"

"Not for a second, but there it is," he said flatly. "So, you'll probably get more questions from the arson squad, as well as from Nadine and now, probably, someone from homicide, probably Detective Paterno."

"Who's he?"

"He's been with the San Francisco PD for years. A homicide inspector who was involved in that Cahill case that was in the papers a few years back."

"I don't remember it."

"Well, it made a splash, a socialite with amnesia. Anyway, it put Paterno in the limelight and he apparently didn't like it. Moved to Santa Lucia about eighteen months ago. All I know about him is that he's good at his job. Plays straight. You can trust him."

"Why wouldn't I?" she asked, suddenly realizing that Shea was warning her.

"Because the questions might get a little sticky, Shannon. I've spent the last hour with Paterno and he's not only interested in the fire at Robert's house but also the one at yours, the fact that Travis Settler's daughter is missing, and he's even dredging up the old Stealth Torcher thing and Ryan's death."

Shea's worry was contagious; she felt a jolt of concern race through her blood. "The Stealth Torcher? Why?"

"I don't know. He's probably just getting himself up to speed. Being thorough."

But she heard the hesitation in her brother's voice. "There's something you're not telling me," she charged.

"Look, really, I can't discuss the investigation with you or anyone else," he snapped, his frayed nerves finally giving way. "I just wanted to give you a heads-up on what's going on."

She wanted to argue but knew it would be useless; Shea wouldn't be budged. She changed the subject. "Have you seen Robert? How's he holding up?"

"About as bad as can be expected. He's eating himself up with guilt. It looks like he was the last one to see Mary Beth alive and, given that their fight outside El Ranchito was witnessed by all of us: Settler, Liam and the manager of the motel . . ."

"He's a suspect." Of course he was—the estranged husband involved with another woman, a man who wanted a divorce from a clinging wife who was fighting him.

"Yeah, but he isn't alone. Quite a few people didn't get along with Mary Beth."

"Not getting along isn't exactly motive for murder," Shannon said, wondering where this was leading.

"So when's the last time you talked to Mary Beth?"

"Me?" Shannon asked, surprised.

"Yeah, you . . . Paterno will ask, just like he'll ask all of us."

"Well, of course I saw her in the parking lot, and then later she called me after I got home." Shannon remembered the phone call. "She sounded as if she'd been drinking and she wasn't making much sense. She was still mad at Robert. I gathered he'd dumped her off, then split. Anyway, she was complaining and looking for him again. You know, the usual stuff."

"She didn't say anything weird?"

"It was all weird, Shea."

"But *she* called *you*, right?"

"Isn't that what I said?"

"I just wondered if you called her."

"No. Why would I?" Shannon said. "But it was odd because she said I'd phoned her and that she was calling me back. I said she was wrong and she got all belligerent, said something ridiculous like she had my number on caller ID or something. I figured she'd just had too much to drink. Why?"

"You're sure about all this?"

"Of course I'm sure, Shea! *She* called *me*," Shannon insisted. When Shea didn't respond, she sensed, again, there was something more he wasn't telling her. Something vital. Maybe even something damning. "What is this? You don't believe me? Check her phone records."

"We are."

"Good!" She pushed herself away from the cabinets, tossing the remains of her coffee down the sink. "That should settle everything." Deciding the conversation was going nowhere, she changed the subject again. "Has anyone else talked to Mom?"

"Oliver stayed with her last night and I stopped by this morning. I don't know if Robert or Aaron have seen her."

"I'll call."

"That would be good." She heard other muted voices, apparently Shea was no longer alone. "What? Yeah. Just a sec," he said, his voice muffled, then he turned his attention back to her. "Look, Shan, I gotta go now. We'll talk later." He hung up before she could say good-bye, but that wasn't unusual. Shea's brain was always two steps ahead of his body.

She hung up, feeling cold from the inside out. Although the temperature was already over eighty, she felt as if her blood was slowly but surely turning to ice.

"Stop it," she told herself sternly, and as she did she heard the sound of a truck's engine rumbling up the drive. Within seconds Travis Settler's pickup rolled into view.

Chapter 18

The Beast was back!

Dani's heart flew to her throat. So engrossed was she in pulling out the darn nail, she hadn't heard his truck arrive. Since he hadn't come back last night, she figured she had the day to herself. Now his boots were clomping on the creaky floorboards of the porch.

She tossed her dirty clothes over the nail, then vaulted from the closet onto her bed. Her heart pounded as she heard the locks click and the door unlatch.

Heavy footsteps pounded through the cabin.

She swallowed hard as she realized she'd left the door to the closet open. But it was too late to do anything about it.

Half a heartbeat later the door to her room opened with enough force to bang against the wall. Terrified, she stared up at him and knew something had happened.

Something bad.

His usual cool was gone, his hair was uncombed, the pupils of his eyes were pinpricks, and there was a desperation to him that scared her to her bones. She hoped to God he wouldn't walk into the closet, see that the nail head was over half an inch above the board.

Looming over the bed, he was sweating, dusty and breathing hard. It was almost as if there was an electric current running through him. "Get up!" he ordered. He jerked a hand to the living area and didn't so much as glance at the open closet. "Let's go."

"Where?"

"In there." There was the hint of a tic over his eye and she didn't argue, though she wondered what had happened. The sun had been up for several hours, the cabin was already warm and he hadn't returned all night, which was odd, different from his usual pattern.

She walked into the living area, a room he usually forced her through at a quick pace.

"Sit," he said, pointing to the broken hearth. "And don't try any funny stuff."

He started building a fire and she knew then that he was over the edge. The room was already hot, but he lit the stacked paper, kindling and chunks of wood anyway, rocking back on his heels and grunting in satisfaction when the flames began crackling and growing, burning bright.

For the first time she got a closer look at the pictures on the mantel. She'd been allowed through this room before, but always only as she was being shepherded outside. Now she saw that there were six pictures, all of them looking as if they'd been taken long ago. Four of the pictures were head shots of serious young men who all had similar traits: shiny black hair, intense, don't-mess-with-me blue eyes and thin lips. Another picture was a snapshot of a couple on their wedding day, the woman wearing a long white gown and a wedding veil, the man in a tuxedo. He could have been one of the guys in the head shots, taken at a different time. The final picture was of a woman, just her face, and Dani felt her heart tighten. She had reddish brown hair, big green eyes and a smile that showed off just a bit of her teeth. Her expression looked as if she was in on a private joke as she tilted her ear, leaning it upon one hand, her fingers buried in the riot of auburn curls.

"Who are those people?" she asked, her mind snapping with questions.

He didn't respond.

"They're all related, aren't they? Brothers?"

He'd been kneeling, staring at the fire, but now his head whipped around fast, as if he'd forgotten she was there, forgotten she was close enough to the pictures to make them out. He scowled. "You ask too many questions."

"Who are they?" she asked again.

"Shut up." He rose quickly and reached onto the mantel. For a second Dani thought he was going to burn the pictures, frames and all, but instead he merely replaced his small torch, then from his pocket he pulled out a miniature recorder and a piece of folded, lined paper. The paper's edge was frayed as if it had come from a tiny spiral notebook. A message was scrawled upon the single sheet.

He squatted next to her and placed the recorder close enough to her mouth that it would certainly pick up anything she might say. "Read," he instructed.

Dani looked at the words written in bold block letters:

MOMMY, HELP ME. PLEASE, MOMMY. I'M SCARED. COME AND GET ME. I DON'T KNOW WHERE I AM AND I THINK HE'S GOING TO HURT ME. PLEASE, MOMMY. HURRY.

Instead of saying the words, she turned her head to look at him. She could smell the scents of smoke and body odor upon him. "My mother is dead," she whispered. She felt a deep ache within her as she thought of Ella Settler, the mother who had been so overprotective, who had made her suffer through Sunday school, who had worked with her doing math and history nearly every night before bed, who had abided no sass. Dani bit the insides of her cheeks to keep her lips from shaking as she remembered how she'd fought her mother's strict sense of right and wrong. Maybe that's why the God Ella had so firmly believed in had taken her mother away. To punish her. Maybe the reason that she had ended up in the hands of this sicko was because she'd been such an ungrateful daughter. She swallowed back the urge to sob and blinked against the hot tears that were touching the back of her eyelids. She couldn't, *wouldn't*, break down in front of this creep.

"Just do it," he growled.

Dani met his gaze. "What're you going to do with this?"

"It doesn't matter."

"I told you, she's dead," Dani said, her voice catching.

"But your birth mother isn't," he snarled and Dani felt as if her heart had just dropped through the rotten floorboards of this forgotten shanty. "Remember, the one you were so hell-bent to find? She's still alive."

"You know where she is?" Dani asked, incredulous. Then she warned herself that this could be another one of the perv's tricks. He couldn't be trusted. Hadn't she found that out about a jillion times over?

All of a sudden she understood. Her gaze flew to the mantel where the picture of the pretty young woman with auburn hair was staring down.

"Figure it out?" he taunted.

Dani shot to her feet. Scooped up the picture and stared down at the woman who, in the shot, couldn't have been much more than twenty. "This is her, isn't it?" Her heart was pounding and she glared down at him. "Where is she? What are you doing to her? Who are all these other pictures of?"

"Just make the recording. That way no one gets hurt."

Dani's fingers gripped the edge of the cheap frame so tightly, the metal cut into her flesh. But she was tired of taking orders, sick of his bullying her around. Her birth mother was nearby! She had to be! That's why Dani had been dragged down here. She stared at the picture of the beautiful woman who had given her life, then given her up. Why? Who was she?

This creep knew.

He'd known all along.

That's how he'd lured her into trusting him, with just enough knowledge to entice her.

"I said make the fuckin' recording and you won't get hurt!"

"Are you threatening me?" she demanded as he ripped the frame from her hands.

"Take it anyway you like. Make the damned recording and you don't get hurt, your mom doesn't get hurt and your dad doesn't get hurt, either."

"My dad? You know where he is?" she demanded.

He didn't respond but the smug smile that pulled at the corners of his thin lips told her all she needed to know.

"Where?"

"Don't even worry about it."

"Where is he?" Then it hit her. "You mean my biological father. Right? I'm talking about my adoptive dad, *he's* my real dad. Travis Settler. That other guy . . . He doesn't count."

Something in his eyes flashed for an instant and his nostrils seemed to flare just a bit. "I don't care who does or doesn't 'count.' Make the recording. You've got five minutes." He looked at his watch, then pulled a big hunting knife from the back of the mantel. Slowly he unsheathed the blade and Dani thought of the big garbage bag that had dripped blood in the dirty white van with the out-of-state plates, the van that he'd first dragged her into and was now parked with the bag and its grotesque contents rotting in the garage somewhere in Idaho.

What good would it do to get herself killed now?

What good would it do to refuse him?

Maybe her natural mother was really, really rich and the recording was some kind of ransom demand.

She took the recorder from him and tried to come up with a subversive way to tell whoever received this tape her location, but she didn't know where she was. This was all happening too quickly. She didn't have time to come up with a signal, or some kind of secret message to let whoever received the tape know anything other than yes, she was alive . . . or had been when the message was recorded.

He stood in front of her, his arms folded over his broad chest, the fingers of his right hand curled over the handle of the knife. There was no way out. She had to do what he wanted.

For now.

Soon she'd escape anyway.

The nail was just about out of the board in the closet.

She clicked on the recorder and as a squirrel scampered over the roof of this dilapidated shack, she started reading. "Mommy, help me. Please, Mommy. I'm scared—"

Angrily he reached forward, snapped off the recorder and rewound the tape in a whir of noise. "Stupid bitch!" His face suffused with color and his laser-blue eyes narrowed on her furiously. "I know you're not that dumb, so no more game playing. Now, do it again and this time, don't just read it like you were in fuckin' English class, okay? Make it sound good. Real. Like you're scared."

"But I don't know how to—"

Suddenly, he bent down, squatting next to her, one arm around her middle, the other with the knife next to her face.

She nearly peed her pants.

His lips so close to her they brushed the shell of her ear, he whispered, "You just need some motivation, a little incentive." The blade pressed against her cheek and it was all she could do not to squeal in fear.

She was quaking, the cool metal of the flat side of the knife pressing against her skin so that she hardly dared draw a breath. Fear slammed through her body and she felt his heat as he pressed his muscular frame against hers. Sweat rose on her skin. Dread curled in her stomach. The fire crackled and popped.

"Okay, now," he suggested, his voice low and nearly sensual as he seemed to have regained some of his calm, "Let's try it again . . ."

* * *

Khan gave a quick bark.

Shannon watched as Travis Settler parked near the garage, then unfolded himself from the cab of the truck. He appeared as intense as he had last night. His features were set and hard, his eyes shaded by aviator sunglasses, his hair less mussed, a few blond strands catching in the sunlight. He wore what looked like the same jeans as the night before, beat-up running shoes, a T-shirt that had seen better days fitting taut across his shoulders, and a take-no-prisoners attitude. He slammed shut the door of his truck and stretched, his T-shirt riding up enough to show off a tanned, flat washboard of an abdomen with a trail of dark hairs disappearing beneath the waistband of his low-slung jeans.

Shannon wrenched her gaze away. She told herself that the sudden heat stealing through her body had more to do with the warm morning than any glimpse of Travis's bare skin.

Muttering at how silly she was, especially given the grim circumstances surrounding her life, she gave herself a swift mental kick, then headed out of the kitchen and away from the window.

Pull yourself together, she silently chided herself as she opened the front door just as he stepped onto the porch.

"Mornin'," he drawled and again her stupid pulse raced.

"Back atcha." She managed a smile and held the door open. Khan shot through and wiggled energetically around Travis's legs.

"Not much of a watchdog," Travis observed.

"Maybe he trusts you."

"Maybe he trusts everyone."

"Nah, Settler, it's just your winning personality. Dogs can sense these things, you know."

His eyes narrowed skeptically. "And dog trainers really know how to peddle BS."

"Sometimes," she admitted, feeling the corners of her lips

twitch a bit. After all the stress of the past few days a little bit of levity helped. "So, before we get started, how about some coffee?"

One side of his mouth quirked up. Khan was still wriggling around his legs. Travis reached down to pat his head. "You must've read my mind."

"Yeah, that's me, the psychic." She led him into the kitchen, plucking mismatched mugs from a cupboard as Khan, glad for company, bounded ahead to survey his empty food dish. She picked up the glass carafe and poured the first cup. "I don't think I have any cream or sugar. At least that's what I 'sense.'"

He chuckled as he set his shaded glasses on the counter. She found herself staring into eyes as blue as a June sky.

"Black's fine."

"Good." Noticing that her hands had begun to sweat, she managed to pour a second cup without spilling and hand him the larger of the mugs. "So have you heard anything new?"

"About Dani?" His smile fell away. The lines of worry that had been momentarily erased returned as deep grooves near his mouth and eyes. "Not a word." He tested his coffee before taking a long swallow and meeting the questions in her eyes. "Well, that's not exactly true. I've talked to the Feds and the locals down here as well as the authorities in Oregon." Frowning into his cup, he shook his head. "But as for anything concrete or new in the case? No. Nothing."

Her heart sank. Even though she'd expected his answer, a small part of her had wished to hear something, any little sliver of hope that might convince her that Dani was alive. Instead she witnessed a deepening sense of despair in Travis's features. Beneath his facade of rugged determination lay both devastation and guilt.

"You'll find her," she said, though she wasn't sure she believed her own words. She just felt that if anyone could locate his daughter, it would be this hard-driven, no-nonsense man with the blade-thin lips, hard jaw and coiled tension evident in the cords of his neck and the way his right hand fisted nervously.

"More ESP?" he asked, raising an eyebrow as he took a long drink and settled both hips against the lower cupboards.

"More like faith."

He snorted. "I could use a tankful of that right about now." Then, as if he'd heard the defeat in his voice, added, "But you're right. I'll find her." He hesitated, looked her straight in the eyes and added with conviction, "Or I'll die trying."

She believed him. "Let's hope it doesn't come to that."

"Amen."

"Have you talked to the police about Mary Beth?"

"Well, since I've been in California, it's more like they talk to me, but, yeah, I had a conversation with a couple of arson dicks this morning."

"Janowitz and Rossi," she guessed. "They interviewed me at the hospital."

"So you haven't met Paterno yet?"

She shook her head.

"You will. I had the pleasure this morning. Paterno's a homicide detective. Since your sister-in-law was killed, this is his baby now and he believes that everything, including the fires and Dani's abduction, is linked."

Her stomach clenched. "Do they know how?"

He lifted one shoulder. "My guess is they'll start looking at you. You're the obvious connection."

She'd been lifting the mug to her lips again, but her hand stopped its upward movement in midair. "I don't know what happened to her."

"Then we'll have to figure it out, won't we?" His gaze lost its hard edge and for the first time since meeting him, she felt that they had a chance of being on the same side.

"Yeah," she said, "we'll have to try real hard."

"Then let's get to it. We'll start with your dogs." He finished the rest of his coffee in one swallow and she left the remains of hers on the counter.

Outside the day was already sweltering, the barest of breezes rustling through the dry leaves still clinging to the branches, shafts of sunlight dappling the ground. What was left of the shed scarred the landscape, the blackened rubble having dried out with the heat of the last few days, one end of the yellow crime scene tape catching in the breeze to wave tiredly.

Travis surveyed the grounds. "You know, whoever set that fire could have done it just as easily in the kennels, or the stable or your house."

"I know. I've thought of that. The animals would have put up some kind of noise, though."

"My guess is that he would have found a way around that. He managed to skulk around here without much trouble."

"Like you."

Travis shook his head. "I never got close to the house."

"But he did," she thought aloud, remembering that horrible night and feeling her skin crawl all over again. She caught Travis staring at her, and saw her own distorted reflection in his mirrored lenses. "And that wouldn't be easy." To underscore her point, she opened the door of the kennels and was greeted by a cacophony of barks, yips and bays. "The natives are restless," she said. "Even though they've already been fed, watered and exercised. You'll all just have to wait and then I'll let you out again," she said to the eager animals, rubbing each dog's head as she passed.

When she was in a serious training mode, especially with other people's canines, she took each dog out one at a time and exercised him, then worked with the animal before going through the same routine with the next one. Only after each dog had gone through his or her lessons for the day would she let them join each other in a free-for-all play that a few trainers discouraged. She, on the other hand, believed that dogs, as pack animals, functioned better if they socialized. Business was business, of course, but play was play. And important. This morning, after she was finished working with Atlas, she would let them run, sniff, pee and cavort at will again. Just as she had earlier.

"Only five?" he asked.

"Six, counting Khan. But yeah, I'm not boarding any dogs right now. These are all my own."

"But they don't have the elevated status of living in the main house?"

"Not all the time. I take turns. But each of these guys . . . oh, and gals, sorry, Cissy," she said, scratching her border collie's shoulders. "They were all raised as puppies in the house. As I said they all come in from time to time, but it gets to be a little much," she said and glanced at Khan. "He, of course, is spoiled horribly. I call him 'the chosen one' and he acts like it." She petted Khan's head and he immediately licked her palm. "See what a charmer he is?" To the dog, she said, "You're really workin' it today, aren't ya?"

Khan wagged his tail as if he understood.

"A dog has to earn the right to sleep in my bedroom."

Travis eyed her. "Khan sleeps with you?"

"Most of the time. Yeah. He's supposed to stay in *his* bed, which I've got under the window in my room, but more often than not, in the middle of the night he slinks onto the covers of *my* bed and I'm usually too tired to argue. The worst of it is, he likes the middle of the bed, so I wake up on the edge, don't I?" she asked and petted him again. Straightening, she glanced at Travis. "That a problem?"

"I guess not, but . . ."

"But what?" she asked, reaching for a leash.

"I was just thinking that a dog in the bed might not be welcome if . . ."

"If what? I want to watch television or . . . Oh, you mean if I have company?" she asked, surprised at the intimacy of the question. "You get right to it, don't you?"

"It just crossed my mind."

She lifted a shoulder. "I guess I'll cross that bridge when I come to it." She snapped the leash onto Atlas's collar, then reached into a locker in the kennel where she'd placed the plastic bag containing Dani's sweatshirt. "Come on, boy," she said to the dog, then, glancing up at Travis, explained, "Atlas is my best tracking dog. So if there's anything here, if Dani's been nearby, he should be able to pick up her scent. But I've got to warn you it's not likely." She led the dog outside. "First, we both know there's a very small chance that whoever has Dani brought her here. So that's strike one. Secondly the area around my house has been contaminated with people, fire and tons of water. And thirdly, it's been several days since we think the perpetrator was on the premises . . . and he's not Dani. I don't think that regular search and rescue guidelines would work here, but we'll try tracking. I'm just saying you shouldn't get your hopes up."

"It's all I've got right now."

Shannon put on a pair of gloves, then, trying to stay clinical and shoving her emotions into a back corner of her brain, she removed her daughter's sweatshirt from the plastic bag. Her heart ached as she let her dog sniff the clothing, and she silently prayed that Atlas would be able to come up with something.

*Any*thing.

Some minuscule shred of hope.

Beside her, Travis tensed.

She gave the dog the command—"Find!"—and Atlas took off, nose to the ground, circling the area, moving quickly, lifting his head only to breathe.

"How will you know if he's caught her scent?" Travis asked.

"He'll let me know," she said, but as she followed and watched Atlas move around the buildings and fields, she feared that the tracking was an exercise in futility.

The shepherd tried.

Atlas circled the kennels, garage, house, stable and burned shed. He slunk, nose to the ground, down the driveway, but never once did he return to Shannon and bark, nor did he indicate that he'd picked up Dani's scent.

He crisscrossed, doubled back, searching an ever-widening

area. Across the paddocks and dry fields, through the woods, along a deer trail, under a fence and into the surrounding fields including the area that was posted with a huge NO TRESPASSING sign, warning that violators would be prosecuted. This very field, where Travis had stood and stared through his night vision goggles at Shannon's house, was slated for development.

But it was useless.

There was just no scent for the dog to follow.

"No go," Travis said after nearly two hours of studying the dog's movements through sunlight and shadow.

He rubbed the back of his neck and sighed in bitter acceptance. "One more brick wall."

"I was afraid of this," Shannon agreed. She was sweating and the pain in her shoulder had increased with the sun's climb in the sky. She patted the German shepherd, told him how great he was and plucked a few burs and grass seeds from his thick coat before giving him a long drink of water from a hose she had connected to the horse trough and a big metal pan. Once the dog had drunk his fill, and with Travis beside her, Shannon returned Atlas to his kennel.

"We knew it was a long shot," she said, but couldn't quell her own sense of despair. Things were spinning out of control, going from bad to worse and they both knew that with each minute that passed, the chances of finding the girl diminished.

"Thanks for trying," he said and when she tried to hand him back the sweatshirt, added, "Keep it. For now. We might get another chance if something breaks."

Her throat tightened. What other chance? she thought, but held her tongue and nodded. "Okay."

"I'll be in touch . . . You sure you don't need a ride to get your truck?"

"I don't think so. Oliver is supposed to be delivering it."

"The priest?"

"Almost a priest," she clarified as swallows swooped near the roof of the stable. "He hasn't taken his final vows yet." Seeing the question in his eyes, she said, "I don't know why he volunteered to bring the truck back, but I imagine Shea's tied up in the investigation, Robert's a mess with Mary Beth's death and Aaron . . . Who knows?"

"If you're sure."

She managed a smile. "I've got your number if I need help, but I doubt it. If all else fails, Nate should be back sometime." She slid a look at the garage and felt a frisson of concern.

Travis followed her gaze. "Where is he?"

"Beats me." She almost confided in him, told him her worries, but there was something in the way he asked the question that caused her to hold her tongue. After all, hadn't Travis Settler come down here thinking she'd kidnapped his daughter? Hadn't he been spying on her just the other night? Though she was starting to feel a kinship with the man, she silently warned herself to tread carefully. "I guess I'll find out when he shows up." She forced a smile that she was certain Settler could see right through.

"Okay, I'll let you know if I learn anything else." He lifted a hand toward the kennels. "And thanks for trying to help me locate Dani."

"Anytime," she said. *She's my daughter, too.* But she didn't say the words. She didn't need to. They both were more than cognizant of the reason Settler had come to Santa Lucia in the first place.

"Let me know if you hear anything."

"It's a deal."

For a second he hesitated and, through the dark glasses, gave her a look that touched a forbidden part of her, searched deep into her soul. She had the sensation that he wanted to kiss her, that only his own reservations, his doubts about her, held him back.

Which was just as well because she had no idea what

she'd do if he reached for her and pulled her tight against him. The thought of it alone made her blood run hotter than it should, and she silently blistered herself with recriminations. So he'd looked at her. So what?

Dear God, Travis Settler was not a man to be fantasizing about. In fact, she thought, standing in the parking lot and staring into the wake of dust his truck left behind, he was probably the last man on earth she should be attracted to. The very last.

Chapter 19

Anthony Paterno drummed his fingers and stared at the notes he'd taken. Five pages of his thoughts were spread across the top of his desk in the Santa Lucia Police Department and he was trying to connect the dots, however frail, between them. The door to his office was ajar and he heard the noises he'd grown accustomed to: the ringing phones, buzz of conversations, kerchunk of printers and occasional burst of laughter over the steady rattle of the overworked and failing air-conditioning system.

The squat brick building was nearly eighty years old, and though it had suffered through several renovations, none had really improved it, Paterno thought with an eye to aesthetics. Function over form, that was the motto of whomever had designed the ugly stucco wings that sprang from either side of the original edifice.

The climate ran hot in this section of the wine country, which was decidedly inland from San Francisco, the place he'd called home for years. No views of the bay nor the

Pacific Ocean, just rolling hills covered with vineyards between clusters of towns that catered to tourists. Pretty country. But warmer than he liked. Adjusting his internal thermometer had taken some time, and he found himself constantly relying on air-conditioning in his car as well as in his apartment and the office. This summer had been the worst, hotter than it had been in nearly three years, the heat never letting up, the temperature, even at night, rarely dipping below eighty.

Water reservoir levels were dwindling, brownouts from the overuse of energy for cooling were common, and the threat of fire was ever-present—the bleached grass fields and arid forests ready, with the aid of a small spark, to burst into flame.

He was often uncomfortable and supposed that dropping fifteen pounds would help, but so far he hadn't so much as lost an ounce, hadn't stepped foot inside the gym here at the station nor at his apartment complex.

Yanking at his tie, he leaned back in his chair, the facts of Mary Beth Flannery's death running through his mind in a continuous loop. It was how he worked. A puzzling case like this one would get under his skin, and he thought of little else, day and night. The cut-and-dried ones didn't create the same itch in him, the same need to outwit the killer, the race against time to stop the murderer from striking again.

Because that's what Paterno thought they had here— someone not only out for blood but something else as well. The guy was playing a game, intentionally leaving clues, taunting the police and hoping to strike fear in those who were still alive.

Why else take the time to scrawl the weird symbol on the mirror in lipstick?

Why else leave a backpack with the identical drawing?

Why else make a point to let the police and everyone involved know that the kidnapping of Dani Settler was connected to Mary Beth Flannery's death?

He glanced at one page of his notes, the ones dedicated to the victim.

Mary Beth Flannery had been thirty-three, a mother of two, and, if gossip was right, soon to be divorced from her husband, Robert Flannery, a firefighter. There was a sizable life insurance policy on her, nearly half a million dollars. But she was balking at divorce, so her death would both free Flannery of his marriage and put a lot of money into his pockets.

And Robert Flannery was in financial trouble. The family house had a first, second and third mortgage on it. Any bit of equity in the small ranch house had been already taken from it. Then there was the credit card debt and a brand new leased BMW.

Robert Flannery had plenty of motive to kill his wife, but why go to all the trouble of such an elaborate, staged killing? That part didn't fit. Unless he was trying to throw the police off and knew enough to make it look like this killing was connected to the burned birth certificate left at his sister's house. But Paterno didn't think Robert had the brains, time, or wherewithal to kidnap the kid. He might be an opportunist taking advantage of an ongoing investigation, trying to muddy the waters after learning that the girl had been kidnapped. But Paterno didn't think that, either.

Robert Flannery struck him as impulsive—a risk-taker, but not a plotter. He may have wanted his wife dead, but he would be the kind of guy who hired someone to do it. Or he might stage an accident himself, but not this bizarre, almost ritualistic act. Paterno felt this was outside the scope of the man's imagination.

So who?

Paterno drummed his fingers some more and frowned.

There were others who probably would have liked to have seen Mary Beth out of the way including Cynthia Tallericco, Robert's mistress, but again, why the over-the-top killing? The planning? The linking to Dani Settler's disappearance?

The interesting part was that Tallericco had been instrumental in helping to put the girl up for adoption.

Coincidence?

Paterno didn't put much stock in coincidence. In fact, he didn't much believe there was such a thing.

Why would Cynthia Tallericco, or anyone, for that matter, draw the symbol on the mirror? Or on the backpack?

After searching the premises, the police had found the backpack left near the sink. It had been singed but had remained intact, so it must have been sprayed with some kind of retardant.

Upon questioning, Robert Flannery had insisted that the backpack didn't belong to either of his kids or any of their friends, but Paterno wondered if the firefighter would even know. School had barely started and Flannery had been pretty involved with his new girlfriend. Chances were he was ignoring his kids as well as his wife while the affair was heating up.

However, the backpack and symbols didn't seem to fit with Robert Flannery unless they were elaborate smoke screens. But Paterno didn't buy it. No, the backpack and scrawled images were the killer's doing, and that killer wasn't Robert Flannery.

So what did he know?

First, Mary Beth had been strangled. There had been water in her lungs, but not enough to drown her, and the bruising around her neck indicated someone had cut off her air supply with his hands. True, her husband Robert had alledgedly been the last person to see her alive, but he had an alibi, the Tallericco woman, and Paterno believed they really had been together.

Second, Mary Beth's place had been torched, with clues intentionally left at the scene.

Third, a search of her phone records revealed that Mary Beth had spoken to her brother Liam and Shannon Flannery within the hour before the fire had been called in.

Fourth, her kids were conveniently spending the night with Mary Beth's sister, Margaret.

He decided to check with all of Mary Beth's family and friends again. Officers were already canvassing the neighborhood, talking to people who lived nearby, looking for anything out of the ordinary on the night of her death.

Her family had called the police station repeatedly. And the press didn't seem satisfied by the answers they'd gotten from the information officer. But they would all just have to wait.

Paterno's chair squeaked as he got to his feet. He leaned over his desk again, his eyes drawn to the weird symbols that were left at two of the scenes. The first was an odd diamond-like shape missing a point. In the middle of the shape was the number six. Or, he supposed, nine, if he turned the shape upside down.

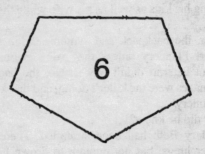

The second symbol was obviously part of a five-pointed star with one point missing. In the lower left-hand corner, there was a blank space, no point, but the number five had been written, boldly drawn. The lower right-hand point was visible, but it had been drawn with a broken line while the rest of the star was in strong, bold strokes. The number two, also written in a broken line, was situated in the middle of the lower right-hand point.

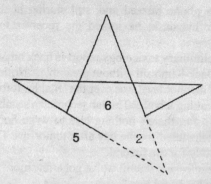

Paterno stared at the drawings and frowned. If he lifted the first image and placed it over the second, it fit perfectly, the number six in the center of the fractured star. Not nine, but six, so that all of the numbers were situated right-side up.

What the hell was the murderer trying to convey?

He picked up his cup of coffee. It was cold, but he downed it anyway, crushed the paper cup, then tossed it into his waste-basket under the desk. Who was this guy? What was his game?

His gaze moved to the next sheet of paper: his notes on Shannon Flannery. She, he was certain, was at the center of whatever was going on. He was aware that the kid she'd given up for adoption thirteen years earlier, Dani Settler, was missing. A piece of the kid's birth certificate had been par-tially burned and left at Shannon's home and not too long after, a fire started on her property. In both cases the symbol for the center of the star had been left.

Was she number six? What did that mean?

Whatever was going on had to do with Shannon Flannery.

And had to do with fire. Why else bother to char the birth certificate, or burn down Shannon Flannery's shed, or take the trouble to set fire to the bathroom where Mary Beth, ac-cording to preliminary reports, was already dead, the result of strangling?

Paterno's phone buzzed and, still staring at the papers strewn over his desk, he jerked the receiver to his ear. "Paterno."

"The preliminary toxicology report is back on Mary Beth Flannery," Jack Kim said without preamble. "Nothing unexpected. Her alcohol level was over the legal limit for driving, but not for taking a bath." The lab technician's stab at a joke fell flat. "So far, there's nothing else to write home about. Autopsy's scheduled for the day after tomorrow. The family wants the body for the funeral."

"I'm not releasing it until we've got a few more answers."

"That's what I told 'em."

"Good." That was always the trouble with victims' families. They wanted answers, the criminal brought to justice, but they also were in a hurried-up rush to put their beloved's body into the ground. Paterno hung up and scooped up his page of notes on Shannon Flannery. He was still waiting to get the case records surrounding her husband's death three years earlier, and when he did, he planned to go over them with a fine-toothed comb, then go over them again. Something about the woman didn't wash. Too many people who'd been close to her had seemed to die or fall off the face of the earth. Where the hell was the father of her child, Brendan Giles? And what happened to her brother Neville? He fleetingly wondered if they'd met some sort of violent end, just like her estranged husband. According to witnesses, the last time anyone had seen Neville Flannery had been barely three weeks after the murder of Ryan Carlyle. He'd quit his job, started acting strangely and then . . . just disappeared.

Unlikely.

Paterno made a note to find out more about Shannon's missing brother. People didn't just up and vanish. Something didn't fit.

So what was it?

He reconstructed what he knew about the murder of Ryan Carlyle and Shannon's subsequent arraignment. The evidence was circumstantial at best, but the DA seemed to have a hard-on for nailing her.

The prosecution's case had been pretty basic. Shannon Flannery's husband had beaten her. There were hospital records of her injuries sustained on two separate occasions. The first time she'd insisted she'd fallen in the horse barn; the second she hadn't tried to hide the fact that he'd struck her hard enough to crack her jaw. She'd filed charges, but he'd gotten out on bail, only to go after her again. That time she miscarried. She managed to get a restraining order against him and was heading for divorce. Before that could happen he violated the court order, refusing to be cast out of his own home.

But she'd been waiting for him, almost as if she'd expected him to show up, and she'd set a trap. With the aid of her brother Aaron, she'd installed a video-and-audio system to capture Carlyle on tape while breaking the law.

Almost on cue the stupid son of a bitch had shown up and started in on her. In Carlyle's rage he'd discovered the video equipment and smashed it into a million pieces.

She'd ended up in the hospital again.

A week to the day after she'd been released, Ryan Carlyle's body had been found, nearly charred beyond recognition. He'd died in a forest fire, which was started, the defense had insisted, either by Carlyle himself, a known fire bug, or by careless campers who had left their fire untended. The tinder-dry forest must have caught fire just as the wind had shifted and Carlyle had been trapped in a canyon surrounded by flames. Two thousand acres of national forest had been burned to cinders. As had Ryan Carlyle.

No physical evidence had directly linked Shannon to the fire.

Though she hadn't had an alibi (she said she had been home alone with her dogs at the time), the defense had cast enough reasonable doubt into the prosecution's theory that Shannon Flannery Carlyle had walked. Or skated, depending upon your viewpoint.

Ryan Carlyle's family, including his cousin Mary Beth, had been up in arms at the outcome of the trial. The press had a field day. Speculation ran hot on whether Shannon Flannery had literally gotten away with murder.

No one, it seemed, felt that justice had been served.

Paterno mopped at his brow and noted that the temperature in his office was over eighty, though the air conditioner rumbled and wheezed, the fan blowing the papers on his desk.

Stretching, he walked to the window where, from the second story, he could look down at the sidewalk below. Pedestrians strolled, pigeons flapped and tiny pieces of glass within the concrete reflected the sun's intense rays. There was a moratorium on all exterior watering and the trees lining the street looked withered, their yellowing leaves hanging limply from near-naked branches. Heat jiggled in waves as he gazed up the street at the cars, vans and trucks moving through the traffic lights, their images distorted and shimmering.

He wasn't convinced either way of Shannon Flannery's guilt or innocence, but he intended to sift through all the evidence once the old boxes of files were brought up from the warehouse where they'd been sealed for the past three years. Maybe then he'd be able to make his own determination.

Not certain what he expected to find in those documents, he hoped there was something that would help him figure out what was going on today. Why did it seem that everyone around Shannon Flannery either disappeared or died? Where the hell was the father of the child she'd put up for adoption? Brendan Giles's family still resided somewhere around here . . . maybe Santa Rosa.

Paterno made a note to contact anyone who knew Giles and find out what the hell had happened to him. As he already had about Neville the brother who had, after Ryan's death, disappeared. Another one who had done a major vanishing act. Without a damned trace. Had Neville been involved in Carlyle's murder? Was he guilty and running from the law? Or had he been silenced, his body dumped? Maybe somewhere in the forested hills or deep in the Pacific Ocean, which was only a couple of hours west.

He would take a second look at the other brothers, too. Though Paterno felt Robert was innocent, he didn't completely scratch him off the list yet. He had motive and opportunity. As for Shea Flannery, the guy was all right, but he was secretive and nervous. Paterno didn't like him, was glad to relieve him of his duty for a while. That left Aaron, who was now a PI because he'd gotten himself kicked out of the fire department. Why? He circled Aaron's name, decided to do some digging into his past.

Then there was the one about to become a priest, Oliver, who had been in a mental institution, not once but twice. Why in the world would the church take someone into the priesthood who was so obviously unstable? Even though the Catholic clergy was in trouble these days, it didn't make sense that they were scraping the bottom of the barrel so deeply that they had to take nutcases into the priesthood.

Oliver had not only tried to slit his wrists as a child, but had become completely undone after the discovery of Ryan Carlyle's body. He'd grown silent, nearly a recluse, and had ended up in the loony bin for several weeks. Then he received "the calling."

Sure.

Another question mark. Another person who had to be interviewed.

Along with Shannon Flannery, her brothers and Mary Beth's family.

Restless, Paterno tried to open the window, but it was painted shut. Frustrated, he leaned against the window ledge and tried to imagine what Mary Beth Flannery's death had to do with a little girl who had been kidnapped in Oregon.

The girl Shannon Flannery had given up for adoption.

It was all tied together, he just had to figure out how. And he would, he decided.

Stretching one arm over his head he heard his spine pop

from too many hours seated at his desk, too many long minutes held in one position while the wheels of his mind turned.

What he did know was that the fires that had been ravaging the area three years earlier, all started by an unknown arsonist the papers had dubbed the Stealth Torcher, had stopped with the death of Carlyle. Seven buildings set on fire. One death. Paterno checked his notes—a thirty-two-year-old woman by the name of Dolores Galvez.

The phone rang and he scowled. He didn't want to be disturbed as he tried to work things out. Yanking the receiver to his ear, he bit out, "Paterno."

"Hey, Tony, guess what?" Ray Rossi asked. "Those prints taken off the backpack? We got a hit from NCIS."

"Let me guess. They belong to Travis Settler."

"Bingo," Rossi said. "Give the man a prize."

"Anything else?"

"Nothing that matched. We figured the other prints were probably the kid's."

"Probably," Paterno said. "I'll talk to him."

Her truck slid to a stop in front of the garage.

Shannon, who had been at her desk, sorting through bills, heard the engine and flew out the door as Oliver, dressed in slacks and a golf shirt, hopped out of the cab. Khan was beside himself with excitement and ran up to be petted.

"Sorry it took so long," her brother said. "I had a little trouble getting Mother motivated."

"Mom?"

"She's on her way." He picked up a stick from the yard and threw it, spinning it end to end across the gravel lot. Khan was after it like a shot. "I needed a way back into town," Oliver explained.

"I would have taken you."

"Mom wouldn't hear of it. Oh, wow . . ." Squinting, he

gazed at the shed and exhaled on a long sigh. "Intentional, I heard."

"Yeah." She heard the purr of her mother's tank of a Buick approaching. Bracing herself for another scene, she watched as Maureen O'Malley Flannery, her bright red hair looking as if she'd just walked out of the beauty parlor, herded her car to a stop not far from Shannon's truck.

Great, Shannon thought, knowing that the visit wouldn't go all that well.

She wasn't wrong.

As she ushered her mother past the rubble and into the kitchen, she heard all about "poor Mary Beth" and "I can't imagine what your brother's been thinking" and "Have you seen the doctor again? How're you feeling?" Shannon offered instant coffee and Maureen gave her a look.

"At this time of day?" she asked. "I think I'd rather have some iced tea, if it's not too much trouble." She took a seat at the round café table.

Quickly Shannon scooped up her bills and calculator, placing them onto a corner of the counter before her mother caught a glimpse of Shannon's finances. It wasn't that she had anything to hide so much as she didn't want her mother worrying, fretting, and asking about her current Visa card balance or mortgage payment.

"I just don't understand it," Maureen started as Oliver, insisting Shannon take it easy and sit at the table across from their mother, found the instant iced tea and began whipping up a glass. "Why would anyone want to harm Mary Beth? And those poor children."

Oliver, ever dutiful, deposited the glass in front of her, but she barely noticed.

"I tell you it's the Flannery curse," Maureen insisted, dabbing at her eyes with a napkin from the holder on the small table.

"You said so last night."

"Well, it's true!" Maureen snapped.

She was known for her will of iron. Her friends had marveled at how she'd handled her strapping, big, hellions of sons and yet Shannon knew that her mother had her own secrets, her own demons to deal with. This morning she was on a roll, taking up where she'd left off the night before.

"If it weren't for bad luck we'd have no luck at all," she said, sniffing.

That had been her personal mantra for as long as Shannon could remember.

"It killed your father, you know. Not just you getting pregnant or all that mess with Ryan. The assault charges, the restraining order, the accusations about that stupid Stealth Torcher, the damned murder, and Neville . . . sweet Neville . . . oh, dear God . . ."

She stopped to cross herself and Oliver placed a hand upon her shoulder as his eyes met those of his sister. They didn't have to say a word, just silently acknowledged that this woman was their mother and she wasn't going to wind down until she was good and ready.

Caught up in her own theatrics, Maureen started to quietly sob. Shannon, despite knowing better, felt sorry for her.

"Not to mention Aaron being kicked off the fire department and now . . . Now the fires have started and Mary Beth is dead. Think of poor little Elizabeth and RJ. What will they do without a mother?"

"I don't know, Mom, but Robert will take care of them."

"I pray that he does." She took in a tremulous breath. "He's been so . . . distracted lately."

"He'll be there for his children," Oliver said. He stood with his hips resting against a cabinet, his fingers curled over the lip of the counter.

"That horrible fire. What else could it be but a curse?"

"Mother," Oliver quietly reproached.

Shannon's headache thundered back with a vengeance. Maybe she needed those painkillers after all.

"And what about the fire here, Shannon? Look at you! Your face still bruised, your arm and ribs."

"What's happened has nothing to do with curses or demons or the devil," Shannon said. "Bad luck, maybe . . . well, certainly . . . and stupid decisions and someone out to get us, yes, I'll grant you that much, but really, not a curse."

Oliver put in his pious two cents' worth. "At least we should be thankful that Shannon wasn't injured any more than she was."

"But Mary Beth wasn't so lucky."

After a few more minutes Oliver mentioned that he had to get back. Shannon tried not to show her relief as she walked them outside, watching as Oliver helped Maureen into the passenger side of her Buick.

Before he left, he pulled Shannon aside, into the shadow of a black oak. "There's something I think you should know." His eyes shifted from one side to the other, as if he wasn't exactly certain how to say what was on his mind.

"What is it?"

He hesitated.

"Enough with the high drama. Please. We get enough of that from Mom, so what's up?"

He scratched his chin. Avoided her eyes. "Well, I'm not certain, at least not a hundred percent, but I think, no, I'm pretty sure that I saw Brendan in the congregation last Sunday."

"Brendan?" She was stunned. A dozen pictures of the father of her child flashed through her mind. Brendan in his tux as he'd picked her up for the senior prom, Brendan waving from the stands at her graduation, Brendan with her in the bedroom of his apartment, Brendan's chalk-white face when she'd told him about the baby . . .

"Yes, Brendan Giles," he snapped, then visibly calmed himself. "Sorry . . . It's just that I hate to bring this up in case I'm wrong. But I think I saw him, well, or someone who looked a lot like him, standing behind the last pew in the back of the church." He shook his head. "I could be mistaken, of course. It's been so long since I've seen him—what?—thirteen or closer to fourteen years? But . . . I think . . . Oh, who knows . . . ?" Oliver swallowed hard, looked up at the sky, worry wrinkling his face. "Maybe I shouldn't have said anything."

"No, of course you should have," she insisted, still bowled over.

His gaze came back to hers. "I just thought you should know."

"Did you try to speak with him?"

"Yes, after the service, I hurried to the back of the church, greeting everyone of course, but . . ." Oliver lifted his shoulders as if the weight of the world had settled upon them. "He was gone. Vanished." He snapped his fingers. "It was almost as if he hadn't been there at all . . . like maybe I'd imagined him there."

"You mean hallucinated," she said slowly.

"Crazy, huh?"

Shannon didn't respond.

The passenger door of the Buick opened. "Oliver?" their mother called. "Are you coming? It's awful hot in here."

"Right there, Mom." He looked back at his sister, his blue eyes tormented. "Gotta go."

"I know."

He gave Shannon a quick kiss on the temple, then left her standing beneath the branches of the oak. *Brendan was back? Just when she'd found out her baby had been kidnapped—* their—*baby?*

Or had Oliver been mistaken?

Or conjured up Brendan's image?

She stared after the bronze sedan as it rolled down the lane, kicking up dust in the hot afternoon.

If Brendan was back in Santa Lucia, he certainly would have contacted his parents. Right? *They* would know if he was here on the West Coast, now, when, coincidentally the child they'd conceived together was in grave danger.

The nightmare she was living was becoming stranger by the moment.

Her guts churning, she hurried into the house and flipped

through the pages of the local phone book. With trembling fingers she placed a call she didn't want to make.

Of course voice mail picked up. Feeling important minutes slipping away, she left her name, number and a plea that someone call her back.

She hoped to God someone would bother.

Chapter 20

"It's Dani's," Travis declared, his throat tight, fear and rage running through his blood as he stared at the backpack. "She had it with her when she went to school that day." Stunned, afraid, he turned his eyes to the detective. "Where did you get it?"

"It was left at the Flannery house, the murder scene."

"She was there?" he whispered, horror-struck.

"I don't think so. I think the killer left it, just as he left her burned birth certificate on Shannon Flannery's porch."

"Why?" Travis asked.

"I don't know. But he wanted us to find it."

"You found no other trace of her, right?" Travis asked, forcing out the words. "She wasn't . . ."

"She wasn't there," Paterno quickly assured him. "No evidence that she'd been anywhere near the house."

Travis let out his breath. Maybe Dani was still safe . . . Oh, God, he prayed so.

"I was hoping you could explain this." Not allowing Travis to touch the backpack, Paterno flipped open the upper flap and upon it, drawn in what looked like charcoal, was a weird star symbol with numbers and broken lines. "You ever see this before?"

"No. I have no idea what that is." Travis gazed hard at the odd etching. "It wasn't there the last time I looked."

"You're sure?"

"Yes."

"Could your daughter have been into drugs or cults or—"

Travis banged a fist on the corner of Paterno's desk. "Listen, detective," he snarled, rage thundering through him, "I've been over this with the police in Oregon and the FBI a million times. Dani did not do drugs. She didn't trust strangers. She didn't run away." The muscles in the back of his neck were so tight they ached. Suddenly he wanted to strangle this presumptuous prick of a policeman. "My daughter is the victim, you got that? The *victim*. Don't twist this around, just do your damned job and find her."

"I think every police agency in California and Oregon is doing just that."

"Then where the hell is she? Huh? With the pervert who did that?" he asked, jabbing an angry finger at the singed backpack. "The guy who killed at least one woman and attacked Shannon Flannery? Is that who has my little girl?" His fingers coiled in frustration. "You and I both know that all of this fucking mess is somehow connected, and my daughter is at the center of it. We also know that every second that passes, her chances of survival diminish, so, Detective Paterno, instead of asking me inane questions about cults and drugs, why don't you go out and find my kid!"

Travis didn't wait for a response. He slammed out the door. One fist was balled and he wanted like hell to slam it into someone's face.

The police were running in circles.

Just like the son of a bitch who had his daughter wanted them to be. The goddamned bastard was playing games. With his kid's life!

But Travis was focused.

Single-minded.

And lethal.

If that fucking freak show had so much as harmed one

hair on his Dani's head, the guy was a dead man. Travis would take him out. No questions asked.

"Beware of Greeks bearing gifts." Wasn't that the old saying? Or was it *geeks* bearing gifts? At this moment in time, maybe either way worked, Shannon thought. Her neighbor, portly real estate agent Alexi Demitri, the man who had sold her the new property up in the hills, proudly handed her a chubby blonde puppy. Shannon had used the time since her mother and Oliver left to call Aaron with the news about Brendan Giles. Aaron had promised to look into it, and when she'd heard a knock on her back door, she'd expected to find Aaron. Instead, Alexi had arrived.

"I just wanted to do something," he said. "You've gone through so much lately." He lifted a hand and motioned toward the space where her shed had once stood. "I heard about your sister-in-law. I'm sorry."

"Me, too," Shannon said, flummoxed by his gesture of good will.

"But you. You're feeling better?"

"Marginally," she said with a smile as she held the wiggling little mass of fur. Her feet no longer hurt and her headache had been reduced to a dull throb, though her shoulder and ribs still reminded her of the fire. She still looked like she'd wound up on the losing end of three rounds with the current heavyweight champion.

The puppy snuggled against her, and she immediately lost her heart to the soft fluff of taffy-colored fur. Khan, ever-present and jealous, looked eagerly up at the pup and whined.

"Shh," she said. "You're still number one."

"When I heard that you had suffered so much bad luck," Alexi said, "I thought I'd bring you something to cheer you up."

A dog? Shannon thought, disbelieving. Though since she'd been hurt she'd received plants, cards and flowers, no one had come up with an animal as a get-well gift. Until now. She thought of all the dogs she had on the property, animals who needed to be trained as she recovered and decided the last thing she needed right now was this pup.

At that moment it licked the underside of her chin, melting her heart. It smelled like a puppy, of course, and was all warm and soft and cuddly. And cute as the dickens.

Maybe Alexi was right. Maybe she did need this little Lab to lift her spirits.

As if he could read her thoughts, Alexi grinned, showing off a bit of gold rimming one of his front teeth. "The pick of the litter, I tell you, and smart? This little girl is smart as a whip!" He handed her veterinary records proving that the pup had been inoculated.

Shannon skimmed the papers, then stuffed them into her pocket.

"So why didn't you sell her?" Shannon asked, leaning against the doorjamb and feeling the heat of the day seep into her bones.

Alexi's dark eyes shined. "I did not sell this one, because I could not bear to give her to a stranger, no matter what the price." He nodded, his nearly bald head bobbing up and down as if he was convincing himself. He fished in his pockets and came up with a set of keys. They glittered in the sunlight. Brand new.

"What about the rest of the litter?" Shannon asked.

"Oh, well, my daughter she took one, and my nephew, he, too, needed a dog. Two died at birth—such a shame—and so I saved this one, Skatooli, the best, for you." He smiled broadly again as he handed her the keys. "These go to the back door, off the woodshed. I had to replace the lock and, as I told you, forgot to bring them to the closing," he explained.

The keys were to the property that she'd just purchased from him, a ranch with twenty acres attached to it, located fifteen miles up the county road. A perfect spot, she'd decided, to expand her working training ground for search and rescue dogs, a place to start over, a place with no memories of the past and now, she thought, glancing to the blackened side of the horse barn, a place that might be safer from whoever had decided to harass her.

"What does Skatooli mean?" She pocketed the keys.

"A Greek endearment." He waved his hands as if the real meaning was inconsequential. "All grandmothers—yiayiàs—call their adored grandchildren Skatoolis . . ." Yet he was blushing, the skin stretched over his pate turning crimson in the heat of the afternoon.

"Skatooli," Shannon repeated as she held her new puppy, a golden Lab. "I don't know what to say. You shouldn't have . . . but thank you." She stroked the pup's soft coat as the tiny tail swept across her chest frantically. At her feet, Khan whined and circled.

"Don't mention it. And please, get better!" His dark eyes were suddenly worried. "This business with the fire and with your sister-in-law . . . it's disturbing . . . no good." Obviously he'd read the newspaper reports or seen on the local television newscast that arson was suspected.

"Amen," she agreed.

"Take care, Shannon. Be careful."

"Always."

"I mean it, you could use a security company to come and set up some kind of system, complete with cameras. Here." He scrounged in his back pocket, came out with a smooth leather wallet and withdrew a business card. "When I'm not selling real estate, I do security work with my brother-in-law." He handed her the card for Safety First, a company with a Santa Rosa address.

"So you sell houses and suggest that your clients invest in a security system?"

He lifted a shoulder. "I do what I can."

"Nice gig."

His smile broadened. "You might consider a system for here *and* the new place. You can never be too secure."

"Safety first," she said, fingering the card while holding the squirming little dog. She remembered the video equipment she'd installed at Aaron's suggestion. The equipment Ryan had destroyed when he'd discovered it.

"Yes . . . exactly." He lifted a hand in a slow wave, then walked to his car, a white Cadillac that was probably twenty years old, gleaming in the sunlight. As he opened the driver's door, he looked over the car's roof and added, "You'll never regret buying the new place."

"I certainly hope not," she said, thinking his comment odd as she watched him climb into his Seville and throw it into reverse.

After completing a quick turn, he nosed the big car out of the driveway. She stood on the porch and watched as it bumped along the rutted tracks that wound through the copse of live oaks shading the drive.

"You know, Skatooli," she whispered, "he's more than a little weird. Good thing you escaped while you could." *Oh yeah, right. Like this was such a safe haven.* She kissed the pup's velvet-soft crown. Pure bred Lab? Unlikely since she was a gift. There was something about Alexi's demeanor—a little bit of the overly clichéd oily used-car salesman—that bothered her. Yet she'd bought the property from him and signed the papers just the week before.

Before everything in your life turned upside down.

She watched the plume of dust rising from beneath the Caddy's tires slowly dissipate and told herself she was borrowing trouble. "Come on inside," she whispered, wincing as the pup wiggled against her ribs. "Careful." With Khan nearly tripping her, she carried the little dog into the house.

The puppy, suddenly aware of the new smells, sights and sounds of her surroundings, trembled and Shannon clutched the tiny thing more firmly. "It's okay," she said as she gently introduced the little one to Khan. With his mismatched eyes studying the fluff of fur, Khan nosed the pup and snorted, as if in disgust, then trotted off to his water dish. "See," Shannon whispered to Skatooli as the old dog slurped noisily, "he likes you already."

She set the pup in the kennel she kept in a corner of her kitchen, saw that she had puppy food and water, then waited. The little dog whined and tried to climb the mesh as Shannon stuck its veterinary records into a file cabinet in the laundry room, then searched again for her damned cell phone.

The last call she'd made was to 9-1-1 as she was flying out the door to the fire and from that point on she couldn't remember what she'd done with it.

If she didn't find it soon, she'd have to cut the service and get a new one.

Though she'd tried it once before, she picked up her home phone and dialed her cell number. It began to ring on the other end, but not anywhere in the house.

Or did she hear something faint through her open window? On the fourth ring she heard her own voice and hung up. Then she hit redial and walked outside. The phone connected and this time she not only heard the ringing in her receiver, but also the distinct tones of her cell. She followed the noise to the open window of her truck before the voice mail answered again.

She tore open the door and checked the interior . . . The phone wasn't in its usual spot, which was the cup holder near the gearshift. Nor was it on the dash or front seat . . . She checked the glove box. Not there. Using a flashlight she kept in a pocket on the driver's side door, she searched again, sweeping the flashlight's beam under the seat and there, hidden beneath the seat-adjustment bar, was her phone, the battery nearly dead.

How had it gotten there?

She hadn't used it since the fire, had dropped it during the attack.

She'd been nowhere near her truck.

Someone had put it there.

Her heart nearly stopped. She had the eerie sensation that she was being watched. She looked around the grounds and saw nothing out of the ordinary. The horses were grazing in the pasture, Khan was nosing around the water trough, the dogs in their runs were sleeping undisturbed in the afternoon sun and Nate was still missing.

Nerves strung tight, she flipped open her phone and tried to check her messages as the battery beeped a warning. Before she could connect, the phone went dead and there was no reviving it. "Damn," she muttered, slapping it against her palm before giving up. Who had found her phone and placed it—no, hidden it—in her pickup without telling her? Someone who had found it that night? Travis? No. Nate? She made a mental note to ask him about it. But when? Surely not the night the shed burned down.

And then she knew.

As surely as if he'd whispered the truth to her, she realized that whoever had started the fire had placed the phone in her truck. The same twisted individual who had left her the burned birth certificate, who had kidnapped Dani, who had killed Mary Beth.

And she'd just erased any chance of collecting his fingerprints, she berated herself. Then she decided that whoever had taken it would have been careful about that, too.

Goose bumps broke out on her skin and she slowly turned, staring at her house, the kennels, the stable, the destroyed shed, searching the familiar nooks and crannies for a stranger, someone dangerous and dark, someone who enjoyed tormenting her.

Who was he?

Why had he killed Mary Beth but spared her?

Because he's not finished. And he wants you to know. He gets off on scaring you.

"Bastard," she hissed. She thought of Dani Settler. *Her* child. Travis's child. *Hang in there, honey . . . We'll find you. We will!*

She strode into the house, hooked the cell phone into its charger, then dialed Nate's cell phone. To hell with giving him his space. She needed him here. Now.

But he didn't answer and his voice mail box was full.

"Damn it all to hell," she muttered. Her thoughts next flew to Travis. She wanted to talk to him, to see him. He'd been gone for only a few hours and it seemed like an eternity.

"Oh, get over yourself," she muttered. What was she thinking? She, who was so hell-bent to get away from her overprotective brothers. She, who had sworn off marriage after the horror she'd endured as Mrs. Ryan Carlyle. She, the girl who had suffered the ultimate rejection when she'd told Brendan Giles she was pregnant. She had no business—no damned business at all—thinking of Travis Settler as anything more than Dani's father, a worried man looking for his child.

"He's nothing more to me," she told the puppy who had finally, in exhaustion, curled into a little ball and was sleeping on the fluffy pillow in the pen. "You're going to be fine," Shannon whispered and wondered if she was talking to the dog or herself.

What she needed, she decided, was some time to think, away from the rubble, away from the phone, away from the ridiculous notion that there were sinister eyes watching her every move.

"I'll be back soon," she promised the little dog, who didn't so much as move upon the pillow. "Sweet dreams."

She found the keys to her truck. She had to get out. She'd been cooped up with her thoughts too long.

She wondered about Nate again. Ever since she'd told him she was buying a new place she'd felt a wall build between them, one emotional brick stacked upon another.

And it was weird that he hadn't been hovering over her since the fire, but maybe that was a blessing, to borrow from Oliver's take on life.

Deciding to do something constructive, she began hauling a load of supplies to her truck that she'd bought earlier, intending to move them to her new place. It was tricky, carrying the boxes of cleaning products, painting supplies, paper towels, toilet paper and such, but she managed eventually to fill the bed of the pickup. Shannon worked steadily, grimly satisfied at her efforts. With hours still before sunset the last case of Lysol was finally tucked behind a wheel well. Despite her tender shoulder and ribs, it felt good to actually *do* something again, to turn her thoughts away from the fires and Mary Beth's murder, at least for a little while.

Whistling to Khan, she opened the door of the cab and he flew across her seat to his position on the passenger side. "Aren't you the pampered one," she said with a smile as she twisted on the ignition. She threw the rig into drive and took off, gravel spraying from her tires as she tromped on the accelerator a little harder than she'd intended.

They drove fifteen miles under a canopy of madrona and oak trees where sunlight pierced through the leaves to spackle the ground. Though she turned on the radio and tried to concentrate on a ballad by some country artist she didn't recognize, her mind spun wildly with images of charred documents, baby pictures, Brendan Giles, Mary Beth's horrid death, Travis Settler—who was too damned sexy for his own good—and odd-shaped symbols burned into wood. What kind of nightmare had she fallen into? What did it all mean? Was Brendan really back in Santa Lucia?

Don't trust what Oliver told you, her mind warned. *He's been wrong before. Hallucinated. Been hospitalized for psychiatric problems . . . It could be happening again . . .*

She was so deep in thought that she nearly missed the turnoff to her new place. The lane was overgrown, brambles and berry vines covering a rusted, permanently opened gate that lopped on uneven hinges. She braked quickly, causing Khan to nearly lose his footing.

"Sorry," she said, then maneuvered her pickup into the private road. Little more than two ruts separated by a stripe of dry weeds that scraped the truck's undercarriage, the lane wound through the trees upward into the foothills. The old pickup bounced and lurched as it made the gentle climb. Shannon, shifting down, made a mental note to order several loads of gravel.

When her life returned to normal. *If* it did.

Around a final turn, the trees gave way to a clearing and a lake of clear water. Near the shore was a rambling cottage that had been built between the First and Second World Wars. It was two full stories, though the upstairs hadn't been used in years. A well-kept barn, stable, separate double-car garage and several utility sheds had been built on the north shore of the spring-fed lake. A boathouse and dock jutted into the water where dragonflies flitted, and trout swam below the clear surface.

From the instant Shannon had set eyes on the place, she'd felt at home, though she couldn't explain why. This quaint, albeit run-down ranch had touched her. True, it needed a lot of TLC and elbow grease, but it was larger than her current home, it was more private and most of all, it held no memories of the past; no ghosts walked the hallways here.

And though the old house needed repair, the outbuildings were in fairly good shape, and the grounds were perfect for the new life she'd carved for herself since Ryan's death. She already imagined how she could expand her business, placing more emphasis on water-rescue dogs and training them on the private lake.

The configuration of the large field behind the barn could be changed to include a circular enclosure for Nate and his horses.

Nate.

Still missing in action.

Theirs was a unique union, she thought. Most people assumed they were lovers—two misfits who lived on the same compound, two loners. The gossips in Santa Lucia who whispered that she and Nate shared a bed were wrong, not that she disavowed any of the tongue-waggers of their speculation. Nate worked with the horses, she with the dogs. Nate had spent eighteen months in prison before his murder conviction had been overturned with new DNA evidence. She'd been accused of killing her husband . . . No, they weren't lovers, at least not yet, and that was her decision, not his. That was probably the crux of their recent disputes, the primary reason he was against her buying the place from Demitri. He thought she was running away.

From him.

Shannon grimaced. She didn't want to think about him and what he wanted from her because she knew, deep in her heart, she'd never fall in love with him. Probably because he might just be the "right" kind of man for her, despite her brothers' protests. But then, she never did go for the right guy. Even now, the only man she found interesting was Travis Settler, and no matter how damnably male he was, that thought was just plain absurd. He had suspected her of stealing his daughter away from him. He had been found at her place on some kind of mission, loaded with military-like equipment and weapons. Since he'd come to California, things had gone from bad to worse and now her sister-in-law was dead.

Travis Settler was definitely a man to avoid at all costs. Getting close to him, even if he allowed it, would be another mistake. And hadn't she made enough for a lifetime?

She had only to think of Brendan, the college boy she'd dated in high school and a friend of her brother Robert and how that had turned out. Then, of course, there had been Ryan, the man she'd married on the rebound—and the biggest mistake of her life. The few men she'd dated since Ryan had been few and far between, no one to write home about.

Remembering her husband, Shannon shuddered. What a nightmare. One of the reasons she'd finally decided to leave her home was to get away from the house they'd shared, a place where unspeakable acts had occurred. Though she'd long ago moved out of the main downstairs bedroom, converting it into a kind of office, and had bought a new bed and placed it upstairs, the memories of Ryan and what he'd done to her still lingered.

This new place, though about a dozen tiers below rustic, was a fresh start. One with bright, broad horizons, she told herself while unloading paint cans, rollers, trays, cleaning supplies and a few essentials such as toilet paper, paper towels and trash bags, hauling them all inside.

The kitchen had yellowed pine walls, the floors throughout were a scarred, scratched hardwood. The chimney was river rock and, she suspected, from disuse was home to either birds or hornets. But, in her mind's eye, she saw the place as it would be with fresh paint, a new glossy surface on the plank floors, repainted cabinets and new tile on the counters.

She imagined a few rugs scattered strategically between her old rocker and antique sofa, a fire burning cheerily in the grate. Best yet, just off the kitchen, through a porch that opened on both sides of the house and doubled as a laundry facility, there was an attached woodshed. Long and narrow with a sagging roof and a door on the far end leading to the backyard, this unused space would become the new kennel for all the dogs she boarded and trained. She would build individual runs that would open into a general exercise and play area.

It would be perfect!

"Heaven on earth," she muttered sarcastically, knowing there was no such thing, as she took the key Alexi had given her and opened the door to the sagging woodshed. The scents of dry kindling, sawdust and dirt filled her nostrils and she made her way to the back door while swatting at the spiderwebs draping from a ceiling that would need to be replaced. She wondered if any of the woodshed's existing walls could be saved, deciding as she reached the back door that the whole one-room shed was probably a teardown. Besides, she would need insulation, plumbing, updated electricity, heat and more windows to let in natural light for the dogs. She would also have to rip out the rotting wood floors and replace them with cement and tile. It would take time and money—lots of both; but Shannon had been saving for three years, determined to move from the place that had caused her such heartache, pain and shame.

She was about to unlock the shed's back door when she

realized it hadn't been latched, the shiny new deadbolt wasn't slipped into its place.

In fact, as she touched the knob, the door itself creaked open, revealing a broken back step and an overgrown yard with a weed-choked path to the gate.

A tremor of unease whispered through her.

Why would Alexi go to all the trouble of installing a new lock, then negligently leave the door unlatched?

A mistake?

Or had someone broken in?

She stepped outside, turning slowly, scanning the house and grounds once again. She dismissed that thought. The only people who would be interested in the place were either teenagers looking for a place to party—although she'd seen no evidence of anyone inside the house, no empty beer bottles or tossed cigarette butts, or other trash—another realtor hoping the sale would fall through, or some hiker or hunter who'd stumbled upon the place and was just curious.

No one evil.

Nothing serious.

She was just projecting because of all the weird stuff that had happened. Because of the fire and attack. "Stop jumping at shadows," she muttered as she locked the door firmly, then tested it. The unlatched door was probably just an oversight. No big mystery.

She left the woodshed and called to Khan, wading through ankle-high grass to the front of the house where the lake, with its still waters, beckoned. The old dock was sound except for a few rotten boards, so she made her way to the edge, kicked off her running shoes and socks and dangled her feet into the cool depths. The water felt like heaven! She undid her ponytail, letting her hair spring free to her shoulders. Closing her eyes, she leaned her head back and sighed.

She didn't feel like explaining to Nate or any of her brothers why she'd felt compelled to move. Nor had she confided in her mother or any of her friends. Buying this place had been a simple decision she'd made single-handedly. She shuddered as she imagined her family discussing the pros and cons of the change in her life. Let them think what they would. She'd decided three years ago to stand on her own two feet, come hell or high water. No more running to her brothers. No more discussions with her mother. No more depending upon anyone but herself. Okay, so Shea and Robert and Aaron had helped her with this last trauma, but from now on, she'd make her own decisions. In the past she'd let her family talk her into things, but no more.

"No more," she said aloud and felt a chill, as if a cloud had slid over the sun. But when she opened her eyes, the sky was still clear, the golden orb in the sky as intense and bright as ever.

Funny.

She rubbed her sore shoulder and looked for the dog, only to find him standing stiffly, hackles raised, eyes trained on the woods just on the other side of the fence line.

Shannon's body tensed.

Frozen, Khan let out a low warning growl.

"What is it?" Shannon whispered as she gathered her shoes and socks. Sitting alone on the edge of the dock, dangling her feet in the still waters she'd felt innocent as a schoolgirl, but that was foolish. Hadn't she learned? Hadn't the attack against her or Mary Beth's death taught her anything? Exposed as she'd been, she could be a target for any—

Stop it! Don't go there! Do NOT go there. You still have to live your life and not feel compelled to cower and hide.

But Mary Beth was dead. Horribly and cruelly murdered. And Dani Settler was missing.

Had she allowed the insanity, the fear, to follow her to the place she'd hoped would become her haven?

Slowly letting out her pent-up breath, she turned her gaze to the shadowy area of trees. There was nothing visible. No one lurking in the umbra. Yet the goose bumps on the back of her arms didn't go away and she felt as if someone was watching her, someone studying her every move.

Angry with herself, she gave a sharp command to the dog and Khan, still growling, tucked his tail between his legs and sprinted for the truck.

"You're being a big wuss," she told the mutt, ruffling his hair after she'd climbed inside. She rammed the Dodge into gear. "Make that a *major* wuss!"

And so are you, Shannon!

Flipping on the radio, she caught the tail end of the weather report as she cranked on the steering wheel, forcing the truck into a wide arc.

". . . continued heat spell with no end in sight. Temperatures will soar into the upper nineties and fire danger remains high . . ." the announcer said as she glanced in her rearview mirror.

Her heart jammed into her throat.

He was there!

Through the dust, a blurry, dark figure appeared in the reflection—a quick image of someone darting through the trees.

She gasped.

Slammed on the brakes.

Whipped her head around to stare through the back window. Dust settled behind her.

Heat shimmered in waves, distorting her view.

Yet no one was visible in the dappled light beneath the black oaks. No bogeyman lurked maliciously in the shadows. No evil presence skulked through the thickets.

She glanced at the dog. Khan looked up at her expectantly. His coat was smooth. Unruffled.

There was no sound other than the soft call of birds over the thrum of the truck's engine and the click of insects hidden in the grass. Shannon forced her muscles to relax. "Idiot," she ground out. She was moving up here to get away from her demons . . . she would not bring them with her. No way.

Slowly, she eased off the brake and with one eye on the rearview mirror continued driving down the lane.

Nothing seemed disturbed.

Nothing was out of the normal.

The rambling bungalow near the shores of the wooded lake disappeared from view as she rounded a corner and the pickup bounced and jarred down the grooved lane.

She had probably imagined the image in her mirror. She'd picked up on the dog's anxiety. He could have seen a deer or a fox, or even a cougar.

But you saw a man.

Upright. On two legs.

Pulse racing, she punched several buttons on the radio, found a rock station, and singing along to some Springsteen song she remembered from her youth, turned onto the highway. She wasn't going to let her overactive imagination run away with her. She refused to let fear control her.

Not this time.

Not ever again.

Chapter 21

Her fingers bleeding through her now toeless and filthy socks, Dani worked hard, putting all her strength into pulling out the damned nail. "Come on, come on," she muttered, knowing she was running out of time. As well as patience. The creep wouldn't keep her here forever; she knew that much. She'd observed him through the crack in the door and he was getting more restless, more keyed up. He paced a lot, striding back and forth in front of the fire, and he'd taken to leaving his knife on the bricks near the firebox, the blade stretching toward the flames, its steel looking red with the reflection of the coals.

She thought about how he'd pressed that blade against her cheek, how he'd threatened her with the razor-sharp edge, and she quivered inside. She would never let herself get into that position again. Never.

Her fingers ached, but she wouldn't give up. "Come on, you miserable thing!" She hunched her shoulders, pulled back and felt the nail wiggle crazily.

"Come on!"

With one final tug the nail was free.

Dani nearly fell backwards.

Heart pounding, she stared at the long spike and curled her sock-clad fingers around the shaft. Yes! Freedom from the creep was within her grasp. She wanted to bolt out the door at this very minute but knew that would be suicide. She might run into him coming back. He'd already been gone for hours this time, and his hours in the cabin had become irregular.

Much as she wanted to race into the surrounding woods now, she didn't dare leave. It was still daylight and she needed to leave at night, after he took off for whatever sick mission he was on.

The last few days she'd been watching him through the slit in the door. She knew where he kept an extra flashlight and his knife, which he usually took with him, but there were other objects she could carry with her, like the little torch he used to light his fire each night. That might come in handy. And the picture of her mother, damn it, she was taking it.

But she didn't have a backpack any longer. He'd stolen that a few nights ago, so what she could carry would be limited. And she still had the creep's cigarette butt, hidden deep in her pocket. If she took some other things from this place, they might have his fingerprints on them and the police would be able to nail his sorry hide to the wall.

She couldn't wait.

But she was getting ahead of herself.

First she had to hide the spike and the best place to do that was to put it back in its hole. She'd reamed the old wood out well enough that now she could extract it again easily.

Smiling to herself she stared down at the long nail.

What she'd really like to do with it was ram it deep into the guy's neck. Or using her tae kwon do skills she could drop the bastard to his knees. Oh, how she'd love to take him out! However, just like he had obviously underestimated her and didn't know what she was capable of, she didn't know anything about him, either. He, too, could have a black belt. He was muscular and strong. She'd seen enough of his body when he went through his nightly ritual to know that. As gross as the spectacle was she did learn some things. He was tough. And a lot bigger than she was. If he took a mind to, he could hurt her.

So she couldn't push him.

But she couldn't just sit around and wait for him to decide he didn't need her any longer.

She stared down at the nail . . . It was nearly six inches, she guessed. Long enough for her purposes.

Soon he would return. Her guts squeezed at the thought of being near him again and the sick sensation in her stomach returned. If she knew she had the time she would take off now. But did she? Should she risk it?

Glancing up at the skylight, she realized that it was late in the afternoon, maybe early evening. Shadows were creeping across the sky so the sun had to be getting low in the western sky. Maybe he wasn't coming back. Maybe she should leave now, while she had the chance. Maybe she wouldn't get another one.

She palmed the nail.

The least she could do was explore the cabin . . .

She thought she heard a truck rumble in the distance.

Crap!

Fear sizzled through her body.

Don't let him get to you. Don't. You only have to put up with him a few more hours.

Quickly she slid her newfound tool into the hole in the closet floor and threw herself onto her bed. She had to wait. Had to deal with him one more night.

Her throat tightened in revulsion.

Tonight.

No matter what.

After he came back and checked on her, fed her, and went through his eerie fire ritual, he would leave. And when he did she'd have enough time to make good her escape.

Later tonight after he left, she would be outta here.

By the time Shannon got home and parked near the garage, her case of nerves had nearly disappeared. She'd spent the drive convincing herself that she was just tired and edgy. And maybe she'd imagined the man at the cabin. With all that had happened in the past few days her nerves were strung past the breaking point. That was it. She thought of a long bath, maybe a glass of wine, lit candles . . . and clearing her mind or, even better, letting her mind wander. Maybe if she had a few minutes alone she would be able to make sense of things, put them in order, push back her fears.

She couldn't let the strain that had ruined her sense of well-being here spread into the dreams she had for her new home, her new beginning.

"It'll be worth it," she told herself as she climbed out of the cab. Khan hopped to the dusty floor of the garage to bolt through the open door and relieve himself on a favorite fence post. All the dogs loved that old gnarled stake and Shannon spent the next ten minutes, in the dark, hosing it down.

"You can't wash the smell away," Nate said and she nearly jumped out of her skin.

The nozzle of the hose slipped in her hands, water spraying wildly as she readjusted her grip.

Suddenly her hair, arms and front of her shirt were drenched. "Damn it," she said, but, in truth, the cold water felt good. Refreshing.

"Sorry."

She caught the hint of a smile, the flash of white teeth against his tanned skin. "You miserable bastard, you do that on purpose, don't you? You *enjoy* sneaking up on people." He opened his mouth to speak and she held up a hand. "Think twice before you start off on some diatribe about it all being a part of your Native American heritage, okay?" She pointed the nozzle at his face. "I'm not unwilling to shoot you where it does the most good." She lowered her aim, siting her new-found weapon at his crotch.

Nate's hands flew up, palms outward. "All right, ma'am," he drawled in a poor imitation of some ridiculous Hollywood cowboy twang, "I surrender."

"Just the words I love to hear from a man," she said, leaning down to twist off the spigot. She felt a sharp twinge, reminding her that her ribs were far from healed. "At least the post won't reek so bad that every stray for a hundred miles will end up wandering down here to take a leak."

"You'd love it if they did and you'd adopt every one of them."

She chuckled and felt a faint twist of pain again. But he was right. She'd never found a stray she didn't take in. "St. Francis of Assisi, I'm not," she said, wiping her hands on the tail of her shirt.

"No?"

"Definitely not."

"Then how about St. Shannon?"

"There is no St. Shannon."

"You sure?" he asked.

"Well . . . no." She lifted a shoulder and whistled for Khan. "It's been a while since I attended St. Theresa's and studied catechism. But I think if someone named Shannon had been canonized, I would have heard." She eyed him and rested one hand on her hip. "So where the hell have you been?"

"In and out. The truck's giving me fits. It's in the shop now. One of the mechanics gave me a lift back here."

"You could have called."

"I did. Your cell. You never called me back."

"I tried, but your voice mail was full. Besides my cell's been missing a while," she said, still disturbed about its sudden reappearance.

"Okay, so I tried to get in touch with you."

Not too hard, she thought, but let it slide.

"I heard about Mary Beth. I'm sorry."

"Yeah, me, too."

"The police think it was intentional, that someone killed her?"

She nodded and all of the warmth and humor they'd shared only moments before drizzled away with the cold truth.

"How's Robert holding up?"

"I haven't seen him since it happened, but according to my other brothers and mother, not well."

"And the kids?"

"I don't know, but it's got to be tough." She leaned her arms over the top rail of the fence. "The police think whoever killed her is the same one who burned down the shed."

Nate's gaze moved from the shed to her face. "And attacked you."

"And probably kidnapped Dani Settler."

"Your daughter."

She lifted an eyebrow. "I don't remember telling you all my deep, dark secrets."

With a shrug, he said, "Santa Lucia's a small town. Everyone knows everyone else's business."

"Including you?"

"Only the people I care about," he said, then, before she could reply, hitched his chin toward the paddock where the small herd of horses was grazing. "I've got something I want to show you."

"What?"

"Just come on." As if expecting her to argue, he added, "Humor me, this once. Believe me, Shannon, I think you'll be interested in what I found out."

Curious, she gestured broadly with one hand. "Lead away." She followed him to the fence enclosing the paddock outside the horse barn. Inside the enclosure the horses were enjoying the last rays of evening sun. Several picked at the dry stubble that still existed in clumps within the paddock while the roan gelding was rolling in the dust, sending up great clouds that partially hid his body, so that his legs, pawing the air, were all that was visible. Still others stood, heads turned in their direction, dark eyes watching.

"Wait here," Nate instructed as he grabbed a leather lead from a hook on the side of the building, then slipped through the gate and approached the small herd standing beneath the bows of a madrona tree. The animals lifted their heads to watch him approach. He walked surely, his voice steady, his movements deliberate and smooth.

Molly, the buckskin who had balked at being freed during the fire, was still skittish. While the other horses went back to plucking at dry blades of grass, she appeared ready to bolt. Her nostrils were flared, her eyes wide, her flesh quivering beneath her tawny coat.

Nate singled her out, stepping closer, and she snorted anxiously, but allowed him to snap the lead to her halter. He patted her shoulder gently, then led her back to the fence.

"She's still nervous," Shannon observed and swatted at a horsefly that hovered near her head.

"I would be, too." Nate was suddenly grave, his dark eyes angry. "Look at her chin and around her mouth," he said.

Shannon's eyes were drawn to the mare's face. Dark eyes regarded her suspiciously. Molly tried to throw back her head as Shannon reached over the fence to pet her, but Nate held the buckskin's head steady. "I don't see anything," Shannon said. "What is it I'm looking for? . . . Oh." Noticing the dark stubble around Molly's mouth, she said, "Wait a minute. Her chin hairs and muzzle hairs are missing."

"Not just missing, but I think they were singed off."

"Singed?" she repeated, spying a few blackened hairs. "In the fire?"

"Before the fire."

"What?" She stared at him, cold dread seeping through her.

"By the guy who attacked you."

"But why?" She asked the question but already her mind was racing to the only reason that made any sense. "Oh, no . . ."

"To freak her out," Nate said flatly. "To make Molly impossible to handle. To force you inside her stall and ensure that you would be trapped with a frenzied, wild, crazy animal." A muscle worked in his jaw as he added, "Whoever did this planned it carefully. Molly wasn't just being stubborn or balking because of the fire. She was reacting to being tortured. See here," he pointed to a bit of darkened skin near the corner of the mare's mouth, an obvious burn mark.

"No." Shannon stared at the horse's muzzle and saw the evidence, so plain to her now. Sudden nausea roiled in her stomach. "What kind of sicko would do this?"

"Someone determined, someone lethal, someone who has one helluva grudge against you. Used some kind of torch or lighter or held up a burning stick."

"Damn it!" She wanted to scream at the blatant cruelty to the mare. She replayed the scene that Nate had mapped out: She'd tried to touch Molly, to pet her, but the horse had reacted by tossing back her head. "Have you told the police?"

"Not yet," he said and Shannon understood his aversion to the authorities. Nate, like she, had been falsely accused of murder in the past. He'd spent eighteen months of his life in prison before DNA evidence had cleared him of the crime. He didn't trust the law. "I figured you might want to tell them yourself."

"I will," she said, anger boiling anew through her blood. What kind of horrible maniac would harm an innocent animal, use the creature's pain to get back at her? Who? And why? She automatically reached into her pocket for her cell before remembering that it was in the house recharging.

Hell! She let her gaze move from Nate's concerned face to the rest of the little herd. "Were any of the other animals harmed?"

"Not that I can see."

"You checked the dogs, too?"

"Yep."

"Good." Though she was pissed as hell about Molly, she felt a bit of relief that there were no other examples of the hideous torture.

"It might be time to get a security system installed, for your house, the stable and kennel."

He unsnapped the lead and let Molly free. Snorting, the mare quickly trotted over to the other horses where she stood, black tail swishing, ears flicking nervously.

"I'll put one in up at the new place. It's going to be renovated anyway. And Alexi Demitri stopped by today. He told me he has a company that will do the installation."

"I don't like him," Nate said without inflection.

"So you've said."

His lips flattened as he stepped through the gate. "You might rethink your plan. You're not moving for a while, and, apparently the danger is now. You might want to do something here as well."

He had a point. She still had a few weeks to live here and the thought that whoever had attacked her had been able to come and go at his will made goose bumps run up her arms. Worse yet, that same man probably killed Mary Beth and was holding Dani Settler hostage . . . if he hadn't murdered the girl as well.

Panic and rage rippled through her. Though she had no evidence that he'd been in her house, she wasn't certain and if he came back . . . Her stomach curdled. "I'll call Alexi immediately," she said.

"So why was he here?" As the sun set and shadows lengthened across the fields, Khan, tired of searching for squirrels in a woodpile, trotted over and whined for Nate's attention. Out of habit, Nate reached down and scratched the dog behind his good ear. "What did Demitri want?"

"He dropped off keys to the woodshed at the new place."

The corners of Nate's lips pinched and the skin grew taut over his high cheekbones. "I thought maybe after what happened the other night, you might not want to move."

"It might be safer up there."

He snorted. "More isolated."

"Look, we've been over this before. Alexi had another reason for dropping by."

"Which was?"

"To offer condolences for Mary Beth. And he also brought me a gift."

One black eyebrow raised as he straightened.

"A pup." She hesitated. "Come on, I'll introduce you to her."

"He *gave* you a dog?" Skepticism laced his words.

"Mmm hmmm." She'd already turned and was walking toward the back door. In three swift strides, Nate caught up to her and they crossed the porch together, old floorboards creaking under his boots.

As she reached for the door, he touched her arm, the first physical contact they'd had since the fire. "Wait a minute," he said, his voice low. "How are you doing?" From his gaze she knew that he meant more than the surface stuff.

"I'm okay." She flashed a smile she didn't feel. "Didn't you once say I was 'tough as nails'?"

He glanced at the ground. "I could have been wrong."

"Nah!"

She opened the door and he dropped his hand back to his side. The problem with Nate was that he wasn't a surface guy; she knew that. His feelings, though often hidden, ran deep. Maybe too deep.

Once in the kitchen, she walked to the kennel where the puppy was already awake again. The little ball of fur was jumping and leaping at the confines of the cage. Carefully Shannon leaned over the wire mesh and scooped up the wriggling little dog. "Skatooli," she said as the puppy licked her face wildly. "Here, meet Nate." Shannon handed the pup to the tall man and, as with just about any animal, Skatooli calmed in Nate's big, calloused, incredibly gentle hands. "Purebred Labrador retriever . . . without papers, of course."

"My ass," Nate said, his voice calm. "That's like saying I'm full-blooded Cherokee or that Khan here is a prize-winning Aussie shepherd." He glanced up, fingers still stroking the little dog, as Khan, hearing his name and for-ever wanting to be the center of attention, did circles around Nate's boots. He whined expectantly before giving off a gruff bark. The tiny pup, startled, yipped.

"I know. But she's sweet, and probably smart."

"I already told you I don't trust Demitri," Nate said again. "That guy has ulterior motives for his ulterior motives."

Shannon sighed. "I got that message loud and clear."

"And you ignored it. As always."

"Not 'as always.' I heed your advice when I think I should. Face it, Santana, it's not just Demitri. You don't trust anyone."

He made a deprecating noise and she chuckled. They'd walked this ground before. "Besides, I like the new place."

"I know. No reason to argue about it again," Nate said. "It's a done deal." The lines around his mouth tightened a bit.

Shannon ignored his disapproval. There was no reason to explain why she wanted a place of her own, a place that held no memories, no ghosts from a past that wouldn't disappear. A place where she didn't wake up in the middle of the night covered in sweat, her body shaking, the nightmares still as vivid and real as they had been for three years. Looking up, she caught Nate staring at her with his guarded dark eyes. He had a way of looking straight to her soul, she sometimes thought, as if he was trying to read her mind.

Careful there, Nate, you might not like what you see.

As disturbing as his insight could be, it was a gift when it came to training animals. Part horse whisperer, part Native-American shaman and part restless cowboy, Nate Santana was the primary reason her business thrived. Nate's silent intensity, his quiet concentration and calm ways were unmatched. Shannon had once seen him stand for three hours staring into the furious eyes of a reputedly "no-good piece of rotten horseflesh," a "devil in a nag's pricey hide," an animal that had been beaten and battered and knew nothing more than to fight. Neither horse nor man had moved and all the while Nate had kept up a low, calming monologue.

In the end, the stallion had lowered his head and shuffled up to the man who was unafraid and quietly healing. That horse, Rocco, a sleek bay with bloodlines that could be traced back to some famous charger from the Civil War, was now Nate's.

That revealed the positive side to her partner.

Once a particularly nasty wasp had been hovering near his head and she'd witnessed him sweep it into his bare fist, then crush the life out of it without flinching as the struggling insect stung his fingers repeatedly.

When it was over, he'd dropped the tiny black carcass onto the ground.

Shannon had never forgotten either incident.

Now she found him staring at her. "Looking at something?" she asked.

"Just tryin' to figure you out."

"It'll never happen, Santana."

He smiled. "Just give me enough time."

They both knew it would never happen and as he handed her the dog and left the kitchen she felt a little tug on her heart.

There was something about Nate's quiet authority, his seeming calm that belied a storm within him. Maybe that was the reason she hadn't tumbled into bed with him. Or maybe it was because she knew he loved her. He'd never said the words, but she sensed them there, lying just beneath the surface.

"Or maybe you're just a head case," she muttered as she watched him through the window and wondered why this man had never reached her the way that Travis Settler had.

Her relationship with Settler, if that was what you could call it, had already intrigued her and she found him exhilarating. If she looked at it logically, he wasn't any better looking than Nate Santana, and she knew very little about him.

But his determination to find his child, his passion to protect her, his all-balls-out approach to life appealed to her at a very sensual level. There was just something visceral and male that got to her.

Probably because of all the heightened drama surrounding him. Surely because he was her daughter's father and probably because she forever fell for the wrong kind of guy.

"Like I said," she whispered to the pup, "a head case."

He'd been foolish.

Too anxious.

Letting his emotions rule his actions.

Everything had been meticulously planned. He'd waited so long for just the right moment to strike, and now this!

He couldn't risk another mistake, he thought, as he slunk through the lengthening shadows in the thin stands of black oak and madrona. Wearing camouflage he slid noiselessly toward the spur of a lane leading to an abandoned gravel pit where he'd parked his truck. He was sweating, his heart pumping, but the thrill of adrenaline raced through his blood.

So close.

He was so damned close!

He jogged easily through the gathering dusk, effortlessly

hurdling a fallen tree that blocked his path. He was in excellent physical condition and would prove up to the task at hand. Hadn't he already proved as much with pathetic Mary Beth?

Anticipation gunned through his bloodstream as he thought of the stroke of luck that Shannon had purchased this particular parcel of land. He couldn't have found a more perfect stage to set his plan into motion if he'd picked the spot himself. At a juncture in the path, he veered to the left and ran another quarter mile to the abandoned gravel pit.

His truck was waiting.

And the prize—no, the bait—was hidden safely away, a wimp of a kid who always acted so scared she could barely face him . . . except for the rare occasions when she showed some spirit, some spunk. He wondered about that. Was she really as frightened as she seemed? Sometimes nearly catatonic? Or was she smarter than he thought?

He'd have to be careful.

No more mistakes, he told himself, slowing his stride and taking in deep lungfuls of air, not another misstep. He was too close.

He'd waited too long as it was.

He thought of his next two victims. Imagined the fires— growing, spiraling upward, hiding the stars with smoke and hot, hungry flames, filling the air with the smells of burning wood and charred flesh.

He closed his eyes, envisioning the sparks shooting toward the heavens.

Oh, yes! Anticipation buzzed through his blood, heating it, filling the void in the deepest part of him.

This time he wouldn't wait so long.

One fire would spark the other . . . like the Olympians carrying the torch from one town to the next.

One on the heels of the other.

Yes!

It was time to notch things up.

Chapter 22

"Trust me," he whispered against the shell of her ear as they lay naked in the darkness. The night sang with the sounds of frogs and crickets. The forest loomed above them. A breeze rattled the dry branches overhead. An October moon slid silently across a cloudless, starry sky.

Her heart was pumping, her breathing shallow as they lay upon a bed of dry leaves that rustled with their movements. Sweat soaked their naked bodies and the wind that swept through the surrounding trees was dry as a dragon's breath and twice as hot. Far off, a dog was barking.

Or was it a wolf?

Sensing she was doing something vastly dangerous, Shannon couldn't stop herself. Her skin rippled with want. Her blood ran hot in her veins. She returned the fervor of his kisses with her own.

She tingled all over. Desire pounded through her brain.

She wanted this man, needed him.

His lips were warm and sensual, his body naked and taut, lean muscles rubbing over her own bare skin. He touched her intimately. Lovingly. His mouth found hers and she responded eagerly. Hungrily. Wanting him. All of him.

Don't do this, Shannon, this man is trouble, her mind screamed. He brings with him death and darkness.

But she ignored the warnings, gave in to the pure animal sensuality of the moment.

His hands were big and calloused. Experienced. They splayed against the curve of her spine, fingers pressing anxiously into the dimples over her buttocks.

Oh, God, she ached for him. Yearned for him. Trembled with need. Perspired as his lips created a warm, wet path, sensuously sliding along her cheek, under her chin, down *her neck, and his tongue pressed into the shallow circle of bones at the base of her throat.*

"You want me," he said and the forest seemed to quiet. His voice was deep, resonant. She could feel it vibrate inside her body. One hand found her breast, toyed with a nipple. "You want me."

She swallowed hard, looked up at him.

"Say it."

She tried to speak, but her voice failed her.

"Say it."

Those magical fingers rubbed her areola more intimately, almost roughly.

The frogs had stopped croaking.

He leaned down and kissed her breast. She bucked upward and he pulled her tighter to him, bowing her back. She clung to him, knew there was no going back. She wanted him. Desperately. Despite the little nag inside her head that said this was wrong.

Dangerous.

Deadly.

And above, a tiny crackle on the forest floor, the thin smell of smoke.

"Say it," he ordered.

"I . . . I want you," she forced out, her breath hot and still in her lungs.

The crickets no longer chirped.

Stop now, while you still can, her mind insisted in the silence.

Deep within she ached, imagined what it would feel like to have him inside her.

It had been so long . . . so damned long.

The leaves rustled ominously as he lifted his head. She stared up at him in the moonlight. His eyes were a dark midnight blue, his hair glinted with silver, his face was tight with expectation. God, he was beautiful.

She slid her own hands down his chest and lower, over his

ribs, along his abdomen, her fingers dipping lower until above her, he sucked in his breath and said, "Yes, oh, yes."

The dog had gone mute.

A thick, dark cloud blocked the moon and suddenly she saw an orange glow on the horizon. A dull roar reached her ears and suddenly smoke filled her lungs, burned her eyes. Trees—their trunks black silhouettes against an ever-moving, relentless, angry wall of flames—surrounded her.

Fire!

She looked up at her lover but he was gone, had disappeared like a puff of smoke.

The fire raged. Hot. Angry. Closer.

And she was alone.

Shannon's eyes flew open. The scream forming on her lips died. Heart still beating wildly, adrenaline thrumming through her veins, she recognized her bedroom, saw the sun streaming through the windows, glanced at the bedside clock and groaned. It was after eight. For the first time since the attack she'd slept soundly.

Until the dream had brought her to consciousness. This time there was no fire, no lingering scent of smoke. The conflagration had all been in her subconscious. *Thank God.*

Pushing herself up in the bed, swinging her bare legs over the side, she considered the dream where she'd nearly made love to a man, a strange man. As the dream was unfolding she'd thought the man had been Travis Settler; she'd responded to him as if they were already intimate, as if they truly were lovers.

"Jesus," she whispered and Khan, nestled in the covers, lifted his head and yawned. Downstairs the puppy whined. "Better get up." Stretching, she thought of the dream again. Had Travis been the man lying naked with her? It seemed so real and yet . . . The facial features of the man who had been touching her, had inspired such lust in her, were blurred.

Faceless.

Nameless.

"You're a head case," she told herself and glanced at the picture of Dani Settler propped up against her bedside lamp. She picked up the page and sighed, the weight of the world once again settling on her shoulders. "We'll find you," she said to the photograph of the smiling girl, and hoped she wasn't lying.

She threw on jeans and a sweatshirt, turned on the coffee-maker, then took care of the dogs including the new little puppy, who couldn't seem to get enough of the puppy kibblets she had on hand. "What is it?" she asked the little one when Skatooli had finished the last morsel and looked upward in anticipation of more food. "Didn't Alexi ever feed you?" She held the puppy for a while, then walked her outside before returning her to her pen and tackling chores that included taking care of the other dogs. They too were fed and given fresh water, then Shannon worked with each animal and finally, hosed out their runs.

By the time she was finished it was after eleven and her own stomach was grumbling. Upon returning to the kitchen, she discovered four phone messages, two from her mother asking her to come to a "family meeting" around five.

"Sounds like a blast," Shannon muttered under her breath. The third call was from a woman looking for a place to board her dog and the fourth was from Anthony Paterno, the lead detective in Mary Beth's homicide. He asked her to call him back and set up a time for an interview. "More fun," she muttered, but punched in his number and when he didn't answer, left a message.

She'd just hung up the phone when she spied Nate crossing the parking lot and heading toward the house. A few seconds later he rapped on the back door, pushed it open and toed off his boots.

"Just thought I'd check on you," he said, flashing a smile. "How ya feeling?"

"Better. At least physically." Her ribs still hurt, and the stitches in her head were starting to itch, but the blinding headaches had abated. Her shoulder ached but the pain wasn't unbearable. "It's still hard to think about Mary Beth."

He nodded and she decided to change the subject as she reached into the cupboard for a couple of mugs. "How about coffee?"

"Sounds good." He walked into the kitchen in his stocking feet and stared down at the puppy, who, meeting his gaze, wagged her tail. "She needs a new name, you know."

Shannon waited as Nate picked up the puppy in his big hands and was rewarded with a face washing.

"And why is that?"

Nate smothered a smile. "I don't think she likes to be called Little Shit."

"What?"

"That's a loose translation of Skatooli."

"You're kidding."

"Nope. I checked it out on the Internet." He replaced the pup in her pen, ignored her whines and even managed to give Khan some badly needed attention. "Maybe some people think it's cute, but personally, I think you can do better."

"You're lovin' this aren't you?" she asked, sending him a mock-scathing look as she poured the coffee and handed him a cup.

"I told you I don't trust Demitri."

"Yeah, I remember." Sighing, she sipped a little coffee and shook her head. "How about Bonzi?"

"Geez, that's just about as bad. What does that mean?"

"Don't know. I just like the sound of it."

"Give the dog a break. Name her something . . . real."

"Like Fido or Rover or Goldie Locks?"

"Goldie Locks isn't bad."

"It sucks, Nate," she said, taking a long swallow of coffee before kneeling at the pup's cage and looking into her brown eyes. "How about Marilyn?"

"What?"

"She's blonde and beautiful and Marilyn Monroe is an icon . . . That's it."

"Monroe would be better."

"Nah. Too male."

"Like Bonzi."

She ignored the jab. "I like it!"

"Marilyn?" he tested the name and raised a dubious eyebrow. "I guess it beats the hell out of Skatooli."

She laughed and they discussed what they planned to do with the horses and dogs for the rest of the week. She didn't say too much about her new place as she knew he disapproved. Fifteen minutes later he set down his cup and went back to work.

"Keep the doors locked, even during the day," Nate suggested from the porch as he pulled on his boots. "I just don't like what's going on around here."

"Neither do I, but I think the house is safe during daylight."

He shook his head. "Too much weird stuff going on." He straightened. "Let's just err on the side of caution, okay?"

"Okay. But if I lock myself out, you'd better have a key handy."

"Just hide one in the garage, on the wall behind the extension ladder. There's a nail there and no one will ever know the spare key is there."

"Good idea."

"And you'll call someone about a security firm, preferably not Demitri?"

"ASAP," she promised.

He gave her a look that said he didn't believe her as he walked across the parking lot and up the exterior steps to his apartment. At the top of the stairs he paused. "I mean it, Shannon, I've got to be gone a lot in the next week or so . . . Find someone."

"I said I would, didn't I?" They stared at each other across the gravel lot.

As he turned to the door of his apartment, Shannon called suddenly, "Nate?" He stopped, gazed back at her. "Why aren't you going to be around? Can you tell me?"

Shannon's pulse beat strong and fast. *Please tell me what you've been doing.* For a moment she thought he might actually answer her.

His lips tightened. He seemed to consider her question hard. But all he said was, "Things aren't always what they seem," and with that cryptic comment hanging in the air, he walked into his apartment.

It was no answer. It didn't even speak to the question. Shannon gazed after him, perplexed and a bit uneasy. Though she defended him to all and sundry, Nate was a man full of secrets.

Where had *he been the night of the fire?*

He tested the lock as he always did, making certain that the hook and eye held the kid inside. He'd been concerned about her throwing her weight against the door long and hard enough to break the latch, but his worries had proved groundless. She was too much of a wimp to do anything as adventuresome as trying to escape.

Or so it seemed.

He eyed the lock and scowled. It was odd, this kid who had melted into a puddle of fear. From what he'd learned about her while communicating on the Internet, he'd expected a tomboy, a girl who had some gumption and guts. She'd bragged about being able to shoot a gun and boasted of a black belt in some kind of martial arts. She'd claimed to be able to ride a horse bareback at a gallop and pitch her own tent, hunt and fish, compliments of an outdoor education from her father.

So far, none of that had proved true.

Unless she was playacting, pretending to be scared shit-less.

He thought hard. Studied the lock with a hard eye.

A lot of people lied on the Internet. All the time. Single people looking for a date lied about their age, or their weight or how much money they made. People inflated their personal stats to satisfy their egos and kids were probably the worst, screwing around in cyberspace pretending to be something they weren't.

He rubbed his chin, glanced at his watch, knew he didn't have much time even though it was still late afternoon. He pounded a fist on her door. "I'll be back soon," he yelled loudly through the thick panels and the girl actually yelped, as if the sound of his voice terrified and startled her.

That just didn't seem to fit. His eyes narrowed and for a second he wondered if he was being conned.

On several occasions, he'd caught her staring at him, watching his every move. He'd even observed her eye pressed against the crack between the door and frame, though he was facing away from her. The spotty, cracked mirror hung over the mantel gave him a view of what was going on behind him as he faced it and he'd been able to watch the door to her room while pretending not to notice her silently watching him. So he'd given her more of a show than was his custom. She probably got off seeing a naked man. Well, fine. He made the best of it. Fear was a great motivator, the perfect psychological weapon.

She had to be smart enough to realize that his muscles meant that he was tough and he'd made a big show out of walking around with his knife, heating the blade in the coals, and then popping off a few rounds of difficult exercises just to silently prove to her how strong and deadly he was.

Just in case she got the wrong idea.

Just in case she had the notion to run.

Not yet, Brat, he thought. Not ever.

You don't know it yet, but you're doomed.

Just like your mother.

"I'm so sorry about Mary Beth," Shannon said, seeing her brother Robert for the first time since the tragedy that took his wife's life.

"Yeah, I know," he replied and looked away, unable to meet her gaze as they stood in their mother's tidy kitchen. It smelled of leftover bacon grease and Lysol, just as it had for four decades. The only odor missing was the aroma of her father's cigars. Though Patrick had been banished to the den near the fire or outside on the porch, the scent of burning tobacco had always lingered in the house, a reminder of who was the patriarch, who ruled the roost.

Thank God he hadn't witnessed this.

Patrick, like his father before him, had been fascinated with fighting fire, with pitting himself against a raging, living, breathing, crackling beast. It had been in the Flannery family's blood for generations.

Now, Robert, his wide shoulders sagging, was the last of the Flannery men to actually fight fire. All five brothers had followed in their father and grandfather's footsteps, but all had either by choice, or stern suggestion, left. Except for Robert.

How ironic that his wife had died during a blaze.

"How're the kids doing?" Shannon asked as conversation lagged.

"Okay, I guess. Elizabeth has nightmares and RJ doesn't talk about it, acts like he expects Mary Beth to just magically show up." Robert's voice caught and he cleared his throat. "The funeral's going to be rough."

"For all of us," Shannon agreed. "You might consider a counselor for the kids."

"Yeah, Cynthia thinks it would be a good idea."

Shannon felt her back stiffen. Though she told herself that she accepted Robert's relationship—it was his life, after all—it seemed disrespectful and somehow discordant to talk about Cynthia so soon after Mary Beth's death.

"Where are they?"

"With Mary Beth's sister . . . Margaret . . . I've got to work out some kind of babysitting arrangement for after school." He closed his eyes, and as if for the first time it occurred to him how much his wife had actually done for him, for his children. "It's a fuckin' nightmare," he whispered, then, hearing himself, added, "Sorry . . . It's still a shock."

"I know." The front doorbell rang and the rest of her brothers came into the house where their mother, thinking the family needed time to reach out to each other before the funeral, had convened them all. Maureen had hors d'oeuvres displayed on the breakfront in the dining room and on their father's bar, which was still stocked with Irish whiskey and every other make of hard liquor.

They made small talk, drank and nibbled on tiny crab cakes, fruit skewered with toothpicks, vegetables and hot wings with ranch dip. Little smokies simmered in a Crock-Pot near a stack of corn chips drizzled with cheese. The television was turned on to the baseball game where the Giants were losing to the Mariners. Her brothers were clustered around the flickering images of men with bats and cleats and big wads of chaw in their cheeks.

To Shannon, the whole scene seemed surreal, as if somehow her mother was trying to make something normal out of the abnormal, trying to find a way of laying Mary Beth and her memory to rest. Before the funeral. Before the Flannery clan would have to face Mary Beth's family at the service.

Well, it wasn't working. Though no one acknowledged the fact, Mary Beth's presence was more viable, more obvious than if she'd been alive. It was as if she were a ghost, listening in to the banal and inane topics of conversation.

All in all, the afternoon was trying. Conversation was strained, small talk favored over anything that might bring out tightly guarded emotions. Their mother alternately forced a fake smile or dabbed at the corners of her eyes with a handkerchief.

Shannon quickly tired of telling her brothers that she was feeling better. Their concerned looks, gentle touches and soft-spoken inquiries only made the situation more uncomfortable. The injuries she'd barely felt this morning seemed somehow more pronounced. Her mother's reference to the family curse was the worst, as bad as nails on a chalkboard. Shannon refused to comment, to be drawn into the conversation, and when Oliver said something about "thanking the Father for the family's blessings," she nearly gagged on a bite of overly salted crab cake. The headache she'd held at bay earlier came galloping back behind her eyes and, rather than get into an argument with any of her siblings or her mother, she retreated upstairs to the bathroom where Maureen kept her extensive selection of pills and remedies.

Shannon popped two coated aspirin dry, then sat on the edge of the bathtub, letting the breeze that slipped through the partially opened window cool the back of her neck. The house was hot. Stuffy. Beads of sweat prickled her skin and she lifted her hair off her neck in her fist.

She heard her brothers clamor onto the back porch. Lighters clicked and smoke drifted upward with the hushed conversation. As she had as a child, she blatantly eavesdropped. It was a habit she hadn't broken, one created by exclusion, because her brothers, though always protective of her, had also kept her away from their inner circle.

Aaron's voice was hushed, but she heard him say "birth order." What the devil were they discussing?

Someone, it sounded like Shea, muttered something about Neville, but she couldn't make it out.

Now she was really curious. She locked the bathroom door quietly, then stepped into the bathtub where she could look beneath the opaque panes to the crack that was open. Past the tattered screen she viewed the tops of two heads, black hair shining in the sunlight. Aaron and Shea, she thought, watching them smoke and converse in quiet tones near the grape arbor that offered a bit of shade from the sweltering sun. Hummingbirds flitted around the bird bath and bees droned in the garden lush with fuchsias, petunias, daisies and lavender.

So where were Robert and Oliver?

Under the porch overhang so they weren't visible to her? With their mother in the house?

Excluded intentionally?

Why did she feel that there was something ominous in their gathering? They'd just stepped outside for cigarettes with their drinks and yet . . .

Rap. Rap. Rap.

Knuckles on the door.

Shannon nearly jumped out of her skin.

"Honey, are you all right?" Maureen asked, rattling the doorknob.

"Yeah." She caught her breath, stilled her heart from the shock of nearly being discovered listening at the window. "I was just looking for some ibuprofen or Aleve."

"In the medicine cabinet."

"I found it." Silently Shannon slid out of the tub and noticed that, thankfully, she'd left no footprints on the gleaming porcelain.

"Are you all right?"

"Just a headache, Mother."

"I wish you'd go see that doctor again."

"I will. In a few days."

Shannon flushed the toilet, then ran water in the sink. A few seconds later she opened the door to find her mother standing near the bureau, staring into the mirror and tucking a few wayward locks into her carefully arranged curls. "You sure you're all right?" she asked, picking up a can of spray and shellacking her hair into place.

"Right as rain," Shannon lied and before her mother could launch into another episode of "Woe is us" and the "Flannery curse," she said, "I've really got to go, Mom. It's been a long day and I've got that new puppy."

"Of course." Maureen was only half-paying attention as she adjusted her scarf. She turned her head left and right to survey her image. As if any of her children would care which way the scarf's folds overlapped around her neck.

"See ya later," Shannon said.

"At the funeral. If you need a ride . . ."

"I should be fine, but I'll call," Shannon said, knowing

her mother would want all her children around her for support. She'd do it. Somehow Shannon would tune out all the negative talk and sit with her mother, hold her hand, provide a shoulder to cry on and what mattered most: the semblance of family solidarity at the service.

She nearly ran into Oliver at the bottom of the stairs.

White-faced, looking shaken he said, "Is Mother upstairs?"

"Yes."

He seemed worried.

"Just fiddling with her hair."

"I don't like her being alone."

Shannon motioned to the staircase with its polished rail and worn steps. "Then go talk to her."

"What about you?"

"I have to go, Oliver," she said and saw a dark cloud cross his eyes, a hint of vexation. "I'll talk to you soon."

"Shannon, wait."

When she turned to look at him, he was staring at her and there was something in his gaze, something tortured, that gave her pause. "What is it?"

He glanced up the stairs and deep lines creased his forehead. "They say forgiveness is good for the soul."

"Are you talking about me?" she asked. "And who are 'they'?"

"I mean—"

Footsteps interrupted him and a second later Robert walked into the foyer. Oliver was about five steps up, Shannon near the base.

"You leaving?" Robert asked Shannon.

"I have to go. Duty and dogs call." She brushed a kiss across his temple and smelled the scents of smoke and twenty-year-old whiskey clinging to him. "Take care and give my love to the kids."

"I will," he said and hugged her more fiercely than he had in a decade.

She glanced up at Oliver, who held her gaze, then, troubled and resigned, continued up the stairs.

She was bothered by Oliver's attitude, but there wasn't much she could do. "Oliver," she said and blew him a kiss. "Later."

"Right," he said, but there was hesitation in his voice.

"Is something bothering you?" she asked.

"Everything bothers me, Shannon. Don't you know that?"

"You want to talk about it?"

He glanced at Robert, met his older brother's gaze. "Nah. I'm fine."

"Sure?" she asked, once again feeling left out of her brothers' secrets.

"Absolutely," he said, and then with a smile and a hint of devilment in his gaze, added, "Go with God."

She laughed. So he did have a sense of humor after all, could still laugh at himself. "Later," she said. She told the rest of her siblings good-bye, then took off, driving her truck five miles over the speed limit, as if she expected one of her brothers to chase her down the street and pull her back into the swirl of tragedy that was her family.

"Don't be an idiot," she told herself, but checked her rearview mirror anyway. She saw the worry in her own eyes and decided it wasn't worth it to try and psychoanalyze why her family sometimes made her feel claustrophobic, or why she often had the screaming urge to run away.

There was just no logic to it.

Not that there was much logic to any part of her life these days. She tromped a little harder on the accelerator and pushed the thoughts aside.

"We think we found the van." Carter's voice sounded grim. Strained. "The one that Madge Rickert saw while walking her dog, the one that had been parked behind Janssen's Hardware Store that Earl Miller noticed, the one with the Arizona plates."

Travis was sitting on the foot of his bed in the motel room. "Dani?" Travis whispered, throat tight, fear pounding through his brain.

"Not there, Travis. But her cell phone was."

"Jesus Christ," he whispered.

"The van was located in a garage of an abandoned farm in Idaho. The only reason we found it is that a neighbor who rents the acreage to grow wheat parked near the garage and he noticed a bad odor. He had his dog with him and the Lab was going ape shit. The garage door had a new padlock on it and the farmer thought that was funny, so he forced it open, found the van and inside it was a big garbage bag filled with bloody clothes. Men's clothes. Lots of blood."

"Whose blood?" Travis forced himself to ask.

"Blanche Johnson's."

Travis closed his eyes, counted slowly to twenty, willing his pulse to stop racing.

"The farmer called Blanche's phone—the Idaho place is hers—and we took the call. Because the clothes were so covered in blood, we're speculating that they were what the perp was wearing when he killed Blanche. We're testing them for evidence, hoping something will tell us who he is."

Travis's hand hurt from clenching the phone so hard. "But you didn't find Dani?"

"No. Just her cell phone on the floor of the garage. The Idaho State Police charged it and tracked its owner. Expedited our investigation. We've got men and dogs searching the area, but from the tire tracks, we figure he had another vehicle stashed and took off in it."

"With Dani?"

"Probably. We found footprints in the dust. Ones consistent with a woman's size seven, the same as your daughter's."

Travis squeezed his eyes shut. *Please let her be alive. Safe.*

"We have other footprint impressions as well, a man's size thirteen, and the crime scene investigative team is going over the van and the garage now. The Idaho State Police are working with the FBI and the local Sheriff's Department. I'm in the loop and I'll keep you posted."

Travis held the phone to his head with one hand, raked his fingers through his hair with the other. "You don't think the blood on the clothes is my daughter's?" he asked, forcing out the words.

"No, I don't, but, of course we don't know for certain, but we will soon. The butcher knife we found in the bag looks like one that was missing from Blanche Johnson's kitchen set, and the link is her place in Idaho. She inherited the place a few years back but hasn't lived there since she was a child. As far as anyone knows, she rarely visited it. The place is a shambles. She's been renting it out for the past couple of years to the neighbor."

Travis listened, his throat tight, his pulse pounding in his ears as he thought of bloody clothes, a dripping butcher knife and his daughter.

"I figure whoever killed Blanche wanted us to find the van . . . He had to have known that someone would eventually stop by, maybe notice the new lock. It's also someone who knew Blanche owned the place. We're checking all of her acquaintances, people who knew her way back when. It'll take some time."

"I'm afraid we're running out."

"Hang in there."

"He's here now. Somewhere around Santa Lucia," Travis said, thinking of the recent fires. "And he's got Dani. He left her backpack at the last fire."

"I know, I've been talking to Paterno. Don't worry, we'll keep digging on this end. I'll call you when I know something more," Carter promised before hanging up.

Travis stared at the phone in his hand. Rage, his constant companion these days, wormed through his brain. He climbed to his feet and walked to the window. It was getting dark and he was restless, had to do something. Anything. He just couldn't sit around this motel room another second.

Snagging his keys from the top of the desk, he headed outside to the parking lot where the security lamps were humming and insects hovered near the bulbs. The heat of the day hung heavy in the air, with no breath of a breeze to bring down the temperature. As people walked in and out of El Ranchito, Latin music and conversation drifted into the night.

Travis paused at his truck and looked across the street. The silver Ford Taurus was missing, the detectives assigned to watch him having been pulled off the case. Or . . . His gaze swept the surrounding area, half-expecting to see another unmarked vehicle parked in the shadows.

None was visible and he didn't really care anyway.

He eyed the spot where Mary Beth Flannery so recently had rested her hips against her husband's silver sports car, the key dangling from her finger, the threat of violence in her eyes.

A few hours later, after leaving with Robert, she'd been killed, her house torched and Dani's backpack left at the scene of the crime.

Why?

What the hell did Dani have to do with Robert Flannery's wife? Shannon's sister-in-law?

Shannon.

Dani's mother.

Travis expelled a slow breath. She'd been on his mind from the moment he'd met her. He'd wanted to hate her. To distrust her. To prove that she'd somehow been involved with the stealing of his child. But that wasn't the case. Oh, she was involved all right, but at a different level. She, too, was a victim, if what he'd witnessed here in California could be believed.

Things aren't what they seem, you know that. Don't trust her, just use her.

The muscles in the back of his neck tightened. For a second he saw her as she'd been this afternoon: sunlight touching her green eyes, her slightly sexy smile—a smile that showed off a hint of white teeth—on lips that glistened a soft pink. She was intelligent, determined and confident as she'd worked with the dog. Travis had noticed the way her jeans had pulled over her buttocks as she'd squatted near the rescue dog. He'd been way too conscious of the skin on her lower back as her shirt had lifted to show just a tantalizing hint of flesh.

It seemed improbable, or even damned impossible, that he should be attracted to her, given the situation. So she was beautiful. Hadn't he learned his lesson about gorgeous women? Hadn't Jenna Hughes slam-dunked him? And this . . . The mother of his kid, this was out of the question.

Just use her.

He shook his head. It seemed not only unfair but unwise. She was still recovering from a beating, the bruises on her face not yet disappeared. She'd been through so much in her life and she was trying desperately to help him find his child. Wasn't she? Certainly it wasn't an act. But he couldn't be certain. Though he no longer believed she was a part of Dani's abduction, she was still certainly a player, albeit unwilling.

Shannon Flannery was the link.

So use her . . . You know she's attracted to you. You felt it today, didn't you? Don't wimp out.

"Son of a bitch," he growled, feeling a bit of sweat along his forehead. He kicked at a pebble, sent it careening into the hubcap of a dented minivan.

Angry with the world and himself, Travis climbed into his truck, fired up the engine and pointed the nose of the pickup toward the street where traffic, thinning with the night, rushed by.

He crammed the Ford into drive and hit the gas.

Chapter 23

Paterno switched off the ignition. Armed with as much information as he could plumb about the Carlyle and Flannery families, he, along with Rossi from the arson division, had driven to Shannon Flannery's little ranch. He'd already interviewed all of her siblings and Mary Beth's family and friends before calling on the infamous widow of Ryan Carlyle.

In his mind all the crimes were linked. The old Stealth Torcher business, Ryan Carlyle's murder, Dani Settler's abduction, the new fires and the murder of Mary Beth Flannery. As he'd looked into old information, he'd found out a few other skeletons hanging out in the Flannery and Carlyle closets, strange things that had remained unexplained for decades.

Just like the number six in the weird symbol left at the crimes, Shannon, whether she liked it or not, was at the center of what was happening.

"Let's go," he said to Rossi and they climbed out of his car. The grounds around the place were well-enough tended. There were lights blazing in the house, but the apartment over the garage was dark and the only vehicle he spotted was the truck registered to Shannon Flannery. He made a mental note that the guy who lived on the property, Nate Santana, wasn't around tonight. The little ranch, though not far from town, had a serene, rural feeling. One security lamp illuminated the gravel lot where her truck was parked and several buildings rimmed the lot. One had been burned to nearly nothing, yellow crime scene tape still surrounding its perimeter. A tall barn nearby had been scorched, its paint blistering on the side nearest the charred debris, some of the windows boarded up.

Paterno walked across the lot. A dog barked from inside the house and before he reached the stoop a porch light blazed on. The door opened and a small-boned, athletic-looking woman stood in the frame. A mottled-colored, shaggy dog, every muscle tense, hackles raised, stood beside her and glared up at Paterno with mismatched eyes.

"Shannon Flannery?" he asked, flipping open his badge, keenly aware of the dog. She nodded. "Detective Paterno, Santa Lucia Police Department. This is—"

"Detective Rossi," she said icily. "We've met."

Paterno ignored the frosty glare she sent to the younger detective. "We're investigating the death of Mary Beth Flannery. If you don't mind, we'd like to come inside and ask you a few questions."

He expected her to try to stall, or to hesitate, even balk, given her history with the police department. Instead, she opened the door wide. "I've been expecting you," she said. "I heard you visited my mother and brothers. Come on in." To the dog she said, "Get on your blanket. Now." With one last furtive glance at Paterno and Rossi, the mutt did as it was bid, claws clicking on the floor as it headed toward the kitchen where a puppy whined and the spicy smell of onions and green peppers erupted. As they passed by the archway he noticed a microwave meal, still steaming in its cardboard box, on a counter.

She led them into a small living room with a worn carpet. Pictures of her family and several dogs covered the tops of small tables scattered around the room. She curled up in a striped side chair with a matching ottoman, and tucked her bare feet beneath her. He sat on the edge of a beat-up old couch and Rossi took a seat in a rocker that creaked beneath his weight.

Shannon eyed the two men warily. "What do you want to know?" She'd known she wouldn't be excluded from their interrogation, but as Rossi began taking notes and Paterno, with her permission, set a small recorder on the coffee table, she clenched inside. She was assaulted by a horrible sense of déjà vu, remembering the last time the police had interrogated her here, in this very room.

But this time she had nothing to hide, had done nothing suspicious.

Paterno started by asking her about her relationship with Mary Beth, and what Shannon had been doing on the night her sister-in-law had been killed. She explained everything including driving to the scene, seeing her sister-in-law's body being removed from the house and her truck being blocked in so that she had to leave it parked on the street.

Yes, she had witnessed the fight between Robert and Mary Beth and seen them get in his car. No, she hadn't called her sister-in-law, though Mary Beth had insisted she had and even Shea thought Shannon had called her.

"But you didn't call her," Paterno reiterated, watching her with hawklike eyes.

It hit Shannon like a ton of bricks. "Oh, Jesus," she whispered, straightening in her chair. "No, I didn't call her, but I lost my cell phone on the night of the fire in my shed. I called 9-1-1, but then dropped the cell when I was attacked. It had been missing for days, since that night. I just found it yesterday and, of course, the battery had run down to nothing. I haven't used it since. Wait just a sec." She unfolded herself from the chair, hurried into the kitchen and knew without a doubt what she would find. Heart pounding, she pulled the cell phone from its charger. Ignoring the puppy who whimpered for her, Khan who lay on his rug, waiting for the word to be released, and the microwave Chicken Oriental dinner she'd just heated, she switched on the phone. Walking slowly into the living room again, she stared at the small screen as it came to life. With a touch of a button she found the list of recently dialed calls.

"Oh, God," she whispered. Hand at her throat she witnessed the familiar number on the display. Robert and Mary Beth's number listed three times in succession. She handed the damning evidence to Paterno. "I found this in my truck, wedged under the seat, but I didn't have it on the days those calls were made." On a note of barely suppressed hysteria, she wondered aloud, "Who would do this? Who would take the phone, make the calls and then hide it in my truck?"

"You have no idea?" Paterno carefully placed her phone in a plastic evidence bag.

Shannon lowered herself onto the ottoman. "No."

"No one you know who would want to set you up?"

"Oh, my God, you don't think I . . . I . . . That *I* killed Mary Beth?" she asked, stunned.

"We don't know what to think," Paterno said with maddening patience. "But you asked 'Who would do this?' . . . I think you're the best one to answer."

"I already gave Detective Rossi and his partner a list of people I thought might attack me and set my shed on fire. It hasn't changed."

"Could you elaborate on your relationship with your sister-in-law?"

Shannon gazed at him blankly. She had no idea what he was really thinking. "We were friends once, best friends, in grade school and high school. She met Robert through me. We all went to St. Theresa's together. My brothers, me, Mary Beth, Liam, Kevin, and Margaret."

"And your husband?"

Shannon clenched her hands. "Yes."

"Ryan Carlyle was Mary Beth Carlyle Flannery's first cousin."

"That's right."

"Her *adopted* cousin."

"Yes," she said, "Ryan was adopted. It wasn't something that he broadcast, but nothing he or his family had tried to hide."

"He had a brother, too, didn't he?"

Where was this going? "Yes. Teddy."

"You knew him."

"In grade school. He was a year older than me."

Paterno checked his notes. "In the same class as your brothers Neville and Oliver."

"Yes," she said automatically and remembered Teddy

Carlyle, a spoiled, loud-mouthed, athletic kid with freckles and slightly crooked teeth.

"They hang around with him?"

"Some," she said. "Though he was more of a friend to Neville. Oliver and Teddy didn't really get along."

"Why not?"

"I guess because he got between Oliver and Neville. Teddy was a troublemaker and he teased Oliver about being shy and bookish. Whenever Teddy was over, there was always a problem."

"So you didn't like him."

"You're twisting my words. I didn't like what he did to the family dynamics, how he came between the twins, but that was their business, not mine. Teddy didn't have much use for me."

"But Ryan did."

"Not then."

"Teddy wasn't adopted." The remark came out of left field.

She felt a shift in the atmosphere, sensed his eyes focus a little sharper. "He wasn't? I guess not, I don't really know. It wasn't something I ever talked about with Ryan." She frowned. "What's Teddy got to do with anything?"

"He died in a car wreck when he'd just turned thirteen. Ryan was at the wheel."

She nodded, feeling the need to tread carefully. "A horrible accident."

"I know. I read the report. Ryan was an inexperienced driver, barely sixteen, coming back from a football game, about this time of year."

"I guess . . ." Shannon said, trying not to nervously pluck at the arm of the chair. Where the hell was Paterno going with this line of questioning?

"According to all the eyewitnesses, and the skid evidence taken at the scene, Ryan swerved to miss a deer, hit gravel, lost control and the car smashed into a tree on the side of the road. Witnesses at the scene testified that Ryan tried to pull the kid out, but the car exploded into a ball of fire. Autopsy reports show that it was too late anyway, Teddy wasn't wearing a shoulder restraint. He died instantly from a broken neck."

Shannon shivered. Teddy had been a trial, always causing trouble between the twins, but it was a shame he'd died so young.

"Don't you think it's weird that Teddy was thirteen when this happened? He'd just turned a week or so earlier, and now your daughter, Travis Settler's kid, she turns thirteen and she's abducted, presumably brought down here, though we can't be sure of that, and now these recent fires . . . similar to the ones that were set by the Stealth Torcher. Doesn't it all seem tied together?"

"I don't know."

"I think it's all connected somehow, you know what I mean? Like knitting, you pull one thread and everything starts to unravel."

"Then pull a thread," she said, tired of the unspoken accusations, the innuendos that she'd recognized during the interview.

"Your brothers, they were tight?"

"Pardon?"

"The twins. You know how that is. They were close."

"Very." She nodded but didn't relax. Just because the questions had gotten easier, she didn't want to be lulled into a sense of security; not with Paterno.

"Didn't the twins hang out with other kids?"

"Some. Especially Neville. Of the two, he is . . . was . . . the most outgoing."

"Was?" Paterno asked. The rocker squeaked as Rossi changed positions. "You think he's dead?"

Shannon shook her head in lieu of an answer.

"He just up and disappeared. Right after the fire that took your husband's life."

"Well . . . about three weeks later, I think."

"You saw him in those three weeks?"

"Of course."

"Talked to him?"

"Yes," she said.

"What about?"

"I can't remember! It's all kind of a blur," she admitted, turning up her palms as she remembered the horror of learning of her husband's death. No, she didn't love him any longer, no she didn't trust him, but no, she didn't really wish him dead. She'd just wanted him to leave her alone, to give her some peace, to quit hurting her in every way possible. But his death, the fire. The suspicion that she'd somehow either killed him herself or set him up had nearly pushed her over the edge emotionally. Yes, she'd seen Neville in that time, but had she really talked to him? She didn't know. Her brothers had, she thought. The last one to see him was Oliver, and that was just before Oliver's breakdown and stay in the psychiatric ward where he'd found Jesus, where through prayer, God had spoken with him, called him into the priesthood.

Obviously Paterno had heard all about it. Just as obviously he wasn't buying a word of it.

Paterno shifted on the couch. "Isn't that odd? Your brother just up and vanishing?"

"Extremely odd." She sighed, glanced out the window to the encroaching night. "I . . . I don't get it. Never have, but during that time I was distracted."

"Because of the murder charges."

"Yes!" She glared at him and the rage she'd felt at the district attorney, at the police department, at the damned system, swept through her all over again. "My entire life was turned upside down. My husband was dead. Murdered. Accused of being a serial arsonist and I'm accused of killing him? On top of that my brother goes missing and no one can find him." She leaned forward, elbows on her knees. "Look, Detective Paterno, this is all old news. I don't know what happened to Neville. No one in our family does. Of course you know my brother Shea because you replaced him in this investigation, and my brother Aaron is a private investigator. They both, along with everyone in the family, have tried to locate Neville."

"And nothing?"

"Nothing." She looked up at him, felt her headache returning. "I thought you were going to ask me about Mary Beth's murder."

The look he sent her was filled with the patience of a methodical but determined man, one who would never give up.

"How did Mary Beth feel when her cousin died and you were on trial for his murder?"

"She blamed me for his death," Shannon admitted. "The whole Carlyle family did, especially Liam. He and Ryan were the same age, played on the same football team, were best friends."

"Along with your brother Robert."

"Robert was in their class, too." She nodded, scooted back in the chair, resigned herself to putting up with a few more questions.

"Tight little group?"

"Most of the time." High school seemed a lifetime ago.

"Mary Beth testified at your trial."

Shannon closed her eyes. "Everyone did." She remembered Mary Beth on the stand, her eyes wet with tears as she testified she'd heard Shannon say she wished her husband were dead. Then Liam had echoed the same words, more vehemently, while extolling Ryan's virtues. Kevin had been quieter but had stared directly at Shannon with such hatred she'd shivered inside, and Margaret, ever the devout, had been visibly shaking, making the sign of the cross repeatedly as she told the court her only cousin's marriage had been rocky.

Of course they hadn't known Ryan had abused her. Hadn't believed him capable of such violence. But then few had.

"Your husband"—Paterno's voice brought her back to the

present—"worked with your brothers in the Santa Lucia Fire Department."

"Yes."

"And Liam Carlyle, too?"

"That's correct."

"And after the fire that took Robert Carlyle's life, not only did Liam quit, your brother Neville did, too. Then a few weeks later Neville disappeared. And you have no idea where he is?"

"I've already told you: no. I wish I did, but I don't. The truth is that I suspect something happened to him."

"Foul play?"

"One day he's with us and acting as if nothing's wrong, the next he's gone." She snapped her fingers. "Just like that."

"How does someone just disappear?"

"Good question. Ask Jimmy Hoffa's family," she snapped, then pushed herself off the ottoman and into the chair. "I wish I knew what happened," she admitted. Looking out the window to the dark landscape and the reflection of her own image showing in the glass, she said, "I wish he was here."

"There was a life insurance policy on him. You're the primary beneficiary."

"The company never paid me."

"Yet . . . It's still pending, right?"

"I suppose."

"And you got the lion's share of his estate?"

She nodded. "Neville wasn't married, had no children."

"But he has a twin brother, an identical twin brother, and you said they were extremely close. They used to play tricks on everyone, trade identities."

"You think he should have left everything to Oliver."

"I'm pulling threads, Ms. Flannery."

Shannon ducked her head. "I don't know why I'm the beneficiary, Detective. Maybe Neville knew Oliver was going to join the priesthood," she said, having asked herself the same question over and over again. "Neville wasn't particularly religious. I don't know. All of my brothers are extremely protective of me, they always have been. I'm the only girl and the youngest."

"Number six."

"What?"

"The sixth child."

"That's true," she said and felt a little change in the air, something shift. The hairs on the back of her arm lifted.

"The same number on the symbol that was left here on your porch, and in the middle of the star design we found at the fire that killed Mary Beth Flannery." Paterno reached into his pocket and took out two pages of paper, each with a drawing on it. He handed them to her. The first drawing she recognized, as it was the shape of the burned birth certificate, the second—a star missing a point, with numbers and broken lines—was new to her.

"You think the six represents me?" she asked, dumbfounded. "What does that mean?" She didn't wait for a response. "If I'm six, what are the other numbers?" she asked, trying to follow his logic and feeling a chill as cold as death. "Members of my family?"

"Possibly."

"But why the broken lines . . . ? Why would I be in the middle of this thing?" she whispered, staring at the pages as if in so doing she could solve the mysteries of the universe, or at the very least, of her own life and the lives of those closest to her. God, it was creepy. "I don't get it. Where did this come from?"

"We found this image in two places at Mary Beth Flannery's house. One scribbled on the mirror in what we think is lipstick, the second on the inside flap of a backpack left at the scene. Travis Settler has ID'd the bag as belonging to his daughter. *Your* daughter."

"What?" she whispered, her lungs suddenly tight. Oh, God, no. She couldn't bear to have Dani even remotely connected to Mary Beth's murder. "I don't understand."

"Neither do I. Yet," he said, then, as his cell phone rang,

he stood and whipped the flip phone from his pocket. "Paterno," he said quickly after placing the phone to his ear. "Yeah . . . No . . ." A quick look at his watch. "I can be there in about fifteen. Yeah, just wrapping up here . . . Got it." He snapped the phone closed and, pointing to the pages still clutched in her fingers, said, "I think that's about it for now. You can keep those."

As if on cue, Rossi rose.

"Is there anything else you want to tell us?" Paterno asked.

"No . . . Well, yeah. I don't know if this has any bearing on anything, but my brother Oliver thought he saw Brendan Giles in the congregation last Sunday."

Paterno frowned, his thick eyebrows slamming together to become one intense line. "Did he talk to him?"

"No." Quickly Shannon related what Oliver had told her.

"It's probably a mistake," Rossi finally said.

"Maybe. It's been years. I just thought you should know."

"Funny your brother didn't mention it to me when I talked to him," Paterno said slowly. "Guess it must've slipped his mind."

"As I said, he's not sure."

"Anything else you think maybe we should know?" he asked, one eyebrow raising.

"Yeah," she said. "One thing, but I'm not sure how it all fits."

"Shoot."

"On the night of the fire here, the one that destroyed my shed, it looks like someone intentionally harmed one of my horses." She explained Nate's theory about Molly, then slipped on a pair of shoes and walked the two policemen into the horse barn where they saw the mare's singed whiskers first-hand.

Paterno's face was shuttered and grim.

"The guy's a real sicko," Rossi said, his face red.

Apparently wounding an animal was worse than killing a woman in Rossi's estimation. Or maybe he'd become jaded over the years, was used to finding charred bodies in bath-tubs. An animal lover herself, Shannon understood his rage, but it surprised her in the detective. Paterno, on the other hand, remained quiet, his eyes dark and contemplative.

As they walked back to the house, Paterno said, "If there's anything else you think of you'll call, right?"

"Count on it. I want this maniac caught as much as any-one. He's got my daughter."

If he was going to say anything else, perhaps mention the fact that Shannon had given up her motherly rights to her child thirteen years earlier, he thought better of it.

Smart man.

She escorted them to their car. As they were climbing into the sedan, she returned to the house where, once she'd closed the front door, she leaned against the panels, thankful the interview was over. Her thoughts turned to Dani Settler again, just as they had continually since she'd first heard the girl had been kidnapped. "Please, please, keep her safe," she prayed, aching inside. Why couldn't the police and the FBI find her? Where was she? Would Shannon ever see her, ever meet the only daughter she would probably ever have, or ever have the peace of mind of knowing that Dani was safe?

That was the big, chilling question.

The thought that she might never meet the girl whose pic-ture she kept on the nightstand by her bed tore at her heart. Surely God wouldn't be so cruel.

Her throat filled with a lump that made it impossible to swallow, and the headache she'd been fighting all day came back with a vengeance.

From the kitchen, Khan gave up a sharp, pay-me-some-attention bark. "Did you think I'd forgotten about you?" she asked as she walked through the archway. She dropped the drawings Paterno had given her on to the kitchen table.

The mottled dog was still sitting on his rug, every muscle tense. "Were you going to sit here until kingdom come?" she asked, amused. He wriggled at the sight of her and Marilyn, from her little pen, barked and tried to climb the mesh.

"Come!" Shannon said to Khan. Glancing through the kitchen window, she saw twin beams from the police car's headlights cut through the night. A second later the engine caught and the car was rolling down the drive. Shannon let out her breath and turned her attention back to her dog. "You're such a good boy," she told Khan.

But he wasn't in the mood for praise or platitudes. Toenails clicking wildly, he bolted to the front door and stood at the window, nose to the glass, eyes focused on the retreating car, every muscle in his body tense. "Yeah, I'm glad that's over, too." She noticed the shriveled state of her already-nuked microwave meal and couldn't stomach the thought of reheating it again. Scowling, she tossed it into the garbage. "So much for gourmet," she said to the puppy. "Hey, you." She patted the velvet-soft head and felt a wet nose against her palm. "Just give me a sec, okay?"

While the puppy whined, Shannon hurried up the stairs, popped two aspirin, and holding her hair away from her face in one hand, washed the small tablets down with water from the tap. She slid into a pair of flip-flops and clapped her way back downstairs.

The pup was yipping noisily as Shannon returned to the kitchen. "Patience not your long suit?" she teased, picking up the fat little animal and getting her face washed with a wet pink tongue.

Shannon actually giggled. What was it about puppies that was so irresistible? Their smell? Their innocence? Their big eyes? Their soft, wiggling body? Or just the whole damned adorable package? "Yeah, yeah, I like you, too."

Khan, ever jealous, was suddenly at her feet, but for the moment, Shannon ignored him as she set the newcomer back into her pen. She refilled the puppy's food dish. Marilyn couldn't devour her dry kibbles fast enough. As soon as the last morsel was scraped up and the pup had lapped some water, Shannon snapped a training leash onto Marilyn's collar and walked her outside. While Khan raced ahead to sniff the bushes and fence line, hoping to scare up a squirrel or chipmunk, Shannon let the pup wander and explore her new environs.

The burned shed was a grim reminder of what was happening. Shannon reminded herself to call Alexi Demitri's security company in the morning, despite Nate's distrust of the man. But Nate, Shea and even Alexi were right about one thing: with everything that had gone on, she'd be foolish not to have cameras and alarms installed. If Alexi's men couldn't come over immediately, she'd ask Aaron to help her. Just as she had in the past.

She cringed a little as she thought about the last time she and Aaron had installed tiny cameras and recorders. She'd known that Ryan would ignore the restraining order and she feared he'd come at her with his fists flying. She'd decided she could either fight back, even shoot him if need be, to protect herself, or she could tape his actions and take the proof to the police and the district attorney.

And the whole idea had backfired.

She drew in her shoulders protectively as she recalled Ryan's rage when he'd discovered what she'd done. Not only had he hurt her, he'd destroyed the evidence by smashing all of the equipment.

A week later he was dead.

Burned in a horrid fire.

And she'd been accused of his murder.

Now, as she wandered the grounds with the dog, she thought about the weird symbols that Detective Paterno had shown her and of course she thought of Mary Beth and Dani.

Headlights flashed along the drive.

Her heart sank.

"Oh, no," she whispered, believing the two detectives had returned. But the rumble of the engine sounded deeper than that of the cops' sedan and within seconds she spotted Travis Settler's truck roll up the drive.

Relief, a refreshing wave, washed over her and she actually allowed herself a smile. However, as he climbed out of the truck and her stupid heart skipped a beat, she caught herself. She recognized trouble when she saw it. And Travis Settler in his faded jeans, leather jacket and grim, don't-give-me-any-bullshit expression was pure trouble.

A couple of days' worth of beard darkened his jaw and whatever was on his mind wasn't good. "I saw Paterno leaving," he said, nodding toward the lane. When his eyes found hers again, they were dark, filled with concern. He touched her good shoulder, the pads of his fingers warm through her sleeve. "Are you okay?"

She felt something break inside her, some tiny piece of resistance that she'd kept around her heart. "Are you?" she asked and he almost smiled.

"Don't know if I'll ever be." He ran his free hand around his neck but his other still touched her in that fragile connection. "They told you about Dani's backpack?"

"Yeah."

He closed his eyes. The pressure on her arm increased. "If that son of a bitch has done anything to her, I swear, I'll kill him with my bare hands."

"Only if you beat me to him," she said. Their eyes met in the gathering darkness, only the eerie light from the security lamp offering any illumination. She thought of her dream, of nearly making love to a man she thought was this one and though she knew it was silly, felt a little thrill rush through her.

"Who's this?" he asked, glancing down at the puppy.

"The newest member of my family. Recently dubbed Marilyn."

Travis almost smiled as he glanced down at the pup.

"Come in and I'll buy you a beer," she said.

The almost smile became a partial grin. "You've got yourself a deal."

Once they were inside with the kitchen lights blazing, some of the intimacy of their meeting outside faded. She handed him a beer, and, because of the aspirin she'd taken, just sipped one of her own as they sat at the table. She chided herself for being such a romantic ninny, and then forgot about her fantasies altogether as he explained about his phone call from Oregon and the discovery of the van in which, it was theorized, Dani had been abducted. In turn, she told him about her recent meeting with Paterno and Rossi and about Oliver thinking he'd seen Brendan Giles in town, and showed him the weird sketches, which he already knew about. She then told him about Molly and what Nate Santana thought.

Travis frowned at the mention of Santana, but drained his beer and asked to see the horse. Once again, this time with Khan leading the way, she headed outside, across the lot and into the horse barn. A few snorts and whinnies greeted her and several of the animals, ears cocked, swung their heads over the stall doors.

"It seems like forever since that night," he said, his eyes drawn to the spot where she'd been attacked. Bloodstains still marked the floor.

"A lot has happened." She unlatched the stall door. "Poor Molly, here, was a victim, too." Carefully she reached for the buckskin's halter and showed Travis the mare's muzzle with its charred whiskers.

Travis's eyes darkened. His lips compressed. "Bastard," he whispered. "Damned son of a bitching perverted bastard!" His fists closed for a second and he looked as if he wanted to strike something or someone. She didn't blame him. They left the stable together. "And you said Giles is back in town?"

"No. I said Oliver *thought* he saw Brendan. When I pressed him, he backed off. I've phoned Brendan's parents and, big surprise, they haven't returned the call. I did mention to Paterno that Oliver thought he saw him."

"Good," he bit out, but was obviously agitated at the thought of Dani's biological father being anywhere nearby.

"There's something else," she said as they headed across the parking lot to the house. A hint of a breeze slipped through the night, stirring dry leaves and dust in its path. "I found my cell phone. In the truck." She explained about the calls to Mary Beth and Paterno taking the phone as evidence.

"When did the cell phone get put there?"

"I don't know. It could have happened when the pickup was parked down by Robert's house during the fire. There were tons of people around and then, as you know, I had to leave the truck on the street."

Travis turned to look at her vehicle sitting in its usual spot. "Where exactly did you find the phone? Show me."

"Sure." She crossed the lot to the truck, yanked open the door and pointed to the seat. "Under there."

"Got a flashlight?"

"Sure . . . Why?"

"I just want to poke around," he said cryptically as she reached into the glove box and retrieved the tool in question. She handed it to him and he clicked it on, then shined the beam under the seat.

"What do you think you're going to find?"

"Probably nothing, but I hope the son of a bitch screwed up and left something that we might be able to trace to him."

"The police didn't look in here."

"They didn't believe you, did they?"

He didn't lift his head, just rummaged around and pulled out an old road map, a few French fries, a magazine and a small plastic box. "This yours?" he asked, holding it up to the light.

Shannon squinted. "I don't think so. What is it?"

"A tape."

Her heart stopped. "You mean like a cassette? The kind you can record on?"

"That's right." His voice was grave and he stared at the cassette as if it were a demon straight from hell. "You got a player?"

"Yeah . . . on the stereo. It's old." She was already half-running toward the house, dread pounding through her. Instinctively she knew the recording was important, probably a message from the killer. "Should we call the police?"

"Not yet. It could be nothing, something someone left inadvertently, like old songs they recorded. We don't want to call Paterno over to listen to bad copies of Bon Jovi or Madonna or the Dixie Chicks."

"That's not what it is," she said, her voice low as she opened the cabinet to the old stereo. Travis knelt before the system. He'd barely touched the sides of the tape all the while he'd looked it over and now he slipped it into the machine.

A few seconds later a girl's voice came through the speakers.

"Mommy, help me! Please, Mommy. I'm scared. Come and get me. I don't know where I am and I think he's going to hurt me!

"Please, Mommy. Hurry!"

Chapter 24

All the blood drained from Shannon's head. She felt faint. She knew the truth, realized what she was hearing even before Travis stated flatly, "It's Dani. That's her voice."

Shannon placed a palm against the wall, steadying herself. Travis squatted before the stereo, frozen. His face was pale as death, his eyes dark with rage. Swearing pungently, he slammed a fist on the table. Pictures rattled and fell. "Goddamn son of a bitch," he hissed through teeth clenched tight and lips that barely moved. He turned his eyes on Shannon.

"She's alive." Tears streamed down Shannon's face at the sound of her daughter's voice. Inside she was shredding, dying to meet the child she hadn't set eyes on in thirteen years. "But there's something else, another sound," she said, cut to the bone as she recognized the familiar rumble.

"Fire. He's got her near fire."

"Oh, God. Oh, God." She was shaking, her mind spinning, her emotions in tatters. Seeing Dani's picture had scraped the edges of her soul, but this, hearing her child's voice, knowing she was out there somewhere, in the clutches of a madman while pleading to her mother for help, the mother who had abandoned her all those years ago. Shannon placed a fist to her mouth and tried not to sob.

Mommy, help me! Please, Mommy. I'm scared. Come and get me. I don't know where I am and I think he's going to hurt me! Please, Mommy. Hurry!

The words ran over and over in her head. "Jesus," she whispered, swiping at her nose, feeling as if everything she believed in, everything she trusted, had been stripped from her. Out in the darkness, alone, was her daughter, held hostage and trapped near flames.

She let out a cry and Travis moved closer, placed his arms around her, forced her against his chest where she broke down completely, her fingers curling in the edges of his shirt, her tears staining the soft fabric, her shoulders shaking uncontrollably.

Strong arms surrounded her, held her tight as she squeezed her eyes against the rain of tears, the pain of it all.

"Shhh," he whispered and one hand gently stroked the back of her head.

It only made it worse. How he must be aching. How he must be breaking bit by bit.

"I . . . I . . . Oh, God, Travis, I'm so sorry," she whispered losing her battle for control.

"It's not your fault."

"Of course it is. If it weren't for me, he wouldn't have taken her. She was calling out to me, did you hear that? To me! Her mother. But why? She doesn't know me. No . . . Now I see. He's making her say those things. Staging what he wants her to say, by the sound of a fire that he was sure we'd recognize. Then . . . then . . . leaving the recording in my truck so that I would know, I would feel her pain . . . Oh, my God . . ." Her knees gave out and he held her upright.

"Don't beat yourself up."

"But it's because of me." She blinked hard, fought the rush of tears, tried to stiffen her spine and square her shoulders. Travis was right. She couldn't fight the monster by falling apart, by doing exactly what he'd hoped. And yet, it seemed impossible to pull herself together, to fight the way she always had all her life.

Whoever was doing this had known how to hurt her, had wanted to cut deep to the heart of her, to see her twist in the worst pain imaginable. She swallowed and sniffed, clutching his shirt so that it was wrinkled and wet, trying to draw strength from this man, Dani's father, the only person on the planet who was wounded by this more than she.

"We have to find her," she said, lifting her head back to stare at him through the sheen of tears. "We have to do every damned thing we can to get her back."

"We will. We are," he said, his voice gruff, his own eyes shining. But beneath the fear, lying under the surface of his pain, was a visible resolve. His jaw was set, his muscles rigid, his nostrils flared as if for battle. "First, you need to go upstairs, to bed. Rest. Pull yourself together. I'll call Paterno. They'll take the tape and dissect it. Maybe they'll find fingerprints, or break down the sound to listen for other noises on the tape, noises disguised or hidden by Dani's voice."

"He won't have slipped up," she said, not daring to believe.

"Everyone does. Now, come on, let me help you upstairs—"

"No . . . I'll be all right. I . . . um, just give me a second to clean up." She couldn't have him taking care of her like some frail, weepy, pathetic woman, even if she was acting like one. She pushed herself away from him and nearly crumpled when he let his arms fall away. "Call Paterno, have him come back here for the tape and to check over the truck or whatever he wants. He can tear this place apart for all I care. I just need a minute . . . to . . . wash up."

"You should rest," he said, "you're still recovering."

"Aren't we all, Travis? Just give me a minute. I didn't mean to break down, it's just that . . . Oh, damn it all . . . hearing her voice . . ."

"I know." He reached for her again, pulled her close and kissed the top of her head. His breath ruffled the hairs on her crown, caused a small tingle of anticipation to run through her blood.

She thought about pushing away from him, of breaking this unlikely embrace, but she couldn't. It was as if they needed to hold each other tight to reaffirm their dedication to their cause, to find their child. Not his kid. Not her daughter. But their child.

She looked up at him, found his eyes staring down at her and a heartbeat seemed to stretch to infinity. Here was a man she could love, she thought fleetingly, a single man whose life was dedicated to his child.

Her throat thick, she pressed a quick kiss to the side of his face and smelled a hint of aftershave as she felt the prickle of beard stubble against her lips. "I'll be down in five. Use my phone if you want."

And then, before she did anything so foolish as to sweep her mouth over his, she hurried to the stairs, barely feeling any of her injuries as she climbed up. At her bed, she paused and walked to the nightstand where she picked up the picture of Dani Settler. Tears again threatened her eyes as she thought of the desperate words, aimed at her, that had been coerced from her daughter's throat. "Don't worry, honey," she said, tracing the curve of Dani's jaw with her finger. "I'm coming . . . your momma's coming."

* * *

It was now or never. The Beast had been gone for nearly an hour and she wasn't going to be tricked by trusting that he would be back as soon as he said.

Even if he hadn't lied, Dani couldn't stand it one more second in this stinky, hot room with the crummy cot and no windows. She'd already lost some time as it was, had planned to leave earlier, but circumstances had prevented her escape. She knew things were changing. He was getting desperate. She could tell by how erratic he was, how angry all the time, how restless. And he wouldn't have forced her to make that tape pleading for her mother to save her unless he was planning to get rid of her soon.

She had no illusions.

To stay was to die.

She had to take her chances.

She was ready. She'd put on all her clothes, filthy as they were, and now, with the nail in hand, she walked to the door that was the gate to freedom.

She was jumpy, her nerves thin and stretched as she slid the nail into the crack between the door and frame and slowly and steadily lifted upward. She felt resistance as the nail encountered the hook that held her door closed, but she pushed upward.

Nothing.

The hook didn't so much as budge.

No, oh, no! Her plan couldn't fail. She had to escape. The thought of leaving this creep behind was all that had kept her from dissolving into a million pieces when faced with being alone with him. Her scheme had kept her going and she wasn't going to abandon it because of some stupid, dumb latch that seemed hell-bent on staying put.

She tried again. Slipped the nail into position. Forced it upward. It hit the thin metal hook again. "Here we go," she said, pushing the nail upward, trying to get more leverage, imagining how the hook was bent so that it wouldn't easily unlatch.

She failed.

"Damn it!" she muttered, then cringed at the sound of her own swearing. She couldn't give in to anger. She had to focus. Remember her lessons from tae kwon do and Master Kim. She took a deep breath. Calmed herself. Stretched out the muscles of her neck, all the while aware that precious minutes were slipping by, that at any second the Beast could return to do his perverted regimen in front of the fire.

She held the nail in both hands, best as she could. Sliding the spike into the crack, she concentrated, then slowly but steadily moved the nail upward. Closing her mind to anything but visualizing the latch lifting upward, the hook sliding out of its eye, the door creaking open. She felt resistance. Ignored it. Kept up the pressure. Breathed evenly. Imagined her escape. Her fingers began to hurt, the muscles of her forearms shaking. She ignored the pain, thought only of the metal pressing against metal. *Open, open, open,* she thought, a personal mantra. *Open, open, open . . .*

She felt a twinge. Something was giving, the hook moving slightly. Her heart leapt, but she kept up the pressure, forced her mind to remain centered on the movement of the latch.

In an instant, it loosened. The hook swung upward, the latch gave way and Dani nearly tumbled into the living area.

She wasted no time. Grabbing the knife and fire-starter from the mantel, she found the flashlight he kept in a box by the rickety chair, then stuffed the picture of her mother—the woman with the curly reddish hair and green eyes *had* to have borne her—into her pocket. All these things had his fingerprints on them. She'd witnessed him touching each item, so she had to be careful not to smudge or disturb them. She still had the cigarette butt that had his DNA on it, but fingerprints would be easier to trace if he was in the database, at least that's what she'd gathered from watching all those crime/detective shows on TV. But she didn't have time for any contemplation right now. She had to get moving.

Quick as lightning, Dani slipped out the back door.

The night was dark, a smattering of stars and a piece of

the moon the only light in these mountains. She thought of predators, of rattlesnakes and cougars, porcupines and bats, but nothing, no animal on the planet, was as frightening or as deadly as the beast she'd just left.

And he'd be pissed. When he found out that she'd gotten the better of him, he'd be pissed as hell. She had to make good her escape or die trying. That was all there was to it.

With the thin beam of the flashlight leading her way, she followed what had to have been a deer trail as fast as she could run without tripping. She was certain he'd be able to track her, she had to be leaving impressions in the dust, but as soon as she could figure out a way to veer from the path she would. Right now, she just needed as much distance from him as she could get.

She headed downhill, thinking that there might be a stream at the bottom and she knew that if she splashed through the water of a brook, he wouldn't be able to find her footprints and, if the old movies were to be believed, even tracking dogs, bloodhounds would be confused. The good news was that he didn't have a dog. The bad news was that in a summer as dry and hot as this one, most streams would be little more than dry creek beds.

Nonetheless she needed to stick with her plan.

Such as it was.

Focus, she told herself. *Focus, focus, focus!*

"This is your daughter's voice. For sure?" Paterno asked. He and Rossi had returned after receiving Travis's request and were now standing in Shannon's living room, listening to the tape.

"I know Dani's voice, Detective," Travis snapped. "And that other sound you hear, the rushing rumble, we think it's the crackle of flames, that whoever the bastard is who has my kid is holding her next to fire to make a point with us."

Paterno's face grew even grimmer. He listened hard, then nodded his agreement. "You're right."

Shannon, as she had each time she'd heard the recording, died all over again. Hearing the sound of the word Mommy coming from the daughter she'd never met brought her to tears. Almost literally to her knees.

"But your wife, her mother, is dead."

"I know that!"

Shannon cut in, "Obviously this was meant for me. Left in my truck with my cell phone. Whoever forced my daugh— Dani into saying those words did it to get back at me."

"Same with the fire in the shed and your sister-in-law's death?" Paterno asked, even though, she suspected, he was way ahead of them. He was just testing Travis and her with his questions, plodding along, watching their reactions. They were all standing, she near the windows, the men in front of the stereo located in a low cabinet pushed against the wall.

"You said I was the center of it all," Shannon said, staring outside, seeing her own ghostlike reflection in the glass. "The number six in the middle of that damned odd-shaped star."

"You believe that now?"

Folding her arms over her chest, she said, "Like you said, I'm the sixth-born in my family. Today I overheard a conversation between my brothers . . ."

"About?" Paterno nudged but Shannon hesitated, feeling as if she was incriminating her own kin, the men who had constantly looked out for her. As Aaron was fond of saying, "Don't worry, Shannon. I've got your back." Had he? What did their conversation she'd overheard on their mother's back porch mean? Anything? And even if she was pointing her fingers at her brothers, was it wrong? A child, her child, was in danger. One woman had been killed. "I just don't get what the whole birth-order thing means."

"What is the birth order?" Paterno asked and, in the reflection, she saw him staring at her, pen in hand.

"You know," she said.

"I just want to make sure I don't miss anything."

She doubted Paterno missed much. "Aaron's the oldest, just turned forty, then Robert's thirty-nine, they're only a little over a year apart, then, um, Shea . . . He's next and I think he's thirty-seven, not quite thirty-eight. Oliver's a year and a half older than me at thirty-four."

"And you're thirty-three?"

"That's right."

"What about your brother Neville?"

"He was . . . Oliver's twin. Thirty-four."

"You keep referring to him in the past tense."

She closed her eyes. "I guess there's a part of me that assumes he's dead," she said quietly. She'd never admitted as much before, always been the one who had told her mother, "He'll return, you just wait and see. When he's good and ready, Neville will walk right through your front door." But now she realized she'd been lying, kidding herself. Deep inside she'd believed her youngest brother was dead. Turning from the window, she stared at the detective, noticed Travis, standing to one side watching her. "If he's alive, then where is he? Why is he hiding? Does he have some kind of secret identity, or amnesia, or is he in the witness protection program or . . . What?"

"Maybe he wants to stay hidden."

"Why?"

"Maybe he's a criminal," Paterno posed. "Maybe he did something so bad, he can't come back."

"Like what?" she asked, then realized what he was getting at. "You think he killed Ryan? Because Neville left shortly after Ryan's death?" She was incredulous, shaking her head. Her voice had risen and Khan, once again relegated to his rug in the kitchen, growled. "Shhh!" she commanded as the puppy then let out a whimper. For the moment, she ignored the animals. "No, it wasn't—*isn't*—in Neville's nature. I don't believe it."

"You mentioned a conversation between your brothers?"

As Rossi bagged the tape, she explained what she'd overheard. "I don't know what it meant, and probably wouldn't have thought anything of it, but one of them, and I can't really say which one, mentioned 'birth order,' another one said something about 'it,' whatever 'it' is, being Dad's fault." She saw the question forming on his lips and she said, "I don't know. I really can't even speculate what they were talking about, okay? You'll have to ask them."

"You got it," Paterno said, wrapping it up. The two officers gathered their things and started heading toward the door. Before they left, Paterno alerted Shannon that the FBI would be out in the morning as this was a kidnapping case. He also said that he would analyze the tape and let her know what he found, and that her truck was being towed into town to the police garage where it would be searched minutely, examined for any evidence left by whoever had delivered her the tape.

Travis stayed with her as the tow truck, carrying her pickup, rumbled down the drive, and finally they were alone.

"Now what?" she asked.

"You need rest." He placed a finger gently on her cheek where the last of her abrasions was still healing. "I'll take care of dinner."

"You can cook at a time like this?"

"No." His lips twisted. "But I think we need to regroup." He tried to appear calm, in control, but a little tic beneath his eye belied his pent-up energy. "We'll talk it out over pizza. They deliver here?"

"Gino's does, but the delivery charge is about the cost of a round-trip ticket to Europe."

"I'll buy."

She realized he didn't want to leave her. "You don't have to babysit me, you know."

"Is that what I'm doing?"

"Looks like it."

He shrugged. "Okay, first of all, you're trapped here since the police took your vehicle, and secondly this seems to be the center of it all. And I'm not just talking about the six in the middle of a star, but this place is where he strikes."

"So you're either hanging around to be my bodyguard, or because you think you can catch him here?"

"A little of both, I guess," he admitted.

"Should I be flattered? Or pissed off?"

He lifted a shoulder. Blue eyes glinted. "A little of both, I guess," he repeated. "Now go, get into 'something more comfortable.' Doctor's orders."

"Who's the doctor?"

"Me." His smile was faint.

"Yeah, right."

"Wanna play?" he asked.

"What? Doctor?" Shannon gazed at him in surprise.

He snorted. "Okay, bad joke. I just thought maybe we should lighten up."

She lifted an eyebrow.

"I've been so focused, so . . . tense and single-minded, I haven't been able to step away from what's going on and look at it with a broader scope." His eyes narrowed. "Don't get me wrong, my sole purpose here is to find my daughter and get her back safely. But I think because I've been so tunnel-visioned, I may have missed the big picture and that larger view might help me locate Dani.

"And you're involved," he went on. "The center . . ."

His mind was working in new circles, gears turning, ideas running through his head quickly. Shannon saw it in his eyes.

"Look, whether we like it or not, you and I, we're in this together. He's forcing us to work as a team and I think we shouldn't fight it."

"Have you been?"

"Hell, yes. I wanted to rush in here all full of myself, with a sense of fatherly duty and determination. I wanted to find my kid myself. I was sick to death of the police and FBI and waiting around for the abductor to make a move. I was friggin' John Wayne! But it hasn't worked out that way and it's probably because the bastard who took my kid is counting on me acting just like that. In a way, I've been playing into his hands . . . And you have, too. So we have to keep at it, but with cool heads, look at this thing with a hard, new eye, be one step ahead instead of behind.

"It's hard. Damned hard. This is my kid we're talking about. The son of a bitch has dropped me to my knees and I have to wonder why. It's not about me, I don't think, but it is about you. So that's the angle we have to examine." He sobered. "I'm not going to kid you, Shannon, this part is going to be rough."

"Like it's been a picnic so far."

His eyes held hers and all of his attempts at lightheartedness drained away. "I hate to say it, but you could be right, maybe what we've gone through, what Dani's endured, is a picnic compared to what he has planned for us from here on in."

He followed his quarry from a distance.

Ever vigilant.

Ever wary.

No one could catch him, not yet, not when he was so close to his ultimate goal. Parking his truck several blocks away, he jogged through the night, then waited in the shadows, hidden by the shrubbery that surrounded the old mission. The groundskeeper had watered and the smell of damp earth reached his nostrils, a welcome scent on this hot, dry night. His every muscle was taut, his nerve endings singing in anticipation, and he felt an edgy little worry as well. The girl . . . Something was up with that damned kid. He sensed it and because of her, the little brat, his enjoyment of the night wasn't as heightened as usual. He couldn't savor this ritual, one he'd been planning for years, as much as he would have liked. It angered him. Having the kid around was getting to him. The kid gave him the creeps—the way she mutely stared at him, studied his every move, and when she did talk, the questions.

But soon it wouldn't matter.

Just another day or two at the most.

Then he'd get rid of her.

He felt a little tinge of satisfaction at that. After she'd served his purpose, she'd be of no use to him. Then he'd take care of her.

But, now, as the night thickened around him, he had to concentrate on this task. Finally, after waiting and planning so long, he would extract some well-deserved vengeance.

It would be an intricate two-step as he'd had to adjust his timetable. No more stretching things out. He couldn't trust the kid and he was running out of patience, couldn't wait for the ultimate goal.

Tonight would be full of surprises . . .

His gaze trained on the street in front of a small, well-kept cottage, he saw the familiar car approach and park in its usual spot.

So predictable.

The car's engine died, the headlights dimmed and the driver climbed out quickly, almost as if he sensed the danger of lingering in any place too long. He hesitated, took a quick look at his little house, then turned and walked quickly toward the church.

Obviously "Father" Oliver had some sins to confess.

The Beast—that's what the kid called him, he'd heard her whisper it when she'd thought he was out of earshot—smiled to himself, expectancy building.

It was better when his victims felt a little spasm of fear, when they sensed their precious time on earth was about to be cut short.

Somewhere nearby an owl hooted.

Bats flew from the tall bell tower, winging overhead.

The target didn't notice, just kept walking swiftly, almost jogging, as if he was desperate.

And afraid.

Head down, intent on his own thoughts, the target hurried to the church steps and fiddled with a large key ring.

Traitor.

The Beast squinted through the darkness where the only light was a sickly pale illumination from a few lampposts scattered along the paths that cut across the watered lawns of the mission. Even the glare of headlights from passing traffic was muted, filtered by the dense bushes and trees sheltering the grounds.

It was perfect.

Licking his dry lips, he felt the zing of anticipation, could envision the blood being spilled, the flames climbing the walls, the crackle and hiss of the fire as it met the oozing red liquid.

Slow down . . . Take your time. It's not finished yet.

As his next victim walked through the portico, then unlocked the door and stepped inside St. Benedictine's Church with its tiled roof and stucco walls, he watched.

Waited.

Readied himself.

After a full five minutes had passed since the thick door had closed, the Beast reached into his small pack and withdrew his knife. His gloved fingers surrounded the hilt and he felt the weight of it in his palm.

A perfect weapon, one that could be used as a threat, to urge a person to bend to his will, or for the act of killing itself.

No one else entered or left the church.

Another two minutes passed and the bells, counting off the hour of midnight, began to peal. *One, two, three . . .*

He started moving, slinking through the shadows.

Four, five, six . . .

While the church bells rang, he used their dulcet tones to cover the sound of his own footsteps. Quickly he crossed the grass, exposing himself for a few short seconds as he made his way to the church.

Seven, eight, nine . . .

Breathing irregularly, his heart pumping in wild expectation, he stepped onto the portico, his hand reaching for the huge door handle.

Ten, eleven, twelve . . .

And then it was time.

A surge of adrenaline raced through his body.

At the stroke of midnight he opened the door to St. Benedictine's Church. With silent footsteps he slipped inside.

The day had been excruciating.

Lies. Perfidy. Adultery. Cruelty. And murder.

Sins teeming and abounding around him while he spent time with his mother and siblings. To offer solace. To provide comfort. But there had been none of that, nor had there been much time for bereavement and grief and murmuring of prayers for safety and sanity. Oh, no . . .

Oliver's stomach lurched, threatening to give up its contents as he recalled the visit at the old house on St. Marie Avenue.

There had been talk, all in hushed tones, about what was to be done. How to "handle the situation." Oliver quivered inside, knew that what was being planned was so very wrong. And yet he didn't have the strength of character, the conviction for the truth and love of Christ that would help him persevere, so he'd retreated here, to his sanctuary, the church where he so often prayed for a courage he would never know.

The weight of falsehood pressed hard against his soul. Swallowing hard, he knew it was time to end the lies, to tell the truth, to stand tall and let the scandal, the punishment, begin.

He, of course, would be denied ordination, perhaps even excommunicated for his sins, but his soul needed washing. Cleansing.

He was weak.

Oh, Holy Father, so weak.

Perhaps death was the only solution, he thought, lighting several candles and watching the small flames flicker and burn. If he confessed his sins, prayed for absolution, the Father might still allow him into heaven. He was, after all, a forgiving God.

Surely death would be better than this perpetual torment on earth. He'd tried before . . . But now . . . Could he commit a mortal sin? Who would receive his confession? Who would absolve him before he died? Father Timothy?

Father, please . . . Help me.

Listening to the peal of the church bells, he dropped to his knees on the hard stone floor of the church with its high ceilings, tall stained-glass windows depicting the stations of the cross and the altar. The scent of burned incense sweetened the air, mingling with the odor of his own nervous sweat. He needed guidance and penance, a means to see clearly his path, a way to be absolved of so many sins. Deftly, he made the sign of the cross, felt the weight of the rosary in the deep pocket of his jacket. "Forgive me, Father. Please, I beseech you, help me find the strength to stop this." He fought a spate of tears and the darkness that pulled at the corners of his consciousness. Depression and fear vied for his soul and he was so tired, so weary from the burden of sin he'd carried for three long years, that he didn't know if he could go on.

He thought he heard the scrape of a shoe behind him and he glanced about. His eyes and ears strained, but no one was entering. He was alone, just nervous, worried about what he had to do. The candles seemed to shift a bit. He saw a mouse dart beneath one of the pews and slip into a tiny crack in the wall. He was imagining things again. Jumping at shadows. Letting the paranoia slip into his life.

Don't go there. Don't give in to the fear, the hatred. Remember Neville, the one who was your other half, whose image was identical to your own, but whose psyche was so different.

Oliver began to weep at the thought of his twin.

Stop it, show some spine, some strength of character. Do not fall apart, do not let Satan control you, do not let the weakness send you away, to the hospital, to a place where dreams are broken and lives are destroyed.

He remembered Our Lady of Virtues from his childhood. The darkness that oozed through the hallways, the secrets behind the locked doors, the resident, ever-present evil that stalked all those who had the misfortune to reside in those darkened corridors.

"Deliver me," Oliver prayed, shuddering inside, once again a frightened little boy. The sound of the ringing bells stopped suddenly, the church again thrown into a dark silence that was pierced only by the sound of his own breathing, the heavy beat of his heart.

Nervously, he slid his fingers into his pocket and extracted his rosary with its worn, well-used beads, hoping to find the comfort it usually brought him. He took a deep breath as he prepared to whisper the prayers that were forever a part of his daily life. His fingers wrapped familiarly over the crucifix of the rosary and again, he made the sign of the cross. "I believe in God, the Father Almighty, Creator of heaven and earth . . ."

Tears of regret filled his eyes as his lips moved and he looked up at the statue of Jesus on the cross. So immersed was he in his prayer that he didn't notice the soft rush of air as a door opened, was deaf to stealthy footsteps approaching, didn't realize someone had slipped into the church for a singular and deadly purpose, didn't begin to understand why tonight, like Christ before him, he was to die for the sins of others . . .

Chapter 25

Dani's heart was beating crazily. Her lungs burned and her legs stung where they'd been slapped by berry vines and stickers as she ran down the trail. She had no idea what time it was or how long it had been since she'd escaped, but she had run until she could run no longer, her body screaming for rest. She had shin splints from going downhill, but she kept pushing forward, trying to get as much distance between herself and the cabin. The farther she got, the more likely she would make it to safety.

Keep going. Just keep going! Gritting her teeth she never completely stopped, sliding a couple of times, stumbling on loose rocks, but fortunately never falling or twisting her ankle. Hurriedly, she swept the beam of the flashlight in front of her, keeping as fast a pace as possible, but she was gasping, the only thing keeping her going now was the adrenaline pumping through her blood.

She didn't know if it was better to run under the cover of darkness, hoping he didn't see her flashlight, or if, after daybreak, she could make better time, see what was ahead, but be visible herself.

Surely she'd lost him.

Certainly now she was far enough away from him that he wouldn't find her.

And yet she remembered his steely determination, the way he did his exercises naked on the floor in front of the fire, sweating profusely, his skin shining with perspiration, his dark hair soaked and in strands, the scars on his back slick and gleaming.

He would never give up.

Not until he found her.

Not until he used her for whatever perverted thing that was on his mind.

That kept her going, running, hurtling down the hillside, following the trail until her head was pounding and her lungs felt as if they would explode. Gasping, she finally stopped at a fork in the scrawny little trail. Listened hard. Straining to hear past the pounding of her own pulse in her ears. Leaning over, hands on her knees, taking in big gulps of air, she tried to relax and get her bearings.

The stars were no help . . . The North Star meant nothing to her. Which way was to safety? She had no idea.

Her breathing slowed.

Sweat ran down her nose, dripping on the dust at her feet. She was so thirsty she could barely breathe.

"God help me," she whispered and thought of her dad. Where was he? And Mom, oh, man, if she could just tell her mother one more time that she loved her. Tears clogged her parched throat and she felt about to break down completely, but she couldn't let herself. Being a crybaby now, dissolving into self-pity wouldn't help a darned thing. She had to keep at it.

Faintly, she heard the sound of bells. Church bells. Tolling through the valley below, but far in the distance. Her heart leapt. She straightened, searching the darkness. Where there was a church there were people; she was zeroing in on civilization! She forced her eyes toward the sound and though brush and trees were in her line of vision she thought she spied lights, a town. Far below. Really far below.

Crap!

How could she get there? She couldn't just barrel through the forest, she had to stick with a trail or she might come across an impossible cliff. Her progress would be slower and she'd risk the chance of getting lost, running in circles. Though her father had taught her a little about navigating by the stars, she could make out only Venus, the Big Dipper, the Little Dipper and the North Star, but it wasn't enough, she wasn't confident to go traipsing though the dark woods where vines and loose rocks and roots could trip her.

So she stuck to the trail and at every fork, she picked the

path that seemed to head downhill, though twice she'd taken an upward-swinging trail, planting footsteps in the dust, then creeping back through the brush, careful not to leave any trace, turned downhill again. It was a simple, probably useless ploy that wasted time, but she hoped beyond hope that she might confuse the Beast when he started chasing her.

She didn't doubt that he would take off after her. He had a purpose for her, something to do with her birth mother, but she had no idea what it was. Something bad. It chilled her to the bone to think about what his plans were, for she knew he was evil. Malicious. And crazy. Obsessed with the people whose pictures he kept framed on his mantel. She reached inside her pocket, touched the one she'd stolen and wondered about the woman in the snapshot. Was she married? Did she have other kids? Why couldn't she have kept Dani in the first place? That particular thought had an ugly edge. She loved her dad and mom, the people who'd raised her, with all her heart, but still . . . She had dozens of questions for this woman. The flashlight's beam was failing, but she started forward again, jogging, trying to put as much distance from the cabin as she could. She couldn't imagine his rage if he caught up to her, this weirdo who got off on peeing in the fire. Didn't want to think about it. She couldn't let that happen. No matter what.

"I have to talk to Oliver," Shannon said, pushing back her chair. The legs scraped against the kitchen floor as she climbed to her feet. She ignored the remaining three slices of pizza congealing in the box on the kitchen table.

"It's after one," Travis pointed out. Still seated at the table, he was finishing a beer, staring at the drawings Paterno had left behind. He was getting nowhere fast. Inside he was still reeling, his guts twisting in the aftermath of hearing Dani's voice.

He'd been through a lot in his life. Hell, he'd been through enough for two, no, make that three lifetimes, and he wasn't yet forty. But this . . . knowing that his kid was out there some-where in the darkness, alone with a vile, malicious murderer, held against her will and enduring God-only-knew-what nearly broke him.

Yes, he was determined to find her.

Yes, he'd personally rip the killer limb from limb and damn the consequences.

Yes, he'd never give up.

But damn it, yes, he was scared to the very bottom of his soul. Fear was his constant companion. Time seemed to be flying by at a breakneck speed. Frustration made him want to climb the walls.

Not listening to his objections, Shannon was already punching numbers on the cordless phone. "Priests are on call 24/7," she said, walking past the pen where the tiny pup was curled up and sleeping soundly, yet making little whim-pering noises, the result of a puppy dream.

The other dog, Khan, was lying under the table, eyes fo-cused on Travis as he hoped for a handout.

"Damn!" Shannon slammed down the phone. The pup let out a yip but didn't awaken. "Oliver's not answering."

"You could have left a message."

"*If* my brother ever hauled himself into the twenty-first century . . . But Oliver prides himself on being the last hold-out. No answering machine. No voice mail. No caller ID. No . . . nothing." She rotated her head and rubbed the kinks from her neck. "He should've studied to become a monk."

"I think a priest's close enough," Travis offered and no-ticed how tired she looked. Her skin was pale, dark smudges were visible under her eyes, and she winced a little when she lifted her arm over her head to stretch. "You should take a break. Get some rest. Go to bed."

"Why? So I can toss and turn all night, hear that tape run through my brain until dawn? Worry myself sick?" she asked, pinning him with an intelligent green gaze. "Thanks, but no thanks."

"Don't you have medication that'll help you sleep?"

"I can't be a zombie," she answered.

"I just don't want you to kill yourself."

"I won't." Finished with her impromptu stretch, she punched numbers on the phone again. "Come on, Oliver. Wake up."

"Maybe he's not home."

"Where would he be?" she asked, then looked over at him and rolled her eyes. "All right, point taken," she said, hanging up and sighing. "Even priests, or soon-to-be priests, have their own lives."

"So why are you so hell-bent to talk to him tonight?"

"Because earlier today I blew him off." She looked suddenly guilty. "He tried to talk to me at Mom's house. There was obviously something troubling him, I could read it in his eyes, but before he could tell me what was on his mind, Robert came into the room and Oliver clammed up." She frowned, tiny lines appearing between her eyebrows. "To tell you the truth, I was glad. Didn't want to get hung up in some kind of heavy conversation. Wanted to escape." She glanced out the window to the night beyond. "But now . . ." Her lips pursed into a thoughtful frown. ". . . Now I think he might have had something important to tell me, something he was desperate for me to know." She leaned one hip against the edge of the counter. "Oliver had just come in from outside, from that conversation where my brothers were whispering about the family birth order and whatever it was being Dad's fault." She walked to the table and picked up the drawings. "It felt so clandestine that I have the feeling that whatever it was must be tied into what's going on with Dani and the fires, maybe even Mary Beth's murder." She tapped on the number six on the half-finished star drawing. "Swear to God, Oliver knows something and he was trying to tell me about it today."

"If you're so sure, then let's find out."

"You and me?"

"Yep." He climbed to his feet, then really looked at her. "You're about dead on your feet."

"Yeah, yeah, so you said." She swatted the air impatiently. "I couldn't sleep if I tried. Could you?"

He shook his head.

"Didn't think so. Since my pickup is with the cops, we'll have to use yours. I'll drive."

He sent her an over-my-dead-body glare. "*I'll* drive."

"Fine. Let's go."

Paterno couldn't sleep.

The damned case was getting to him.

No two ways about it.

He stripped down to his boxers and T-shirt, found a glass in his kitchen and scooped up a handful of ice from an opened bag he kept in the freezer. With practiced hands he unscrewed the top of a bottle of rye whiskey he kept on the counter, then listened to the familiar crackle as the liquor hit the ice cubes. Swirling his drink, he refused to pay any attention to the few rinsed dishes sitting in the sink. Instead, he walked into his living room where the television was turned to two channels, ESPN on the main screen, CNN in the inset in the lower right-hand corner.

Jesus, it was hot. His air conditioner was on the fritz and his second-story apartment was sweltering. He opened the slider door to his deck but felt little relief.

Traffic was slow and quiet, the street below empty. He took a sip of his drink and felt the smooth liquor slide down his throat as he noticed a moth fluttering near the deck light. He slammed the screen shut and stared into the night.

So what was it he was missing?

Turning to his desk, he sipped his drink and stared down at his notes, arranged in disorderly piles. The drawings, yeah, he made nothing of them except that he had an inkling the points of the star had to do with the Flannery brothers . . . What else? The missing one was the missing brother, right? The broken lines . . . Maybe that was because Robert was in the middle of a divorce . . . No, it was because the person who died wasn't part of the formation, just linked by marriage . . . Or was it? Shannon was in the center . . . her brothers circling around her . . . Oh, crap, did that make any sense? No. If it was a birth-order thing, wouldn't the numbers run chronologically, age-wise? But the way he saw it, number five, without a point, was positioned next to the broken point of number two, with six in the middle. Any way you cut it, two shouldn't be next to five. It should be surrounded by one and three . . . if his theory was correct. But then, who said a killer was sane?

Maybe he was way off base with the birth-order thing. Maybe there was another reason that the number six was significant and assigned to Shannon . . . or the kid? Maybe that was it. It was Dani Settler's birth certificate, not Shannon's. Maybe he'd made a big leap, following a gut instinct when there was nothing to base it on.

He had to step back.

Start over.

Forget any reference to "birth order" by the father.

His gaze moved to the next pile. Notes on the Stealth Torcher . . . No one killed in all those fires except for one woman. It was almost as if the arsonist picked buildings he knew were abandoned.

Paterno took another swallow and let a piece of ice flow into his mouth. He crushed the cube and thought, then thumbed through the three pages of notes on the Torcher . . . One woman died: Dolores Galvez.

Why did that name ring bells? There was something . . . But what?

He sat at the desk, and pulled out a box of notes he'd copied from the original investigation. The pages were yellowed and smelled musty from three years of storage and as he flipped through the reports he thought of all those fires, so close to Santa Lucia. At that time not only Patrick, Shannon's father, was a firefighter, but so were his sons. All of his sons. Paterno double-checked. Aaron, Robert, Shea, Oliver and Neville. And two other familiar names as well: Ryan and

Liam Carlyle. First cousins. "Incestuous little group," Paterno told himself. He didn't like them as a whole, including the deceased. Ryan Carlyle had been a piece of work and his cousins weren't much better. Though she didn't deserve the fate she'd been handed, Mary Beth had been a bossy fishwife. Her sister, Margaret, was a pious prig while Kevin, one of her brothers, was a real odd duck, a loner who kept to himself and though he had degrees up the wazoo, worked as a clerk for the Federal government. Liam, the eldest, the one closest to Ryan, also kept to himself. He'd been married and divorced a couple of times and after quitting the Santa Lucia Fire Department had landed himself a job doing arson investigation with an insurance company in Santa Rosa.

And Teddy, Ryan's younger brother, was dead, killed in a fiery single car crash with Ryan at the wheel when he was thirteen.

Nope, Paterno thought, he didn't like the Flannerys or the Carlyles.

Ryan had, arguably, been the worst. A wife beater. No two ways about it. Paterno had heard a small bit of tape that had been retrieved from the final fight between him and his wife, Shannon. Most of the equipment and recording had been destroyed, but the police had reconstructed one little bit of the tape where Shannon was yelling at her husband, and sounding as if she was fighting for her life. That scrap of audiotape had been used as the basis for the theory about why she might have killed her husband . . . Yes, it had proved motive, but, in Paterno's estimation, not enough. The prosecution had persevered, insisting that Shannon had sought help from either a killer-for-hire or others who had abetted her—those others being her brothers, whose only alibis had been each other.

It had been a weak case and looking back at it now, Paterno wondered why the DA had decided to try it. Pressure, he decided, staring at the transcript of the tape.

He dug further until he found information on the sole victim of one of the fires set by the Stealth Torcher.

Dolores Galvez had been thirty-two, divorced, with no children, a waitress at an Italian restaurant that had gone under since her death. Dolores had one brother who lived in Pasadena. Her parents, as of three years ago, lived in LA. There was a note that her brother had thought she'd been seeing someone, but he'd never met the guy, never heard his name, just knew that Dolores was "in love." She'd been reticent to tell the brother anything about the guy and he'd shrugged it off because his sister had been one of those women who fell in love easily—"a couple of times a year"— was the quote. But in all the notes about Dolores there was no mention of the man she'd been seeing at the time of her death. All the old boyfriends had been checked and had come out clean.

After the tragedy, the mystery man hadn't come forward. If he'd attended the funeral, no one had bothered to make note of it.

Paterno didn't like it.

It didn't feel right.

But nothing about this case did.

He hoped the lab would come up with fingerprints off the cassette of the kid's voice, or at the very least separate the sounds so that they might have a shot at hearing noises that would help pinpoint where the recording took place, but he didn't have much faith. Shannon's cell phone might give up some clues; the numbers recently called and those received would be on the screen and he'd already requested her records from the cell phone company. And then there was her truck. Would whoever had left the phone in the truck been careless enough to leave fingerprints or trace evidence?

He doubted it.

So far, this guy had been careful. He'd given the police only what he wanted them to have. Maybe the FBI would find something more from the van found at Blanche Johnson's Idaho property. Something that would lead them back to the whack job who was holding Dani Settler and probably killed Mary Beth Flannery as well as Blanche.

There was a chance they would get lucky.

Paterno wasn't banking on it.

He rubbed his face with one hand and felt eighteen hours' worth of beard stubble as he glanced through another stack of notes about Blanche Johnson's murder.

What was the message that had been left at the scene, in blood no less? *Payback Time.* What the hell did that mean? And what did it have to do with Shannon Flannery?

Paterno felt he was spinning his wheels.

He'd have to call the authorities in Oregon in the morning and then have a chat with the elusive Nate Santana. See what that guy knew. He'd been gone a lot recently. Never around. And he was an ex-con, whether he had beat the rap or not.

Finishing his drink, he gave up for the night, walked to the slider and pulled it shut. The damned moth was still beating itself silly around the lightbulb.

"Give it up," he muttered, snapping off the light. He didn't know if he was talking to the fluttering insect or himself.

"Let's try to call again," Shannon said as Travis parked his truck behind a white Toyota Camry parked on the street in front of the small, darkened cottage.

"It doesn't look like he's home." But Travis handed her his cell phone.

"His car is here." Punching out the number, she nodded toward the car in front of them. "Come on, Oliver," she whispered, waiting and then gnawing at the corner of her fingernail as the phone continued to ring. No light came on in the house. She snapped the phone closed. "Something's wrong."

Before he could say a word, she was out of the truck and up the concrete walk to the front door. As Travis slid out of the truck, she rang the bell repeatedly. Where was Oliver? she wondered. Her mind raced with ideas—maybe he had duties to perform, last rites or tending to the sick, but wouldn't he have taken his car? A friend could have picked him up, or he could be with one of her brothers, she supposed, but it didn't feel right. She stole a glance at the Camry parked in its usual spot and a cold knot of fear coiled in her stomach.

"Oliver," she said and pounded on the door. "It's Shannon. Open up."

Nothing.

"Oliver!" Her fist was poised to strike the door again when Travis stopped her, his fingers surrounding hers.

"You'll wake the neighbors."

She glanced along the deserted street. "I know where he keeps a key," she said and before Travis even thought about arguing with her, she was down the two steps of the porch and hurrying along a path to the back of the house. Reaching over and unlatching the gate to the fenced yard, she tried to keep her fear at bay. Oliver was fine. She just had to find him.

But she thought of Mary Beth and Dani and the fact that Oliver had so much wanted to talk to her today. Kicking herself for not listening to him, she walked to the back porch, reached under the lowest step and found the key. Within seconds she was twisting the lock and with Travis at her side, walked into her brother's small, stuffy, spartan house.

She switched on the kitchen light.

Everything was as she would have expected. Not a dish in the sink, no stack of unread mail on the counter, neither of the two dinette chairs pushed away from the table. Aside from the hum of the refrigerator and the ticking of a hall clock, there was no noise.

"Oliver?" she called. A cold shiver of fear chased down her spine.

In the living room a Bible lay open on a table next to his chair, the seat shiny from years of use. The fireplace was cold, never used, and on the walls were various pictures of Christ and Mary.

Her feet creaked upon the worn carpet as she walked quickly to the two bedrooms. One, his office, was as barren as the rest of the house with only a desk, a daybed and books, all sorted neatly on shelves. She'd seen them before: texts on religion, theology, psychology and the like. The next room, his bedroom with its small, neatly made bed and a bureau that he'd kept from his youth, was empty as well, the bed not slept in.

"Where is he?" she asked as her eyes swept the open door of the bathroom. Empty. Neat. The blue hand towel lying near the sink folded with military precision.

"I don't know." Travis walked back to the living room, to the table where the Bible was. He snapped on the light and skimmed the pages.

"Anything there?"

Shaking his head, he said, "Nah. Don't think so."

"It's so late." She frowned and was ready to call and alert one of her brothers, was already on her way to the phone hanging on the wall in the kitchen, when she stopped and thought. Tried to get into Oliver's head. She studied the crucifixes decorating the walls, the palm leaves, the artifacts. "If you were about to take your vows as a priest and you were worried about something . . . Something major was eating at you . . ." she thought aloud as she crossed the living room and turned the venetian blinds open to stare across the small front yards to the mission grounds on the other side of the street. Lights shone upward, displaying the bell tower and the crosses mounted high on the peaked roofs. "If you were really troubled, where would you go?"

"I don't know. I'm not Catholic," Travis said, but he walked to the window and, following her gaze, stared at the mission.

"When you're upset, you, Travis Settler, where do you go when you want to sort things out?"

"I usually take a walk. Outside. Someplace quiet where I can think," he said.

Shannon nodded, her finger pointed through the slats of the blinds. "I think he's in the church at the mission. Across the street."

"Could be," he said.

Shannon was already striding through the kitchen, exiting the house the way they'd come in. She was running now, feeling a sense of urgency. Why hadn't she stopped and listened to Oliver at their mother's house? Didn't she have a few seconds to give to her brother when he was so obviously tormented?

Stop it, Shannon, don't beat yourself up. You still have no idea what was on his mind!

She dashed across the street and Travis was right beside her. They found a brick path and headed into the compound, an old mission that was still used by the church. This church was small, not nearly as large or modern as the main church, St. Theresa's, located half a mile north, but it was close and Oliver's car was nearby. This *had* to be the place.

The portico was shadowed as they approached, no sound from within.

Shannon wrapped her fingers around the big handle of the door and pulled. It opened silently and she felt a stir of trepidation, the same feeling she always experienced when stepping into a place where she wasn't welcome, where there were NO TRESPASSING signs posted or implied. The church was like that—though friendly and warm and holy, filled with singing and prayers and organ music and hope during its hours of operation—dark and chilling, silent when no one was around. She'd always felt that way, ever since she was a little girl.

Her brothers, altar boys, had felt more at home inside the apse and nave, but she'd always felt alienated when the pews were empty, as they were now.

She stepped inside and stared up the aisle to the altar where candles flickered and the looming figure of Jesus hung on the cross, blood dripping from His forehead where the crown of thorns rested, His palms and feet, too, smeared with red, the slash on His side oozing.

For those without faith, who didn't understand Christ's

sacrifice for humanity, the image could be frightening. As a small child, it had scared her to death.

She reached for Travis's hand, linked her fingers through his and sent up a prayer for strength.

"He's not here," Travis said.

"But the candles are burning," she whispered, motioning to the stand where several votive candles wavered as they passed. Glancing up at Travis's shadowed features, meeting his gaze with her own, she said, "Someone lit them."

"Shannon, the church is empty."

"This part of the church is empty. We don't know about the rest."

"You want to go poking around in all the little nooks and crannies?"

"Don't you?"

"It seems sacrilegious."

"It is." Pulling on his hand, she started down the center aisle of the nave, her gaze darting left and right, searching for anyone or for anything out of place. With each step her heart pounded in deeper trepidation and the hairs on the back of her arms raised, warning her. "Oliver?" she called in a voice slightly above a whisper. "Oliver, are you here?"

She paused. Listened.

Nothing.

Travis shook his head, but she started forward again, pushing aside her ridiculous reservations. This was a building, God's building, and surely He would want the truth known. At the altar, she looked up, made the sign of the cross as the image of Jesus stared at her, but she didn't genuflect. Just gripped Travis's hand more tightly in her free hand.

She walked to one wall and opened the door to the small chapel, a place for private worship where she thought Oliver might have decided to speak to God. The room was dark. She fumbled for a switch and threw the lights. The room was empty.

"He might not be here," Travis said, giving her hand a small, comforting squeeze.

"Let's make sure." Leaving the muted lights in the chapel burning, she walked toward the front of the church again, past the transepts, then peered behind the altar. Nothing. Just silence and the smell of ash and incense, a burning scent that permeated the stale air.

She eyed the sacristy but saw nothing other than the vestments and vessels used by the priests. On one wall, she saw the confessionals: two dark booths. Pulling Travis after her, she made her way to them. She remembered entering as a child, telling Father Timothy on the other side of the screen how she'd sinned: saying a bad word, or talking back to her mother or lying to her brothers. Then she'd waited for the priest to come up with a soft-spoken penance.

Now, she approached the booths.

Heart thudding, she opened one creaking door.

Nothing.

Holding her breath, she approached the other, her hands trembling as she yanked back the door. It, too, was empty.

Carefully, she walked to the side where the priests took their seats and opened each door, only to find them, too, vacant.

"Oliver?" she called again, her voice louder, echoing off the rafters, sending a chill through her own body.

"He's not here," Travis said gently, but then, she felt his fingers grip her hand more tightly. She saw him lift his head, turning his face toward an arch leading to a dark hallway.

"What?"

"Shhh!" he said, tensing, starting toward the arch. "Do you smell that?"

"What?" She sniffed the air, picked up a thin hint of smoke.

"The candles . . ."

He shook his head, released her hand, and motioned her to stay behind him as he crept toward the dark opening. *This is nuts,* she thought. *We're in a church. And we're acting as if we're in some teenage horror flick.*

Yet she didn't say another word. As she crept behind Travis into the darkened hallway, her heart was knocking loudly, blood pounding in her ears. The odor of smoke, which she'd attributed to the votive candles or a residue from old incense, became more intense.

Fire?

Goose pimples raised along her spine.

Oh, please, God, no. Not here! Not again!

Travis stepped around a corner to a short hallway and a door that was ajar. Through the crack in the doorway she saw shadows, golden and shifting, moving against the wall and stairs leading downward to the basement.

"No!" she cried as the smell hit her fully and she heard the first crackle of hungry flames. "Oliver!"

Travis tossed her his cell phone. "Call 9-1-1! Now!" He threw open the door and hurried down the stairs.

Shannon was right on his heels, already punching in the numbers, nearly stumbling on the steep wooden steps. Smoke rose up the staircase, the smell of burning kerosene was thick. Fear pulsed through her. Oliver! Where was Oliver? *Here?* "No," she said, over and over, "Please, no!" Images of Mary Beth's burned body being carried out of her house, being stuffed into a body bag, seared through Shannon's brain.

Travis landed at the bottom of the stairs, his boots ringing on the concrete. "Jesus!" he whispered, almost as a prayer, then turned away. "Go upstairs! Now!" She was on the bottom step, staring ahead. "Shannon, no!"

He tried to shield her with his body, but it was too late. She looked over his shoulder and nearly collapsed as she spied her brother, ringed by small flames, hanging by the neck, swinging gently from a rafter. His body turned, the rope holding him creaking. A folding chair beneath him had been knocked over, as if he'd committed this heinous act himself, and surrounding him, in a wide circle, was a fire of debris, burning low and dying.

"No!" Shannon cried. "No!"

"Call 9-1-1!" Travis ordered again.

In one swift motion, he yanked his shirt over his head. Beating at the flames, he jumped across the line of the smoldering fire. Righting the chair beneath Oliver's body, he climbed upon it.

Frantically, Shannon hit the dial button.

"Nine-one-one, Police Dispatch," a woman's calm voice said. "What's the nature of your emergency?"

"There's a fire and a . . . a man who needs help, possible attempted suicide. He's hanging but we're getting him down."

"A hanging *and* a fire?"

"Yes! Send help! To the church at the corner of Fifth and Arroyo! St. Benedictine's!" she said, then repeated, "There's a fire and a man seriously injured! In the basement of St. Benedictine's Church." Shannon was hyperventilating, taking in smoke, watching Travis saw at the thick rope with his knife.

"Ma'am, that's Fifth and Arroyo?"

"Yes! Send someone now!"

"Stay on the line, I'm dispatching now. What's your name?"

"Shannon Flannery!" she said, with the sense of déjà vu chasing down her spine. It hadn't been that long since she'd made the last call, when she'd been attacked in her horse barn. "The man who's injured is Oliver Flannery! Send an ambulance! Hurry!"

"Vehicles are on their way," she was assured as Travis's knife finally sliced through the rope. Oliver fell into a crumpled heap on the dirty cement, the fire burning bright and deadly around him.

"Ma'am, could you stay on the line?"

Travis was on the floor beside him in an instant.

Shannon dropped the phone. Shaking, coughing, disbelieving she stepped forward. "Oliver," she cried.

"Don't! Stay back! Or find a fire extinguisher!" Travis

held up a hand and leaned down, listening for the sound of breath, feeling for a pulse. Oliver's head lolled to the side, his eyes open and staring, glassy and unmoving.

Inside she broke into a thousand pieces. Memories of summertime, butterflies, fishing poles and running through open fields with her twin brothers cut through her mind. Oliver laughing. Neville urging them both to run faster.

Her throat worked and she backed up, hitting something, a post at the bottom of the stairs.

Travis looked up, shook his head.

Even before he said the words, she knew with mind-numbing certainty that Oliver would never take his final vows, never become a priest.

Her brother was dead.

Chapter 26

"Let's get out of here." Travis placed an arm over Shannon's shoulders and steered her away from the church and the madhouse that had erupted with the discovery of Oliver's body. Fire trucks, police cars and an ambulance had screamed to the scene, and with their noise and flashing bright lights a crowd of neighbors and the curious had collected around the restricted area that was cordoned off by police officers and crime scene tape. Emergency vehicles filled the small parking lot near the side door. Barricades blocked either end of the street between Oliver's house and the church.

Father Timothy, thin gray hair spiking upward, rimless glasses not hiding his bloodshot eyes, had arrived after being phoned by one of the neighbors. He looked disheveled and was unbelieving, aghast and angry that "such a horrible atrocity" had happened not only in his parish but inside the holy walls of St. Benedictine's Church. He, alone, had spoken to the press who had arrived en masse, white news vans with satellite dishes rolling in to deploy reporters with microphones, cameramen and bright lights. Competing stations had arrived and the reporters were all vying for the best shot of the church, the latest news and/or an exclusive interview with anyone who knew what was going on. Shannon and Travis had repeatedly declined the requests.

The night was hot and dry, no breath of wind, the heat seemingly fueled by the evil that had been committed. Shannon forced her thoughts away from the image of her brother's drained body twisting from a bell-tower rope.

Somehow she and Travis had managed to give their statements to an officer of the Santa Lucia Police Department who had been one of the first on the scene. They'd both promised to make themselves available for further questioning and Shannon knew she'd soon have another face-to-face with Detective Anthony Paterno. What could she tell him? That because of her, someone was killing, abducting or terrorizing people close to her?

Why?

If only she'd been able to talk to Oliver, if only she hadn't been in such a hurry to leave her mother's house. What would it have taken to give her brother five minutes of her time? Guilt was still eating at her when she spied two of her brothers huddled together beneath the branches of a large sequoia tree planted near the parking lot.

"Give me a second," she said to Travis and crossed a patch of grass and shrubs to get close to them. Robert, though not on duty, and Shea, still relieved of his, had shown up separately and had answered questions thrown at them by the police, the same questions that had been asked of Shannon.

Did they know anyone who would want to do this to Oliver?

When was the last time they'd seen him, talked with him?

Did they know anything about his personal life? Lovers? Friends? Enemies?

Had anyone been angry with him?

What had been his regular routine?

Had he strayed from it?

How did they know to come here? Or, in Shannon and Travis's case: How did they find the body? Why did Shannon want to talk to her brother at one in the morning? Why wouldn't it wait?

White-faced, shaking their heads, lips thin and pressed together in something between rage and despair, her two brothers were still reeling at the loss of Oliver.

"Both twins," Robert said, his eyes downturned. "Gone. And Mary Beth, poor Mary Beth."

"It looks like the same perp," Shea confided, lighting a cigarette and blowing smoke from the corner of his mouth. Robert nodded, then hit Shea's arm with the back of his hand. "Can I bum one of those?"

"Sure." Shea's dark gaze slid from Shannon to focus on the bell tower, but Shannon figured, like her, his thoughts were a million miles away. He handed Robert a crumpled pack of Marlboro Lights. Robert, hands trembling slightly, shook out a filter tip and lit up.

"Of course it's the same psycho," Shannon said. That was the one thing she was certain of. The only thing. "There couldn't be two maniacs running around, trying to kill off members of our family, making weird burned marks as some kind of sick calling card."

"You think that's what he's trying to do?" Robert asked.

"Don't you?"

"Then why Mary Beth? And why . . . Why not . . . ?" He let his question drift away.

But she caught his drift. "Why not kill me the night he had a chance?"

"Yeah."

Good question, Shannon thought, not for the first time. Why had she been attacked and spared?

A mistake?

She didn't think so. Killing her would have been easy that night. All the murderer would have had to do was turn the sharp tines of the pitchfork on her rather than beat her with the handle.

A warning, then?

No, this guy struck fast and hard. The grisly murders of Mary Beth and now Oliver had been meticulously planned.

A glimpse of the future?

She inwardly shrank. The killer wanted her to know fear. Dark, soul-clawing terror. And he'd managed that.

And tonight . . . Witnessing Oliver's death scene had been mind-shattering. Seeing her brother swinging softly from a crossbeam—blood staining his palms, a short wall of flames surrounding him as he'd been suspended overhead— had burned into her brain. She'd screamed, her stomach had wrenched, her knees had given out, and it had been all she could do not to throw up.

After cutting Oliver down, Travis managed to drag the would-be priest's body out of the circle of flames, but no amount of resuscitation attempts had worked. Oliver was dead. Grotesquely murdered. The EMTs hadn't been able to revive him and the police had discovered, after the flames were extinguished, that the ring of fire surrounding his swinging corpse hadn't been a ring at all, but a star missing several points. Numbers, marked as they had been on the backpack and mirror, had been drawn in kerosene and probably burned first, before the final shape had been lit around his body. The shape had been similar to the other drawings except in this case one more spoke, the upper right-hand point as you looked at the star, was missing. In its stead had been a number four:

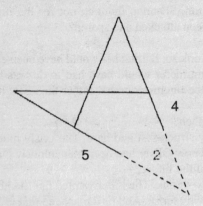

Shannon felt sick at the image.

Someone had gone to a lot of trouble.

Someone was making a macabre point.

Someone was out to get every member of her family.

Not just your immediate family—Mary Beth as well.

Travis spoke as Robert and Shea silently smoked. "Whatever is happening includes more than just your family, since my daughter was abducted."

Robert exhaled gray smoke. "But she's Shannon's daughter, too. Still blood."

"True, but another woman was killed in Oregon. Dani's piano teacher, Blanche Johnson."

"Wasn't she murdered so that he could kidnap your daughter?" Robert asked Travis.

"Maybe. Or, it might have been a separate act. Dani wasn't at Blanche Johnson's house that afternoon. At least there's no evidence of that. She was missing from school before her scheduled lesson, which had been cancelled anyway."

Shea shook his head and frowned.

"So why was the woman killed?" Robert asked.

"That's what the police are trying to figure out."

"Was there any image left behind? Like the complete star or something?" Shannon asked, still trying to make sense of the tragedies.

"No star, just a simple message, left in blood and written on the wall: Payback Time."

"Jesus, payback for what?" Robert muttered. "What the hell does that mean?"

"Is Dani part of the payback?" Shannon asked, hardly able to say the words.

Travis's scowl deepened. "We don't know. Yet."

Shannon held on to his arm and glanced up at him. What more did he know that he hadn't shared?

"Look, I'll break the news to Mom," Shea said as the silence grew awkward. He tossed the remainder of his cigarette onto the pavement and ground it out with his heel. "I'll stop by tonight." He looked over his shoulder to the news vans still parked on the scene. "She gets up early and I don't want to have her wake up and see what happened here on the television."

"She'll be devastated," Robert muttered.

"Aren't we all?" Shannon asked.

"I think we all had better brace ourselves," Shea said as a cat slunk between the bushes, then trotted across the street. "It's not over yet."

Shannon's stomach clenched. Goose pimples rose on her skin. Who was the madman? What did he want? Dear God, couldn't they find Dani Settler and end this? "Has anyone called Aaron?" she asked.

"Why wake him?" Shea asked with a shrug. "He'll get the news soon enough. I heard about it from someone in Dispatch and Robert, you were called by Cuddahey, right?"

"Yeah, Kaye called me when the call came in to the station. I'll tell Aaron tomorrow. Right now . . . I just want to get home. To my kids."

"I'm shoving off, too," Shea agreed soberly. "Nothing more we can do here. Shannon, you need a lift?"

"I'll take her home," Travis interjected.

Neither brother commented, but as Travis and Shannon walked the short distance to the street where his truck was parked, she felt her brothers' gazes following her. She heard a reporter call out to her, but she just kept walking. She was in no mood for inane questions, or recriminations or dredging up of a past she knew would be regurgitated in the news all over again.

Bone-tired, she just wanted to go home.

With Travis.

She was glad for his strength, for his clear-headedness and though she realized it was a silly fantasy, she felt as if she and he were bound together, working toward the same cause, searching for the monster who held their child.

She slid into the cab, yanked the door closed, leaned her head against the backrest and closed her eyes. It had been a long day and an even longer night. She wanted nothing more than to sleep for a million hours, to chase away the demons, to block out the horrible images she'd seen, to start over.

Which was impossible.

Travis maneuvered his rig around the barricades at the end of the street. They rode in silence with the wheels skimming over the pavement and the engine rumbling. With practically no traffic at this time of night, the drive to her little ranch took less than twenty minutes.

Nate's truck was missing.

Again.

In the middle of the night.

In the shop? She doubted it. Nate's apartment looked dark, but then wouldn't it be, if he was inside and asleep?

As Travis slowed his truck to a stop, Shannon wondered if Nate had taken a lover; a woman he hadn't yet mentioned to Shannon. Why else the late hours? The long stretches of time when he was missing? It crossed her mind that he might be involved in crimes against her family, but he had no reason. No, she couldn't lose faith in him, but she'd damned sure talk to him the next time she saw him, get to the bottom of it. What had been his last feeble excuses? He had been "in and out," his truck had been "giving him fits," he'd "tried to get in touch" on the cell phone but couldn't get through. And his voice mail box had been too full to leave a message with him.

Things aren't always what they seem.

It wasn't enough of an answer.

Not when murder and mayhem had taken over.

So what was it he was hiding? That thought bugged her. In all the time that he'd worked for her, he'd taken very little time off, but just before the first attack, he'd told her he'd be gone for a while, that he needed some time off. She'd said "No problem" and had agreed to take care of the horses for the week he'd be away.

Then he'd shown up here on the night she'd been attacked, before he was scheduled to return, and helped to save her. Afterward he was, as he'd said, "in and out," though he never neglected the stock. He'd be gone at all hours of the day and night, but the animals were fed and watered, maybe not on their usual schedule, but taken care of nonetheless.

So what had he been doing?

Travis cut the engine and she reached for the door handle.

"I need to check on the animals," she said, then tossed him a glance over her shoulder as she slid outside. "Want to help? I could use the company."

"You got it."

She stepped out of the cab. The night was warm, still holding on to summer, just the hint of a breeze offering relief, a partial moon visible through the canopy of branches overhead. The buildings were quiet and dark, the shed still a blackened skeleton and reminder of the fires that had taken the lives of those close to her.

She felt bone-weary but there was work to be done. For now, she looked past the shed and the tragedies. Travis walked with her as they found the horses dozing and woke every dog in the kennel by switching on the lights. But all seemed to be as it should.

"So where's Santana?" Travis asked as she closed the door to the kennel and started for the house.

She glanced up at the darkened rooms over the garage. "He could be home, he mentioned he was having trouble with his truck, but . . . I don't know, he's been acting funny lately. Gone a lot."

"Describe 'funny.'"

"Distant. Secretive." She paused at the door and frowned. "Nate and I have always done our own things. We don't get into each other's lives too much, probably because we've both been overscrutinized by the press and the police, or whatever. And he's always taken care of the animals first, even during all of this, whatever it is."

"But . . ." Travis urged.

"But something's not right. Definitely not right." She hazarded a glance at him. "Nothing seems to be these days."

"I know." They stood for a second as they reached the darkened porch. Shannon stared up at him, looked into eyes silvery blue with a bit of moon glow.

His gaze shifted to her mouth.

She swept in a breath as he suddenly bent his head and brushed the side of her cheek with his lips.

Her heart nearly cracked at the tenderness of it all.

"You'd better get some sleep," he said, warm breath brushing across her skin.

"What about you?"

"I thought I'd crash here. On your couch."

"Again you think I need babysitting?"

A slash of white showed in the darkness as he grinned. "I think *I* do."

She almost laughed, despite everything else, and it felt good. "I don't think you'd ever need a sitter, cowboy," she said. To her surprise, he drew her into the circle of his arms, pulled her tight against him and rested his chin on the top of her head.

"Oh, darlin'," he whispered thickly, "if you only knew."

She heard the beating of his heart, echoed by her own and started to pull away, only to have his arms tighten around her. It was as if he'd been waging a silent emotional battle and had finally, unwillingly, given in.

"Oh, hell," he growled, then captured her mouth with the pressure of his own. Gone was the tentative touch of his body to hers. His hands twined in her hair and he held her close, so close she could barely breathe. Hungry lips melded to hers.

She kissed him back. Eagerly. Without a thought to anything but the persistent pressure of his mouth against hers and the feel of his body. Hard. Sinewy. All male. She didn't think where this might lead, just that right now, this very instant, she needed to be wanted, to be touched, to be kissed.

To forget.

Her fingers clutched his shirt and she opened her mouth to the invasion of his tongue. Her mind spun. Pure, wanton fantasy became reality until she heard a sharp, demanding bark from the other side of the door.

Groaning, she pulled her head away from his. "Khan," she said.

Travis chuckled. "Never have I taken a backseat to a dog," he said, amusement crinkling the corners of his eyes.

"If you hang around me, you'd better get used to it."

His hands dropped and she turned, shaking her head at the ridiculousness of the situation, then unlocked the door. Khan bounded through the door. He wiggled and wormed through her legs, barking happily.

"Yeah, you're spectacular," she said. "We all know it."

The dog insisted on attention from Travis, too, and only after having been petted and scratched, talked to and praised, did he bound off the porch to find a bush or fencepost on which to relieve himself.

"Isn't he great?" she teased.

"The best."

So the cowboy did have a sense of humor. Even in the

face of such a ghastly situation. Which was good. Shannon was a firm believer that black humor was better than no humor at all.

From inside the house, the puppy yipped. "Duty calls," Shannon said and walked into the house, snapping on lights, pushing the horror of the night into a far corner of her mind. She wouldn't let herself dwell on that last image of Oliver, nor would she let the desperate words of the tape she'd received, the pleas for her to help from the child she'd never met, run through her mind. Not right now. There was time enough for that later.

"Hey, Marilyn, how're you?" she asked, reaching into the pen and picking up the soft little puppy. Her face was washed over and over again. "Yeah, yeah, I missed you, too. Soooo much." Shannon spent the next fifteen minutes dealing with the puppy, feeding her, holding her, talking to her and walking her outside.

Travis rummaged in a cupboard that served as Shannon's liquor cabinet and fixed them each a stiff drink.

The puppy was wide awake, ready to be up for hours. Or so she thought. "I know, now you're all hyped up, right?" Shannon said, kissing Marilyn's soft little head. "Wrong." She played with the two dogs for a few more minutes. Once they were both calmer, she straightened and gratefully accepted the drink, a short glass with some kind of amber liquor poured over ice cubes.

"Scotch," Travis said and they touched the rims of their glasses together. "To . . . better days."

"And nights."

"And finding our daughter."

There it was. Right out in the open. The simple fact that they shared parentage of a missing girl.

"Yes. To finding Dani." Shannon's throat tightened and she nodded, fighting sudden tears. Staring at Travis over the rim of her glass, she took an experimental sip.

Despite the ice, the liquor burned a warm trail down her throat, heating her blood, easing the tension that had become her constant companion the past few days. She should have felt uncomfortable with him, she supposed, but didn't. When she finished her drink, it seemed the most natural thing in the world to leave her glass in the sink, stand on her tiptoes and gently scrape her lips over his. "Thanks."

"For?"

She cocked her head. "Oh, you know."

"Nope."

"Being here. I, um, usually don't worry about being alone. In fact, I prefer it, but tonight, with all that's gone on . . ." She flipped a palm into the air. ". . . it's just nice that you're here."

"You know, I feel the same way," he admitted, then looked away as if suddenly embarrassed. "I know damned well that the smart thing for me to do is call one of your brothers or friends or someone else to stay here with you. I should pack it in and go back to the motel." He nodded, as if agreeing with himself, then looked back at her. "But I don't want to."

"And I don't want you to."

She suddenly swallowed hard. Felt incredibly vulnerable. Biting her lip, she heard him mutter something under his breath. "Damn it, woman," he growled, one strong arm slipping around her waist to pull her tight against him. His mouth slanted over hers and he kissed her hard, with an urgency that made her tremble. Everything about him was tough. Strained. Tense. Her knees threatened to give way and she could scarcely breathe, couldn't think, didn't care.

It had been so long since she'd been with a man, so very long, and this man, though he was the worst possible choice, was the one she wanted. Desperately.

She closed her eyes as he kissed her temple and sighed against her ear. "What is it about you?" he whispered before his lips touched her eyelids.

Something inside of her cracked.

Emotions she'd dammed rushed through.

Dear God, she wanted him, wanted to get lost in him, in sex, in the fusing of two live bodies.

His lips found hers again. One of his hands pressed flat against her spine, the other caressed her neck, thumb stroking her throat, fingers wrapped around her nape.

His breathing was rough and shallow, and pressed against him, she felt his erection, pushing against his jeans, insistent against her.

"Oh, lady," he said, holding her close. For a heartbeat she thought he might tell her that this was a mistake, that they were losing their heads, that they couldn't be distracted. Crushed, she opened her mouth to speak just as he lifted her off her feet, looked over his shoulder and, holding her close, ordered, "Stay!" to the dog.

Khan didn't move a muscle.

"I can't believe it," she whispered, her heart pounding in expectation, one hand caught behind his neck. "He doesn't pay attention to anyone but me."

"I've got a way with animals." Travis's smile was a wicked slash of white. With a slap of one hand he cut the lights, then kicked the door to the kitchen closed. Her boots fell off, one at a time, clattering to the floor as he mounted the stairs, carrying her upward to a room where she'd never made love, never felt a man's presence. Since claiming and renovating the upstairs after Ryan's death, not once had she allowed a man to step into her private sanctuary.

Until now.

Her throat worked as they tumbled onto her bed and she felt a little jar of pain from her ribs. He began kissing her again and the pain disappeared, chased away by a new hot emotion, a yearning that began deep within. His mouth was warm and sensual, touching and tasting of her, causing her flesh to chill and heat at the same time.

She kissed him eagerly, tasting the salt of his skin and smelling a musky blend of aftershave and smoke that had lingered. Anxiously her fingers dipped beneath his collar, touching hard, sinewy flesh.

His tongue slid between her lips, pressing against her teeth. She moaned, opening her mouth to him, feeling the tip of his tongue touch her own, flicking and teasing, causing desire to flow through her veins.

He reached beneath her shirt, a finger tracing the edge of her jeans where the waistband hugged her hips. Her nerve endings screamed, and when his fingertips slid beneath the fabric, skimming the top of her hips, she squirmed to get closer, yanked his shirt over his head, ran her hands down the sweaty, sinewy strength of his shoulders and arms.

He was so male.

So sleek.

So hard.

So determined.

And she wanted him.

He stared down at her, then kissed her again, his midnight blue gaze locked with hers as he jerked on the waistband of her jeans. The zipper gave way in an eager, expectant hiss.

She was breathing fast and hard, desire building, fires stoked. Both his hands forced their way between her skin and the denim, touching, probing, one set of fingers sliding down her abdomen beneath the thin barrier of her panties, the other hand lightly skimming her buttocks, making her wriggle.

"Ooh." Heat oozed within her. "Ooh . . . oh, Travis," she cried.

Still kissing her, he slid his finger into her cleft, into the moistness. She gasped, bucked up and he applied more pressure, widening her, making her ready. His other hand flattened over her buttocks, holding her in place as he stroked her, touching deep inside, causing her to gasp in the back of her throat. "Oh, God," she cried, her fingers digging into his shoulders as he kept up his ministrations, his knee now separating her thighs, his hand still working its magic.

It was impossible to take a breath, to think of anything but that one pulsing, needy spot and the way he was touching her, salving her while at the same time she wanted more, so much more. Her heart was beating wildly, her blood pumping white-hot through her veins, her pulse skyrocketing. The more he touched her, the more she wanted, the more she writhed. Sweat soaked her skin and she felt that at any second she might explode. Hotter. Faster. Wilder. In a blinding instant she convulsed, crying out, clinging to him, her mind splintering.

Slowly Shannon exhaled her pent-up breath. She opened her eyes to stare into his before falling back onto the bed, drenched in sweat, her breath raspy, her blood tingling in her veins.

As her breathing slowed, she flung one arm over her forehead. "For the love of God," she said, "for the love of God." She glanced at him and smiled. "I think maybe you've done this before."

He laughed then, his own breath uneven. "Maybe a time or two."

"Yeah . . . I'll bet. Wow." She sighed. "Wow."

He stretched out beside her, levering up on an elbow, a half-smile visible in the darkness. She wrapped one hand around his neck. "Come here, you," she whispered. "Two can play at this game."

"You think?"

"I know."

"Then game on, darlin'," he said, kissing her forehead. "Game on."

She couldn't resist. Bit her lower lip. Touching his cheek, she slowly dragged one finger down his jaw, then lower still along his neck, tracing an imaginary line. "Tell me if I do anything that bothers you," she said, and he laughed again.

"Try."

"Hmmm." She slid her finger lower, down the hard muscles of his chest, along a washboard of abdominal muscles while following a fine, dark arrow of hair that dipped beneath his jeans. She hooked the finger over the waistband, feeling his abdomen retract, offering her further access.

"I think it's your turn now," she said, her breath fanning his chest as she stared up at him through the fringe of her lashes. He sucked in his breath as she tugged on his jeans, hearing the soft pop, pop, pop as the buttons gave way and his fly opened.

"Watch it, lady," he warned, voice low. "You're playing with fire."

"You, too . . ." She pushed her hand into the opening of his fly, fingers scraping the muscles of his thighs. He rolled closer to her, his mouth pressing urgently against hers.

Kissing.

Touching.

Caressing.

Her hands moved naturally. Feeling his hardness, tracing the length of his shaft, her breathing irregular as she wrapped a hand around him and cupped his buttocks.

"Jesus," he whispered.

She started working his jeans down his legs but he was impatient and with a groan rolled away, quickly kicking off his Levi's. And then he was lying naked against her. Long, muscular thighs rubbing against her. He was hard, taut, his muscles gleaming with sweat, his manhood hard and ready.

Her breath caught in the back of her throat.

He stared down at her, leaned over and kissed first one breast, then the other. He suckled eagerly, hungrily, his mouth warm and wet, his teeth and tongue skimming over her flesh. Her mind closed to anything but the pure animal want that was driving her, the need to be close to him, the ache that only he could salve.

Love me, she thought, but didn't say the words.

She felt him shift, straddle her and then, his lips finding hers, he pushed her knees apart and came into her, thrusting deep, pushing hard, creating a swirling, consuming heat. Eyes locked with his, she met each of his hard thrusts with her own. Watched in fascination as he loved her, pushing harder, faster, harder, faster, harder, faster until with a gasp she convulsed again. Every muscle in her body jerked. She closed her eyes as her mind spun crazily. Travis stiffened, his cry ragged and hoarse. "Shannon," he whispered and fell atop her.

Pain rocketed down her side. Sharp, biting pain. She bit back the urge to cry out, but he understood, rolled quickly to his side. "Sorry," he said, pulling her close to him. "You okay?"

"Mmm." The pain in her ribs subsided and even if it hadn't, she wouldn't have cared.

"You're sure?" he asked, concern evident in his voice.

"Yes, cowboy . . . I'm sure." Closing her eyes, she felt his breath on her hair. Snuggling nearer to him, wrapped in the smell of sex and musk, this man in her bed, she thought fleetingly that she'd never fall asleep, that she was too jangled, too keyed up.

She was wrong.

Exhaustion took its toll.

With Travis Settler's arms wrapped firmly around her, she drifted off.

Chapter 27

The kid was gone!

He couldn't believe it. Reeling through the tiny rooms, he searched, looking in every possible hiding place. Closets, cupboards, any little hidey hole. Nothing! He double-checked.

She was just plain gone.

He swore in frustration. No! This couldn't happen. Not now!

The damned cabin was empty, the door to her room open wide.

Shit, hadn't he locked it? Yeah, he remembered double-checking the latch, just as he always did. But somehow she'd wormed her way out of her prison.

"Fuck!" Despite all his best efforts that little bitch had managed to escape! Ungrateful kid. He stormed into her room again, shined his flashlight over the floor and dirty blankets, then kicked a pillow across the room. The thin fabric gave way as the pillow crashed into the wall. Old feathers flew, making a damned blizzard of white down. "Son of a bitch!" He threw down the flashlight as a dull roar started somewhere in the back of his head, like the sound of the surf. Raking his hands through his hair, he felt the fury start deep inside, a white-hot heat boiling up until his vision narrowed into blackness. He couldn't lose her! Couldn't! She was the key to his entire plan.

The bait.

Rage burned in his gut.

Because of her, he couldn't revel in the satisfaction of Oliver's death. He should have had the luxury to savor the killing, to replay the moment Oliver, kneeling in the church and absorbed in a pathetic prayer, had felt the rough fibers of the rope slide around his neck, had turned his head quickly to meet his killer's gaze.

There had been a moment of recognition.

Of understanding.

And acceptance.

Almost as if the would-be priest had expected to die.

Almost welcomed it.

The Beast sneered, remembering how he'd yanked on the noose, dragged a flailing, suddenly desperate-to-live man through the church. Choking, gasping, clawing at the thick rope surrounding his neck, Oliver had decided life was better than death.

Things had changed, though. Oliver had passed out before the Beast had hauled him down the stairs to the basement. Now he remembered carrying Oliver's limp body down the rickety steps. Once in the basement, he'd dropped Oliver onto the floor. It had taken a few minutes to set the stage. He'd tossed the old rope over an exposed beam that had once been used to ring the church bells, then pulled Oliver to his feet, setting him on a folding chair below the beam. When Oliver finally awoke, he would see what was happening, watch in terror as the fire was lit into the form of a star missing a few spokes. Then he'd feel some kind of weird pain and look down to see his own blood drizzling to the floor to pool beneath the chair. Oliver would panic, meet the Beast's eyes as the chair was kicked out from under him, and realize that his soul was going straight to hell. That was the plan.

But Oliver hadn't reacted as he'd hoped. Hadn't squirmed and flailed, hadn't clawed at his neck again, nor scrabbled for his life. It was as if in the brief time he was unconscious, he'd found acceptance . . . even absolution.

Oliver had opened his eyes and seeing the flames growing and crawling over the sticks, rope and rags surrounding him, knowing he was bleeding from his wrists, he'd met the Beast's gaze, smiled, and before the Beast could react, calmly stepped off the chair and kicked it backward. The metal chair had clattered noisily to the cement floor as Oliver had hung himself calmly and quietly. It had been as if Oliver had been ready for death. No, not quite right, as if he'd fucking *embraced* death.

That part had been unexpected.

Creepy.

Bothered him now.

Acceptance of death wouldn't do.

Welcoming death was just plain wrong.

Unnatural.

The Beast wanted a fight.

He wanted to witness a struggle. He wanted to delight in their panic, sense their horrifying, gut-wrenching, blood-curdling fear.

Only then would his need for revenge be satisfied.

He needed someone to fight for his life, to battle him, to make him feel the surge of power that came when the flames grew and consumed and he, the Beast, was the victor.

Oliver's own sacrifice had tainted his plans.

Brought a bad taste to his mouth.

And now this! The kid breaking away.

Completely unexpected!

Of course Oliver had always been a nutcase. From day one.

But the kid . . . Now, she was a different story. Cagey and fearless, as it turned out, patient and determined, an adversary worth battling. Shannon's daughter. He felt a zing as he anticipated chasing her down, running her to the ground.

She would lose.

Of course.

Slippery little brat! He had to find her! Had to!

Ready to face the new challenge, he calmed his pulse, readied himself for the hunt. Walking into the living area, he glanced up at the mirror and sensed something was wrong. In a second he realized one of his framed pictures was missing. The photograph of *Shannon*. He checked, to see if it had fallen over or been tucked behind one of the other framed photos, but no, it was gone.

His teeth ground together and the fury he'd managed to rein in just seconds before unleashed in a black, consuming wrath. That miserable, little piece-of-crap kid had taken the photo!

Oh . . . She would regret it . . .

When he caught up with her, he'd make sure she understood that she'd crossed the line with him. This was to never happen again. Who the hell was she to take the damned picture?

If he could just kill her now. Quick, fast, get rid of her, but he couldn't. That wasn't part of his plan, laid so carefully for years.

A scheme, because of her, now scattered in pieces.

No, he reminded himself. *The plan didn't fail. You did. You underestimated her.*

Just fix it. Fucking find her!

One little miserable, lying teenager wasn't going to stop him. He'd hunt her down. And when he did, she'd know who she was dealing with.

He slammed a fist into the wall. He wanted to find her right now and shake the life right out of her, watch her squeal in fear and pain.

Stop! Think! Calm down.

You can locate her. You picked this place because escape would be next to impossible. She hasn't gotten far. Just outsmart her.

His mind racing, he forced himself to take calm, deep breaths, to think of this as a challenge. A hunt.

How much of a head start did she have?

Not enough, he figured. He hadn't been gone long enough for her to have traveled too many miles. Though the forest was dense with good cover, she would stick to trails or old roads to keep from getting lost. It was dark . . .

He glanced to the place where he kept his flashlight. Gone.

Quickly he searched the rest of the house. She'd taken a knife and a lighter, but no extra batteries. Her flashlight would fail quickly, before dawn, no doubt, and the lighter she'd nabbed wouldn't help her. He considered the fact that she could start a fire, attract attention, but she wouldn't. For fear of attracting him and starting a blaze that, in these tinder-dry woods might consume her.

There was only one rutted, old forestry road up here and though there were hiking and deer trails, they all convened at one spot.

The bridges.

One for the train.

Another originally built for logging, for trucks.

Both used to span a narrow part of the canyon, each one less than a quarter of a mile from the other.

The only other way off the mountain was around the back side, but one had to climb upward before finding an equally daunting precipitous path down. He banked on the fact that the kid would head downhill rather than up.

So he'd just have to find her.

He headed outside.

His truck was already loaded with the essentials: his rifle, ammunition, hunting knife, boots, gloves, night vision goggles and rope.

He'd catch the little bitch by morning.

Nothing and no one was going to ruin his plans.

He'd come too far.

Dani's flashlight was useless, the weak beam giving out completely. Exhausted, she found a tree and sat behind it. Maybe she could sleep, for just a few hours, until dawn. She couldn't move in the darkness.

But he'll find you. You know he will. You have to keep going. Just keep moving.

She wanted to break into a million pieces, to cry and pray for her father to come find her. But it was too late. She was in this alone. Tears started to track down her dusty cheeks, but she told herself to keep going. This was no time to be a wimp. She'd just have to inch along—that was it, follow the trail and . . .

She felt a rumble.

The ground shook.

The trees trembled.

Holy crap, was this an earthquake? She couldn't believe her bad luck. On top of everything else, would she have to endure a friggin' earthquake?

She shot to her feet, wondering what to do, which way to run, and then she heard it, the familiar rush of a train barreling through the night.

Where? She looked around frantically. *Where?*

Louder and louder it came, the thunder of its wheels upon the tracks deafening, an incredible roar.

A light shined through the forest as the train approached. Moving quickly, ignoring her sore muscles, Dani ran through the trees and underbrush that suddenly gave way to the tracks, laid over a big swath of cleared land. The light was nearly upon her and with a deafening rush, the engines clattered noisily by, rushing at a breakneck speed, dragging a long tail of freight cars behind.

No chance to hop the train or ride a rail, she thought, wishing desperately that she could somehow climb aboard, stow away in the big metal containers and leave these miserable woods behind. At the next stop she'd go to the authorities, the sheriff or any cop on the street, and tell them about the whack job and what he'd done to her.

Of course it was all fantasy.

The train flew by, disappearing into the night. Her heart sank. Despair and desolation converged on her. This was so useless. So damned useless.

Don't give up now. You can do this, you can!

She squared her shoulders. Setting her jaw, she climbed up the short embankment and started walking on the tracks. She could barely see them beneath her feet, but was able, by keeping her steps even, to walk without tripping. It might take a long time, but eventually the train tracks would lead to civilization.

She set out in the direction from which the train had come, the way she'd been heading, away from the cabin. Away from him.

But she had to hurry. She knew the Beast was out in the night somewhere, sensed that he was following her, closing in on her.

"Bastard," she said in a whisper and just kept moving, telling herself that she was being a paranoid freak and to get over it, not give in to her fear. Move. That was it. Just keep going. She walked for what seemed like miles before noticing that the sky was beginning to lighten, a gray dawn slowly but surely stealing through the hills, birds beginning to chirp, the sun rising behind her.

Which was good. And bad.

She'd be able to see, of course, and could walk faster if she could keep up her strength, but he'd be able to spot her more easily, too. With the sun as her guide, she'd know which direction she was traveling, not that it mattered much because she didn't know where the nearest town was located.

Her mouth tasted like sand and all her muscles ached. She was sure she could kill for a Dr Pepper, or a slice of cheese pizza or one of her dad's special tacos. When she got home, she'd raid the refrigerator big time. There wouldn't be enough chicken nuggets and French fries and homemade tacos to satisfy her.

When she got home.

If she got home.

Don't think that way.

He hasn't caught you yet, has he?

And even if he was chasing her she felt a tiny bit of satisfaction tempering her fear. She couldn't help but smile at the thought of how ticked off he would be when he found her missing. She would have loved to have seen his face. *Yeah, well, take that, you weird sack of crap, and piss it all over the damned fire.*

She reached into her pocket and touched the picture of her mother—well, she thought it was her mother. How did the woman in the framed snapshot figure into this? How did Dani? Who knew? Probably no one, not even the fire-pisser. That psycho was so warped he probably didn't know what his plans were.

Don't kid yourself. He knows exactly what he's got in mind and you're a part of what's going on.

Keep going.

Keep moving.

Her feet were sore and as the sun began to climb, she knew it would be another hot day. Even now, though it was early morning, she could feel the heat beginning to grow and any hope for fog to hide her, or clouds to offer some kind of respite, would be false. As her father always said, "It's gonna be a scorcher."

Her dad.

Where was he?

Why hadn't he come for her?

She felt sorry for herself again and angrily brushed away her tears. She was tired and hungry and scared. She thought about the trips she used to take with her dad when they'd gone on four-day hikes into the mountains. Of course those hikes had been way different. They'd had food and water and sleeping bags and . . .

She rounded a corner and two deer, as startled as she was, bounded into the underbrush. Heart knocking, she told herself to cool it, quit jumping at shadows, when her gaze landed on the bridge.

She stopped short.

Her heart nearly quit beating. It was one of those narrow, wooden railroad bridges spanning a steep chasm between sheer cliffs. Below, over a hundred feet, she thought, was a dry creek bed weaving through the mountain floor and there was no other way down.

"Damn."

Fear coiled over her heart.

Dread filled her.

Surely there was another way . . . But as she looked around, she realized she was stuck. Either go back the way she'd come or cross.

How tough could it be? She'd just walked miles along the tracks and never once had fallen off. Getting across was only a matter of nerves. Of not looking down. Of planting one foot in front of the other. Of not panicking.

But, oh, man, was that a long way down!

Maybe there was another way across, or maybe she could find a path to climb down to get to the bottom and she could follow the dry river bed. Desperately, she swept her gaze over either side of the canyon. Sheer, ragged rock walls flanked the deep chasm and were topped with brush and trees.

Not far to the south was another bridge, a narrow one that had been built for cars or logging trucks or whatever vehicle wanted to scale these hills. She walked backward for about a hundred yards or so, searching for a path that might lead through the forest to the road. She checked the spot from which the deer had leapt, but she saw no evidence of a trail. And even if she did, who was to say it would take her to the road?

The road the Beast probably uses.

That's where he would be. He probably thinks you were trying to find the road and just used the trails to throw him off. So go for it. Cross the damned railroad bridge. Now. Get it over with.

Gritting her teeth, she made her way to the edge of the trestle again, then squatted and placed her hands on the rails, feeling for any sense of movement, listening hard, hoping that if there was another train coming she would sense it. The rails didn't tremble at all. Nor could she hear the huff of an engine or the clack of wheels on tracks. All in all, aside from the twitter of a bird or the rustle of a chipmunk or squirrel in the brush, there was no sound.

Just do it. Go on. Quit being such a wuss!

It was now or never.

Tentatively she started out, making certain each of her footsteps landed squarely on the wooden slats, seeing, through the spaces in between, the land give way to clear space and a terrifying drop. Carefully, she stepped on one narrow tie at a time.

Keep going.

Heart pounding, she inched farther over the chasm, noticing that her breathing was shallow, that her heart was frantically beating, that her nerves were stretched to the breaking point. All of her concentration was on her movement, slow, but sure, even farther over the wide crevice, one foot, then the other, one foot, then the other.

Out in the open, without the hills or trees to shade her, the sun beat hot against her crown and sweat ran down the sides of her face. She didn't dare swipe at the beads that stung her eyes for fear she'd lose her concentration or, worse yet, her balance.

What had her mother often said? "Every task is as easy or as hard as you make it." *Yeah, right.* "Easy as pie, honey."

Her dad had told her, not without a sense of pride, that she was fearless.

Wrongo, Dad. Inside she was quivering like a leaf in a stiff breeze.

Halfway across now.

She took a long breath, then stepped forward again. Maybe she was going to make it. On the other side she wouldn't even stop to rest, just keep going along the tracks, hoping and praying that there would be a town, or at the very least, a farmhouse in the distance.

Another step.

And another.

Closer still.

She looked up and thought she saw a movement in the brush along the sides of the trestle. A glint of something . . . glass caught in the sunlight?

She stopped. Barely twenty feet from the end of the bridge. She looked more closely to the spot where she'd seen the glimmer of light, a reflection of some kind, but there was nothing in the brush and shrubs, no movement in the shadows.

Yet the hairs on the back of her neck raised.

Her skin crawled and fear inched up her spine.

He couldn't have figured out where she was, could he?

Couldn't have driven his truck down the road and, banking on the fact that she'd gone in this direction and wouldn't risk using the road, had ended up here?

No . . . that was giving the guy too much credit.

Or was it?

She hesitated. Bit her lip. Squinted at the hillside in front of her. She took one more tentative step forward and stopped again. Something wasn't right. She could feel it. Did something move in the shadows beneath the tree? Another deer?

Yeah—with glasses. No way.

She took a step backward. One more.

He was there!

The damned Beast was there.

Her eyes widened in horror.

He rushed from the brushy shadows, a big, muscular man in camouflage and sunglasses, striding straight for her, fearlessly, onto the trestle bridge, his footsteps causing it to shake.

Somehow the Beast had found her.

No!

Spinning quickly, she twisted her ankle but hurtled forward, trying to get her feet under her, intent on racing back the way she came. But the expanse was huge, the drop paralyzing, the slap of his boots on the trestle like claps of thunder. Her heart kicked into overdrive. She wouldn't give in to him, wouldn't. She started running, faster and faster, feeling him coming closer.

"Stop! You crazy little bitch, stop!"

Oh, God, no, she couldn't have come all this way only to have him catch her now—

The toe of her tennis shoe caught. Screaming, she pitched forward and saw the deep chasm beneath her. Far below the rocks gleamed in the sunlight.

A strong hand surrounded her arm, grabbed painfully and hauled her to her feet.

"Hey!"

He threw her over one shoulder. "Stop it, you little brat, or you'll get us both killed!" Her head was dangling down his back, her hair falling in front of her face as he held her legs and turned seemingly effortlessly, heading toward the ledge where he'd been hiding, the brushy end of the bridge where she'd thought she would find salvation.

Tears of frustration fell to the ground and she beat at his back with tired, angry fists.

"Keep it up, you bitch, and I'll drop you, I swear I will," he promised and she quit, her hands falling to her sides, fingertips nearly sweeping the ground, great wracking sobs welling up from her body. She was doomed, she knew it. No, she didn't think he'd kill her right away, but it was only a matter of time. If she had any guts at all, she would try to fling herself away from him, over the edge, hoping that both of them would fly into space. Yes, she'd die, but at least she'd take the psycho with her.

But she didn't.

Instead she gave up.

Let him haul her off the bridge. He carried her down a path and through the forest for nearly a mile to the spot where he'd parked his truck. It waited at the side of the road, baking in the sun.

She was silent on the drive back to the cabin, too tired to plan another escape attempt, no longer trying to be brave, letting tears track down her cheeks.

He drove like a maniac, the truck bouncing along the rutted road, dust pluming from beneath the wheels. He didn't seem to care if she saw where they were headed. She knew why. He was going to kill her soon and since she'd already been outside, seen the lay of the land, secrecy no longer mattered.

He parked in his usual spot, lit a cigarette, then, prodding her with a damned rifle, marched her along the beaten path to the sorry little cabin. Inside he flung his cigarette butt into the fireplace, then nudged her, with the tip of his gun, toward her bedroom. The prison cell. "Strip," he ordered, and she balked.

"What?"

"Go in there and strip. Throw out your clothes and your shoes."

"No, please, don't!"

"Do it!" His face was a mask of grim determination. He pointed the gun right between her breasts. "I'd like nothing more than to kill you right now, but I'm giving you a reprieve. Be a fucking good girl, go into that room and toss me your clothes. And don't empty the pockets. I know you have my things and I want them back." She glared up at him mutinously and he pushed her with the rifle. "Now!"

She did as she was bid, stripping down to her underwear and balling up her clothes. Her fingers closed around something hard. The nail. She held it tightly, counting her heartbeats, drawing strength. She then tossed her clothes through the crack in the door.

"Shoes," he reminded her.

Angrily she flung her favorite sneakers through the open space and heard them clunk somewhere near the front door.

"Underwear."

"No . . . Wait."

"Underwear!"

"But I—"

She heard his rifle cock.

"Take off everything or I'll come in there and do it for you."

Sick pervert.

Humiliated, silently swearing she'd kill him if she ever got the chance, she stripped from her bra and panties and hurled them through the small space between the door and its jamb.

A second later, she retreated to the relative safety of her cot and pulled the dirty blanket over her.

The door slammed shut.

The latch clicked.

Locked in again, but she still had the nail.

She heard him in the other room, moving about. Probably getting ready for his sick ritual, but she didn't dare look at him through the crack today, didn't want him to catch her watching, felt awkward and mortified that he might see her nakedness. So she lay in the bed, exhaustion taking its toll. She started to fall asleep.

BAM! BAM! BAM!

The entire building shook.

For a second she didn't know what he was doing and then it hit her. He was hammering. Against her door. No doubt nailing a crosspiece between the walls and door.

Making certain she was sealed inside this hot, airless jail.

Chapter 28

Travis opened an eye.

Sunlight was streaming into the room.

Shannon was nestled against him, her naked body cupped by his, her gorgeous rump pressed firmly against the juncture of his legs. He remembered making love to her, the desperation of the act, the release, the rapture of it. Sex had been what they'd both needed. He wrapped an arm over her and kissed her nape. She smiled and let out a soft, contented sigh.

The smell of her was all around and though he knew he should get up, that he had to face the day, the sight of her beside him, sunlight playing in the fiery strands of her hair, her breasts full and unbound, was more than he could resist. He traced the edge of one areola with his finger and she sighed, the nipple puckering expectantly.

His damned cock was already hard at the sight of her; the pressure of her buttocks so near, made it ache for want of release. He toyed with her nipple and she smiled.

"Watch it, cowboy. Don't start what you can't finish," she said groggily and he was undone.

He leaned over, found her lips and kissed her with a heat he hadn't felt since he was a horny teenager.

Slowly her eyelids raised, exposing intelligent, verdant irises that dared him to keep at it. "Feelin' randy?" she asked.

"Very."

One reddish eyebrow arched and he gently squeezed her nipple, watching as her pupil sharpened. "Do you always wake up this way?" she asked.

"Yes, ma'am," he drawled and she laughed, flung her arms around his neck and kissed him as if he were the last man on earth. His body responded and they wrestled on the rumpled bedclothes, arms and legs entwined, breathing labored, lips exploring and tasting, pressure building. When he could stand the teasing no longer, he entered her with a long, hard thrust.

Her body was moist and hot, muscles contracting around him. He moved, and she found his rhythm, keeping up with him, staring at him, fingers digging into his arms, gaze locked with his.

He felt her body start to quiver, saw her catch her breath and he could hold back no longer. In a rush, he came into her and rather than falling atop her, crushing her already-bruised ribs, he landed on his elbows, gently pulling her atop him. She turned her head, snuggling at his shoulder. Her heartbeat was an echo of his own as they slowly descended, her breath mingling with his. Only when she'd finally let out a long sigh did he roll her to her side.

She gazed up at him. Her eyes sparkled impishly and one side of her mouth twitched upward. "Dibs on first shower," she said, kissing his forehead and before he could grab her, slid from the bed.

Naked, she hurried into the bathroom and he was left lying on her bed, wondering what the hell he was doing. As he heard her twist on the faucets and water begin to run, he thought for a fleeting second that he was falling in love with her. Immediately he banished that wayward idea. He'd sworn off women after his failed attempt at hooking up with Jenna Hughes. It was just as well that had never happened, but this . . . Shannon Flannery . . . the birth mother of his daughter. Worse yet.

And yet he heard her singing off-key in the shower and it was all he could do not to walk into the bathroom, slip into the small enclosure, and with their bodies lathered and slick, lift her from her feet and make love to her with the hot water cascading over them.

The idea was so appealing, Travis had already rolled off the bed when he noticed the picture of Dani, the one he'd given Shannon at El Ranchito, the flyer announcing that Dani Settler had gone missing.

The old pain resurfaced. Instantly he sobered and the last few hours suddenly seemed to be frivolous.

With all the fear and dying and pain, he'd lost sight of his mission, if only for a few hours. Now, however, it was back with a vengeance.

He grabbed his Levi's. The old pipes moaned as the water was turned off. Travis looked up to find Shannon, a towel wrapped around her, her hair wet and dripping, step into the room.

God, she was beautiful.

Even without a bit of makeup, her face still lightly bruised, she was still incredible. "Your turn if you want."

"I think I should have joined you. Then we'd both be done."

"Nuh-uh," she shook her head. "We'd have stayed in there until we ran out of hot water. It's better this way. Besides, while you're cleaning up, I need to see to the animals. Khan's nose is definitely going to be out of joint, Marilyn needs to be fed and taken outside, and then I've got a lot of horses and dogs who are waiting for me."

"Doesn't Santana take care of them?"

"Yes, but lately . . ."

"I know, he's been acting 'funny.'"

Some of her lightheartedness faded. "Come on," she said. "Maybe you'll get lucky and I'll make you coffee *and* breakfast."

"I think I already did 'get lucky.'"

A smile lifted the corners of her mouth. "Me, too."

Shannon hurried down the stairs, started the coffee, took care of the two dogs inside the house, then headed to the kennels. Khan dashed ahead, knowing the routine. Nate's truck wasn't in its usual spot, but the horses were outside.

She fed the dogs and took them outside to run their legs off. "Feeling neglected?" she asked Atlas. The big dog nudged at her leg while Khan was busy barking at a squirrel who scolded from the branches of an oak tree. She scratched Atlas behind his ears and he groaned. "You like that, don't you? I know . . . tonight, it's your turn. And yours, too," she said to Cissy, who, as usual was lying in wait, body pressed to the dry grass, unmoving as she stared at the larger dog, ready to stalk the German shepherd if he ever gave her the time of day.

"Come on," she said, finding the dogs' toys. She played catch and fetch and generally enjoyed being with them. They filled a need in her that now—because she knew about Dani—had shifted. For years she'd believed she would never have children, never know what it was like to care for a child. In some ways, the dogs and horses had taken up the emotional slack.

Now, things had changed and though she loved these animals fervently, and she couldn't wait to move them to the bigger, better surroundings, she realized they would never take the place of her child.

She threw the ball with her good arm, until she'd run out of steam, then accepted the fact that she couldn't put off the inevitable forever. She needed to phone her mother, visit and console her, then square off with Nate if she could find him.

As for Travis . . . Shannon cast a look over her shoulder to the house and sighed. Last night they'd become lovers, but it didn't mean anything other than that they were two lonely people caught up in a horrific tragedy together.

It was odd but pleasant. She'd never been one to jump into bed with a man at the drop of a hat; in fact, after her experience with Brendan Giles, it had taken a long time for her to trust again. And then, unfortunately, she'd again chosen the wrong man in Ryan Carlyle.

The two men she'd seen since had been disasters. Especially Reggie Maxwell, the man who had neglected to mention his wife and kids. No wonder she'd given up on men.

Until last night. And then, it seemed, she'd thrown away all of her rules. Because of Travis? Or because everything she believed in was being tested and destroyed?

She watched the horses in the paddock for a minute and as she did, her mind spun with the conversation between her brothers she'd heard less than twenty-four hours earlier. All those whispers about "birth order" and "Dad's fault." She'd convinced herself that Oliver had meant to confide in her.

She stared at the buckskin, but in her mind she thought, again, about the order in which her siblings had come into the world: Aaron, Robert, Shea, Oliver, Neville. She thought about the spacing between them, wondered about the miscarriages her mother had endured, but couldn't think of anything . . . Nothing made any sense.

She needed to talk to one of her brothers about it, most likely Aaron. She wondered how he'd taken the news of Oliver's death. It was telling, she thought, that in the face of Oliver's death, rather than wanting to run to her family, to be a part of the grief and consolation, she wanted instead to run the other way.

Without any answers, Shannon slapped the rail, then walked through the stable. The stalls were clean, fresh straw strewn on the floor. Nate had definitely been around. How did he figure into all of this? Maybe their unspoken agreement not to pry into each other's lives wasn't such a hot idea.

The door at the far end of the building opened and she nearly jumped out of her skin. Half-expecting Travis, she was surprised when Nate himself appeared, his silhouette dark, his body thrown in relief by the sunlight behind him.

She'd been so absorbed in her thoughts, she hadn't heard his truck roll in.

"Jumpy this morning?" he asked.

He was wearing a short-sleeved T-shirt that had once been red and Levi's with tattered pockets, almost the height of fashion, though he didn't know it.

"Do you blame me?"

"No." He was serious as he walked toward her. "I just heard about Oliver on the news." His eyes were shadowed and red, as if he'd been up all night. "I'm sorry."

"Me, too."

"I don't know what to say."

The image of Oliver's bloodied body, swinging from a crossbeam, leaped from the safe place in her mind where she'd stored it. Her throat clogged.

"You want to talk about it?"

She shook her head and blinked hard. "No. I know I have to go and see my family and . . . discuss it, and I'll probably have to talk to the police again, and try to avoid talking about it with the press, so for now, I'd rather pass." She felt a hollowness inside, an empty place that she knew could never be filled.

"Fair enough."

"And don't start in on me about a security system. I plan on calling a company today," she said, then cringed. "Right after I talk to Mom."

"How's she doing?"

"Don't know yet," Shannon said, with more than a bit of guilt. "I haven't talked to her yet. Shea was going over last night. I'm sure she's devastated."

"So are you," he said so gently she nearly broke down.

But she didn't. Instead, she said what was on her mind. "So where have you been, Nate? And don't give me any cock-and-bull story about being 'in and out,' I know that much. You've kept taking care of the animals. Like this morning. You weren't here when I got in, which was really late, nearly three, I think, but somehow you came back, saw to the stock, then left again. What's that all about?"

"I thought we agreed not to pry into each other's lives."

"That was before people started being killed! Come on, Nate! Before I was attacked, before Molly was tortured." She pointed through the open door at the far end of the barn to the paddock where the buckskin was restlessly grazing.

"You think I had something to do with what's going on?" he demanded.

"I don't know! That's the problem!"

"I'm no killer," he said evenly.

"Well, good," she said, unable to hide the sarcasm in her

voice. "But there's something going on, Nate." She pointed a finger at his chest. "Something you've been hiding."

His jaw slid to one side. "I said, I'm not a murderer."

"So then you won't mind telling me where you've been, what you've been doing, and why the hell you're in and out of here like a damned ghost."

He looked at the ground.

"You know, you're almost acting as if you're involved with a woman and don't want to tell me about it."

His lips compressed and he frowned at the floor.

"That's it, isn't it?" she asked on a note of discovery. "I think that's great! But you don't have to sneak around, for God's sake."

He reached out suddenly, one hand circling her wrist. "Remember when I told you things aren't always what they seem?" he asked, then, as if he realized what he was doing, released her. "Well, this is one of those times. Yes, there's another woman, but it's not what you think." He rubbed a hand around his neck. "Maybe it's time I leveled with you."

"Past time. You're the one man I thought I could really and truly rely on in this world. Even more than my brothers."

A tic had started to develop under one eye.

"Let's go inside," he said, his gaze skipping from her to the floor to the open doorway where sunlight blazed and the horses grazed.

The morning had seemed calm and safe. But a sense of foreboding came over her and she knew that feeling was going to change.

He started for the open door. "Settler should hear this, too."

Paterno sat at his desk. He'd studied the crime scene at the church and was convinced by the scuff marks that Oliver had been caught in the nave, probably praying, and dragged to the basement. His fingers were raw from struggling with the rope at his neck. His wrists had been slit at impossible angles for him to have done it himself. No doubt he was murdered by the same perp who seemingly had made a half-assed attempt to have the death appear like a suicide. But no, Paterno wasn't buying that. The killer was smart enough to know that no one would be fooled, he was just reminding everyone that his victim had once tried to kill himself by slitting his wrists.

At least that was Paterno's take on what had happened. "Nutcase," he muttered, then turned his eyes back to his cluttered desk. He'd been studying the information they'd collected on the recent murders as well as Ryan Carlyle's death. He went back to it, sifting through the damned information again while he waited for the lab reports, ducked calls from the press and doodled on a notepad. He wrote down whatever thoughts came into his head about the case, drawing stars, one after the other.

Rossi walked into the room with two paper cups of coffee. It was late morning, Paterno had slept only three hours the night before, and even the sludge that passed as Java down here smelled good. He'd already downed three cups, two at home and one here. "The son of a bitch is trying to give us a clue," Paterno muttered, pointing at the figures that had been found at each of the fires, including the most recent one, where the number four had replaced the long triangular point of the star.

Rossi nodded. He handed Paterno one of the paper cups. "But what?"

"Beats me," he said, taking a sip and staring at the images. "But it means something and it has to do with birth order, according to Shannon Flannery."

"Looks more like the spokes are protecting the center piece. Birth order . . . Do the numbers represent the brothers by birth order?"

"It's possible."

"That's a weird thing, though, isn't it?" Rossi shook his bald head. "The guy's just fuckin' with us."

"Why go to all the trouble?"

"He's a friggin' psycho. Got time on his hands."

Paterno's head snapped up. "Good point. Whoever did Oliver took a lot of time at it. He had to have been waiting for a while. If this guy's got a regular job, or a family, he must be dead on his feet by now." He drank a long swallow, then frowned. "And where the hell is Travis Settler's daughter?"

"Wish I knew," Rossi said.

"I wish anyone but the killer knew." Paterno looked at a map of the area he had mounted on his wall. With blue push-pins he'd marked all the residences of the Flannery and Carlyle families. Using red, he'd indicated where fires had been set, black where a murder had been committed. In Shannon Flannery's case, she had two red pins and two blue—for the two fires and for being a member of both the Flannery clan and the Carlyle family. At Robert and Mary Beth Flannery's residence, he'd inserted a red, two blue and a black pin on the map.

So far the system hadn't told him much. He'd done a similar thing on the computer, hoping that some fancy program would help him locate the kid, or the killer or some damn thing. So far, nada.

"So what do we know?" he thought aloud, sipping from the cup. "We've been figuring that the guy has to have the kid nearby, so he can get back and forth to the crime scenes, but that might not be true. Dani Settler might not be alive. The tape he left in Shannon Flannery's truck could have been made at the time of the abduction or any time thereafter. It doesn't prove she's still alive, just that he abducted her and she was alive when the tape was made. We know he didn't leave her in Idaho at the farm, so we assume he brought her to California, but that's still just an assumption."

"But he has to live nearby," Rossi ventured. "And know the victims pretty well. He's figured out their schedules, knows where they live, or where they go, like in Oliver's case. He anticipates where they'll be and finds a way to get inside."

"In each case, there's a fire involved. So it's someone who has a fascination with fire."

"We're checking the database for all known arsonists who aren't locked up, looking at those who have recently been released. Haven't come up with anyone yet."

"It's a long shot anyway, this is more personal. As for anyone fascinated with fire, you've got the whole damned Flannery family," Paterno said. "Shamus, the grandfather, when the department was all volunteer, then Patrick, his son, and later all of Patrick's boys signed up."

"Until they dropped out."

Paterno nodded. "Now we're down to Robert. He's the only one still in the department. How about that?" He raised an eyebrow as he leaned back in his chair. "The Flannerys—They're not exactly retiring as heroes. The old man, Patrick, he didn't retire unblemished. He was pretty much forced into it."

"Why?"

"From what I gather, he used to bend the rules. Had a problem with booze and made some bad calls. Funny thing is, this happens just about the time the whole department starts to disintegrate. The old man's forced out and his sons start leaving like rats off a sinking ship." Paterno held up a finger. "Shea takes a position with the police department." Another finger joined the first. "Aaron, he gets the boot for 'insubordination,' whatever that means, Neville quits on the spot and a few weeks later disappears and Oliver finds God." Fingers three and four joined the first two. "Four brothers and the old man, out, just like that."

He drank a long, hot swallow, his eyes squinting at the map. "And that's just the Flannerys. Then there's the Carlyles. Ryan ends up burnt to a crisp and the evidence points to murder. Afterward, Liam quits the SLFD to take a job with an insurance company. Gives up all his benefits and starts over at a helluva lot less pay. I might even understand it if he was a family man and wanted a more nine-to-five life with a safer job, but he's got no kids and was divorced from wife number two at that time." Paterno fished through his notes, until he found those on the Carlyles. "Since that forest fire, Liam moved on to wife number three, but that's already rocky. They're split."

He frowned to himself. "So that's what happens to the fire department. They're practically decimated, have to recruit new blood."

His eyes lingered on the notes about the Carlyles, another group of loners. "The other brother, Kevin, with an IQ in the stratosphere, is content with a government job, has never been married and is possibly gay, though he's never officially come out of the closet. The sister, Margaret, is a religious fanatic who goes to mass every damned day and then there was Mary Beth. Dead. Another victim."

"Maybe Liam got tired of putting his life on the line. After all, his cousin died in a fire."

"But not while trying to put out the blaze, not in the line of duty," Paterno pointed out. "Besides, most of the firefighters I know love the job, they're dedicated, it's in their blood." He looked up at Rossi. "They don't quit."

Paterno didn't like the way the whole thing played out. Standing and stretching, he walked over to his map and scowled. There were just so many things that didn't fit. "You know, Rossi, I still don't get why the DA tried to pin the case on Shannon Flannery. I wasn't here at the time, but I've looked over the file. The case was thin as melting ice."

Rossi shook his head. "I was new to the force at the time, had just moved from San Jose. The DA, Berringer, was looking for a win, the department was having public relations problems and the Stealth Torcher business was making the whole community nervous. Of course the press couldn't leave it alone, and there was a lot of pressure to solve the case and put it away. Make the public feel safe again.

"Berringer, he really wanted to put it to rest and I think he believed that somehow Shannon Flannery had done the job. He was obsessed with it, had a real hard-on to break her. She didn't have an alibi, but had a big-time motive: Carlyle beat her. Bad enough that she lost a baby. She'd had a restraining order against him, which he broke and, even though he had a girlfriend, he was fighting the divorce. His whole life was in the toilet. She was going to go after him for battery, but before that case could come to court, he was killed and Berringer was hell-bent to prosecute."

"Still, not enough to press charges."

"Then there was an anonymous tip that Shannon's car had been seen out by the old logging road that night, not far from the murder and the fire. An elderly woman had concurred. There was the suggestion that Shannon couldn't have pulled this off herself, that she either hired someone to help her or her brothers did it. Their only alibis were each other and she maintained her innocence to the end. I think Berringer thought she would crack, confess, and they would plea bargain, but it never happened, and the anonymous caller never called back. Another witness, a woman who thought she'd seen the car out there, turned out to be legally blind, couldn't tell a white van from a yellow station wagon in broad daylight. Not too credible on the stand.

"Yep, it was a thin case, should never have gone to trial and cost Berringer his career."

Paterno had heard the scuttlebutt, of course, once he'd started digging but it helped to have Rossi lay it all out again. Made things clearer. What it came down to was that Berringer was an idiot.

His phone rang and he braced himself. Reporters had been calling all morning and no matter how many times he referred them to the department's public relations officer, they didn't give up. Then again, it could be the lab, or someone with information on a case, a fellow officer. He drained his coffee, crushed the cup, tossed it into his wastebasket and grabbed the receiver. "Paterno."

"Shane Carter," the guy said.

Paterno recognized the voice of the sheriff from Oregon. "How are ya?"

"Been better. Look, I thought I'd give you a heads up. The FBI will be calling as well."

"Great." Just what Paterno needed. The Feds. Most of them knew their shit, were okay, but the guy from the local field office was a prick. No two ways about it. "What do you have?"

"It turns out that Blanche Johnson had two ex-husbands, one's dead, the other we haven't located yet. A few boyfriends, scattered around the Northwest, some we're still trying to track down. No other family aside from a couple of kids, both boys. The older one ran away when he was a teenager, the other, we think, she gave up as a small child, maybe a baby, possibly a toddler, when she was in Idaho. We're running that down now but it's taking a little time as the adoption records were sealed back then. That kid would be about in his middle thirties now."

"Keep me posted," Paterno said as he hung up. He couldn't see how Blanche Johnson having a couple of kids could come into play, but he filed the information away. The way this case was going, who knew.

He glanced at the map again. To all of the pushpins. "I think you're right, Rossi, our guy has got to be nearby and if the kid is alive, she's not far, either." He pointed to several places on the map. "He's got to be able to move around here quickly. In and out, no one sees anything suspicious and he can get away, back to wherever he lives without drawing attention to himself. Comes and goes as he wants, at all hours."

He stepped back from the map, trying to get a fuller view, hoping that he'd see something revealing, a pattern, like if he strung a string to each of the red pins on the map he'd see the beginnings of a five-sided star emerge, or that someone lived in the very center of all the fires or some other obvious clue. But no.

Nothing struck him.

No bolt of lightning.

But it would. He was getting closer. He could feel it. He looked down at his notes and frowned, staring at all the little stars he'd drawn. "Hey, Rossi," he said, "why don't you draw a star for me."

"What?" The younger detective looked at him as if he'd lost it.

"Humor me," Paterno said, staring at the drawings by the killer. "Draw me a star . . . in fact, make it two."

Travis poured himself a cup of coffee and sat at the table where the drawings that Paterno had left still lay. His hair was still wet. What the hell did they mean?

His cell phone jangled and he picked it up. It was Carter, but there was still no news about Dani. A field officer from the FBI would keep him posted. Paterno had been called and Carter had given him the same news he now gave Travis: Blanche Johnson had two ex-husbands, a handful of boy-friends and a couple of kids. Carter promised more information later in the day.

They hung up. Travis absorbed this information, wondering how it fit in. Through the window he spied Nate Santana walking toward the house with Shannon, and his gut twisted. They took off their boots and entered the house, familiar with each other, as if they'd done it a million times before. He felt more than a twinge of jealousy. He remembered how Santana had touched her on the night of the fire, how he'd taken control, how it had seemed that he and Shannon were lovers, which she swore wasn't the case.

But now Shannon's face was hard and set. She cast a glance at Travis and he knew instantly something was wrong. More bad news. "What is it?" he asked, climbing to his feet.

"Nate has something to get off his chest," she said.

Travis gazed at Santana. The man hesitated, then nodded curtly. "It might affect you as well," Santana admitted.

"So tell us," Shannon prodded. "What the hell's been going on?"

"I *was* involved with another woman," he said. "You got that right." Travis felt a build up of tension in the air. Where the hell was this going? "The only problem is that she's dead."

"What? What are you talking about?" Shannon asked. "Who's dead? Mary Beth?"

"No!" Santana clenched his fists and walked to the window, looked outside. "Dolores Galvez."

"Who?" Travis asked, but the name was ringing distant bells.

"Dolores died in a fire nearly three-and-a-half years ago," Nate stated flatly, his emotions on a tight leash. "She was the only victim in the series of fires attributed to the Stealth Torcher."

Shannon visibly paled. She grabbed the back of a chair for support. "Oh, my God," she whispered, staring at Santana. "You mean . . . Ryan killed her?"

He shook his head. Turned and faced them both. His jaw was set, his lips razor-thin, and the fury burning in his eyes ran deep. "I don't think so," he said, his fingers curling over the windowsill until his knuckles showed white. "Ryan Carlyle wasn't the arsonist who took her life, Shannon. He wasn't the Stealth Torcher."

Chapter 29

"What do you mean? Why don't you think Ryan was the Stealth Torcher?" Shannon asked, stunned, as she stared at the man she'd thought she'd known for nearly two years. At her feet Khan whined for attention, but for once, Shannon ignored him. The house felt suddenly stuffy. She brushed past Nate to the window, cracked it open, hearing a crow cawing from the roof of the stables as if laughing. "How would you know that he wasn't?"

Nate leaned against the counter, his hips pressed against the lower cupboard. "I don't know, not a hundred percent yet, but I'm working on it."

"Working on it?" she repeated. Things started clicking in her head. She remembered meeting Nate at a horse auction, how they'd struck up a conversation, how they'd seemed to have so much in common, how in subsequent meetings he'd mentioned that he was looking for a place, hoping to become a partner in a business involving training animals, how she'd mentioned that she was looking for someone to work with the horses . . . She felt suddenly sick inside when she realized she'd been played for a fool. She felt totally and utterly betrayed. "You set me up," she whispered as the ugly truth dawned. This man whom she'd defended to the teeth was suddenly a stranger to her.

Travis scraped back his chair. "What the hell's going on?"

Nate held up a hand. "Let me explain."

"Then get to it." Travis was on his feet and the kitchen seemed suddenly small. Claustrophobic.

"Let's go outside, I can't breathe in here," Shannon said. She opened the back door. Khan bolted outside and she followed, her head thundering with lies, the deceptions, all the half-truths she'd heard for so many years. From people she'd trusted. People she'd believed in.

She slipped into her boots and stood on the porch, hearing the shuffle of feet as the men, both coiled like rattlers ready to strike, followed her. "Okay," she said once Nate was standing under the overhang of the porch. Behind him she saw the shed, black and burned, and wondered what, if any, part he had in its destruction. "So . . . go on."

Nate rested a hip on the top rail surrounding the porch. "The long and the short of it is that I met Dolores in a restaurant where she was a waitress. We started dating and things heated up. Quickly. We were getting serious and fast, but she wanted to keep it quiet, hadn't broken it to her family because she'd had a pretty bad track record. One divorce, two broken engagements. Her family didn't exactly trust her judgment when it came to men, and now, looking back, I can't say as I blame them. At the time it made me crazy." He let out a mirthless laugh. "It was ironic in a way. I'd always been a man who didn't want to be tied down, thought marriage was a death sentence, liked doing my own thing, you know, being free and easy, but then I met Dolores and a dozen red flags should have popped up in my head." His jaw tensed, slid to the side. "They did, every last one of 'em, but I ignored them. Thought she was 'the one,' if there is such a thing."

Shannon couldn't believe her ears and yet the lines of strain on Nate's face convinced her he was telling the truth.

"So one night, we're supposed to meet at this old, abandoned restaurant. She picked the place, I don't know why. But I got tied up. I was running late from my job, traffic was hell, she didn't have a cell." His fingers curled hard over the rail. He closed his eyes as if envisioning the entire scene. "I got there half an hour late and the place was ablaze. She was already dead."

"And you never stepped forward?" Shannon was incredulous.

"I didn't trust the cops. Period. Telling them we were lovers wouldn't have brought her back. It just would have caused trouble. I would have had to meet her family, explain why we'd decided to meet there, which to this day I don't know. I think it was random, she'd worked there years before, thought it would be safe. Jesus . . ."

"I can't believe this," Shannon said. She glanced up at the garage where Nate lived. "I trusted you with my life," she whispered. "We've lived twenty yards from each other, worked together and never once did you say a word!"

Travis asked in a deadly voice, "So what happened?"

"Like I said, when I arrived at the restaurant it was already fully engulfed. Firefighters were hosing it down. I was frantic and pushed through the crowd. I heard a reporter interviewing people. The gist of the conversation was that the fire was set by the Stealth Torcher. And then I saw the body bag and I knew it was Dolores. I called her brother. Anonymously. So that he could claim the body. I couldn't bear to look at her."

"Or to have the balls to come forward," Travis stated flatly.

"I was an ex-con. Sure I've been exonerated, but I just bet the charge is still on some police computer next to my name. I figured the best way to help out was to nail the son of a bitch who set the fires. To find the damned Stealth Torcher."

"On your own?" Shannon felt so betrayed she could scarcely speak.

Travis said, "You thought you could catch this guy when the professionals couldn't? A police department with trained investigators and expensive equipment and specialists? Is that what you're saying?"

"I'm saying they hadn't done such a great job of it."

"What made you think you could do better?"

"I didn't know if I'd do it better, but I sure as hell planned to try. I grew up learning how to hunt and track, spent time as a mountain guide. To help pay for college, I spent my summers fighting forest fires. During the winter, while going to school, I was a member of the volunteer fire department. I figured that's qualification enough."

"And your murder charge? That wasn't a lie?" Shannon asked.

His eyes drilled into hers. "Unfortunately, no. The time in jail? Yeah, that happened too. Just the way I told you."

"But you bumped into me on purpose after my own trial, after it came out that the police thought my husband was the Stealth Torcher."

He nodded. Looked at the boards of the porch as Khan, hunting squirrels, sniffed around the side of the house and woodpile.

"You set the whole damned thing up and lied to me," she

said angrily. Travis put his hand on her arm, but she jerked away, tired of men manipulating her.

"I thought getting close to you might help me figure out what was going on, give me an inside look," he admitted, his face flushing angrily. "But it backfired, okay? Because what I discovered from being with you was that Dolores wasn't the only woman in the world for me. She wasn't 'the one.' Hell, I don't even know if I believe that anymore because I fell for you. Hard."

"I don't believe you!"

"It's the truth."

"Jesus Christ, Nate. You could have told me."

"If he told you, he'd blow his cover and then he wouldn't get the information he needed," Travis said. He stood near her, his eyes squinting against the sun, his hair showing streaks of gold, his mouth a thin, hard line.

"You got that right," Nate said, glaring back at him. "But then, you understand, don't you? You're using Shannon to get what you want."

"No."

Something in his denial rang false. Shannon took a step back. "You, too?" she whispered, thinking of their lovemaking, how she'd playfully teased him this morning. She'd known the reasons he'd come down here had to do with his child, the one he'd called "theirs." Yet in the light of day it now seemed sappy, a ploy to get her to trust him.

"It's not like that," Travis said.

"Of course it is, Settler," Nate cut in. "You came here because of your kid, met Shannon and thought you'd hang out, get close, figure out what she knows."

Shannon knew Nate's words were true. Hadn't she suspected as much from this man who had been lurking on her property, spying on her the night she'd been attacked? But she'd put those feelings aside, let herself believe, if only for a little while, that they cared for each other, could learn to love each other. What an idiot she'd been! Again. She felt as if she'd been kicked in the gut. "Go ahead, Nate," she said, her gaze cutting from Travis, with his damned sun-streaked hair, bedroom blue eyes and solid jaw, to the man she'd worked with. "Tell me what else you think you know. Did all the time we spent together pay off?"

He took the shot and didn't flinch. "I think one or more of your brothers is involved in the fires."

"What!" she said in disbelief. "My brothers?"

"Ryan Carlyle wasn't the Stealth Torcher. He was just the fall guy."

"What the hell are you trying to peddle now, Santana?" Travis growled.

"This is nuts!" Shannon couldn't believe what she was hearing. "You think that Aaron, or Shea or Robert is . . . the Stealth Torcher? That one of them started the current fires and is killing off other members of my family? That . . . that . . . what? That Aaron or Shea or Robert attacked me, killed Mary Beth and Oliver?" Her voice rose in fury and something near hysteria.

"You're out of your mind, Santana," Travis agreed tautly.

"I don't think so."

"So how is this theory connected to my daughter's kidnapping or Blanche Johnson's murder? Did one of Shannon's brothers have my kid send a plea to her in a tape?"

"I haven't figured it all out yet. That's why I wasn't going to tell you."

Shannon said through her teeth, "So you were just going to keep acting weird? Keeping odd hours. Showing up and leaving again in the middle of the night? For the love of God, Nate, where the hell have you been? In the newspaper archives? Or . . . the library? Or sneaking around my family's houses? Running down leads on this Stealth Torcher? Playing detective? How in the world did you think you were going to 'figure it out'?"

"I haven't been to the damned library," Nate snarled. "The truth of the matter is that ever since I found out your daughter was abducted, Settler, I've been out looking for her."

"And you didn't tell me?"

"You would have just gotten in the way."

"Shit."

In the paddock a horse neighed and Nate glanced toward the animals before going on. "Look, it seems to me that Dani is the center of what's happening here. The first clue was her birth certificate. Left here . . . at her birth mother's home."

"And you think one of my brothers has her?" Shannon could scarcely credit it.

"It's definitely linked."

"No one in my family would hurt a child. Any child."

"You don't know your family or what they're capable of," he shot back so loudly that the crow, still sitting on the roof of the stables, took off in full flight.

"You believe my daughter's alive," Travis said.

"Yes."

Shannon felt a bit of relief. "Because of the tape?"

"No." He shook his head, the black strands gleaming in the sunlight. "Because if he'd already killed her, he'd have no leverage on you and I think, with what's happened here— the attack, the burned birth certificate—this has as much to do with you as anyone. I don't know what the words written on Blanche Johnson's wall in blood mean, and I haven't figured out the star and the numbers, but I think it has to do with your family."

Shannon strode to the far end of the porch and watched as Khan sniffed around the burnt shed. "How could one of my brothers go to Oregon and . . . and Idaho, and not be missed around here?"

"A person can drive to that part of Oregon in less than twelve hours, twenty-four round-trip. If he flew, say in a private plane, it's only a few hours."

"None of my brothers is a pilot."

"But they have friends."

"This is getting crazier by the second," she said, turning to face him, arms crossed over. "You're trying to make it fit.

It's not some major conspiracy, like, like the Kennedy assassination or what happened to Princess Diana! Who would go to such lengths?"

"Who would?" he agreed.

"Not one of my brothers!" she said emphatically, wishing the conversation was over. "I can't believe one of my siblings hates me so much as to have nearly let me go to prison! And all of this!"

"What about Neville?" Travis asked.

Shannon froze. "Neville?" A new, cold breath of fear swept across the back of her neck. "But he's . . . He's not even around."

"And why is that?" Nate asked.

Travis didn't want to buy anything Nate was saying, but there was something here. He could feel it.

"I don't know."

"What do you think, Shannon?" Nate stared at her.

The day seemed to go from bright to gray as a lone cloud passed over the sun. "Look, Nate, don't you go all weird on me, too, okay? I have no idea what happened to Neville, but he's not skulking around knocking off the rest of my family."

"Why did he leave?" Travis asked.

"I've asked myself that a million times," Shannon said wearily. "I think . . . I have to assume that he's dead." Neither man said a word. "Wait a minute . . . No. Even if Neville is still alive, he would never kill Oliver. Or Mary Beth. That's enough of this! You," she said, pointing to Nate, "need to talk to the police, tell them what you know and please, for the love of God, try *not* to incriminate my family!" She started for the door, wanting this conversation to be over, when Nate's voice stopped her short.

"Didn't Oliver tell you that he'd seen Brendan Giles recently?"

"Yes, but so what?"

"Brendan's in Nicaragua," he said as Khan trotted onto the porch.

"Oh, please. How do you know that?" She was starting to think Nate was going off his rocker.

"I talked to his parents."

"And they told you?" She remembered that neither of Brendan's folks had bothered to return her calls. Or had they? Had they called and Nate picked up the phone? "They refused to talk to me."

"I visited them in person, told them I was a private investigator and that if they didn't talk with me I would go to the police, have the cops come and start talking to them. So they decided to open up, tell me what they knew. I saw pictures and e-mails."

"Which anyone could create from anywhere," Travis pointed out as he leaned against the panels of the front door. "Fake photos are easy to come by, and with all the digital imaging and computers that are available now, it wouldn't be hard to create an e-mail address that looks like it comes from a third world country. Not if you were technically savvy at all."

Nate nodded. "That's true, but I believed these people. I don't think they were harboring their son. They told me that they haven't actually seen him in over ten years."

"And suddenly he's contacting them. At this time? Damned coincidental, don't you think?"

"They've been communicating with him for four years," Nate said. "Even before Ryan was killed. Long before this new spate of fires. The Gileses just haven't broadcast that they've been in contact with Brendan."

"And why would that be?" Shannon asked.

"They didn't say, but I think they're worried that he's involved in something illegal. Maybe drugs."

"Oh, great," Shannon muttered, throwing up a hand. "This is just getting better and better."

"So the point is, why would Oliver lie to you about seeing Brendan?"

"He didn't say he was certain, just that he *thought* he saw Brendan in church."

"The Gileses aren't Catholic," Nate pointed out. "It was a smoke screen, Shannon. He was hiding something."

She felt the need to defend her brother. "He isn't . . . wasn't the Stealth Torcher!"

"Agreed. Otherwise he'd still be alive. But I'm willing to bet that he knew who is and if Oliver knew, chances are that one of your other brothers knows as well."

"Again with the conspiracy. Maybe you should apply for a job with the CIA."

"Maybe I should." Shooting her a killing glance, he reached into his pocket and yanked out his cell phone. "It's a pretty simple matter to check out." He held out the phone. "Let's call Aaron."

"What's your plan?" Travis asked.

"Why Aaron?" Shannon demanded.

"Because he's the firstborn. The oldest. Probably knows what's going on."

As he held the receiver toward her, Shannon could hear the dial tone. Her mind whirled. *Firstborn. The oldest. Birth order.* A cold sweat broke out on her skin and she felt a drip of dread. A recorded voice instructed the caller to hang up and try again, but what Shannon heard were the hushed whispers all the while she'd been growing up, the quickly stifled secrets. An icy chill sliced through her heart. Pieces that had been floating through her mind, teasing her, giving her headaches, started to tumble into place.

"Hang that up," she ordered Nate, and when he didn't immediately disconnect, repeated herself. "Hang it up now!"

Shaking inside, she walked into the house, grabbed a piece of paper from the notepad on the counter, then sat down and wrote down the names of her brothers, one below the other. As she did, she heard Nate and Travis walk inside, the floorboards creaking with their footsteps.

"What's going on?" Travis asked, a hint of concern in his voice.

"Look." She added her own name to the list, writing it below Neville's.

Aaron
Robert
Shea
Oliver
Neville
Shannon

"Oh, God . . . this . . . this is nuts," she whispered as she stared at the names arranged vertically. Her throat closed so tightly she could barely breathe. She remembered hearing the rumors as a child, the nasty gossip that had slunk through the halls of St. Theresa's. That her father was a bad seed, that he had intentionally set fires, earning awards and commendations for his bravery before the truth was discovered. Always the charges had been dismissed and he'd even laughed the allegations off, calling them "sour grapes" from some of his peers.

Had they been?

Her stomach turned sour.

A memory of Mary Beth, wearing her St. Theresa's uniform in the locker room of the school gym, sliced through her brain. Shannon had been in one of the stalls, changing. She'd looked through a crack between the edge of the curtain and the wall, which gave her a view of the mirror mounted over a row of sinks. Mary Beth had been leaning over a dripping sink, her nose nearly pressed to the mirror as she'd applied mascara to her already-thick lashes. She'd been confiding to Gina Pratt that her father, a member of the Santa Lucia Fire Department, had said that Patrick Flannery was a "firebug." That everyone in the department knew it. Shannon had raced to get dressed and hurried after her "friend," only to have Mary Beth insist she'd been "kidding."

And now . . . She swallowed hard.

"What?" Travis said. His hand was on her shoulder, and she tried not to think about it, about the tenderness of the gesture. It was all a fake, she reminded herself. He'd gotten close to her for reasons of his own, just as Nate had. Shrugging off his hand, she slid her finger slowly down the page on the table, touching the first letter of each of her siblings' names before stopping at her own. A-R-S-O-N-S. Coincidence? Her father had been known for his practical jokes, but this wasn't funny. Not at all. In fact, it was downright hideous. "ARSONS."

Travis, his expression dark, stared at her. "What are you saying?"

"I heard my brothers talking about 'birth order' and it being 'Dad's fault.' If what Nate is saying is true, could . . . ? Oh, God—" The thought was reprehensible. She thought she might throw up. "Could my father really have been the Stealth Torcher?"

"Possibly," Nate said.

Travis said, "But he's dead. And there are new fires that everyone thinks might have been set by the same arsonist."

"That's right." Nate stared at Shannon. "So who would be the most likely candidate to follow in Daddy's footsteps? Literally take up the torch?"

"No one," she insisted, but for the first time she doubted herself.

Travis's cell phone rang and all speculation stopped. He flipped it open, and standing next to him, Shannon recognized the out-of-state number for the Sheriff's Department in Lewis County, Oregon.

She didn't dare breathe.

Travis pushed the phone to his ear. "Settler." There was a long pause as Travis stared at Shannon, all the while listening to the one-sided conversation. Eventually, he said, "Thanks," and flipped the phone shut. Stuffing the cell into his pocket, he said, "Another piece of the puzzle. Carter says they got a judge to unseal the adoption papers for Blanche Johnson's second child. Turns out he was adopted by a childless couple down here named Carlyle. They named him Ryan."

Chapter 30

"Okay, okay, so what's with the stars?" Rossi asked as Paterno, carrying pages that he'd put in front of his fellow officers, secretarial staff, and even an alleged car thief who was being booked, returned to the office. He'd asked each one of them to draw a star without lifting the pen. To a one, they'd stared at him as if he'd lost his marbles, but they did as they'd been asked, some making him the butt of jokes about his sudden need to go back to kindergarten. He hadn't listened or cared.

"Here's what it looks like," he said to Rossi as he loosened his tie. Geez, it was hot in here. "Eleven out of thirteen people made the stars the same way you and I both did, starting at the left-hand corner, moving upward to a point, then drawing straight down at an angle, up again over to the left, then straight across to the right and finally down to the original starting point."

Rossi tried to look interested and failed. "There's a point to this?"

"I think so," Paterno said. "Maybe more like five points. Let's just say that if you draw a star this way, without lifting your pencil, the first point would be at the top, see"—he demonstrated—"where you start going downward after going up. So that's number one, but as we continue down, we make the next point at the lower right-hand when we angle up sharply, so that point is number two. Got it?"

"The lower right is number two. I get it. But I don't see what you're trying to do."

"Hang on. You will." With his pen still pressed to the paper, he glanced up. Rossi, focusing on the pen, was starting to slowly nod his head. "So then we go upward to the upper left-hand corner where we veer sharply right, creating the upper left-hand point, or . . . ?"

"Number three." Rossi was taking note.

"Right! And back to the right we go straight across, only to turn downward and so the upper right-hand point is four and"—he brought the pen back to the point of origin, completing the drawing of the star with a point in the lower left-hand corner—"so here's number five down at the left and the middle is now complete, making it area number six." He nodded to himself, as if double-checking his figure, then started writing names in the appropriate spots. "Now, if you correspond the numbers of the points as they were created with the birth order of the Flannery kids, you get something that looks like this:

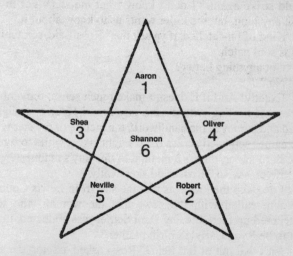

"And if you notice, the ones who were killed or are missing, numbers five and four, Neville and Oliver, are where the missing points should be. Because they're already gone."

"So Neville's dead."

"I would bet."

"Then what's with the broken line, for number two?" Rossi pointed at the page.

"It must mean that the killer took out Robert's wife, Mary

Beth. Why? On purpose? A mistake? To make a statement?"
Paterno scowled thoughtfully. "I don't know, maybe it's to
show her thin, failing connection to her husband, and if that
were the case, then our perp would have to be very close to
what was happening, privy to the inner workings of Robert's
love life. Or maybe he was pissed at her, too, and the line
will only become solid when he kills Robert."

"If that's what this is all about."

"Right." Paterno was on a roll. There was a certain electricity—almost a smell—he experienced when he was about
to break open a case. He felt it now, that stirring of excitement, the thrill of figuring out some sicko's MO before he
could strike again. "I don't know what the star's got to do
with anything, but the killer wants us to know about it."

"Kind of far-fetched, if ya ask me," Rossi said, scratching
at his soul patch.

"Got anything better?"

"No."

"Exactly! And if it doesn't make much sense, remember,
we're not dealing with a sane guy here." Paterno straightened and surveyed his handiwork, the picture of the star with
the names scrawled across it. "It might take a while to figure
out, but I swear, there's a method to this guy's madness."

"If you say so," Rossi said skeptically.

"I do. And the kicker is that the sheriff in Lewis County,
Oregon, called with the news that the woman who was
butchered up there the day Dani Settler was abducted, turns
out to be Ryan Carlyle's birth mother."

"Isn't that out of left field?" Rossi asked, tracing the star
with one thick finger.

"What it is, is another connection to Shannon Flannery."

"But what does it have to do with the kid being abducted?"

"That's something we've got to figure out." Paterno
looked at his rudimentary drawings. What was the killer trying to tell them? All he could make out of it was that
Shannon Flannery was at the center of it all.

The phone rang and, still staring at the drawings, he lifted the receiver to his ear. "Paterno."

It was Jack Kim, the tech wizard in the lab. "I think we've got something down here you might want to hear," he said.

"What is it?"

"Something interesting on that tape of the girl that you brought in. Come down and listen for yourself."

He wasted no time. Heading out of his office, he told Rossi, "The lab's got something on the tape of the Settler kid."

"Wait up."

They wended their way through glassed-in cubicles that did little to mute the sound of clacking keyboards, jangling phones, buzzing conversation and the wheeze of the old air-conditioning system. Rather than wait for the elevator, they took the stairs, hurrying down three flights of steps, the soles of their shoes ringing on the scarred wood as they descended into the lab where, if nothing else, it was several degrees cooler.

Paterno walked unerringly to the windowless, sound-proof audio room where the technician, Jack Kim, was waiting for him. "What have you got?" the detective asked.

"Listen to this." He played the tape and they heard Dani Settler's pleas over the crackle of flames for her mother to help her. Kim stopped the tape and rewound it. "Okay, now listen again. We've isolated the sounds and listen to what you hear when I mute her voice and the fire." He adjusted several levers and knobs, then played the tape again.

Paterno braced himself. He was certain he was going to hear the abductor whisper something, but instead he heard the faint rumbling sound that he'd thought was part of the fire.

"What is that?" he asked, but his mind was racing ahead. It was a familiar noise.

"A train," Rossi said. "He's got her near a railroad stop or tracks."

"Jesus Christ, you're right. Play it again." They listened

again. "Okay. Let's keep this quiet," Paterno said. "No leaks. Not even to the family. We don't want any chance of the jerk-off learning we're getting close. Thanks," he said to Kim, clapping him on the back. "I owe ya a beer."

"You owe me a half case, but who's counting?"

"I guess you are."

Kim flashed a smile. "Always."

"Does the FBI know about this?"

"I'll call the field office, but they've got a copy of the tape. My guess is they're all over this."

Rossi and Paterno left the basement and headed upstairs where Paterno sat down at his computer and pulled up maps of the area. "Well, this really narrows it down," he muttered sarcastically. "Damn trains run through every town up and down the valley and then head out through the hills."

"We have to assume that he's got her somewhere isolated, because we hear the sound of the train, but no traffic," Rossi pointed out. "Nothing else. Since we can hear a train, shouldn't we also be able to hear a car passing or a neighbor's dog, that kind of thing?"

"If a car were passing at the time of the recording. If a dog decided to bark just then."

"Well, what we do know is that when that tape was recorded, she wasn't hidden in some soundproof bunker or basement. Wherever she was, either outside by a campfire, or inside in a place that isn't all that insulated for sound, we can hear the train and nothing else."

"You got yourself a point," Paterno said as he gazed at the computer screen and all of the railroad tracks that surrounded the city. Not so many, really, but miles and miles of it. "It's a start. A piss-poor one, but a start." He reached for the phone. Figured it was time to talk to the FBI himself.

Shannon grabbed her purse and keys. She'd double-checked on all the animals, not really trusting Nate—though, to be honest, he'd never once neglected the animals.

So that was one point in his favor.

But he was a liar. And a user. And God knew what else.

She'd taken the time to call Alexi and arrange for security systems to be set up at both her places by the end of the week, and she'd called her brothers, leaving messages with both Aaron and Robert, but finally tracking down Shea, who was at their mother's and promised to stop by.

But first things first.

She needed wheels. Her truck was still impounded so she asked Travis to drive her into town so she could find a rental.

"You don't have to do this," Travis said as they headed into town. "I'm happy to drive you."

"I want my own car." With Nate's confession and theories, she'd decided not to trust anyone. Including Travis. Besides, she didn't want him tagging along wherever she went; she wasn't one of those women who needed a man with her every second of the day . . . especially a man to whom she was sexually attracted and who had his own agenda.

"You're letting Santana get to you," he said, braking for a corner as they reached the outskirts of town.

"I just need some space, okay?"

He lifted a hand off the wheel. "Don't shut me out, okay?"

"Why? Because we slept together?" she asked, hating the bite to her words.

"No. Because we share a daughter."

"Do we?" she threw back at him as he slowed for a light and traffic converged around his truck. "I think you've got that wrong. We share nothing. I gave up my rights to her a long time ago." Bristling, she flung her arms over her chest as if to protect herself. What had she been thinking? Buying into the "our daughter" trap. Dani belonged to Travis. Period. Though Shannon would do anything she could to find the girl, and wanted desperately to meet the baby she'd brought into this world, she knew her hidden little fantasy—that somehow they would all be a family together, that Travis would be the father, she the mother, and Dani the loving, darling daughter—was a pipe dream that would never work. Never. Not even if all parties were willing to try.

"There it is," she said, pointing to a small business, located between a strip mall and a donut stand, which advertised that they rented wrecks, older cars not in prime condition. He pulled into the pockmarked lot and she was out of the cab before the truck came to a complete stop. "Thanks," she said coolly, then heard herself and decided to own up to the fact that she cared about this man, cared more than she should have. "Really. I appreciate everything you've done."

"I could—"

She held up a hand. "You've done enough. Really. I'll . . . I'll call you later, or you call me if you find out anything about Dani."

"Shannon—"

"Not now. Please. Neither one of us has time. Let's just find Dani and go from there, okay?" she asked, staring at the lines on his face. Damn, it was a good-looking face. But he, like all the men in her life, was untrustworthy.

She slid out of his truck, slammed the door and stood in the dusty parking lot. The late afternoon sun caused ripples of heat to rise on the street, distorting her view of the traffic, neon signs and storefronts. Forcing a smile, she used her hand as a visor, watching as Travis threw the truck into reverse and pulled out of the lot.

Stupidly, she felt a tug on her heart. As if she really loved the guy. "Fool," she muttered, kicking at a pebble in frustration. She walked into the glass-fronted building and noticed the fleet of cars parked behind a wall of chain-link. Some of the cars were dented and showed wear, but others seemed right as the proverbial rain.

Within half an hour, she was at the wheel of a five-year-old Mazda in great condition and nosing it toward her mother's house.

* * *

He was irritated. Edgy. Mad at the kid. At himself. Because of the time he'd lost, he had to give up some of his plans. There were others who had to pay, but they would have to wait. Until after.

Now, because of the damned kid, he'd have to move up his timeline.

Though it was near ninety, he lit a fire, stripped off his clothes and felt the burning heat searing his skin, bringing back the horror that he replayed over and over in his mind, reminding himself that he had vengeance to wreak.

The flames on the wood in the cabin's fireplace grew hotter and he began to sweat, pulling off his clothes, feeling the heat even more.

Flames . . . all the flames . . . he remembered them, remembered watching them consume his victim . . . how they'd swirled and grown, snapping through the forest. The man had been unconscious as the fire had crawled up and around him, smoke roiling in angry black clouds to the sky.

In a whoosh, the wind had come up and the fire had turned, starting to cut off his escape. He couldn't wait any longer. He ran, upward along the trail, feeling the searing heat, noticing, in the corner of his eye, the flames arc and then, quickly, without notice sparks rained from the sky. In his hair, on his neck, igniting his clothes.

Pain seared across his back and he stopped in the trail, dropped to the ground and rolled, back and forth, trying to extinguish the fire, feeling the heat as the forest crackled and burned around him.

He'd been foolish.

Waited too long.

He would die with his victim. Ryan Carlyle and an unidentified man . . . though it wouldn't take them long to figure it out.

He forced himself to his feet and plunged forward, his shirt burned away, his skin blistered raw and throbbing. One foot in front of the other, upward, to the spot where he'd parked his car. For a second he worried that the car would be encircled in flames or catch fire, that the gas tank would explode and he'd have no way out but on foot.

But as he crested the hill, his lungs burning, he saw the vehicle and knew he could escape.

His back raged with pain and would no doubt be scarred.

But he would survive.

And he had.

To wreak his vengeance.

His lips curled into a cold smile at the memory.

Straightening, he slowly extinguished the flames with his own piss. He liked the feel of it, the power he had over the fire. He liked to hear the angry hiss as he shot his stream over the coals. He thrummed with energy.

Now was the time.

Now.

As he finished, he walked naked to the door of the room where he held her. Pounding with a fist, he yelled, "Okay, it's show time." Using the claw end of his hammer he pulled off the two-by-two he'd used to imprison her. The long nails creaked as they pulled out. The board clattered to the floor.

He found her clothes and shoes, then tossed them into the dark room, not even trying to locate her. She couldn't have escaped and now, at last, she would serve her purpose. "Hurry up," he said.

Though nightfall was still hours away, he had a lot to accomplish.

Shannon drove in the little Mazda without the benefit of air-conditioning. With the windows rolled down she guided the little car through familiar streets. Nate's insinuations rang through her head: That her father had been the Stealth Torcher, that one of her brothers was following in dear old Dad's footsteps as the new and improved version of a twisted, murdering arsonist.

Did that make sense?

Was it even possible?

She knew the date Dani Settler had been abducted. Had double-checked. All of her brothers were accounted for, though their alibis were for each other. All of them, it seemed, had had the opportunity. Shea had taken two vacation days that he had tacked on to a weekend and he'd gone fishing. Alone. Robert had time off because of his schedule. Aaron worked for himself.

And now Oliver was dead.

Some of the shock and pain was wearing away and, as the hot September wind tangled her hair, she was angry as hell. She didn't believe for a minute her brothers were capable of the things Nate had suggested, and she was angry with him for his crazy ideas, angry that he'd lied and used her, and was feeling the same way about Travis. Hadn't he gotten close to her only because he was looking for his daughter? Hadn't he initially suspected her of abducting Dani? She'd seen his face this morning, the guilt when Nate had accused him of using her. So she was simmering at him as well as at her brothers for keeping secrets from her.

Worse yet, she was furious with herself.

For being so damned trusting.

Her fingers tightened around the hot steering wheel of the Mazda, and she took a corner a little too quickly, nearly gliding into the oncoming lane where a teenager wearing earphones blasted her with his horn.

Shannon barely noticed. Her thoughts were miles away to her dead father, a gruff man with Santa Claus white hair, a ruddy face and the perpetual scent of Irish whiskey and cigars. He'd been quick with a smile, quicker to anger, and had used a thin black belt on her brothers to keep them in line. Never had he even hinted at whipping her, but when one of the boys screwed up, he'd slowly walk upstairs to his room where the belt hung in his closet, return downstairs, his heavy tread creaking each step, then, without a sound, nod toward the back porch and the offending son, either shaking and crying or stiff with rebellion, would march outside.

Patrick had been a firm believer in "spare the rod and spoil the child," just as his father had been. But it seemed unbelievable that he might have been a criminal. An arsonist. A murderer.

Could she believe that Patrick Flannery had been the Stealth Torcher? No . . . No . . .

So what about the anagram of the first letter of your names?

Had he named his kids with a cryptic anagram as some kind of sick, ironic joke? Who was this man who had sired her?

She slowed for a red light, nervously tapped a tattoo with her fingers on the steering wheel, tried to stem her rage. The fact of the matter was she was pissed off at just about everyone she knew, living or dead. How about Brendan Giles, the coward who had left her at the first whiff of learning she was pregnant? Or Ryan, whose only form of communication had ended up being his fists? Or her twin brothers, the ones she felt were closest to her, both of them now deserting her, whether intentional or not.

"Damn it all to hell," she growled, tromping so hard on the accelerator as the light changed that the Mazda's tires screeched.

She passed St. Theresa's school and wouldn't let her mind wander down those hallowed, dark halls. A few seconds later she pulled up to a spot in front of her mother's house. It looked so much the same as it had when she'd grown up here she started to wonder whether it, too, was a lie. As she extracted the key to the Mazda and dropped it into her purse, she began to think that nothing she'd trusted, nothing she'd believed in had been what it seemed.

She stormed up the sidewalk. She was in no mood for excuses, no mood for platitudes, no mood for anything but the truth.

She took the porch steps two at a time. At the front door, she placed her hands on the thick oak panels and took a deep breath. Knocking twice, she yanked open the unlocked door and stepped inside.

The smells of her youth assailed her: the lingering odors of burning candles and cigarettes; a faint scent of fish cooked, no doubt, on Friday, though no one but her mother seemed to observe that old tradition.

For the first time since she could remember, she didn't feel a wistful bit of nostalgia when she spied the family portrait, taken when she was seven, which hung over the mantel in the living room. It was framed in gold-painted wood, a picture taken when all the siblings had lived under this roof. In the portrait, her brothers stood around a bench where she was seated with their father and mother. The boys wore matching sport coats and nervous, toothy smiles. Some had acne, others a bit of facial hair, all carbon copies of their father with their blue eyes, black hair and strong Irish chins. The twins stood on either end, looking so much alike that she knew that Oliver was the one on the left end of the photo standing next to Aaron only because it had been discussed over Thanksgiving turkey year after year, when the dining room table had been lengthened and stretched through the entry hall and into the living room to accommodate all the members of the once-growing Flannery family.

But no longer.

Because of some madman.

Neville was missing.

Oliver and Mary Beth dead.

"Shannon?" Shea appeared, looking over the half wall to the entry hall. His eyes were shadowed and pained, his skin tight over his face. "Glad you could make it," he said with a trace of sarcasm.

She ignored his dig and hurried up the worn carpet of the stairs. She wasn't going to have any guilt tossed on her. She'd called twice, explained when she'd show up. "How is she?"

"How would you expect?"

"Not good."

"She's taking this pretty hard. Oliver and she were . . ."

"Close."

He nodded. Stuffed his hands into the back pockets of his pants and looked as if he'd been pacing a hole in the carpet outside the bedroom door. The monotonous tick of the grandfather's clock in the entry broke the silence. "I called her doctor this morning and ran by the pharmacy for some tranquilizers," he said. "She's taken a few, so she's a little out of it."

"Where's everyone else?" She'd half-expected the house to be filled with her brothers, Shea's wife, maybe even Cynthia or Robert's kids. As it was, the dark old home seemed tomblike.

Shea lifted a shoulder. "Aaron called her, said he'd be over later but hasn't shown up yet. Robert . . . Shit, who knows with Robert these days? He's a mess."

"Aren't we all?"

He snorted his agreement. "I think I'll take a break out on the porch," he said, reaching into his front pocket for his pack of Marlboro Lights. "She"—he hitched his chin toward the open bedroom door—"will probably fall asleep if she already hasn't." He shook out a filter tip and jabbed it into the corner of his mouth. "There's an older lady Mom knows from the church, Mrs. Sinclair, who's going to come and stay with her for a couple of days. She used to be a nurse. Father Timothy arranged it, and I thought it was a good idea." Glancing at his watch, the cigarette bobbing between his lips, he said, "She should be here soon." He started for the stairs.

"Don't go anywhere," Shannon said. "I need to talk to you." Before he could ask any questions, she walked into the darkened bedroom where her mother lay under a thick duvet despite the oppressive heat inside. The draperies were drawn, the only light coming from a table lamp near the bed.

Maureen looked small and pale in the big four-poster

she'd shared with her husband for over forty years. A half-drunk glass of water, an empty tea cup and several bottles of pills sat next to a box of tissues, her Bible and her rosary. On the night table, too, was an ashtray with several cigarette butts and a half-empty pack of Salems, the brand Maureen had given up when she'd quit smoking over twenty years earlier.

Shannon's heart dropped through the floor. Never had she seen her mother like this, so utterly devastated, not even while at her own husband's funeral.

Maureen's eyelids were at half-mast and her red hair, always such a source of pride with her, was mussed, unkempt.

"Hi, Mom." Shannon walked to the bed, stepped around a wastebasket filled with crumpled tissues, sat on the edge of the mattress and took her mother's hand in her own. "How are you doing?"

Her mother didn't respond and Shannon's heart broke.

"I know it's hard."

Still nothing.

"Mom?"

Maureen's eyes turned toward her, but they were unfocused and rimmed with red. A bit of a smile played at the corners of lips devoid of color. "Shannon," she whispered, her frail-looking fingers clutching hers in a death grip. "Oliver. Sweet, sweet Oliver."

"I know, Mom, I know."

"Why?"

"Oh, God, I don't know. It's senseless."

Tears bled from the corners of Maureen's eyes. "He's in God's hands now," she said and blindly reached for her cigarettes with her free hand.

"Mom, please, you shouldn't smoke in bed . . . or smoke anywhere. It won't help."

Her mother's hand fell to her side, lying atop a floral duvet cover, it appeared ridiculously thin. "It doesn't matter," she whispered, her voice thick.

"Of course it does."

"I'm just so tired," she said.

"You should rest," Shannon suggested, then pressed on. She had to know the truth. Even though her mother was grieving, in pain, and groggy from the sedatives. "But . . . Can you tell me about Dad?"

"Your father?" One eye opened and her pupil, half-dilated, seemed to sharpen.

Shannon took in a deep breath. Her fingers tightened slightly over her mother's frail hand. "Was he the Stealth Torcher?"

"The what?" She was slipping away again, her eyelids obviously heavy.

"The arsonist?" Shannon waited, but her mother had drifted off. "Mom, why were we named what we are? Why are we . . . ?"

"What, Shannon?" Shea's voice, though low, seemed to boom across the room. "Are we what?"

She dropped Maureen's hand, kissed her temple quickly and then walked to the doorway where her brother lingered. "You were eavesdropping."

"You were asking Mom strange questions," he charged, his expression unreadable.

She shut the bedroom door. "I said we need to talk. Let's do it. Now." One step ahead, she hurried down the stairs, through the kitchen and out the back door to the porch, the very spot where her brothers had huddled and whispered together just yesterday. It seemed like a lifetime ago.

"I want you to be straight with me," she said, in no mood for small talk.

"About what?" Cupping his hands over the end of his cigarette, he lit up.

"The Stealth Torcher. Us . . . our family." As Shea stood on the porch in the shade and smoked she laid out everything Nate had told her that morning. He didn't interrupt, didn't ask a question, just listened while yellowjackets buzzed in the apple tree in the backyard and blue jays bathed in a nearby birdbath, splashing water. Finally she said, "So how much of this is true, Shea?"

He took a final drag and shot a plume of smoke from one corner of his mouth. "I don't know what good ruining Dad's reputation would do now."

"You're telling me he *was* the arsonist?" She'd thought she'd braced herself but when faced with the truth, she had to hold on to the rail and steady herself.

"I don't know. I think so." He squashed his cigarette out in the moist soil of a planter box overflowing with pink petunias.

"And our names?"

"All part of the great cosmic joke."

"You *knew*?" She was aghast.

"I *suspected*."

"But Ryan . . . ?"

"Was no innocent." He swatted at a mosquito that was buzzing near his head.

"When he died, the fires stopped."

"Dad was scared, I think."

"You don't know?"

Shea shook his head. "I'm not sure of anything," he said and looked away, over the top of the fence to the neighbor's yard where an aboveground pool was visible, an empty air mattress floating on the surface.

"Who killed Ryan? Did Dad? And then set me up?"

Shea squeezed his eyes shut. "No."

"You know something, Shea," she charged. "Something that's killing this family one member at a time. We've already lost Neville, haven't we? And now his twin, not to mention Robert's wife. Who's next, Shea? You're an officer of the law, for God's sake, you have to do something!"

"I can't," he yelled. "Don't you get it, Shannon? I can't say a damned word."

"Why?" she demanded. "People are dying and . . . and . . ."
And then it hit her. As hard as if a semi had driven over her.
Nate was right. Shea was involved.

Chapter 31

There was no way around it.

Shea stood on his mother's porch, looked down at his sister and wanted to die a thousand deaths. Maybe he had already. "Okay, Shannon," he said. Defeat rested heavily on his shoulders. "You win. You're right. I can't keep this up any longer . . . It's just not worth it. But before we go into any details, I want my lawyer present and then after I discuss everything with him, I'll talk to Paterno. I'm only going through this once."

"As long as you come out with the truth," she said. Her green eyes charged him with all kinds of unspeakable things. Funny thing was, with everything that was going on, he would have thought she would be afraid of him.

Not so, his little sister.

"Not here," he said, looking around the home where he'd grown up, where he'd felt the clap of his father's hand on his shoulder when he'd caught the winning touchdown for the high school football team, where he'd seen his mother's gaze, always full of reproach when he'd come in late stinking of beer, where he'd felt the bite of his father's belt as it cut across his buttocks when he'd been caught doing something he shouldn't. There were holes in the walls, plastered over, but still visible, that were the marks of his fists when a blow he'd thrown at one of his brothers had gone astray. There was a gouge near the door where he'd broken through the chain lock when Neville had locked him out and there was a spot on the roof he thought of as his, outside the attic window, where he'd sat many a night under the stars, horny as hell, and thinking how bright his future might be.

And it had all come crashing down to this.

"Where?" she asked.

"Let's go to Aaron's."

"He's involved, too?" she asked.

But he could tell from her expression that she'd already guessed or been told most of the truth.

"To his back teeth."

"And Robert?"

"Of course."

She was obviously stunned, but she held up her chin and said, "Then let's get to it, okay? If any one of you knows where Dani Settler is, I'll—"

"There's no need to threaten, Shannon," he said, some of his anger returning. "I get it, okay? Let's just do this and for the record, I don't have any idea what happened to the kid."

She clearly didn't believe him, but he didn't give a shit. He called his brothers and the lawyer. They all agreed to meet at Aaron's house over on Fifth Street. He and Shannon waited in intense silence until Mrs. Sinclair arrived to take care of Maureen.

Thank God he didn't have to face Father Timothy again or be reminded of how Oliver had ended up swinging from the crossbeam in the basement of St. Benedictine's.

They drove separate cars to Aaron's. The family lawyer, Peter Green, was just sliding out of his black Mercedes. In one hand he carried a briefcase. He looked worried as hell, his bald pate wrinkled from the eyebrows up as he pocketed his keys. Approaching Shea in front of the house, he said, "I think you're making a big mistake."

"Mine to make, Pete," he said. "Let's go inside."

Shannon waited on the walk and together they entered Aaron's tiny house, a one-bedroom stucco bungalow built around the 1920s.

Robert and Aaron were already in back, on the patio, standing in the shade of a madrona tree, smoking and whispering. They both looked like hell.

"What's going on?" Aaron asked, his eyes darting from Shannon to Peter and back to Shea. He drew on his cigarette as if it was his last chance in this lifetime for a hit of nicotine.

"It's time to come clean," Shea said, and Aaron blanched. Robert scowled. "We can't hide it any longer." He settled wearily into a patio chair next to a dusty table with a broken umbrella. Peter and Shannon took seats next to him. Expression tense, Aaron stood beneath the overhang of the patio. Robert sat on the top step, chain smoking and looking about as miserable as a person could. "Shannon's figured out a lot of what's going on," Shea said, filling them in. "It's time we talked to Paterno. We'll let Pete do the talking for us, see what he can do." He glanced back at Shannon. "You want the truth, go ahead and ask."

"All right," she said, leaning forward on her elbows. "Let's start with the obvious. Where's Dani Settler? Why has she been kidnapped, and who the hell is the Stealth Torcher?"

Shannon listened with growing horror as the story of her brothers unfolded. Shea began the narrative. "You were right," he said. "Dad started this whole Stealth Torcher business. I'm not sure he would have ever owned up to it, but I was working at the Santa Lucia Fire Department at the time and noticed that whenever one of the fires attributed to the Torcher happened, Dad was missing for a while. I found some stuff in the garage, the same kind of accelerant that the Torcher had used, the fuse material. I confronted him and he explained that he'd had to do something, become a hero, so he wouldn't lose his job. He had a lot of years in with the department, wanted a promotion so that he could retire on a bigger salary, and so he created his own scenario where he could be the hero."

Robert closed his eyes and hung his head. Aaron avoided looking at her.

"But then someone died," Shannon whispered.

"Yes. A woman by the name of Dolores Galvez."

"Dad started that fire?"

Shea nodded. "Yeah."

"Is that right, Aaron?" she asked, noting that her oldest brother's face had turned the color of chalk.

"Dad didn't know anyone would be in there."

"And you all knew about this when it was happening?" Her voice rose in outrage.

Peter held up his hands. "Listen, I don't think you need to be discussing this with anyone. You could incriminate yourselves. I'm advising you to speak to no one, only to me."

Shannon's fist banged against the table.

Peter jumped.

All her brothers' heads jerked up in unison.

"My daughter is missing. Some psycho has her and it's connected to this Stealth Torcher thing. Now if Dad was the arsonist, who's the copy cat? One of you?"

"What?" Robert asked, blinking rapidly. "You think I could have killed Mary Beth? Oliver?" He jumped to his feet and walked to the table, pushing his face within inches of Shannon's. "No, Shan. It's not me!" He slapped his chest. "I've done a lot of things in my life I'm not proud of, but I didn't take your kid."

"What about Ryan?" she asked and Robert shrank away from her. "Who killed him? Dad? Is that what you're saying?"

"Robert, don't," Peter warned.

"I—I don't know." Robert's eyes were round.

"Did you know that he was Blanche Johnson's son? That she gave him up for adoption?"

"Jesus, no. I mean, I knew he was adopted, we all did, but . . . What does that mean?"

"You tell me."

"I can't!"

He looked frantically at Shea, and Shannon felt a shift in the atmosphere. Her three brothers exchanged glances.

"I'll get us all a beer," Aaron said.

Shannon held Shea's gaze. "What is it you're not telling me?"

Peter, on her other side, was slowly wagging his head side to side, trying to discourage his client, but it was too late. Shea appeared to be a man at a confessional.

"The five of us brothers talked it over and decided we could do the same thing Dad had done, but not for self-aggrandizement but to . . . make changes for the better."

"You mean like Robin Hood . . . ? Take the law into your own hands and square things up in the world? Jesus, listen to yourselves! Talk about self-aggrandizement!"

Shea's lips flattened. "Do you want to hear this or not?"

"Okay, okay," she said, holding up her hands, still stunned at the news. "What kind of changes?"

Aaron returned, deposited cans of beer in front of everyone. But the cans remained closed, except for his, which opened with a hiss. "We formed a group. And if someone had something he needed fixed, we met . . . in kind of a committee and someone executed the plans. Usually the one who brought it up."

"Things that were illegal," she guessed, her heart pumping crazily.

"Shea," Pete cut in one more time. "I'm warning you, as your attorney, that you shouldn't say anything else."

"Shannon needs to know," Shea said fervently. "There's a kid's life at stake." He gazed steadily at her. "The first suggestion was to get rid of Ryan Carlyle."

"What!" she cried.

"He killed your baby," Aaron defended. "Then beat you up. Was fighting the divorce."

"You murdered him?"

"Actually," Shea said, "it was Neville's idea."

"Neville?" She thought back to her brother, the stronger one of the twins. Yet she couldn't imagine him being involved in killing someone. "Are you saying that you five, including Neville *and* Oliver, formed what, a murder club?" She was quivering all over. There was a roar in her ears. She scooted her chair back.

Robert popped his beer and said, "We only met a few times."

"But you killed Ryan," she whispered, "and let me take the blame."

"No." Robert shook his head vehemently. "It wasn't like that."

"We all met that night in the forest," Shea said, his tone steady, cutting Robert off. "We decided that Ryan would die. And he did."

"You killed him," she repeated, appalled.

"Neville killed him," Shea said softly. "And then found out that he couldn't stick around, that his guilt was driving him out of his mind."

"You know where he is?"

Shea shook his head and her other brothers showed great interest in their beer cans.

"Neville killed Ryan," she said, "and you all knew about it. Knew the truth, even condoned it, approved it. Like you guys are God, or . . . or judge and jury, determining who lives and who dies." She got up from her chair so fast that her unopened beer fell on its side and rolled across the glass tabletop. "I can't believe this," she whispered, then a bit of understanding hit her. "Oliver couldn't stand it, could he? It sent him over the edge and into a mental hospital."

"Oliver was always weak," Shea said.

"Being sensitive isn't the same as being weak!" Shannon couldn't believe these *killers* were her brothers. "And you let me go to trial! I was arrested. And all the while you, my own overprotective brothers, set me up."

"You would never have gone to jail," Shea insisted. "The case was weak. You should *never* have been prosecuted."

Aaron said, "We had an agreement, if the verdict went against you, we'd come forward."

"With this cock-and-bull story that Neville did it and he's missing?"

"Shannon—" Robert tried, but she wasn't listening.

"This is vile and illegal and downright evil," she hissed. "And . . . So . . . What? You started up again?"

"No!" Robert said emphatically.

"So, who's doing it now? Who's setting the damned fires?" she demanded. Fury snapped through her veins. "Who's playing judge and jury and God now, killing the people closest to us? Who has my daughter? Who killed Oliver and Mary Beth and Blanche Johnson?"

Her brothers remained silent.

"*Who?*" she demanded again, and Shea held up a hand.

"We don't know, Shannon. I've told you everything I know, now I think I'd better talk to Detective Paterno."

"Wait a minute, Shea. Let's discuss what you want to say, what kind of agreement you'll need," Pete said.

Shannon stalked from the patio. She'd heard enough. Her head was thundering again and she couldn't take one more second of her brothers' sick pact or their lawyer's desperate scramble to keep them from admitting their own guilt.

She climbed in the rental car, pulled a quick U-turn in front of Aaron's house, then headed out of town, past well-tended lawns and homes where people were just sitting down to dinner or watching TV or having reasonable discussions, where life was carrying on as it was normally supposed to.

Normal.

She doubted she'd ever feel normal again.

Sitting at his desk at home, ice cubes melting in his drink, Paterno stared down at the autopsy report of Ryan Carlyle. He'd intended to compare what the ME had found on Carlyle to the reports on Blanche Johnson, Mary Beth Flannery and Oliver Flannery. He'd pulled some strings and the ME had performed Oliver's autopsy ahead of schedule. A lot of the toxicology reports weren't back yet, but the preliminary autopsy report was almost complete.

"Good enough for government work," he joked as the remains of his dinner—a man-sized TV dinner of chicken and French fries—sat on the counter, untouched. The dishes were piled in the sink, but he didn't care. Not when his mind was somewhere else, and tonight, it was definitely far away.

He laid copies of the reports on his desk and compared them. Two women and two men. Killed in very different manners.

He took a sip of his whiskey, felt it warm his gut. Then he adjusted a pair of reading glasses onto the tip of his nose. Usually he didn't bother, but some of the print was pretty fine these days and his eyes, well, shit, not just his eyes, but his knees and damned back were giving him trouble.

Blanche Johnson had been butchered. She'd bled to death, her carotid artery severed with a serrated blade, probably a knife, the weapon as yet undiscovered. Mary Beth Flannery had been choked, bruises on her neck verified. Speculation was that her killer had been big and strong and had surprised her in the bath. She'd been submerged in the water after death and the fire had come later. Oliver Flannery had also died from having his oxygen supply cut off, the result of a slow hanging by a rope once used for the chapel bells. He hadn't bled to death despite the cuts on his wrists, nor had he inhaled much smoke. On the other hand Ryan Carlyle had died of smoke inhalation, just before his body had been burned to a crisp.

All different modes.

Could they have been killed by the same person?

Carlyle's death had been staged to look like an accident, but it had been done clumsily, almost as if the killer had wanted the police to know that the man hadn't just gotten trapped in a forest fire.

Whoever the killer was, he wanted to show off.

And he had a specific agenda. Otherwise Shannon Flannery would already be dead.

So why the three-year gap?

What had started it up again?

You could have a different guy . . . You're assuming the perp not only killed Carlyle but these people who were close to him.

Two people were unaccounted for: Brendan Giles and Neville Flannery.

It looked like Giles was, indeed, in Central America.

That left Neville Flannery. The missing brother.

But why return to take some kind of vengeance on his siblings? Had they done him dirt? Had he snapped? Could he be so twisted as to track down Shannon's kid? Is that what took him three years? To find the girl and kidnap her?

Something bit at the back of his mind. Like a gnat gnawing. He looked at the pictures of the Flannery family that he had on file. All the boys had the Black Irish good looks, like their father; family resemblance ran strong, and those twins . . . spooky how much they looked alike.

He was crushing ice between his back teeth and stopped.

Was it possible that Oliver and Neville had switched places? Is that what was bugging him?

Paterno took a swallow of his drink, crunched more ice between his teeth as he considered. Why would the brothers trade places? It seemed far-fetched. Was the brother who had been hung indeed Oliver—the religious one, the soft-spoken one, the kind one?

And why had someone kidnapped the kid? To what end, he wondered, the ice cracking between his molars while he thought. To what damned end?

Who was the killer? And why such a long time between the first one, Ryan Carlyle, and the next one, Mary Beth Carlyle Flannery?

He frowned as nothing came to him.

Picking up the ME's report on Ryan Carlyle again, he read each and every line. At the bottom he saw something that gave him pause. Stapled to the report was the identification form. He read it over. There had been a temporary ID made because a piece of a California driver's license had been found at the scene, which had somehow escaped being completely destroyed. The license had belonged to Ryan Carlyle. His ID had later been confirmed by Patrick Flannery and Shea Flannery. Not his wife, Shannon. That was odd, Paterno thought, but then Shannon and Ryan had been separated at the time, she'd been in the process of filing for divorce. Still, she was next of kin. Identification would have been hard, the guy had been burned nearly beyond recognition. The pictures in the file were enough to make his stomach turn.

Still, something was off. He knew it.

And the only person who might be able to explain it was Shea Flannery.

The Beast was driving. And he was hyped up. Excited.

In the passenger seat Dani tried and failed to see much beneath the blindfold he'd pulled tight over her eyes. She was as frightened as she'd ever been in her life.

Somehow she had to find a way to escape, to get away. And soon.

The Beast had something major planned.

Earlier he'd forced her to get dressed, then, taking no chances, had tied her hands behind her back and bound her ankles together. She'd managed to slide the nail into her pocket and he hadn't bothered to check, but it wouldn't do much good now. It was a pathetic weapon at best and with her hands tied there was no way she could use it.

He was pissed at her.

He'd told her as much.

Because of her escape attempt, he'd had to alter his plans and he didn't like it. She thought he might do something because he was so angry: hit her, or beat her or worse. So far, that hadn't been the case.

After he'd bound and blindfolded her, he'd gagged her, then left her on the porch and spent some time inside the cabin. She'd heard him moving furniture. Soon after he'd hauled her down the hill to his truck, stuck her inside and started driving. All the while, she'd smelled gas, the fumes seeping through her gag to burn her nose and mouth.

The scent was everywhere, seeming to emanate from him and she felt cold as death when she thought what he might do with it.

She could see only a sliver of light beneath the crack at the bottom of the blindfold. She could tell it was getting dark and she hated to think what he'd planned for her.

Whatever it was, the gas was an essential ingredient.

It scared her to death.

Shannon spied Travis waiting for her and her stupid heart did a crazy little flip. "Idiot," she told herself as she pulled the Mazda into her parking spot near the garage. What was it about that man that she couldn't get enough of? *There's a phrase for that, Shannon. It's called self-destruction. Emotional self-destruction.*

"Bring it on," she muttered as she threw the key in her purse.

Seated on the top step of her front porch, long legs stretched in front of him, Travis followed her with his eyes, scratching Khan behind his ears, watching Shannon pull to a stop. Damn, but he looked good.

There was just something about his lanky build and easy smile that got to her. All of the tension seemed to ease from her shoulders as she climbed out of the car and he pushed himself upright.

"Traitor," she said to the dog. "How'd he get out?"

"Santana has a key."

"And he let you inside."

"He let the dog out," Travis clarified, "but for the record, I think he trusts me."

She raised one eyebrow. "I doubt it. Nate doesn't trust anyone."

"He's in love with you." His eyes were an intense laser blue.

"So he's said."

"And you?"

She sighed, strolled up to him and said, "Oh, you know how it is, you can't force your heart to do things it won't. You see, I've got this other guy I'm interested in."

His surprised smile stretched wider as she reached him, his shadow stretching over her. "Are you?"

"Hmmm. But he made me mad. Real mad. Lied to me."

His smile fell away. "I never lied to you. Never misrepresented myself."

"Just feigned interest in me to find out what made me tick, what I knew about Dani."

"Only partially right. I did want to know all those things, but I never 'feigned' interest in you. I didn't have to. I was interested right from the get-go." His arms surrounded her, then he pulled her close. She smelled the faint scent of some aftershave. He rested his forehead against hers, their eyes the barest of inches apart. She was lost in the intensity of his gaze, the blue fire burning. "I didn't want to be interested in you. Hell, no. That wasn't something I'd planned, but from the first time I saw you, in the window, leaning over the sink, and I was out in the field, sizing the place up before the fire, I knew I was in trouble."

She sighed. "I thought you were the last man, the very last man on earth I should get involved with." She smiled up at him. "But here we are."

She touched the side of his face with one finger and he groaned.

"Oh, hell," he growled and pulled her tight, his lips claiming hers in a kiss that seemed to ricochet through her body, creating immediate and intense heat, bringing up vivid memories of making love to him.

She wanted to tell him everything, spill out her heart. Tears filled her eyes.

"What happened?" Travis asked, but she shook her head.

Travis gazed down at her. He took her hand and pulled her into the unlocked house, purposely leaving Khan outside. He guided her upstairs and she willingly went.

It was crazy, she knew, spending time in bed with him, but she wanted it, needed it so badly. The touch and feel of him was so real, so tangible, that it pushed the unreal, the horror, away from the front of her mind.

Afterward, they had dinner. He'd bought steaks and champagne. She had one potato in the pantry and a few tomatoes clinging to the vines in pots on the back porch. He barbecued. She poured champagne and as the potato roasted and the steaks sizzled on the grill, they brought each other up to speed about what they'd been doing.

"I'm sworn to secrecy," she said as she chopped onions and the puppy, let out of the pen and allowed to roam around the kitchen, explored her new surroundings.

"Who would I tell?"

She looked at him. To hell with her sick, scheming brothers. Travis was the one who cared, the father worried sick about his daughter. Quickly she told him about her father and brothers and the Stealth Torcher. He just stared at her. When she finished, he shook his head.

"So your father killed Dolores Galvez accidentally, and then gave up setting fires. The boys took up the sword, so to speak, and though they were appalled at what your father had done, they decided to take things one step further. They killed your husband, then let you go on trial for it."

"Essentially."

Travis turned back to the champagne. With a loud pop, the cork exploded out of the bottle and frothy champagne bubbled out. "You believe it all?" He poured them each a glass and handed one to her.

"Most of it. There are still some holes. I'm not sure my brothers were being completely honest with me." She clinked the rim of her glass to his, then took a sip of the cool, effervescent liquid. "But why should they start now?"

"Those holes are as wide as the Grand Canyon." He stared out the window to the night as it crept over the land. "It doesn't fit. No matter how you push the pieces together, something's not right."

"They'll talk to Paterno and maybe he can get the truth out of them."

"But they've already lawyered-up."

"Mmm." She took another swallow of her drink before tossing the onions and tomatoes together.

"I think they're just covering their collective asses."

She didn't argue. Couldn't. She'd had the same hit.

"Something's off."

Shannon nodded, then surprised at her hunger, she sprinkled olive oil, basil, salt and balsamic vinegar into the bowl as Travis walked outside to fork the steaks from the grill. She ate like she'd been starved. A psychologist would probably tell her she was feeding a need, a gaping hole. It was something she couldn't sate.

She finally pushed her plate away and later, when she and Travis lay in bed, nestled together, only a sheet over their naked bodies, a picture of Dani on the nightstand, Shannon wondered, *Where the hell was their daughter?*

Chapter 32

Something was wrong . . . so wrong . . . She wandered through the house, their mother's house, searching for someone, for something.

"Neville?" she called. "Oliver?"

Where were the twins?

She heard meat sizzling, smelled bacon frying, but there was no one in the kitchen, the stove wasn't lit.

"No bacon, Shannon! It's Friday! Shame on you," her mother said, but Maureen was nowhere nearby and when Shannon reached for the door to the basement, it was locked, wouldn't budge. "You never did follow the rules, did you?" her mother was saying and the voice came from the den.

"Mom?" Shannon yelled, but when she reached the room where her father smoked cigars, it was empty, just the odor of smoke lingering, as if her father had been there seconds before, puffing on his favorite type of cigar. The cigars were there, in a glass humidor on his desk, right next to a picture of Dani.

Shannon's heart froze.

Where was her little girl?

She heard a baby crying and headed up the stairs, her mother's disembodied voice chasing after her. "The wages of sin is death . . ." But the baby was crying and there was smoke in the air.

"Dani!" she cried, her legs feeling like lead as she trudged up stairs that went up and up and up. She held on to the rail and it felt slick. When she looked at her hand, she saw it was bloody, that rivers of blood were pouring down the handrail, down the stairs, and still there was smoke and a baby crying.

Looking up, she gasped. At the top of the stairs she saw Oliver, hanging by his neck, smoke and flames surrounding him, a naked infant, her little girl, in his bloody hands.

"No!" Shannon cried, taking the steps two at a time and getting no closer. "Don't! Oliver!"

His eyes flew open.

He stared down at her, his face melting and morphing hideously.

With a jolt, she realized he was Neville and he took the

baby and threw her high into the air, above the flames, higher and higher into the smoke the crying infant flew.

Panic tore through her. She screamed as she lost sight of her baby. "Nooooo!"

Her eyes opened.

It was night.

Dark.

"Oh, dear God," she whispered, shaken as she turned into Travis's arms.

"Shh." He pulled her tight and kissed her crown. She quivered against him, feeling the heat of his body, smelling the pure male scent of him over the thin aroma of smoke lingering from the nightmare.

A dream. A horrid, visceral, blood-chilling dream. That's all it was. Nothing more.

And yet . . . she still smelled smoke. She felt Travis's arms tighten around her. She opened her eyes and found that he was awake, an orange glow reflected in his eyes.

It was dark . . . except for that sinister glow.

Her heart slammed in her chest.

Suddenly she smelled the smoke. Real smoke, no distant memory of burning cigars or bacon grease from her dream.

And she knew. Oh, God, she knew.

The Stealth Torcher was back.

A shriek sliced the air, the prolonged squeal of the smoke detector.

"No!"

Travis was already on his feet, jerking on his jeans.

Shannon rolled out of bed, her bare feet hitting the floor with a thud. Throwing on clothes, she raced down the stairs. "Call 9-1-1," she yelled over her shoulder as she flew into the kitchen.

Khan whined and the puppy, too, was agitated. Why hadn't she heard the dogs? Exhaustion? The champagne? The lovemaking? She couldn't think about it as she threw open the back door and crammed her boots onto her feet. Khan, barking madly, shot out of the door.

"You stay," she said to the pup and spied Travis, cell phone to his ear, shouting out orders to whoever was on the other end of the line.

"That's right. Shannon Flannery's house!"

She rattled off the address and he relayed it into the mouthpiece as he pulled on his boots, then hung up.

"I'll let the dogs out," Shannon said, grabbing a red fire extinguisher from the wall and slamming it into Travis's hands. "Get the horses. I'll get the hose."

She started across the parking lot, sick inside. There wasn't one fire, but two! One in the stable, the other in the kennel.

"You son of a bitch," she growled under her breath, then yelled, "Nate! Santana! Wake up!" She couldn't take the time to pound on his door, not with the flames already spreading through the buildings where the animals were penned, trapped. She saw Travis head into the stable as she flung open the door to the kennel.

The dogs were wild. Barking, yipping, panic gripping them. But the fire was contained at the far end of the building. She grabbed a fire extinguisher from the wall and started spraying, releasing the dogs as she passed. "It's all right," she soothed, knowing in her heart she was lying. She unlatched Atlas's gate and he tore past, shooting for the open door. At the next kennel, Cissy was quiet, patient. But the instant Shannon opened the door, the border collie took off for the open door just as an explosion rocked through the building and Shannon was flung to the floor, her head cracking against the cement.

Travis! The horses!

Through the window she saw flames skyrocket through the roof of the stable.

Travis threw open the door of the horse barn. Fire, smoke and intense heat radiated toward him from the far side, the paddock side of the building. The horses, trapped in their stalls were panicked, shrieking. Smoke lay thick and black, stinging his eyes, blinding him as it billowed toward him. Coughing, spraying retardant in front of him, Travis started with the first stall, unlatching the gate, inching forward.

A buckskin horse hurtled past him, hooves clattering on the cement as she headed at full gallop toward the open door to the parking lot.

He moved six feet to his left and found another stall and quickly unlocked the gate. Again a huge animal raced past him, nearly knocking him down.

Shit, he couldn't see anything, but so far, there was more smoke than flames. He moved forward, one stall at a time, horses racing toward him and at the far end, when the smoke cleared he saw her.

His daughter. Bound and gagged, standing just inside the door to the paddock.

He couldn't believe his eyes. She was alive! And so close. She was shaking her head violently, terror in her eyes as he stepped forward. A heartbeat later he knew his mistake as a thin line at his ankle level broke.

He threw himself forward.

An explosion rocked the building.

He was blasted from his feet.

He landed against a stall door and stunned, saw fireballs shoot through the building.

Dani! Where was she?

"No!" Shannon screamed. Not Travis! She ran from the kennels to the stable, seeing the horses flying out of the burning building. "Travis!" she screamed frantically, coughing, the smoke stinging her nose and eyes. "Travis!"

Far in the distance, she heard sirens.

"Hurry, damn it," she thought, racing into the burning building. "Travis!" The smoke was so thick and black, she couldn't see, couldn't breathe. Flames crawled up the walls and one lone horse screamed in terror.

Pushing herself forward, feeling the heat, she saw the

final stall. The horse, a bay gelding, was terror-stricken, running in circles, rearing and whistling. "Hang on," Shannon said, spraying retardant, choking and forcing herself forward. "Travis!" she cried as a window shattered. Glass sprayed wildly. Shards rained on her hair, scratched her face. The horse screamed in terror. "Travis!" Where was he? Jesus, please let him be safe. "Travis!"

The gelding was out of his mind. His eyes were wide with terror, rimmed in white. Lather, now red with blood from the flying shards of glass, stained his dark, wet coat. "It's okay, boy," she said soothingly, all the while searching for Travis. "Shan . . . . Calm down."

Her lungs were scorched, on fire. Her fingers fumbled with the latch. *Come on, come on!* Where the hell was Travis? *Where?*

Finally the latch gave way, she pulled the gate open and the horse shot through, running wildly, careening down the hallway. "Travis!" she called again as she sprayed at the flames, watched in horror as they climbed up the walls.

BAM!

Another explosion sent her feet out from under her. She saw the roof, aflame, start to collapse.

"Oh, God, no!" Scrambling, crawling backward, she tried to escape. Her boots slid as splinters of glass drove deep into her palms. She had to get out. "Travis!" she cried. She couldn't lose him. Couldn't! With a groan a burning beam listed, started to fall.

Shooting to her feet, Shannon ran after the horses, hearing the sirens wailing. Closer. *Oh, please! Hurry, hurry, hurry!*

She flung herself through the doorway, gasping and choking, tears streaming from her eyes as she searched for Travis. The horses and dogs were running down the road, in jeopardy of being hit by fire engines racing toward the inferno.

What had happened? What?

She looked to the corner of the woods and she spied a girl. Standing alone, shivering and shaking, her hands and feet bound, her mouth gagged, visible because of the hideous orange light climbing skyward.

Dani!

Shannon recognized her in an instant.

Her daughter.

Alive!

Oh, baby!

Her heart squeezed and she rushed forward, racing across the gravel of the lot, ignoring the fact that blood was running from her face, from her hands. "I'm coming," she yelled, coughing, still dazed as the sirens shrieked and smoke poured into the night sky. Who had done this to her? Why?

Dani, crying, was shaking her head wildly, but not moving. As if she was pinned to the spot. She was frantic. Crazed. No doubt from her ordeal. "Hang on!" Shannon said, staring into the girl's terrified eyes.

Only when she was within ten feet did she realize that Dani wasn't shaking her head from fear, but because she was trying to say something, to warn her.

A trap?

She stepped forward and heard a horrifying whoosh. In a heartbeat a ring of fire surrounded her, separating her from the girl as gas ignited the ground around her.

Spinning, she saw her attacker.

Her heart plummeted.

A man in black, wearing a hood over his head, looking like Satan himself approached her. She tried to scramble backward as eyes gleamed through the slits over his eyes. "Who are you? What do you want?" she cried, but he didn't say a word. "Where's Travis?"

She started to run, but faced a wall of flame.

And then he was on her. She fought hard, flailing, trying to wound him, writhing and squirming as the flames crackled and hissed around her. She couldn't let him win. She had to get to Dani. To Travis. But he was heavy and strong, forcing her onto the ground, seemingly unconcerned about the fire. Her shoulder screamed in pain.

He grabbed a handful of hair, pulled back and the stitches in her scalp ripped. She struggled desperately to fling him off and smelled gas.

Gasoline?

Here? In this conflagration?

Her eyes widened in horror. He was pressing her chest and abdomen on the ground, his long body over hers. Reaching around her head with his free hand, he stuffed a gasoline soaked rag over her nose and mouth. She tried to bite his hand and failed, the taste of gasoline filling her mouth. She gagged and he snarled against her ear, "Fight me, and you'll fry."

She didn't doubt him for a second.

She tried to scream, to get away, but the fumes of gasoline, so dangerous, were close to the flames and filling her nose, her mouth, her throat. "That's right, Shannon," he hissed in a voice that was chillingly familiar. "Try anything smart, and I'll light a match and watch as the flames crawl straight into your lungs."

She froze. Fought the urge to pass out.

A few more minutes.

Only a few more minutes.

The fire trucks are near!

Hang on, she told herself as blackness pulled at the edges of her consciousness. *Don't let this bastard win.*

But it was too late. She couldn't draw a breath without being overwhelmed by the fumes.

Her head was swimming. Her stomach roiled.

Despite her best efforts, she lost consciousness.

Dani screamed, her lungs feeling as if they would explode, her mouth gagged. The woman—her mother—was being dragged away by the Beast and the flames were getting so close. She kicked at the rope that restrained her, held her tight to the ring of fire where he'd swooped down on her mother.

Dani was staked to the ground. He'd used one of the spikes for tethering horses to keep her in one position. The rope holding her to the stake was short, didn't give her much room to move. Damn it all! She'd fought him when he'd brought her here, tried to get away. She'd jabbed the nail at his eyes and felt it sink through flesh. He'd howled in pain and fury, but he'd still held her fast, tightening her to the stake while blood poured down his snarling face. She'd thought he might kill her then, but he'd kept on his mission. While she was tethered, like some kind of bait for a predator, her efforts to free herself in vain, she'd watched in horror as he set his plan in motion. Lights in an upstairs room went out, then the Beast started bringing over the gallons of gasoline he'd lugged from the truck, which was parked half a mile away on a back road.

She'd tried to warn someone.

Screamed long and hard until her throat was raw.

Because of the damned gag no one had heard her and though a few of the dogs had barked, no one had paid any attention.

Until he'd set the fire and come back for her. To use her as damned bait!

She'd seen her father and the woman running across the parking lot, going into the buildings that the Beast had booby-trapped.

"No! No! No!" she'd yelled as he'd positioned her near the horse barn. Dani had cried and stomped her feet, but the creep had held her fast. Until her father, in the barn that was burning, had seen her. He'd tried to reach her, but couldn't.

Terror had filled her. The Beast had killed her father. He couldn't have survived.

But the pervert hadn't been finished. He'd brought her

back to this small clearing and staked her where she would be visible from the parking lot. Animals had begun streaming from the buildings. Then the explosions had begun.

Desperately she'd kicked and fought, tried to pull away.

Now she lunged forward and ended up falling flat on her face, her eyes only inches from flames that were crawling closer, eating the dry twigs and leaves and grass that surrounded her. Dust and soot filled her nostrils and every muscle in her body ached. But she couldn't give in.

She trembled, scooting backward, knowing she was doomed.

That prick had finally done it. He'd found a way to kill her. *Bastard!* she thought. *Sick, perverted creep!*

What could she do?

How could she save herself?

She heard the sound of sirens . . . Please, please, would they see her in time? She tried to get to her feet again. Only to fall.

The flames were licking closer when she saw movement.

A dark shadow.

Her heart sank. The psycho had come back for her.

"I've got you," a strong male voice said, and pulling a sharp knife from his pocket, he sliced through the tether. Grabbing her, he hauled her from the flames just as the first fire engine, lights flashing, siren screeching, roared into the area.

The truck slid to a stop.

Firefighters poured from the big vehicle as an ambulance arrived.

"Are you okay?" the man holding her asked as he pulled off her gag.

She nodded. "Who are you?"

"Nate Santana. I know your father and . . . and your birth mother."

"My dad," she said, tears filling her eyes.

"Shh. He's okay." He placed her on the ground and cut

her wrists and ankles free. "I got to him first." He managed a thin smile. "He's gonna be glad to see you. Come on."

He nodded toward the house while other trucks arrived. She saw her dad propped up against the porch, gasping for air. At the sight of him, she broke into a run. "Dad!" she cried and before he could climb to his feet she threw herself at him, landing in his arms, clinging to him and sobbing wildly.

"Dani," he whispered, his voice rough as he held her as if he would never let her go. "Dani." Tears ran from his soot-streaked face and though he fought it, she felt him begin to sob. "Are you okay? Honey?"

"Yeah."

"Did he hurt you?"

"No . . . Dad . . . he . . . I'm okay." She looked up at him with her wide green eyes. "Really."

His voice cracked. "You're safe, now. Oh, God, you're safe, little girl. I won't let anything like this ever happen to you again! I swear."

She was crying, too, clinging to him as he, still holding her, climbed to his feet. Around them the firefighters snaked hoses, started pumping water, barked orders. The horse barn was ablaze, flames threatening the garage. Firefighters trained nozzles on the roofs of the surrounding buildings. Gallons of water shot into the air, wetting down the roof of the house, garage and kennel, while firefighters battled the flames roaring in the stable.

"Hey you," a female firefighter yelled, pointing their way. "Get out of the way! Is there anyone else here?"

"Shannon," Travis said, looking around. His heart lurched when he didn't see her and realized that all the stock was set free. "She's here—"

"No! He's got her," Dani blurted out.

"What?" God, she looked thin and pale. It was all Travis could do not to hold her and rock her and forget everything else.

"He took her away."

Oh, God no! "What do you mean?" he demanded, but he knew, deep in his soul, he knew what his daughter meant. Abject horror clawed at him.

"He's got her!" Dani said, her eyes filled with a wisdom far beyond her years. Travis's blood turned to ice. "The woman with the curly red hair, the one in the picture . . . She's my mom, isn't she?" Her little chin was thrust out, her eyes pinning him, daring him to lie, looking so much like Shannon, his heart cracked.

"Yes," he admitted, thinking how desperate Dani had been to find her birth mother and now that she had, Shannon was missing, in the clutches of the psycho who had abducted her. For a second he felt as if his entire world had collapsed. Having come this far, having found his daughter, knowing Dani was safe, only to lose Shannon. He squeezed Dani as if afraid she would vanish into thin air.

"The Beast has her. We have to save her!"

"We will, honey. We will," Travis vowed, hoping that, as water ran beneath his feet and the air was filled with the stench of damp, charred wood, he wasn't lying.

Santana pinned Dani with intense eyes. "Who's the Beast?"

"The psycho!" Dani clarified as if Nate was an idiot. "That weird pervert who tricked me!"

"Shit," Nate said.

The female firefighter, her face already streaked beneath her helmet, her expression severe, bore down on them. "Is there anyone in the house or any of the buildings?" Silhouetted by the backdrop of angry flames hissing and sparking to the heavens, she looked from one to the other.

"No." Travis shook his head.

She glanced at Nate for confirmation while firefighters shouted, yelled orders, and dragged hoses through the soggy mud and trails of water, all the while spraying great flumes upon the buildings. Dogs barked wildly, horses shrilled and the lights of the engines strobed the night.

"No one," Nate shouted over the din. "Everyone's out. But there's a woman missing. Shannon Flannery. The owner of this place." Nate pointed to Dani. "This is Dani Settler, the girl the police have been looking for. She says that the guy who abducted her brought her here, used her as bait to get at Shannon, then abducted her." His face was hard and set, a mirror of the firefighter's as he stared down at Dani. "Isn't that right?"

"Exactly." Dani nodded and her fists balled.

Travis's heart tore. He held his daughter tighter. "You're safe now," he whispered, though fear for Shannon nearly strangled him. Where had the monster taken her? Was she alive? He thought of Oliver and Mary Beth and Blanche. The madman wouldn't be satisfied until he'd killed Shannon, too. Oh, God, they had to find her. *Had* to!

The female firefighter stared down at Dani. "I think you'd better tell that to the police. I'll call the station and make sure whoever's in charge is told."

"Detective Paterno," Travis said, feeling the minutes passing by too quickly, knowing that with each passing second, Shannon was being dragged farther away. "Just let Paterno know what's going on. We don't have time to wait."

"Who kidnapped you?" Nate asked Dani.

"The Beast. I don't know his name, but he had a picture of her and he . . . he took her. He'd planned it for a long time." She looked up at her father. "I was the bait. But he didn't want me. He wanted her."

"Where did he take her?" Nate demanded.

"I don't know. But . . . I think to the cabin," she said.

"What cabin?"

"The one where he kept me." Her smoke-streaked face was tense. "If he didn't take her there, then I don't know. He didn't say."

Tires crunched on the driveway and Travis looked up to see a news van stopping not thirty feet away.

"Goddamned press," the firefighter said.

"Do you know where the cabin is?" Travis asked his daughter and she shook her head.

"I don't think I can find it." She bit her lip, but she didn't break down.

Travis, gently, though panic was rushing through him, said, "Tell us what you know about it."

"It's . . . it's a long ways away, in the mountains. He locked me in a room with the windows boarded up," she said as smoke continued to billow upward. "It was old and really, really crummy . . . uh, rustic. No electricity. No real plumbing. He, um, he made a fire every night and a train went by sometimes." She looked up at Travis and her expression changed. Hardened. "I got away once and I followed deer trails, like you taught me. I headed downhill, always downhill and then I found the railroad tracks and started following them, you know, hoping that I'd come to a town or something." Her eyes clouded over at the memory. "I should have gotten away. I almost did. But I came to a bridge and that's where he caught me."

Nate tensed. "What kind of bridge?" he asked quickly. "Can you be more specific?"

"A railroad bridge. I told you—"

"A trestle? Made of wood and beams, right?"

"Yeah." She nodded. "It went across a really deep canyon and . . . And not far away, there was another bridge that you could see, not for a train but one for cars and trucks."

"I know where that is," Nate said, glancing up at Travis. "It's not that far. Ten, maybe twelve miles north of here."

Travis was already moving toward his truck, ignoring a reporter stepping from the news van. "Let's go."

"We need a dog." Nate whistled sharply, repeatedly. He turned to the firefighter. "Call Paterno, tell him everything you heard here, especially about the cabin. Tell him about the trestle bridge, the nearest town is Holcomb, I think, the closest landmark is Stinson Peak. There's a road that runs parallel to that section of the railroad . . . It's . . . hell . . . what is it?"

"Johnson Creek Road," the firefighter supplied.

"Right."

Nate nodded quickly as Atlas, the huge shepherd, bounded from the shadows. The big dog, despite the fire, made a beeline for Santana.

The firefighter was already reaching for her cell phone.

The flames were dying, but the air was still thick with wet ash and smoke. Travis said to Dani, "I assume he brought you here in a vehicle."

"A truck," she affirmed. "I got him, though."

"Got him?" Travis said and her lips pursed.

"With a nail. I jammed it into his face. I tried to get his eyes but I don't think I did." She looked up at her father. Tears shimmered in her eyes, reflecting the gold flames of the dying fire. "I wanted to kill him . . ."

"It's okay," he said as she blinked. "You're safe."

"But *she* isn't. He's going to kill her, Dad. I know it." Guilt riddled her expression.

With one arm he pulled her tight against him. "Not if I have anything to say about it. And it's not your fault, Dani. None of this is your fault."

"But if I didn't go online, if I didn't start searching for her, she would be safe. I wouldn't have been kidnapped."

"Don't think like that. Okay? We've got to go after that son of a bitch."

She nodded rapidly.

"Good. Now, can you tell me where he parked his truck?"

"Over there." Without hesitation she pointed through the trucks parked haphazardly in the driveway and past the fence behind Shannon's house. "On the other side of those fields," she said, indicating the subdivision. "In a back alley."

"Let's go. You show us the way," Travis told his daughter.

The female firefighter snapped off her phone. "Paterno's on his way."

"Good." Travis and Dani were already hurrying with Nate to Nate's truck.

"Hey wait." Travis glanced over his shoulder as Nate

threw open a door. Beneath her helmet, disapproval twisted the woman's features. "Your daughter should stay and wait for the police."

Travis wasn't listening to anyone. "We don't have time," he said as Nate fired the engine. Travis and Dani piled in and Nate stepped hard on the throttle, shooting past a worried-looking reporter who was motioning to a cameraman. Nate picked up speed, tearing down the driveway as sirens wailed in the distance.

Fear clawed at Travis. He had his daughter back, yes, but now Shannon was missing, caught by the same horrid psycho who had held his daughter.

He had to get to her.

Before it was too late.

Chapter 33

Shannon's eyes fluttered open.

She coughed, her nostrils burning.

Where the hell was she?

She tried to move but couldn't. As her head cleared and her eyes adjusted to the half-light, she realized she was in a small cabin of sorts. It was dark, the only illumination an eerie, blood-red glow from coals in an old, decrepit fireplace.

She coughed again at the acrid smell that permeated her nose and lungs.

Gasoline!

Instantly her brain snapped into gear. She struggled. Tried to stand. But she was tied to a chair. Her hands were bound behind her. Her feet were lashed to each of the front legs of the chair.

"No!" she yelled, her own voice startling her.

Images flashed through her mind. The fire in the stables. Her daughter tied to a stake. A ring of fire. A dark, hooded man swooping down on her.

Terror grabbed her by the throat.

This was wrong . . . so wrong.

"Awake?" a deep, evil voice asked.

She froze.

The voice was familiar. Hideous.

A ripple of disgust and fear swept over her skin. She was mistaken. She had to be. No way could the terrifying voice from her past be here . . . no . . . oh, God, no!

"Ryan?" she whispered, terror freezing her veins.

"So you do remember?"

Oh, please, God, no!

Like a wraith, he moved out of the shadows. He was naked, his body gleaming in the weird glow, as if he'd spent time anointing every inch of his skin with oil.

She gazed in disbelief. Blood ran down one side of his face. He was wounded near his eye which was purpling and swelling. This had to be a horrid, twisted nightmare.

His smile, white teeth and thin lips were the embodiment of evil. "So you haven't forgotten me."

"But you . . . you . . ."

"I'm supposed to be dead, aren't I?" He walked closer. Taut, strident muscles moved beneath skin stretched tight, as if he'd worked out every day since she'd last seen him. Revulsion and panic stormed through her. *Think, Shannon, think. Don't let him win. You have to fight.* She closed her eyes for a second, tried and failed to get her bearings.

"Surprise, surprise." His voice was silky and smug.

"I don't understand." She opened her eyes. Stared at the face she'd once loved and now despised. He was aberrant, a sick, demented freak. Somehow, someway, she had to save herself.

Outside it was dark as pitch, the windows showing nothing but blackness. Wherever they were it was remote. She couldn't expect any help. The cavalry wouldn't be riding up.

Don't give up. Do not let this bastard win!

"Of course you don't understand," he said, walking in a broad circle around her, not getting close. She saw his back, hideously scarred and she shivered. "But then you never understood me, wifey, now did you?"

The gas! Where the hell was the gas? Heart thudding with fear, Shannon searched the shadows, saw no sign of a can . . . had he poured it out? It was too dark to see, but in the fire's reflection she noticed dark lines on the floor. What was that? He hadn't poured the gas out, had he? And why did it burn her nostrils? As if it were . . . oh, God, she looked down at her clothes. Surely he hadn't . . .

"The trouble was, Shannon, you were never as smart as you liked to pretend. You thought you'd gotten away with it, didn't you? The perfect murder?"

"What are you talking about?" She needed to keep him engaged in the conversation. She needed a way out, an escape route. But her clothes! Had he soaked her clothes in gasoline? Was that why he was naked and she was still dressed? "Wha–what murder? You know I didn't try to kill you. What did you do, stage it? Why? Did you want to disappear?" She had trouble concentrating. Fear spread through her like a plague and sweat slid down her spine.

"I had to. You know it. You were behind it."

"I don't know what you're talking about."

"Don't play innocent with me!" he said, snapping. "Your brothers, ever your protectors, decided to get rid of me. *Your* brothers. *My* in-laws." He hooked a thumb at his naked chest. *"My coworkers, supposedly my goddamned friends.* All their dirty little secrets."

"What secrets?" she asked, but she knew it had something to do with the star, something to do with the acronym.

"Don't play dumb! ARSONS . . . Aaron, Robert, Shea, Oliver, Neville and finally Shannon," he said, spitting her name as he circled her. He was worked up. His hands were waving now. She tried to keep his face in her eyesight, watch for any indication of what he was going to do.

But she knew, didn't she? The smell of gas warned her of her certain, painful death.

"Can't you drive any faster?" Travis demanded as the truck barreled up the narrow, winding logging road. Outside it was black as death, the headlights of Nate's truck cutting through the thick darkness.

"You want us to get there alive, don't you?" Santana growled, but he punched it and the wheels of his truck spun wildly, digging in.

"There it is!" Dani said as a narrow bridge came into view. "This is where he was parked."

Travis's heart nosedived as he imagined his daughter with the madman who now had Shannon.

They'd driven steadily through these forested hills and with each minute elapsing he was going out of his mind. He prayed that Shannon was still alive and that they would find her, that Dani was right and he had taken her back to his lair.

Wherever that was.

Otherwise he might never see her alive again.

Fear congealed his blood and he held fast to his daughter. *Let her be alive,* he silently prayed. *Let us find her . . . oh, Jesus, please!*

Shannon pulled at her restraints so hard her wrists ached.

Ryan was pacing. Explaining. Obviously glad to unburden himself.

"Your brothers, they went through this big, ridiculous ceremony . . . standing at points of a star in the woods, like they were part of a secret society, and one by one, they pledged to kill me. Can you imagine?" He leaned closer, his nose an inch from hers. "Because of you. Because they wanted to protect you, from me. And I was your husband! Your husband! You were supposed to love me! Honor me! Obey me! You remember those vows, bitch?" he raved. His hand lifted as if to strike her.

She stared up at him fiercely, her heart pounding, her nerves strung tight. Silently, she dared him to do it. As he had in the past. His face twisted in fury, his swollen eye making him look like the madman he was.

"I would have died that night if it wasn't for Oliver and his conscience. He told me. Let me in on the secret. Explained what was going to happen. Begged me to leave town."

"But you didn't."

"You know me, Shannon, I don't run." He sneered. "I get even. It was simple really. Neville was about my size. He didn't suspect a thing."

"Neville?" she whispered, bracing for the truth.

"The reason no one knew that I survived that night is because I became Neville. I abducted him, interrogated him and found out that his crazy twin was telling the truth. Then I traded places with him, wearing his stupid disguise and arriving at the meeting in the woods to find out that it was true. All of your brothers were planning to kill me. They had this big show, and the leader, Shea, according to Neville, though no one was supposed to know, mapped it out. They all vowed to murder Ryan Carlyle that night, you get it?" he demanded, still circling, his rage emanating from him, the smell of gasoline nauseating. "I just beat them to it. I left my wallet with Neville. Buried it out of range of the fire but close enough to find. I figured Neville's body would be burned beyond recognition. Lucky for me, your family wanted to keep some secrets themselves. They identified Neville's remains as mine."

"They wouldn't do that. They wouldn't lie about Neville."

"Yeah? Maybe they didn't know for sure. But nobody wanted to look at dear, old Neville's dead body too closely. No autopsy. No DNA testing. Just identify it as Ryan Carlyle and everybody leaves happy."

Shannon wouldn't believe it. She tried to close her ears, think only of escape.

"That's when this happened," he jerked a thumb at his back. "I tripped getting away, and slid into the fire myself. But I managed to get out. Neville didn't."

Shannon shrank away from both the real vision of Ryan's scars and the mental vision of Neville's burning death.

"Had to treat it myself . . . But it's been a good reminder. It's kept me focused. Helped me never forget that I had to return. Payback time."

Shannon's body jerked as she remembered Travis telling her about the bloody words scrawled in Blanche Johnson's house.

Travis . . .

Please God keep him and Dani safe, away from this maniac.

Shannon's insides shredded as she realized that it was because of her actions that they'd been put in danger.

"That's right, wifey, payback time, for that bitch that gave me away and for you and your family. And mine . . ."

"Mary Beth?" Shannon whispered, realizing he must mean his cousin.

"Turncoat bitch. She was supposed to defend me! But your lawyer twisted her words around, confused her." His nostrils flared. "She was always stupid."

"So you killed her."

"It was more than that," he said, pleased with himself. "I wanted Robert to feel the pain, to know he was behind her death, that because of his womanizing, he wasn't there to save his wife." His eyes narrowed and he said smugly, "I think it worked, don't you?"

Ryan glared at the woman, his prisoner, who had once been his whole life. She, like the others, was a traitor and deserved the fate he was about to mete out.

Everyone had turned on him. Especially this bitch seated

on the chair, tied and restrained. She was scared; he could see it in her eyes, the way she watched him, but more than that she was defiant. As always. She'd never had the sense to cower from him, to let him have his way.

Stupid woman.

Worse yet, she was still beautiful. Heart-stoppingly so. He'd always loved her wild hair, her big eyes, her sexy smile. That smile had been his undoing.

He studied her. If he had the time, he'd fuck her first, remind her that he was her husband, leave her sore and aching, making certain she understood that *he* was the one in command. Afterward, while she was still panting and bruised, he'd kill her.

She was no better than the rest of them. Worse even. Hadn't she vowed to love and obey him until "death do us part." *Well, baby, death was just about to do its thing*. With one strike of a match, the gasoline would ignite and she would feel the pain he'd suffered, the heat of the fire, the terror of knowing she was going to be consumed by painful, angry flames . . .

Shannon had to keep twisting her head, watching him over her shoulder as he circled her. She pulled at her bonds when he wasn't looking. Weren't they moving? Wasn't there the tiniest bit of slack? If she had enough time, worked with them, could she pull her hand through? That's all she needed: one hand. Just enough of an edge to grab a weapon and kill him.

"Neville didn't die in the fire," Shannon reminded him through clenched teeth. "If it wasn't you, it was someone else, because Neville was seen after the fire." She was desperate to keep him talking and walking, distracted. She needed time to free herself.

"Correction," Ryan said, holding up a finger. "Oliver, *posing* as Neville, was seen."

"You're lying!" Shannon gasped. "Oliver would never do anything like that. He loved Neville. Loved God!"

"You can't believe that poor, pious Oliver would stoop so low as to pretend to be his brother for a couple of weeks?"

She shook her head. "No."

"He was saving his own hide. Think about it. Did you ever see Neville and Oliver together after my death?"

Shannon's mind reeled backward to those first horrible days when she was accused of murder, when speculation ran high that she'd killed her husband. Her brothers and parents had been around. But now, with the march of time, the images were blurry. She couldn't be sure.

"You didn't see him! No one did. Because Neville was dead. And Oliver was a master at slipping into Neville's skin, pretending to be his twin, and he hid it from everyone but eventually, he cracked. Again. Poor *innocent* Oliver couldn't keep up the pretense and he landed in another loony bin."

"You don't know anything!"

"Think again. You know how they say confession is good for the soul? Well, that's what Oliver did just before he died. In the church basement, he bowed his head and confessed everything to me."

"You son of a bitch!" she growled, yanking at her arms and legs. Pain screamed through her body. "You sick, psychotic son of a bitch!" she yelled, her head spinning.

"Is that any way to talk to your husband? Your lover?"

Her stomach, already nauseous from the stench of gas, curdled at his endearments for her. Staring up at him, she strained so hard she could feel the cords in her throat stand out. "This is so much crap, Ryan. I don't believe you. Oliver, if he knew you survived . . . he would have warned me."

"He knew I was alive even if the rest of them didn't. But they all suspected something . . . they just weren't sure about Neville because of Oliver's impersonation." Ryan leered. "But face it, honey, they all let you twist in the wind for my death. They planned my demise, but they let you go on trial for murder!"

She felt cold inside. Despite the heat.

"Swell guys, your brothers."

"They couldn't have known."

"Oliver sure knew. He didn't rat me out, even when he found out I was back. When I confronted him in the confessional . . . you know, the priest-parishioner confidence thing? I reminded him he couldn't tell or he'd suffer God's wrath."

She was stunned. "You used the church . . . Oliver's faith . . . against him?"

"No, bitch," he said, suddenly angry. "I used his *guilt!*"

Shannon gazed at this horror who had once been her husband. "You killed them all. Neville, Mary Beth . . . Oliver," she said dully, the terrible truth of it sinking in. There was no way out. She, too, was doomed. The smell of gasoline was overpowering. Revolting. Oh, God, please not her clothes . . . but whatever he had planned, it would be excruciating. He intended to extract every bit of revenge he could and she knew her death was not only imminent, it would be hideous. She had to keep him talking and try to find a way to deceive him, to get a jump on him, to save herself.

"I'm just getting even, wifey," he pointed out, still circling her but keeping his distance. "I waited a long time for this. Leaving the country then wasn't as hard as I thought. I'd already gotten myself some fake papers, so it was easy enough to steal a car and drive north. I ditched that truck and bought a junker north of Seattle and just kept driving. It was easy enough to hide in Canada. No one looks for a dead man."

She worked her hands, racked her brain for more conversation. "How did you live?"

"Oh, I worked in sawmills, drifted around. All the while I was just planning for the right time, searching for the way to make it work. Then I remembered: the best way to get back at you was to go through your daughter. The one you gave up."

Shannon tried not to react. *Oh, Dani. Please be all right.*

"She was a piece of work that one, a bitch just like you." He pointed a finger at the puncture near his eye. Blood ran down his skin. The eye was so swollen she doubted he could see well. "She had the nerve to come at me with a nail."

"Is she all right?"

"Of course not," he said without any emotion and tossed the framed snapshot of Shea into the fire. "Burned to a fuckin' crisp. Just like I was supposed to be three years ago!"

He was lying! He had to be! Her fists, beneath the cords restraining her, curled in desperation. If he wanted to kill her, well, then so be it. But not her baby. Not Dani!

She lifted her head. Glared at him with murderous eyes. "You didn't hurt her."

He smiled maliciously.

"If you did, I swear, I'll kill you."

"Tough talk considering the situation."

"You bastard!"

"Sticks and stones, baby," he spat. "Sticks and fuckin' stones!"

"This is the way? You're sure?" Nate demanded as the truck roared down a gravel road.

"I—I think so." Dani had only traveled down it twice. As the Beast had driven her from the cabin, she'd tried to memorize landmarks. There had been a big rock that had stuck out in the road, a boulder, and she'd seen that, and then a tree split and charred by lightning at a fork. She'd pointed out the way, but it was so dark . . .

"It's all right," her father said, but she knew it wasn't; knew that her birth mother's fate relied on her memory.

"And the road doesn't even go up to the cabin." She swallowed hard. "How are we going to find the cabin in the dark?"

"Atlas will help us," Nate said. "He'll find her."

Staring through the bug-spattered windshield, Dani hoped he was right.

* * *

Adrenaline surged through Shannon. Again she strained at her bonds. Was it her imagination or did they slip just a fraction more?

He walked to the fireplace. Slowly he picked up the framed pictures that had been resting atop the mantel, items she hadn't noticed until now. He fanned them and waved them in front of her face.

She blinked at the pictures and a new terror rose in her.

"Recognize everyone?" he asked.

"My family?" she said, aghast. *What now?*

"All that count." A muscle worked along his gleaming jaw. "Shit! I'd planned to kill them first but that damned kid . . . I couldn't stand another minute with her, so I had to go after you. She was the bait."

She remembered seeing the girl during the fire. Silently, she prayed for her safety. "She wasn't part of this. Whatever it was you had against us, my daughter wasn't a part of it!"

"But your brothers were part of it. Every last one of them wanted me dead. Didn't care how I died or how much pain I had to endure." With a deft turn of his wrist, he flipped Aaron's picture into the grate.

Glass shattered. Sprayed. The fire hissed angrily.

Shannon yanked at her bonds the brief second his head was turned. Her forearms ached from the strain, but she was certain the restraints gave a bit more. Crackling flames consumed Aaron's image.

Another flip of Ryan's wrist. Robert's snapshot hurtled into the fireplace to smash against the burning logs.

Shannon pulled on her restraints some more.

Crash!

Tiny, glittering shards of glass spewed onto the floor, reflecting the fire's glow. They sizzled and she thought about the gasoline. So volatile . . . Where the hell was it? She didn't dare ask, didn't want him to know her fear. Dear God . . . was that another line on the floorboards? Had he soaked the tinder-dry wood with the incinerant?

Ryan tossed another picture, this one of Oliver, into the

flames. Smack! Again the glass splintered, the fire roiled, surging furiously, sparks rising.

Shannon twisted her wrists against the biting cords. She saw that Ryan intended to kill her with the same fire devouring the photos of her brothers. It was some symbolic thing, the same with his nakedness. Part of the ritual to destroy her family. Her gaze darted around the tiny cabin with its plank walls and broken windows. Dry as a bone, it would, if lit, become a horrifying inferno. And her clothes would go up instantly.

"No way out," he said, taunting her, as if he'd read her thoughts.

God, he loved this. Torturing her. Making her twist in the wind. Just as he'd enjoyed killing them all. First Neville, then Mary Beth and Oliver. If he'd planned it right they all would have died . . .

You can still do it . . . you still have time . . . but first just kill Shannon. Remember what she did to you. How she set you up with the police. Show her no mercy. Kill her. Now. Do it!

He licked his lips in anticipation, felt that familiar buzz, the rush of the act. It was time. Sex would be good.

But the bitch needed to burn.

"I knew nothing about what my brothers had planned," Shannon said desperately, her mind spinning as she tried to keep him talking. There had to be a way out of this! *Had* to!

"Oh, that's right, you're the innocent." He snorted in disgust. "But you set me up, babe. Remember? With Aaron and the cameras? Tried to get me to break the restraining order. Even taped it on video. So that the police would haul my ass to jail."

He was angry now. Agitated. His lips curling, his good eye's blue gaze knifing into her, the other swollen completely shut. *Way to go, Dani!* Maybe she could use his lost sight against him.

He was a monster, all gleaming, and proud of himself, his back . . . But, oh Jesus, his back scarred and ravaged from fire.

He saw her gaze, how she was repulsed. "As I told you, compliments of your brothers." He grabbed another picture, this one of Neville. Furiously he threw it. The frame cracked and glass smashed. Sparks flew out of the fireplace. The smell of gas was everywhere.

And then, as the flames rose and illuminated the small room, she finally understood why he kept his distance from her, walked around her in such a broad circle. The lines she'd noticed before were clearer now. She knew with deadly certainty that the floor of the cabin had been doused in gasoline. Not in a ring, as she'd thought, but in the diamond shape that was the middle of the star—the image he'd burned with Dani's birth certificate.

"You and Mary Beth," he said. "Bitches."

He picked up the last picture, the one of Shannon, stared at the image. "Your daughter swiped this from me," he said, disgusted. His gaze slid to Shannon's. "I got it back." Furiously, he flipped the picture onto the logs. The glass cracked, but didn't shatter. In horror, Shannon watched as her own image started to smolder from the outside, the paper turning brown before igniting.

"ARSONS," he intoned. He reached into the fire to pick up a burning splinter from one of the frames, then stepped carefully over his line of fuel so that he could get close to her. Her skin crawled as he held the small flame in front of her face. She recoiled, twisted and writhed, tried to avoid it being anywhere near her, near her clothes . . .

Do something, Shannon! This is it! Your chance! Otherwise you'll die! He'll kill you like he killed everyone else! The least you can do is take him with you, kill the son of a bitch!

"Aren't you glad to see me?" he asked and leaned closer, as if to kiss her.

Shannon threw herself forward with all her strength. She rammed the top of her head into his chin. A loud ear-splitting clunk erupted. Pain shot down her spine.

Ryan screamed and staggered. "You bitch!" he cried, dropping the flaming piece of the picture frame onto his own skin. "AAAHHH!" Yowling, he started beating at himself, hitting at the flames. She butted him again, the chair coming off of the floor.

His legs shifted and she nailed him again. Hit him hard. Screaming, arms flailing against his body, he slipped and fell. His body ignited the gasoline.

In a *whoosh*, flames engulfed him.

He screamed again, this one a horrible, nerve-scraping screech that echoed through the night.

The smell of seared flesh filled the room.

Shannon didn't wait. Strapped to the chair, she bounced her way across the burning line, hopping toward the window, feeling fire reaching for her skin, her clothes.

Oh, God. Oh, God. Oh, God!

Biting back a scream, she kept moving. Closer to the window. The heat nearly suffocated her. She was crying, sweating, knowing her chances were desperately slim.

Flames crackled and sped along the trail of gasoline. Faster and faster, higher, the dry floor burning.

Keep going! Keep moving!

Ryan's shrieks rose into a siren of horrible, anguished cries that ascended with the fire.

Don't look back.

Hop! Hop! Hop! To the wall. At the window she saw the reflection of the fire, of the man behind her, thrashing and black inside a wild, roaring ring of flames.

It was too late for Ryan.

Using all her strength, Shannon threw herself and the chair against the window. Glass cracked and shattered as she propelled herself toward the porch. Her head landed with a thud. Blackness threatened to overtake her. The legs of the chair caught on the frame.

"No!" she cried, pushing forward, ignoring the pain in her shoulder, the same one she'd injured before. Glass cracked and splintered around her as she strained forward. Flames burned behind her. She pushed through, tumbling the chair over the frame and outside. Heat helped blast her through. She rolled onto the porch, still bound to the chair. Her head and shoulders banged against the wooden floor.

Oh, God, the rail! How would she get past the rail?

Behind her, Ryan screamed and flames tore through the dry, dusty building. Flames were eating the walls. In a matter of seconds the porch would be engulfed.

The only way off the porch was at the steps near the door. Clamping down on her teeth, she inched forward. Toward the stairs, dragging the damned chair with her, coughing from the smoke.

Pain shrieked up her body and the warmth of unconsciousness tugged at her brain, seducing her to give up the fight. "No way," she growled, trying to stay awake, to fight as she inched forward, determined to save herself.

She thought of Travis.

Of their lovemaking.

Of Dani.

The child she'd not seen since birth and tears filled her eyes. *Please God, give me the strength to get back to them. Please, please, protect them both and don't, oh, please, don't let her be dead.*

Behind her, so near its breath threatened to engulf her, the fire crackled and snarled. But above the roar, she thought she heard voices . . . human voices and a dog's bark and something else—a whooshing sound that seemed out of sync with this isolated spot.

Impossible.

Hallucinations.

Wishful thinking.

Keep moving. The steps are closer. Ignore the heat, the flames. Just keep going.

Whop, whop, whop!

The noise was louder now.

Intense. Somewhere, in the darkness, voices shouted through the night. She thought she was imagining it all, that in the blaze of smoke and fire, she'd lost her mind.

"Let's go!"

Nate? Oh, please . . .

Blackness tugged at her mind. Her body wracked with a fit of coughing.

Keep moving!

Heat blasted.

"Find!" someone cried. "Find Shannon!"

Travis?

Her heart cracked.

"Come on, boy!"

Was she dreaming, or was that Travis's voice shouting?

"Shannon!" he yelled, closer now as she started to pass out. "For Christ's sake, Shannon, hang on!"

Her heart leapt. She tried to roll away from the house, but the rail, now charring and burning, stopped her. Through the seared wooden bars she saw the glimmer of determined eyes in a large furry head. Atlas! The dog barked as Travis ran up behind him and commanded him to stay.

A second later Travis burst through the flames, catapulting himself onto the porch. His boots pounded on the floor as he yanked out a knife, cut her legs and hands free and scooped her into his arms. Heat and flames roiled around them.

"I'm here," he said, burying his face in her hair as he carried her, running, along the porch and leapt down the two steps. She blinked and saw the cabin, surrounded by dark woods, engulfed in flames. Above them the sound of a helicopter's rotor beat through the night.

"Hang on, darlin'," Travis insisted.

"Dani?" she whispered. "Is Dani—?"

"Safe. In the truck."

"Alive?" she choked out, her heart leaping, relief washing over her.

"Yes. Alive. Safe!"

Tears of relief filled her eyes. "How did you find me?" she cried, the roar of the fire behind them filling her ears.

"Dani was held here at this cabin. Nate knew the area. You trained Atlas well, and the forest service helped out. I'll tell you about it later. Where's the maniac?"

"Inside."

Travis looked over his shoulder to a cabin that was fully engulfed, fire crackling and crawling toward the night like fingers from hell. "Good."

Over the roar of conflagration she heard sirens approaching. It was too late for Ryan. This time, she was certain, he'd died. Gasping, sobbing, clinging to Travis, she started to shake and cry. It was over. Her daughter was safe. Travis was here and finally, finally Ryan, the abuser, the murderer was dead. At his own hand. She looked back to the burning cabin. The only noise was the hungry roar of the fire. Ryan's screams had died with him.

"He can't hurt you any more," Travis said as if reading her mind. "Never again. I swear." Shannon clung to him and kissed his lips. When she pulled her head away, he grinned his slow, sexy smile. "I've got you, darlin'," he said, a catch in his voice as he carried her along a path away from the burning cabin. "I've got you and I'm never gonna let you go again."

She looked up and saw Nate and Dani standing at the side of the truck. Sirens shrilled as huge trucks, lights flashing, bore down on them. The girl took a step forward.

"Dani!" Shannon cried, her heart aching at the sight of her daughter.

At that moment, the teenager started running forward, racing through the brush and dry weeds. Through the sheen of her own tears, Shannon saw that Dani, too, was crying, tracks of tears staining her dirty cheeks. She flung herself at her father. "I'm so sorry!" she cried, her arms surrounding both of them. "I'm so sorry . . . Shannon."

Shannon sniffed and nearly laughed at the absurdity of Dani's guilt. "Shhh," she whispered, her throat clogged. "It wasn't your fault."

"But, I—"

"You found me. Brought your dad and me together."

Travis gently disengaged his daughter. He started to carry Shannon to a waiting ambulance, but Shannon reached for Dani's hand. Dani held on tightly. Mother and daughter stared at each other, hungry for the sight of each other's faces.

Her throat thick with emotion, Shannon said, "I hope, if you'll give me a chance, we can all make up for lost time."

Dani nodded jerkily.

Then Shannon looked up at Travis, a smile trembling on her lips. He kissed her fervently.

"We have a future together," he said in an unsteady voice.

"All of us," Shannon whispered.

Dani didn't respond, but she refused to let go of Shannon's hand, and that was the loudest answer of all.

Epilogue

Christmas Eve

"And so this is Christmas . . ." John Lennon's voice played through the new speakers, swirling around the decorated tree and into the rooms of the new cottage by the lake.

It was Christmas Eve morning, over two months since the

night Ryan Carlyle died. Since then Shannon had learned that Ryan had been the son of Blanche Johnson, the woman who had given him up for adoption at birth, the woman whom he'd slain. Blanche had also raised a second son, another murderer who had been on a killing spree in Oregon last winter.

It was a long, terrible horror. And now it was over.

A lot's changed, Shannon thought as she padded barefoot into the kitchen and ground coffee beans on the old counter that would soon be replaced. All of her brothers were facing charges stemming from fires set by the Stealth Torcher, and there was an ongoing investigation as to Neville's murder. Though Ryan had killed him, her brothers were involved in the coverup to varying degrees.

It didn't look good for them, she thought, and because of it, Robert's affair with Cynthia Tallericco had ended, and Shea's second marriage was definitely on the rocks.

And their mother had collapsed. Luckily, after a short hospital stay and with Father Timothy's help, Maureen had been moved into an assisted living home where she was, despite all the tragedy, adjusting and making friends.

Shannon hit the button and the coffeemaker screeched as it pulverized the beans. Through the cottage window, she looked out to the lake where Travis, Dani, and her friend, Allie Kramer, were fishing from the dock. Allie's family was visiting from Oregon and staying at the house where Shannon had once lived and now Nate Santana was thinking of purchasing.

Marilyn, formerly Skatooli, now half-grown, was staring into the water and wagging her golden tail while Khan, the traitor, who had adopted Travis eagerly, was nearby sniffing the shore, trying to scare up squirrels.

Horses were lazily grazing in the newly constructed round pen, and while some of the dogs were in their kennels, others were outside, lying near the house, or sniffing for squirrels and rabbits.

Atop the sagging roof was a miniature Christmas sleigh, while a stuffed, life-sized Santa hung perilously from the gutters. No sign of Rudolph or the other reindeer. It looked as if they'd run for their lives.

While the other dogs were sunning themselves outside, Atlas was inside, lying on a rug near the fireplace where soft red coals gently glowed.

Glancing over at the dog, Shannon smiled as she poured water into the coffeemaker. She would have thought with all she'd been through that burning a fire in the grate would have been traumatic. Not so, thank goodness, and now seeing lights and a holly and fir swag on the mantel she felt an inward warmth spread through her. The latest injuries had healed. Even her shoulder was almost as good as new.

She punched the button to start the coffee. Atlas lifted his broad head while thumping his big tail on the floorboards. "Life could be worse," she told him. "A lot worse."

Dani and Allie had camped out in the attic of this little house, planning the expansion of the area into a suite for Dani, and probably, Marilyn.

The coffee percolated, filling the air with a warm scent and Shannon looked around her new home. With Travis's help she'd moved into the cabin near the lake and though the little cottage was far from renovated, it seemed like home. A real home. She walked to the window and gazed out to the lake where Travis, Allie, and Dani were fishing.

Her family.

Such as it was.

Travis hadn't thought twice about staying with her. Since Dani was starting high school, he'd decided it was a perfect time to move and surprisingly, he'd not gotten many arguments from his daughter. Her daughter. *Their* daughter.

They were talking about marriage but had decided to take it slow. Maybe in the spring. Travis's place in Oregon was for sale. The real estate agent informed them that a couple was "really interested" and an offer, "nearly certain." They would see.

As she watched, a Jeep rolled up the drive. Shane Carter was at the wheel with Jenna Hughes beside him. They'd come to celebrate Christmas with Travis and Dani in California. In the backseat was Jenna's daughter, Cassie, who, though taller, was nearly a carbon copy of her mother.

Shannon hurried outside and down the steps of the porch as Shane parked the Jeep near the garage. Several of the dogs, including Khan, barked and greeted the newcomers as they piled out of the car.

"How do you stand all these animals?" Cassie asked, but she was teasing, her smile wide as she petted every head that came her way.

"I don't know," Shannon said, "but I love them all. It nearly kills me when I sell one."

"I wouldn't sell any of them, not ever." With Khan leading the way, Cassie made a beeline to the dock where Allie was reeling in a fish.

"Merry Christmas," Jenna said, unloading the car.

She was petite and striking, Shannon thought, even more gorgeous than her Hollywood image. Stripped down to bare lipstick, worn jeans, and the glow of a woman in love, Jenna was the kind of woman who would turn heads no matter what. She'd also turned out to be a warm friend.

"Merry Christmas." Shannon hugged her as Shane followed his soon-to-be stepdaughter toward the lake.

Jenna watched her eldest daughter. "It's amazing how resilient kids are. Last year, I thought she'd never get over what happened to her, to us, during that ice storm, but she's surprised me. She's doing well in school and," Jenna's smile widened, "she's got a new boyfriend. One I like."

Shannon laughed. "It'll never last."

"I know. I'm sure that because I get along with him and his parents, the relationship is doomed." She stuffed her hands into her pockets. "So, how's Dani doing? She went through a rough time, too."

Shannon raised a hand and tilted it in the air. "Sometimes good. Sometimes not so good."

"But she's coming around? I mean moving down here and all?"

"I think so. She misses Allie, but she's made new friends and she even slipped and called me 'Mom' the other day." Smiling, Shannon shook her head. "I couldn't believe it."

"That's great."

"It feels good," Shannon admitted. She let her gaze wander to the dock where the girls were talking to Shane and Travis. She felt the same familiar tug on her heart every time she saw her daughter with her father. He was so good with her. Shannon had a brief thought of the boy who had fathered Dani and was glad that the rumors about Brendan Giles had proven false. He hadn't returned. Someday, when she was older, if Dani wanted to know about him, Shannon would give her all the information she had. For now, though, Travis Settler was the girl's only father.

Khan, realizing that his position of honor with Shannon was in jeopardy, raced to her side and growled at Atlas. The big shepherd, didn't seem to notice, just wagged his tail.

Leaning down, Shannon patted both dogs' heads. "You're such good boys," she said as they crowded around her, slapping her legs with their tails.

A burst of laughter erupted from the little crowd gathered on the dock.

"Love the Santa," Jenna said to Shannon as she pointed at the roof of the house.

"Travis's doing."

"I figured."

Jenna and Shannon walked toward their families as the sunlight reflected on the glassy surface of the lake. Dani and Travis turned to look at her and Shannon couldn't help but smile.

So it would take time to heal all the old wounds. Who cared? She had all the time in the world. What were the words in that John Lennon tune . . . "A very merry Christmas . . ."

Yes, she thought, gazing at Travis and Dani, so it would be.

A very, very merry Christmas.

Dear Reader,

Thanks for picking up FATAL BURN! I hope you liked reading the book as much as I did writing it. You might remember that Travis and Dani Settler were secondary characters in DEEP FREEZE, the prequel to FATAL BURN.

As you know most of my books are linked, some more than others. Often times a favorite character of mine appears in a subsequent book. And I'm going to do it once again, this time with one of the most popular characters I've ever created.

Remember Detective Reuben "Diego" Montoya from HOT BLOODED and COLD BLOODED and THE NIGHT BEFORE? He's always taken second seat to another popular character, Detective Rick Bentz. For years readers have written me and asked, "When is Montoya going to get his own book?" Well, now he does.

In April of 2006 SHIVER will be on the shelves. Montoya is back in New Orleans, now a senior detective. Although he's grown up a bit, he's still the swaggering, sexy, rebel cop that he was in previous books. This time he meets his match in Abby Chastain, a woman with a murky past and a disturbing future.

A string of bizarre murders takes place and they center around Our Lady of Virtues, a now-abandoned mental hospital. Set outside of New Orleans and now falling into ruin, Our Lady of Virtues is the same hospital where Oliver from FATAL BURN was sent and came back scarred. There are secrets within the walls of Our Lady of Virtues, dark and deadly secrets that have now come back to haunt anyone who had the misfortune of being a patient there. Abby Chastain's mother died at Our Lady of Virtues under mysterious circumstances, and now Abby realizes Faith Chastain's death was only the first.

A killer is stalking the old, musty hallways of the decrepit hospital and everyone, including Abby and Montoya, is at risk. With each step, he gets just a little closer and the danger becomes more grave.

I think you'll like SHIVER. Those of you who wanted to see Montoya in his own story will love it. Want to know a little more? Just turn the page for an excerpt from the book. Then, log onto www.lisajackson.com for a unique look into the deadly hallways of Our Lady of Virtues and SHIVER.

Keep reading,

Lisa Jackson

In each of her gripping bestsellers, Lisa Jackson has brought readers to the edge of their seats and proven herself a master of romantic suspense. Now the New York Times *bestselling author of* Hot Blooded *and* Cold Blooded *delivers her most powerful novel yet, bringing back New Orleans detective Reuben Montoya as he matches wits with a twisted psychopath whose very presence makes his victims SHIVER . . .*

Detective Reuben "Diego" Montoya is back in New Orleans. Thanks to years of working with the dark side of society, his youthful swagger is gone, replaced by straightforward determination. He'll need it, because a serial killer is turning The Big Easy into his personal playground. The victims are killed in pairs—no connection, no apparent motive, no real clues. Somebody's playing a sick game, and Montoya intends to beat him at it.

His only lead is the ex-wife of one of the victims. Abby Chastain is a woman haunted by painful secrets. Twenty years ago she watched in horror as her mother, a patient at the Our Lady of Virtues Mental Hospital, plunged through a window to her death. Abby has always dreaded that she too would one day go insane . . . especially now, back in this town, where she's begun to feel watched, as if the devil himself is scraping a fingernail along her spine. Something about Abby—her spirit and her honest fear—gets to Montoya. His gut tells him his prime suspect is innocent, just like it's telling him there's something significant about the once-grand hospital now decaying in a gloomy thicket of ancient live oaks. Abby Chastain can help unlock the mystery—if only Montoya can get her to trust him enough to face the ghosts of her past.

As more bodies are found in gruesome, staged scenarios and the FBI moves in, Montoya's in a desperate race to find a killer whose crimes are getting more terrifying, and closer all the time. Plunging deep into a nightmare investigation will uncover a shocking revelation—a deadly connection between Abby and Montoya and an asylum where unspeakable crimes were committed, evil once roamed free, and a human predator may still wait. For the past is never completely gone. Its sins must be avenged, its wrongs righted. And this time Detective Reuben Montoya may pay the price . . .

**Please turn the page for an exciting sneak peek at
SHIVER
coming in April 2006!**

Prologue

She felt his breath.

Warm.

Seductive.

Erotically evil.

A presence that caused the hairs on the back of her neck to lift, her skin to prickle, sweat to collect on her spine.

Her heart thumped. Barely able to move, standing in the darkness, she searched the shadowed corners of her room frantically. Through the open window, she heard the reverberating songs of the frogs in the nearby swamps, and farther still the rumble of a train on faraway tracks.

But here, now, he was with her.

Go away, she tried to say but held her tongue, hoping beyond hope that he wouldn't notice her standing near the window. On the other side of the paned glass security lamps illuminated the grounds with pale bluish light and she realized belatedly that her body, shrouded only by a sheer nightgown, was silhouetted by the eerie bluish glow from those lamps.

Of course he could see her, find her in the darkness.

He always did.

Throat dry, she stepped backward, placing a hand on the window casing to steady herself. Maybe she had just imagined his presence. Maybe she hadn't heard the door open after all. Maybe she'd jumped up from a drug-induced sleep too quickly. After all it wasn't late, only eight in the evening.

Maybe she was safe in this room, *her* room on the third floor.

Maybe.

She was reaching for the bedside light when she heard the soft scrape of leather against hardwood.

Her throat closed on a silent scream.

Having adjusted to the half-light, her eyes took in the bed with its mussed sheets, evidence of her fitful rest. On the dressing table was the lamp and a bifold picture frame; one that held small portraits of her two daughters. Across the small room was a fireplace. She could see its decorative tile and cold grate and above the mantel a bare spot, faded now where a mirror had once hung.

So where was he? She glanced at the tall windows. Beyond, the October night was hot and sultry. In the panes she could see her wan reflection: petite, small-boned frame; sad hazel eyes; high cheekbones; lustrous black hair pulled away from her face. And behind her . . . was that a shadow creeping near?

Or her imagination?

That was the trouble. Sometimes he hid.

But he was always nearby. Always. She could *feel* him, hear his soft, determined footsteps in the hallway, smell his scent—a mixture of male musk and sweat—catch a glimpse of a quick, darting shadow as he passed.

There was no getting away from him. Ever. Not even in the dead of night. He received great satisfaction in surprising her, sneaking up on her while she was sitting at her desk, leaning down behind her when she was kneeling at her bedside. He was always ready to press his face against the back of her neck, to reach around her and touch her breasts, arousing her though she loathed him, pulling her tightly against him so that she could feel his erection against her back. She wasn't safe when she was under the thin spray of the shower, nor while sleeping naked beneath the covers of her small bed.

How ironic that they had placed her here . . . for her own safety.

"Go away," she whispered, her head pounding, her thoughts disjointed. "Leave me alone!"

She blinked and tried to focus.

Where was he?

Nervously she trained her eyes on the one hiding place, the closet. She licked her lips. The wooden door was ajar, just slightly, enough that anyone inside could peer through the crack. From the small sliver of darkness within the closet something seemed to glimmer. A reflection. Eyes?

Oh, God.

Maybe he was inside. Waiting.

Gooseflesh broke out on her skin. She should call out to someone, but if she did, she would be restrained, medicated . . . or worse. *Stop it, Faith. Don't get paranoid!* But the glittering eyes in the closet watched her. She felt them. Wrapping one arm around her middle, the other folded over it, she scraped her nails on the skin of her elbow.

Scratch, scratch, scratch.

But maybe this was all a dream. A nightmare. Wasn't that what the nuns had assured her in their soft whispered voices as they gently patted her hands and stared at her with compassionate, disbelieving eyes? A dream. A nightmare of vast, intense proportions. Even the nurse had agreed with the nuns, telling her that what she'd thought she'd seen wasn't real. And the doctor, cold, clinical, with the bedside manner of a stone monkey, had talked to her as if she were a small child.

"There, there, Faith, no one is following you," he'd said, wearing a thin patronizing smile. "No one is watching you. You know that. You're . . . you're just confused. You're safe here. Remember, this is your home now."

Tears burned her eyes and she scratched more anxiously, her short fingernails running over the smooth skin of her forearm, encountering scabs. Home? This monstrous place? She closed her eyes, grabbed the headboard of the bed to steady herself.

Was she really as sick as they said? Did she really see people who weren't there? That's what they'd told her, time and time again, to the point that she was no longer certain what was real and what was not. Maybe that was the plot against her, to make her believe she was as crazy as they insisted she was.

She heard a footstep and looked up quickly.

The hairs on the backs of her arms rose.

She began to shake as she saw the closet door crack open a bit more.

"Sweet Jesus." Trembling, she backed up, her gaze fixed on the closet, her fingers scraping her forearm like mad. The door creaked open in slow motion. "Go away!" she whispered, her stomach knotting as full-blown terror took root.

A weapon! You need a weapon!

Anxiously, she looked around the near-dark room with its bed bolted to the floor.

Get your letter opener! Now!

She took one step toward the desk before she remembered that Sister Madeline had taken the letter opener away from her.

The lamp on the night table!

But it, too, was screwed down.

She pressed the switch.

Click.

No great wash of light. Frantically, she hit the switch again. Over and over.

Click. Click. Click.

She looked up and saw him, then. A tall man, looming in front of the door to the hallway. It was too dark to see his features but she knew his wicked smile was in place, his eyes glinting with an evil need.

He was Satan incarnate. And there was no way to get away from him. There never was.

"Please don't," she begged, her voice sounding pathetic and weak as she backed up, her legs quivering.

"Please don't what?"

Don't touch me . . . don't place your fingers anywhere on my body . . . don't tell me I'm beautiful . . . don't kiss me . . .

"Leave now," she insisted. Dear God, was there no weapon, nothing to stop him?

"Leave now or what?"

"Or I'll scream and call the guards."

"'The guards,'" he repeated in that low, amused, nearly hypnotic voice. "Here?" He clucked his tongue as if she were a disobedient child. "You've tried that before." She knew for certain that her plight was futile. She would submit to him again. As she always did. "'The guards?' Did they believe you the last time?"

Of course they hadn't. Why would they? The two scrawny pimply-faced boys hadn't hidden the fact they considered her mad. At least that's what they'd insinuated, though they'd used fancier words . . . *delusional . . . paranoid . . . schizophrenic . . .*

Or had they said anything at all? Maybe not. Maybe they'd just stared at her with their pitying, yet hungry, eyes. Hadn't one of them told her she was sexy? The other one cupping one cheek of her buttocks . . . or . . . or had that all been a horrid, vivid nightmare?

Scratch, scratch, scratch. She felt her nails break the skin.

Humiliation washed over her. She inched backward, away from her tormentor. What was happening to her was her own fault. She'd sinned somehow, brought this upon herself. She was the one who was evil. She had instigated God's wrath. She alone could atone. "Go away," she whispered again, clawing more frantically at her arm.

"Faith, don't," he warned, his voice horrifyingly soothing. "Mutilating yourself won't change anything. I'm here to help you. You know that."

Help her? No . . . no, no, no!

She wanted to crumble onto the floor, to shed her guilt, to get away from the itching.

Fight! an inner voice ordered her. *Don't let him force you into doing things that you know are wrong! You have will. You can't let him do this to you.*

But it was already too late.

Close to her now, he clucked his tongue. In a rough whisper, he said, "Uh-oh, Faith, I think you've been a naughty girl again."

"No." She was whimpering. There it was . . . that horrid bit of excitement building inside her.

"Oh, Faith, don't you know it's a sin to lie?"

She glanced at the wall where the crucifix of Jesus was nailed into the plaster. Did it move? Blinking, she imagined Jesus staring at her, his eyes kind but silently reprimanding in the semidarkness.

No, Faith. That can't be. Get a grip, for God's sake.

It's a painted image, that's all.

Breathing rapidly, she dragged her gaze from Christ's tortured face to the fireplace . . . cold now, devoid of both ashes and the mirror above it, now an empty space, the outline visible against the light green paint. They said she broke the mirror in a fit of rage, that she'd cut herself. That her own image had caused her to panic.

But he'd done it, hadn't he? This devil whose sole intent was to torture her? Hadn't she witnessed the act? She'd tried to refuse him, and he'd crashed his fist into the looking glass. Mirrored shards sprayed, hitting her, then crashed to the floor like glittery, deadly knives.

That's what had happened.

Right?

Or not? Now, feeling the blood beneath her nails, she wondered.

What is happening to me?

She stared at her bloodied hands. Her fingernails, once manicured and polished were broken, her palms scratched and farther up, upon her wrists, healed deep gashes. Had she done that to herself? In her mind's eye she saw her hands wrapped around a shard of glass and the blood dripping from her fingers . . .

Because you were going to kill him . . . trying to protect yourself!

She closed her eyes and let out a long, mewling cry. It was true. She didn't know what to believe any longer. Truth and lies blended, fact and fiction fused, her life, once so ordinary, so predictable was fragmented. Frayed. At her own hands.

She inched backward, closer to the window, farther from him, from temptation, from sin.

Where was her husband . . . and her children; what had happened to her girls?

Terror burrowed deep into her soul. Confused and panic-stricken, she blinked rapidly, trying to think. They were safe. They had to be.

Concentrate, Faith. Get hold of yourself! Zoey and Abby are with Jacques. They're visiting tonight, remember? It's your birthday.

Or was that wrong? Was everything a lie? A macabre figment of her imagination?

She took another step backward.

"You're confused, Faith, but I can help you," he said quietly, as if nothing had happened between them, as if everything she'd conjured was her imagination, as if he'd never touched her.

Dear Lord, how mad was she?

She spun quickly, her toe catching on the edge of a rug. Pitching forward, she again caught her reflection in the window and this time she saw him rushing forward, felt his hands upon her.

"No!" she cried, falling.

Glass cracked. Shattered.

With a scream she fell into the dark nothingness of the hot Louisiana night.

<u>BOOK YOUR PLACE ON OUR WEBSITE</u>
<u>AND MAKE THE</u>
<u>READING CONNECTION!</u>

We've created a customized website just for our very special readers, where you can get the inside scoop on everything that's going on with Zebra, Pinnacle and Kensington books.

When you come online, you'll have the exciting opportunity to:

- View covers of upcoming books
- Read sample chapters
- Learn about our future publishing schedule (listed by publication month *and author*)
- Find out when your favorite authors will be visiting a city near you
- Search for and order backlist books from our online catalog
- Check out author bios and background information
- Send e-mail to your favorite authors
- Meet the Kensington staff online
- Join us in weekly chats with authors, readers and other guests
- Get writing guidelines
- AND MUCH MORE!